Dance to the Storm

Dance to the Storm

Maggie Craig

Alligin BOOKS

First Published 2020

ISBN **978-0-9934126-0-8**

Cover design by Cathy Helms of Avalon Graphics.

Typeset in 10.5 point Adobe Devanagari
by 3btype.com

For Kirsty and Robert and the readers,
with apologies for waiting so long to let everyone
know what happened next.

Acknowledgements

My grateful thanks to the following people:

Neil Guthrie, author of *The Material Culture of the Jacobites,* for sharing with me some of his expertise on touch-pieces;

Hilary Johnson of the Hilary Johnson Authors' Advisory Service and her readers for their valuable critiques;

Cornerstones Literary Consultancy and Eleanor Leese for much appreciated editorial input. Eleanor is both an editor and an author, writing as Ellie Darkins.

Edinburgh

December 1743

1

He wanted to laugh. He wanted to dance. He wanted – God help any music lovers within earshot – to sing. He wanted to run out of the guard-house, raise his face to the falling snow and shout out his joy to the invisible heavens and the High Street of Edinburgh. Most of all, he wanted to stay here and keep on kissing Christian Rankeillor.

Her cool fingers were coiled around his wrist, under his Dresden ruffles. A moment before, the starched white embroidery frothing out at his cuffs had brushed her cheek, and she had shivered. Not because she was scared, as he had initially feared, but in anticipation. Her response to this first kiss they had shared had been all he could have hoped for and a lot more than he deserved. Trust. Innocence. Passion. 'Twas an arousing combination. His anatomy was already responding, even as his brain was telling him he had to hold himself in check. She might be scared if he went too far. Besides which, they weren't alone.

Robert Catto's eyes dropped to Geordie Smart the cook boy, snoring softly with his head resting against Christian Rankeillor's shoulder. The lad had fallen asleep there half-an-hour before, worn out by his own adventures this evening. Her free arm curved around the child, she sat between him and Catto. The lavish rose-pink skirts of her evening gown were a startling splash of colour against the smoke-blackened settle, one of two which faced each other across the guard-room. Catto pressed his forehead against her own. 'All right?' he murmured.

She didn't answer him with words, only sought his mouth again. This time it was she who deepened and prolonged the kiss, setting his blood and his body on fire and testing his good resolutions to the limit. His brain was losing this battle.

He wanted more. Much, much more. His hand already lay on her shimmering skirts. Those spilled over his own satin-clad knees, covering the dark-green breeches of his evening clothes. Expansive though her gown was, its skirts and the petticoat below formed only the lightest of blankets. The barrier between his long fingers and the smooth skin of what lay between her thighs was no barrier at all.

It might be a long time since he had last made love to a girl wearing a hooped petticoat, rather than one in a simple skirt and bodice he was paying for the pleasure, but he hadn't forgotten how to navigate his way through the layers. Although what if the movement woke Geordie up? Catto had been in brothels where no one paid any attention to the wide awake children of the whores, gave no thought at all to what those children heard and saw. He'd always felt a certain delicacy about that.

Lost in a haze of rising desire, still he wondered if he could. Oh God, just a little touch... his fingertips nudging tight curls, sliding through that enchanted forest to the irresistible paradise within. In the midst of the kiss, he heard himself utter a little moan of desire. Just a little touch, that was all. He would go no farther. Doing his thinking for him, his hand skimmed down to the hem of her skirts, rose underneath them over smooth white stockings to her knees, slid over one knotted garter to the prize of bare skin. It was as smooth as her stockings, warm and enticing.

She stiffened and broke the contact, her eyes flying open. 'Robert...' she breathed. 'Please... I've never... We can't...'

Not too hard to work out what she had never done, which wasn't helping the situation in the slightest. Quite the reverse. Yet his hand stilled. No girls who seemed in the least wise unwilling. That had always been a golden rule. And God Almighty, there was so much more than that to think about here.

He wanted this girl. He wanted to protect her too, and from more than a rough tumble and a careless coupling. She was in deadly danger. Not least from him. He drew back, laid the offending hand flat against the rose silk and creamy lace of her elbow-length sleeve and looked into her startled green eyes.

'Listen to me,' he said, pushing her a little away from him. 'You have to listen to me.'

2

'Anna, what in Hades are you doing out here? You've missed so many dances! Several of your would-be cavaliers are now firmly convinced you really are the heartless wee baggage it amuses you to pretend to be—' Meg Wood stopped in a rustle of sky-blue silk, her eyes on the long windows set into the outside wall of the stairwell that led down to the ground floor and the curve of the West Bow. 'Och, would you look at that snow! Should we be thinking of heading home? Anna?' she added, her bright face clouding as she whirled round to look at her friend. 'What's the matter?'

For Anna Gordon, stiff and unsmiling, sat perched on the edge of one of the yellow brocade sofas placed on either side of the double doors leading into the ballroom of the Assembly Rooms. Mirroring her, Charlotte Liddell sat on the other side of the wide and open doorway. She snapped out an order to the gorgeously dressed young black boy in the powdered white tie-wig who acted as her personal footman. As he hurried off into the ballroom to do her bidding, she stood up and stalked across the varnished golden floorboards of the landing, coming as close to Meg Wood as the hooped petticoats under their evening gowns would allow. Her face was twisted with venom.

'She's waiting to see what's happened to your friend Kirsty Rankeillor. Who was arrested by the Town Guard some time ago now.' Charlotte Liddell's blue eyes darted towards Archie Liddell, standing watching them next to a door further along the corridor. His arms folded across his chest, he looked nervous but determined. Charlotte raised her voice. 'Whereas I'm waiting till my cousin sees sense and works out on which side his bread is buttered.'

Meg Wood turned towards Anna Gordon, who was also now on her feet. 'Kirsty has been *arrested*?' Her voice rose in disbelief. 'For what reason?' she demanded. 'And by whom?'

'The Captain o' the Town Guard,' Anna said in her rich Buchan accent, answering one question and not the other. 'He escorted her down the stairs some time ago.'

'Captain Robert Catto?' Meg asked, a frown creasing her brow. 'The gentleman of whom she spoke to us? About whom she has somewhat mixed feelings?'

'The very same.'

Charlotte Liddell's eyes narrowed. Focussed on each other, neither Anna Gordon nor Meg Wood noticed the sharpening of interest.

'Where has he taken her?'

'I have no idea. But I'm staying here until I find out. Archie won't tell me anything other than that he expects the Captain to return here to the Assembly Rooms at some point. You go back to the house if you want, Meg. I'll stay here.' Anna raised beautifully curved dark eyebrows. 'If Archie will permit you to leave. He's already stopped two other people, an older gentleman and lady. Told them not to say anything to anyone else, forbye. I understand the caddies are under orders not to move without his express permission, either.'

'No matter,' Meg said. 'If you're staying, I'm staying. But what's going on, Anna? Stopping people from leaving the ball, Kirsty being arrested? I don't understand.' Her frown of puzzlement deepened.

The other girl pulled her back towards the sofa, turning her so Charlotte Liddell could see neither of their faces. 'I'll tell you when that vicious bitch isn't listening,' she murmured. 'For now, we must say as little as possible, Meg. For Kirsty's sake. Her father's, too.'

It took only seconds for realization to dawn. 'Oh no,' Meg cried, one hand flying up to her mouth. 'Tell me this isn't what I think it is, Anna! Och, Anna, in the name of God—'

'Meg!' Anna's voice was an urgent whisper. 'Hold your tongue!'

Meg Wood blinked, shocked into silence. Anna Gordon tugged at the sleeve of her blue gown and drew her down onto the sofa. 'We cannot speak of this now,' she said, still speaking in a hushed voice. 'Not now, Meg, I beg you!'

Meg Wood's eyes searched her face. Then she gave a quick little nod of agreement. The two girls watched Charlotte Liddell, who had turned her steps and her attention to her cousin. Her ivory-coloured skirts swayed wildly, a measure of her anger.

'Release my brother and his friend immediately, Archie. Or it'll be the worse for you. I'll not tell you again.'

Tall and lanky, Archie looked down at her. 'I cannot do that, Charlotte. I have orders from my Captain to guard this door and let no one in or out.'

'Your Captain? *Your Captain?*' she repeated, her voice rising in a sneer of disbelief. 'Who is the Captain of the Town Guard to command the Liddells?' The look she was bestowing on Archie grew even more contemptuous. 'The Town Guard? Town rats, more like. For your information, I have sent Hector Grant to fetch our man of business. Mr Charles Paterson will be here at any moment. And didn't you just hear me order the little black tar baby to go and find Professor Monro and bring him out here to the corridor?'

'Professor Monro?' Archie asked, unwisely. 'How did you know—' He caught himself on.

Charlotte Liddell jumped on the unfinished sentence like a cat pouncing on a mouse. 'So it's true, then? Though I can scarce believe it! Cosmo and Arthur have been injured?'

'I have nothing more to say to you, Charlotte. Go and sit quietly over there.' Archie Liddell pointed to the empty couch. 'If you please. You will achieve nothing by making an exhibition of yourself.'

'Well done, Archie,' murmured Anna Gordon. 'High time someone told Charlotte Liddell to haud her wheesht.' Then, awkwardly, when a stiff Meg Wood neither looked at her nor gave her a reply: 'Although Archie's for it now.'

Sucking in an outraged breath, Charlotte Liddell bunched her hands into fists at her waist. 'How dare you speak to me like that, Archie Liddell? *How dare you?*'

Archie drew in a breath of his own but his cousin didn't give him the chance to answer her, spitting out more angry words. 'I sent for Professor Monro because he is the most senior gentleman here at the ball tonight. One,' she added with withering scorn, 'who easily trumps the orders of your Captain. Are you telling me my brother and his friend require the services of a physician, Archie?'

Archie squared his shoulders. 'I'm telling you nothing, Charlotte.'

'If your precious Captain has harmed Cosmo or Arthur, I'll have him charged with common assault and thrown into the Tolbooth!'

'I don't think so, Charlotte. Nor shall I unlock the door to either Professor Monro or Mr Paterson. Only Captain Catto can give me the order to open it.'

Charlotte Liddell hissed like a snake. 'I always knew you were a fool, Archie.' The expression on her face grew calculating. 'You'll be looking to take articles when you finish at the Old College in the summer, won't you? That's how you hope to make your way in the world, improve your lot. Which,' she added, her voice dripping with contempt, 'you need to do because your father was stupid enough to marry a poor woman for love. Do you think any lawyer in Edinburgh will take you on if Mr Paterson tells them you are not to be trusted to do your duty to your family and your rank?' She looked him up and down. 'Shame though you have brought on both.'

Standing there in his shabby evening clothes of rubbed purple silk, Archie Liddell paled. On the yellow sofa, Anna Gordon laid a tentative hand on her friend's arm. Meg Wood reacted only by growing even stiffer. She continued to stare straight ahead, her eyes fixed on the long windows on the stairs and the snow falling down to earth behind the glass.

3

'We need a plan.'

She gave him an odd little smile. Despite the impossibility of the situation in which Kirsty Rankeillor and he now found themselves, there was mischief there and more. The shared experiences of this last turbulent week and dramatic evening. Regret. Sadness. Some shyness, too. Not surprising when he considered where his hand had so very nearly gone, even in the midst of the danger surrounding them, even with Geordie slumbering next to her. Within Robert Catto's head, a tiny spark of amusement flared. As he had so often thought, he really was a hopeless case.

'Tell me, Captain, do you have such a plan tucked up your elegant sleeves?'

Giving him back the words he had tossed across the guard-room at her not so long ago on this snowy December evening, Kirsty Rankeillor flicked the ruffles at his wrist with one of those cool fingers. As the heel of her hand settled onto the back of his, he drew his breath in on a hiss and saw her face cloud in contrition.

'It hurts?'

'It hurts,' he confirmed. 'But don't take your hand away.' He felt her adjust her touch, so that her fingers rested as lightly as possible upon his bruised skin. The rush of pleasure grew yet more intense. That took him by surprise. For so long he had satisfied his urges directly and without ceremony. He paid a girl, told her what he wanted, and took it. He hadn't thought himself still capable of deriving so much pleasure from the mere touch of a female hand on his.

Pleasure and … comfort. That was there too, along with a feeling of acceptance he hadn't known in a very long time. Pleasure. Comfort. Acceptance. Odd words to spring to mind. An odd combination of words. Yet they fitted. They had meaning, were as solid as stone.

Although this house they were building higher with every passing moment stood upon sand, not rock. How could it be otherwise? Wrong time, wrong place, wrong people. The two of them were gazing hungrily at each other from opposite sides of an ever-widening chasm. He was an engineer, had thrown more than one bridge across gullies and flooded streams. He could see no way of bridging this gap.

You must walk a tightrope, lad. Although I have absolutely no doubt that you can do that.

That was what Duncan Forbes of Culloden had said. The Lord President might have had no doubts. Catto had plenty, especially when he saw the abyss now opening up at Christian Rankeillor's feet. One false move, one step in the wrong direction, and she would plunge down into it. One mistake on his part could tip her over. Black despair replaced his previous elation. Struggling to contain his emotions, he posed a prosaic question.

'What about your forehead?' He lifted his chin to indicate the graze on her temple. That was where the stone hurled through the guard-room window by someone in the Daft Friday crowd had struck her.

Daft Friday, the start of the Daft Days of Yule, when normal behaviour was turned on its head. Boys pulled on their sister's dresses, girls stepped into their brother's breeches. Both sexes and all ages danced through the graveyard, singing defiance to death itself. Both sexes and all ages drank way more than their fill. That made a crowd bold, like the one that had followed Catto and his prisoners down from the Assembly Rooms to the Town Guard House.

That crowd had become a jeering mob, thirsting for some sport with the hated Town Guard, but outside the cracked window the High Street was quiet now. Everyone had scuttled back indoors. The snow that was still steadily falling was keeping them there. Catto had offered the initial encouragement to retreat. Shouldering his musket, he had coolly asked which one of them they would like him to shoot first.

The mob had dispersed, pursued by a group of the Town Guard. Turning on his heel, Catto had walked back into the guard-house only to find the tables had been turned. For a brief period, it was he who was the prisoner. That was no longer the case. Although, damn it all to hell and back again, the changed situation had allowed the escape of two of the men he had arrested up at the Assembly Rooms on suspicion of sedition and plotting armed rebellion against King George. They had been aided and abetted by his own carelessness: and Christian Rankeillor.

One of those men was the Jacobite agent whose *nom-de-guerre* was Mr Fox. The other was Jamie Buchan of Balnamoon, resident at Edinburgh Royal Infirmary and apprentice to surgeon-apothecary Professor Patrick Rankeillor, father to Christian Rankeillor. When she had refused to go with them, Balnamoon had handed her a pistol and told her to use it on Catto. She had, but had aimed to miss. Or so she claimed. Her hand had been trembling so much it had been hard to tell.

'I'm fine,' she said now. 'I shall clean it and apply some salve when I get home.' A frown creased her smooth brow. 'You *are* going to allow me to go home?'

'As a matter of urgency. That's the only chance we've got of keeping the events of this evening quiet.'

'But I remain your prisoner.'

'Aye,' he agreed. 'You remain my prisoner. More's the pity,' he added grimly.

She swallowed hard. 'But you will do your duty. Because you always do.'

'Aye,' he agreed. 'I shall do my duty.' She had told him that earlier too, offering the opinion that his duty was the only thing he had ever had to hold on to. Right at this moment he might be wishing with all his heart he wasn't made that way but she had read him all too accurately.

'What about your other prisoners, the ones up at the Assembly Rooms?'

'They can keep for the moment. I have them under guard. Getting you home is my priority.' Which he should have done well before now, tucking her out of sight in her own house down in Infirmary Street, hard by the city wall, until he had decided what he was going to do with her.

Her frown deepened. 'But you must also see to them as a matter of urgency, must you not? Especially now they know about you and... and...' Once more she faltered, stumbling over her words before settling for: '... about you and Mr Fox.'

Catto's own quick frown had thrown out that warning, although he had not silenced her completely. 'Archie Liddell and your Sergeant Livingstone have also learned that about you this evening. And I suspect you would rather nobody knew.'

'I trust them both not to blab like gossiping girls,' he said tersely.

Did he? Since he had been recalled to Edinburgh a month before, at the special request of Duncan Forbes of Culloden, Lord President of the Court of Session, he had been reminded every day of the truth of one maxim. Trust no one. Especially not with the secret he had spent all his adult life keeping to himself.

Almost to himself. There had been that night a couple of years back when a lethal combination of drink and distress had loosened his tongue. He had told the worst possible person, too. Fred Scott, his fellow officer in Guise's Regiment. A man whose eyes gleamed at any perceived weakness in another man, storing it away till he could find a way to use it against you. Fred Scott had already done that, looking at his brother officer over their commanding officer's head when Catto had been trying with all his might to resist this secondment to Edinburgh to captain the City's Town Guard.

Want me to tell him what you told me that drunken night, Catto? That'll call your loyalty into question for evermore.

For Mr Fox was in reality John Roy Stuart, Robert Catto's long-estranged father. John Roy was also a close confidant of the man the Jacobites called King James and his enemies called the Old Pretender. Enmeshed in the intrigue which swirled like ribbons of November mist around the Stuart court-in-exile in Rome, the man had long been a Jacobite plotter at the highest level. After everything Catto had uncovered tonight and in the preceding week, there could be no doubt that John Roy was an emissary from Rome to Scotland, actively planning armed rebellion against the House of Hanover. The Lord President's fears had been vindicated.

Despite his Highland blood and ancestry, as a soldier, engineer and practical man, Catto refused to believe he was to the slightest extent fey. Yet he knew there had been an undercurrent of foreboding in his reluctance to return. Now that foreboding had become hideous reality.

For Christian Rankeillor and her father, guilty of conspiring to foment armed rebellion and giving aid and succour to a known rebel. For himself, bringing him face-to-face with the painful past he tried so hard to forget. For his military career, if his connection to such a notorious Jacobite plotter became known. For Scotland, which might be plunged into violence and bloodshed.

He had seen warfare in Europe, too much of it. Not only death and hideous wounds on the battlefield but brutal attacks on the civilian population, the rape of women and girls, burning houses, wrecked villages, slaughtered animals and ruined lives. He didn't want to see any of that in Scotland. His beloved mother's country. His beloved grandfather's country … his own country. He tried very hard to convince himself he couldn't care less about this benighted bloody place. Only he knew that he did.

'When we get to Infirmary Street you will allow me to apply some salve to your hand. Is it very painful?'

'I've experienced worse. Any doctoring can wait till tomorrow.' Christ, did she not realize the extent of the danger in which she stood? A minor injury to yet another part of his own anatomy was nothing compared to that. The blow had been delivered here in the guard-room, courtesy of the stock of a pistol brought down hard on the back of his hand. He'd swapped his musket for his sword by then and the blow had driven the blade from his grasp. Jamie Buchan had made off with the sword, damn his eyes. Catto had fought his way out of a few tight corners with that length of steel.

His eyes went to the gun, lying where he had put it on the settle opposite. 'Twas a Doune pistol, all steel, lock, stock and barrel. Decorated with engraved hearts, it was a firearm that would be prized by many. Robert Catto didn't want to even touch the bloody thing again. He remembered it and its partner too well, from a long time ago. The brace of pistols had caused trouble then. As this one was causing trouble now. A witches' brew of memories and emotions bobbed to the surface. Like malevolent seals with the leering faces of eyeless skulls, they seemed to grin inanely, taunting him. *Thought you'd got rid of us, did you? What a poor sodding fool you are, Catto.*

He could not deal with these feelings now, could not allow tonight's encounter with his past to bring them to the forefront of his mind. He needed a clear head. For her sake and his own. Aye, and for the sake of his duty too. Not to mention the survival of the Protestant Succession. Dear God in Heaven, this situation was serious in the extreme.

He wasn't sure he cared much which king sat on the throne or with which corrupt and self-serving courtiers and politicians he surrounded himself. Hanoverian or Jacobite, Catto couldn't see there was much difference. German Geordie had won the argument, though. The House of Hanover had routed the House of Stuart on more than one occasion. The Jacobites were yesterday's men. Or so he had thought. Until this week.

'Robert?' she asked, frowning at him. 'What is it?'

'Nothing.' He shook his head, trying to rid himself of the pictures the private playhouse in his brain seemed determined on showing him.

'How long have we been sitting here?'

'A few moments, no more. Or maybe half a lifetime.' He could not allow many more moments to elapse. He had to get her home and himself back up to the Assembly Rooms as soon as he could. He had tarried here too long as it was. She was quite right. The longer he delayed, the greater the danger. In more ways than one. Yet still he could not stop himself from sliding his free hand around the back of her neck, under her luxuriant hair. Dark as mahogany, its shining curls fell over his fingers like peaty Highland water, cool and clean. An oasis in the middle of the desert his life had become.

Until now. Until he had met her.

This girl whom he had arrested this evening, red-handed and in the act of conspiring with others to commit treason against King George.

This girl with whom he was fast falling in love.

This girl whose life he now held in his hands.

4

Archie Liddell silently told himself to stay calm. He had his orders. All he had to do was stand his ground till the Captain returned to the Assembly Rooms. His adversaries here were hardly going to man-handle him out of the way. Three of them were standing in front of him now, demanding he open the door to the small supper room in which Cosmo Liddell and Arthur Menzies of Edmonstone were confined.

His cousin Charlotte had always been a spiteful wee bisom. From their childhood, she and her brother Cosmo had never left Archie in any doubt that he was the poor relation. Times without number, she had thought it great fun to pull his hair or stick her foot out to trip him up and send him sprawling painfully onto hard floors, cracking his knees on wood and stone. Then, when an adult appeared and asked what had happened, she would be all big beguiling blue eyes and sweet innocence.

Archie's so clumsy. All arms and legs. He's always falling over his own feet.

Her threat to spike the guns of his legal career before it had even begun had chilled him to the marrow. She was repeating it now to her lawyer, Mr Charles Paterson.

The man of business raised his hands in a placating gesture. 'Now, now, Miss Charlotte, allow me to advise you not to say anything you might regret later.' He threw a glance at Archie. Was he fooling himself to see reassurance in it?

There was none in the expression on Professor Alexander Monro's face. 'Be quiet!' he commanded. His stentorian voice and air of command was enough to silence even Charlotte.

'Let me understand this, young man,' the Professor boomed, swinging round to Archie. He just managed not to step back, so powerful was the older man's physical presence.

'You have detained The Honourable Cosmo Liddell and Mr Arthur Menzies of Edmonstone. Whose families,' the Professor continued, his face very close to Archie's, 'have long been generous benefactors to Edinburgh Royal Infirmary. To make matters worse, according to Miss Liddell here — though I can scarce believe it — both gentlemen have sustained injuries at the hands of the Town Guard. At the Infirmary's Daft Friday Ball?' The deep voice rose in questioning disbelief.

An irreverent thought flitted through Archie's head. Those injuries had actually been sustained at the feet of the Town Guard. He glanced at Sergeant Livingstone, standing next to him in front of the door to the supper room. With Robert Catto's complete approval — Livingstone hadn't needed formal orders — the Sergeant had administered a kicking to both Cosmo and Archie, where it hurt most, suiting the punishment to the crime. For they were guilty not only of conspiring with a known Jacobite but of the brutal rape of a young girl.

Their friend Hector Grant of Soutra would be in line for the same punishment, only Archie suspected that after alerting the lawyer, he had made good his escape. If he had any sense, he'd have gone to ground somewhere in Edinburgh. Archie wasn't sure Hector did have any sense, although neither had he ever been sure if he was quite as daft as he often acted. The same went for Arthur Menzies of Edmonstone. Even more so in Arthur's case. There was a look in Arthur's eyes sometimes, the swift gleam that hinted at secrets known but not to be told. Archie was horribly afraid he now knew what some of those secrets were.

'Explain yourself, laddie!' demanded Professor Monro.

'He cannot!' put in Charlotte Liddell. 'He just keeps saying the same thing over and over again. Like a parrot! He can only open the door on the orders of his Captain. Who is a nobody!'

Archie glared at her. 'Mr Catto is Captain of the Town Guard of Edinburgh, Charlotte. And he has very good reasons to detain Cosmo and Arthur.'

'Then kindly tell me what they are. Forthwith!' snapped Professor Monro.

'I cannot, sir. Not without permission from Captain Catto.'

Professor Monro's nostrils flared. 'Where is this Captain Catto, pray? I've never heard of the man. Why is he not here to explain himself?'

'He is at the guard-house, sir. Whither he had to escort—'

The other prisoners. That's what Archie had been about to say. A tap in the middle of his back from Livingstone, unseen by anyone else, stopped him. That warning touch also reminded Archie of a maxim Robert Catto had passed on to him.

Tell people as little as possible. Knowledge is power. Whatever you learn, keep it to yourself for as long as you possibly can. Get other people to tell you what they know instead. Leave silences they will feel obliged to fill.

Shockingly, two of those other prisoners who had been escorted to the guard-house were Jamie Buchan of Balnamoon and Kirsty Rankeillor. Archie counted both as good friends. He had another horrible fear, that Jamie and Kirsty had crossed a dangerous line this week, very probably in company with the mysterious Mr Fox.

Archie had heard what Cosmo Liddell had said about that gentleman's connection to Robert Catto. He wished he hadn't. The Captain's father? He could scarce believe it. Mr Catto kept his cards close to his chest but of one thing Archie was sure. He hated Jacobites and their Cause with a passion.

The young man lifted his head, aware of eyes upon this group in which he stood. This discussion, if you could dignify it as such, had turned the heads of two men standing in the open double doorway of the ballroom. The long case clock on one side of the landing showed it wanted but forty minutes till the ball was due to finish. If more people spotted the snow and how heavily it was falling, the decision might be made to finish earlier. That could happen in the interval between one dance and the next. As, once the musicians stopped playing, raised voices out here might well attract more unwelcome attention.

Archie Liddell had to make a decision: and he had to make it now.

5

A little way down the hill of the High Street at the guard-house, his hand still curved around the nape of her neck under the dark fall of her gleaming hair, Robert Catto sat looking at Christian Rankeillor.

'I wish…' he began, and stopped.

'What do you wish?'

'I wish for what I cannot have. So what is the point of that?'

'Do not retreat back into yourself. Tell me what it is that you wish.' Soft as a summer meadow, her eyes held a plea he found himself unable to resist. He drew in another breath, his shoulders stretching the green and silver swirls of his embroidered waistcoat. The Lord President had paid for the evening clothes, insisted on Catto wearing them.

Want you to make a good showing, laddie. Once they start noticing you, we want them to really notice you! Show the buggers the Town Guard's coming up in the world and a force to be reckoned with!

Fine feathers make fine birds. Or in Catto's case didn't. He should have told Kirsty Rankeillor not to trust him. Duty had not allowed that. Duty was one thing. Here and now, in the guard-house late on this snowy December evening, he could at least give her honesty. He could not know when they might next have the chance to talk together like this, alone but for the sleeping boy.

His duty required him to inform the Lord President of the events of this evening and this past week as soon as humanly possible. Every piece of information he had gathered. Every name. Once he had given over hers, there would be no going back. Her fate would be out of his hands. The thought came with a swift stab of fear and the conviction that if he had something to say to her he had to say it now.

'What do you wish?' she asked again.

Throwing his customary emotional caution to the winds, he told her what was in his heart. 'I wish you and I had met in some other place and at some other time.'

'You wish we had stumbled upon each other in a garden full of sunflowers?'

'I wish for exactly that!' There was a catch in his voice as he remembered that special place, his grandfather's walled garden. He could so very easily see himself and Christian Rankeillor strolling there together on a warm summer's day along the grassy and gravel paths laid out between the nodding sunflowers, the big yellow blooms with the friendly faces he remembered so well from his childhood. And God al-bloody-mighty, he had to put a stop to this right now. He dropped his hand and slid along the smooth dark wood of the settle, putting a few inches between them.

'We must make a move.' He looked across at the jagged crack in the casement and the falling snow behind it. 'Whether it stops snowing or not.' He glanced down at Geordie, curled up on the settle with his head against Christian Rankeillor's shoulder and snoring softly.

'Should I wake him?'

Catto shook his head. 'I shall go and see how the land lies first. Check there is one sedan chair still out there. Hope to spot at least one of my men returning to the guard-house who can play the second caddie with me.' He gave one of the folds of her wide skirts a tug. 'You can hardly walk through the snow in this ridiculous garment.'

She made a face at him. He had offered his opinion several times on the stupidity of fashionable female clothes. Two chairs had been carried down from the Assembly Rooms, Kirsty Rankeillor in one and ... Mr Fox ... in the other. Hobbling on an injured leg as John Roy Stuart had been, Catto presumed he must have been carried further, probably down to the Netherbow. That was the city gate you would choose if you were heading for the port of Leith, a ship and escape.

Jamie Buchan of Balnamoon too must have had a second caddie, one to help him carry John Roy Stuart up to the Assembly Rooms in the first place. That unknown man had to have been on watch outside, freezing in the December evening in some doorway on the other side of the West Bow, seen the departure of the prisoners from there and followed on to the guard-house. Catto's mouth tightened. Those prisoners whom he had allowed to slip through his fingers and whom the relentlessly falling snow was now stopping him from pursuing. Anger at his own stupidity and anxiety for Kirsty Rankeillor sharpened his voice.

'Once we get you home you will do as I say as to how we proceed from there.'

Her mutinous chin went up. He'd seen the gesture several times in the past week.

'We are on opposite sides, Robert.'

'Kirsty, for God's sake!' His voice was low and urgent. 'There can be no sides! Only the winning one, and it has already won. Long since!' God in Heaven, he could only hope he was right there. 'I arrested you this evening. Several people heard and saw me do it. You cannot rely on your friends in high places to simply wipe that out. Even if one of them is the Lord President!'

'The Lord President,' she repeated. 'To whom you answer, do you not?'

'Yes.'

'A straightforward answer to a straightforward question. Now there's a novelty in this day and age.'

For the second time she was throwing his own sarcastic words back at him. He was good at sarcasm. Well-practised.

'Aye,' he said grimly. 'The Lord President is the gentleman to whom I answer. For which you should be bloody grateful, madam. Only with his help and influence can we hope to mitigate the results of your folly.'

'My folly?' she burst out. '*My folly?*'

'Aye, and your father's too,' Catto flung back. 'How could Professor Rankeillor have allowed you to become involved in such a dangerous undertaking?'

'He had no choice! Nor did he know we were going to—'

The sleeping boy shifted and mumbled something. She glanced down, murmured soothing words. When she looked up again Catto was ready for her.

'He had no choice?' Keeping his voice low so as not to further disturb Geordie's slumbers, he locked eyes with her. He knew his steady grey gaze could unnerve people. He had to unnerve her. Hellfire, he had to scare the living bloody daylights out of her.

'He did not know what you and Balnamoon had planned for tonight? Was that what you were about to say?'

Pain flashed across her face at the mention of that name. Catto grabbed her shoulder and gave her a shake. He could not afford to feel sorry for her. By God, he could not, and neither could she! 'Was that what you were about to say?' he demanded again.

'I cannot answer you, sir.' There was no trace now of a smile on her lovely face. For a few horrific seconds, his vision blurred, and the lovely face became one of those hideous eyeless skulls. 'You must know that.'

'You must know the opposite,' he warned. 'I have questions to put to you and I shall have answers. Believe me.' Then, when she did not respond: 'What if someone else questions you? Someone who will not scruple to force an answer out of you? By whatever means necessary?'

'I did not think you to have many scruples in such matters!'

This time he caught a flash of fear in those glittering green eyes. Good.

'Kirsty,' he said, speaking in a low and earnest murmur. 'You and I have a common interest in keeping the events of this evening as quiet as possible. Can we agree on that? Me because I have failed to stop the escape of a Jacobite agent from Edinburgh. You, because you helped him do it. If – when – you are questioned by a third party you must say you were coerced into helping, that it was not your choice, that your father and Balnamoon made you do it.'

He saw the words of protest forming on her lips, placed the tips of his fingers against her mouth to stop them. 'No, hear me out. That has to be your defence. It's the only one with a hope in hell of saving you. I'd wager your father has already insisted it's what you *must* say. Oh, and for God's sake, madam,' he said wearily, seeing her reaction to those words, 'you must try to conceal your true feelings much better than you do. Everything you think shows on your face.'

She pulled his hand away from her mouth. 'So I should wear a mask, as you do?' Her voice was a bitter little whisper. 'Tell me, sir, does your clearly well-rehearsed ability to conceal and deny your own true feelings make you happy? *A Jacobite agent*? Is that the only way you can bring yourself to describe him?'

Somehow we'll find a way.

We?

The two of us.

It was no time at all since they had exchanged those words. Joy had bubbled up inside him, warming his frozen heart. Now they were back to *sir* and *madam* and there was no way for them to find.

Rising to his feet, he drew himself up to his full and impressive height. 'I shall also make sure your friends are aware of the need for silence. I have questions for them too and shall also insist on answers. If they are not still at the Assembly Rooms by the time I get there, I shall call on them at the Duff town house either tonight or tomorrow.'

'They are not involved!'

'Do not treat me like a fool.' His voice had grown harsh. 'I might believe that of Miss Wood. I certainly do not believe it of Miss Gordon. I know who her father is. Patrick Gordon, banker in Banff. A man with dangerous loyalties.'

'As you know where Anna and Meg are lodging in Edinburgh.'

'Well, you already knew that I knew!' Robert Catto blew out an exasperated breath. 'Would you expect otherwise? I would be failing in my duty as Captain of the Town Guard did I not know such things.'

'And your duty is everything to you, is it not?'

'You have already made that observation this evening. As this conversation is doing nothing but wasting time we do not have.'

'You've been having us all watched this week,' she said, continuing to gaze up at him as he looked down at her. 'Before you laid your trap and watched us walk right into it.'

'You chose to walk into it.'

'We thought you were on our side.'

'Maybe I am.'

'You really expect me to believe that? After the events of this evening and what you have told me of your past? Whatever games you are now playing, 'tis too late for that, sir.'

'Kirsty,' he said, leaning forward again and balancing himself with a hand on the back of the settle. 'I'm not playing games. Rail against me later, curse me for all eternity, slap my face, do whatever you like. Right now, we need to work together. In this at least, I am on your side. 'Tis not only your father who is in danger. You are even more directly guilty of giving aid and succour to an enemy of the King, a man actively engaged in fomenting armed rebellion, and of helping him escape justice. That's treason, Kirsty. And they could—'

When he skidded to a halt, she said the words for him. 'They could hang me for it.'

'Aye,' he agreed, his expression grim. 'They could hang you for it.'

'And what might they do to you?' she countered. 'When they find out who the Jacobite agent is? Who is going to believe you did not allow him to escape?'

They were still staring at each other when the guard-house door was pushed open. Cold night air and a flurry of snow blew into the room.

6

'I'll see to the horses. You have a good hold of Mr Fox?'

Jamie Buchan of Balnamoon raised a hand and nodded an answer in acknowledgement of that murmured message and question. With another murmur bidding goodnight, the rider moved off, leading the other two horses towards the stables at the back of the building. The clip-clop of their hooves was muffled by the carpet of snow lining this narrow close which led down to the Shore, the harbour on the Water of Leith.

Balnamoon turned to the narrow but solid door in front of him. 'Twas the side entrance to a coffee house that fronted onto the Shore. From round there on the quay came snatches of fiddle music, singing and drunken shouts. Daft Friday revelry was continuing on into the night and by the sounds of it more than coffee was fuelling it.

Here in the close all was quiet. Jamie Buchan raised his hand to the door. Three short knocks. A brief pause. Two more knocks. It was opened almost immediately. They were expected. Once the door was closed, Jamie propped the sword he held in one hand against its hinges, the better to be able to support Mr John Roy Stuart. In silence but for a few hastily suppressed groans of pain from him, the man on the inside helped get him up the narrow staircase and into a room furnished with a wide bed, a roughly hewn small square table and two upright chairs. Bread, cheese, a claret jug and wine glasses stood on the table, lit by two wall sconces above it.

'Light can't be seen from outside?'

Their host indicated the shutters of the only window in the small room. 'Tightly shut and no cracks atween the boards. Forbye which, this room overlooks the stables, no' the close. Chamber pot under the bed. Are ye needing onything else afore I ging back to my customers? Wi' a bit o' luck they're blootered enough no' to hae noticed my absence for the last half hour awaiting your arrival, but my wife and the lassie will be run aff their feet getting them served. We dinna want anyone reporting onything out o' the ordinary having happened here tonight.'

'Help me ease him down onto the edge of the bed before you go. Let's get your cloak and topcoat off, sir. Inch back a wee bittie farther,' Jamie Buchan advised once John Roy Stuart had been divested of those and lowered down onto the bed. 'Then we'll get your legs swung up onto the bed. This might hurt.'

'That was something of an understatement,' John Roy said lightly once the manoeuvre had been accomplished. He had not cried out, but there were beads of sweat on his forehead and bite marks on his lower lip.

'We canna have any noise the morn,' said the other man with a worried frown. 'It'll be gey quiet then, everybody sleeping it off. It'll be no use me pretending I dinna hae an upstairs room if the watch from the Leith guard-house come looking for you and hear footsteps above their heids.'

'Nobody's going to come looking for anyone tomorrow,' Jamie Buchan said. 'Not in this snow.'

'Even if they do,' John Roy said, his eyes become steely, 'there will be no footsteps above anyone's head. I shall not be moving much in any case.' He glanced at Jamie. 'My young friend here will leave his shoes off and move about as little as possible. My mission is too important for me to betray it by such a foolish mistake.'

'Aye, sir,' came the hasty response. 'I'm no' doubting that ye ken your ain business.'

'*Our* business,' came the correction, the friendliest of smiles replacing the stern words and look. 'And I thank you most sincerely for your help in accomplishing it.'

As the door closed behind the man, Jamie Buchan viewed his patient's badly swollen ankle. The injury had been sustained almost a week since, when he and Patrick Rankeillor had hurried their charge into his hiding place in the unused corridor at the back of the Royal Infirmary. 'The ride down here has not helped.'

'No,' John Roy agreed. 'Nor coming up those stairs.'

'We must keep your leg elevated.' Jamie Buchan walked round the bed and fetched the pillow from the other side of it.

John Roy gave a soft laugh. 'You remind me of my kind doctoress, under whose orders I have been all week. That was her constant refrain.' He pulled a face, mocking himself. 'Mine that I did not want to be elevated in a more permanent fashion.' The amusement faded from his face. 'I fear we have left the young lady in peril. Which is poor reward for the sterling service she has rendered to us and the Cause.'

Carrying the pillow, Jamie Buchan came back round the bed. 'This may also hurt for a moment, sir, but hopefully with the result of making you more comfortable. I am going to raise your leg now to put this underneath it.' He folded the pillow to give it more height and put it in place. 'Kirsty is devoted to the Cause. She is also a very capable young woman.'

'I don't doubt it,' John Roy Stuart said, getting his breath back after a gasp of pain occasioned by the placing of the pillow. 'I have seen her worth over the course of this past week. Unfortunately she is currently a very capable young woman staring the Captain of Edinburgh's Town Guard in the face. Bound at the wrists and the ankles though we left him. I cannot see how Miss Kirsty can easily resolve that situation.'

By shooting him dead. I left her with a loaded pistol, told her to aim for his head or his heart. I wish I could think she's had the stomach to use it.

Jamie Buchan walked over to the table and began cutting bread and cheese. No need to worry about the sound of his footsteps tonight. Muted though it was by the thick boards of the floor, the revelry below floated up to them in ribbons of sound.

'She can hardly keep him prisoner indefinitely. Especially not in his own guard-house. I fear he may already have reversed the situation.' John Roy's voice grew very dry. 'It seems Captain Robert Catto is also very capable.'

Jamie moved back across to the bed and held out a plate of bread and cheese. 'He may indeed be capable but I was naïve. He fooled me into believing he was on our side. And now he knows you are here in Scotland, sir.'

If he isn't already dead. Which is to be preferred. Funny how he could be having these thoughts, while his hand remained steady as a rock. Even under the level gaze of the man looking gravely up at him.

'You would wish he could be stopped from apprising anyone else of that fact.'

'Surely you would wish that too, sir.' Jamie adjusted his hold on the plate John Roy had not yet taken from him. His hand might be steady but his fingers were slick with sweat.

'I could not have allowed you to do what you wanted to do, lad.'

'I did not *want* to do it. I thought it needed to be done.' His thoughts flew where he did not want them to go, back to Jeannie Carmichael. The young prostitute had seen him and Patrick Rankeillor hiding John Roy in the hospital and had threatened to tell Robert Catto. In so doing, she had signed her own death warrant, leaving Jamie Buchan with no choice but to silence her. The girl had struggled with all her might to stay alive, surprising him by how much fight she had in her. He hadn't expected that, not after the amount of gin he'd coaxed her into swallowing.

'I have told more than one of our friends we may all have to do things we would never have dreamt of doing before this is over. As I am very sure I do not need to tell you, sir.'

'Aye, the Cause can be a cruel mistress. Have us consorting with some odd bedfellows, forbye.' He fixed Jamie with a grim look. 'I do not care for men who declare that when a woman says no, she means yes.'

He was quoting Cosmo Liddell, who'd said that when Christian had accused him of the rape of Alice Smart, young Geordie's sister, back up at the Assembly Rooms.

'Cosmo has money,' Jamie replied, his voice dull. 'The Cause needs money.'

'Always.' John Roy sighed. 'More's the pity. That's still no excuse, though.'

Into the silence that fell between them, a snatch of song rose up from the merrymakers below. *Never let a sailor an inch above your knee, Nor ging wi' him oot walking doon by the river's haugh, For if ye dae ye can safely say, Your thingummyjig's awa'...* The rest was lost in raucous laughter, applause and whoops of delight that slowly died away. In the upstairs room, the moment stretched.

'You took a life, lad?' John Roy asked gently. 'To keep me safe?'

The younger man nodded, tight-lipped.

'The first time, I jalouse.' Then, after a second nod: 'Do not be too harsh on yourself. This path we tread is a difficult one. Seldom well-lit, forbye. It can be hard to see what is up ahead, lurking around the next bend. You are pondering, young Dr Buchan. Or may I call you Jamie, since we are now comrades-in-arms? Let me take that plate from you.'

Glad of the excuse to turn his back, Jamie returned to the table to fetch his own supper. He was afraid the expression on his face might betray him. He was not thinking only of what had been done. He was thinking of what might yet be going to happen tonight. On his instigation. Even if Kirsty hadn't had the stomach to fire the pistol. Dear God... How had it come to this?

Behind him, the voice which intertwined the lilt of the Highlands with hints of a long residence in France held compassion. 'We must not torment ourselves with such thoughts, young Jamie. We are soldiers, fighting a just war. Things happen that we do not wish to happen. We are forced to make unpalatable choices. Even if our humanity sometimes balks at those.'

Jamie took a deep breath, brought himself back to the here and now. 'As yours did, sir. This evening.'

'More than my humanity, lad. I could not have stood by and watched you kill him. You can surely understand that.'

'He arrested you. Knowing full well what fate might be in store for you as a result.'

'His feelings towards me are understandable.' John Roy gave what Jamie recognized from French students he had known at the university as a very Gallic shrug. *This is all very regrettable but there's nothing to be done about it. No point in discussing it further.* 'It's a sad story, one with which I shall not trouble you.'

'He will warn the Lord President. Alert him of your presence. Probably has already worked out that you'll be heading for Inverness.'

If he hasn't already been stopped dead. One way or the other.

'While the snow continues to fall, as it seems set to do, the Lord President will remain in blissful ignorance. Nothing will be moving in or out of Edinburgh over the next few days, maybe even a week. The city is effectively cut off. Since we have made it to Leith, that gives us some breathing space.'

'If we can embark tomorrow and are not ourselves stuck here.'

'You will travel with me? I thought the plan was for our other friend to be my escort.' John Roy gestured with his head towards the close and the outside world. 'The young gentleman who saw to the horses.'

'I cannot stay here. Not now.'

'No,' John Roy said. 'I suppose not. I shall be glad of your support. As long as the ship's captain can see where he is going we shall be fine. Snow does not impede at sea as it does on land. We shall have a head start on any pursuer.'

Jamie turned to look at him. 'Is a head start enough?'

'It will have to be. Shall we have a glass of claret to go with our cold supper?' Surveying his plate without much enthusiasm, John Roy raised russet eyebrows. 'I expect there was a fine hot supper at the Daft Friday ball. A man can get tired of bread and cheese. But must needs be grateful for any sustenance.'

Jamie poured the wine and returned from the table. John Roy took his glass and raised it. 'Now I would propose a toast. To the King-over-the-water.'

'And to his son, our Prince,' Jamie responded. 'May God bless them and keep them and allow them to enjoy their own again,' he added, filling up with emotion. How many times had he made this toast? Always covertly, often simply *To the King*, skimming the glass over a bowl of water placed on the table for that purpose to signify the toast was to King James beyond the seas in Rome, not the usurper George in London, the man to whom Jacobites grudgingly accorded only the title of Elector of Hanover.

'Aye,' John Roy Stuart said. 'And to our Prince.'

'Will you tell me of him, sir?' Jamie asked eagerly. 'I long to learn what manner of man he is. From one who knows him well.'

'The best of men,' John Roy replied, his handsome face breaking into the broadest of smiles. 'Brave. Stout-hearted. Charming. Fluent in several languages. An excellent shot. At home in the grandest palace and the humblest cottage. Ready and willing to answer the call. Ah,' he said, 'now I see the question in your eyes as to when that call will come.'

'Are you able to tell me, sir?'

'It will be soon.'

'With the help of the French?'

John Roy nodded. 'They are already assembling a fleet at Dunkirk.'

'That soon!' Jamie Buchan released the words on a long breath of hope and longing.

'Aye. That soon. Probably February.'

'A direct strike against London?'

'Aye,' John Roy said again. 'With us holding ourselves in readiness here to rise in response and take Scotland. There is much work to be done so our friends around the country know to make themselves ready and are standing by to act as soon as they get the word.'

In that moment, despite everything that had gone awry, despite his now forever-blackened soul, Jamie Buchan felt a thrill of excitement course through him. At last. At long last. A rising to restore the Stuarts to their rightful place was in the planning and almost in the execution. He thanked God he was alive in this hour and could play his part in it. And he would do whatever was in his power to bring about a restoration and regret none of it.

The older man raised his glass again. 'To our success,' he said. 'I shall tell you everything you want to know about the Young Gentleman tomorrow. For tonight we shall eat and we shall sleep so we are rested for our journey tomorrow. In the course of which we shall steal that fine march on those who seek to stop us.'

'Aye,' Jamie agreed. Raising his own glass to meet the other, he hoped with all his heart Robert Catto was not going to live to see the dawn tomorrow.

7

Robert Catto and Christian Rankeillor turned so abruptly towards the guard-room door that Geordie was almost tipped onto the floor.

'What?' the boy half-shouted as she grabbed at him to keep him upright. He stepped back to avoid a crack on the shins from the swaying hoops of her petticoat and nimbly regained his balance. 'Och, miss,' he said, 'I'm right sorry. Did I fall asleep wi' ma heid against your shoulder?'

'Livingstone?' demanded Catto, hastily straightening up from where he had been leaning with one hand braced on the back of the settle.

'Lieutenant's Liddell's compliments, sir. There's a wee bit of a problem with the prisoners up at the Assembly Rooms.' Turning back into the room, Livingstone inclined his powerful white-haired head in the direction of the guard-room cell. The question was clear. *What about the other prisoners, the ones you brought down from the Assembly Rooms?*

'Not now, Livingstone,' Catto murmured. His head was swimming, the pictures he'd been trying so hard to hold at bay spinning around inside his skull.

Images of Christian Rankeillor on the scaffold. Of her dropping into empty air, her feet kicking wildly in the vain attempt to find purchase. Dancing the Tyburn jig. That's what they called it in London. Here in Edinburgh, they hanged folk at the Grassmarket. He could see her there, surrounded by a raucous, jeering crowd, slowly strangling after minutes that would seem like hours, her head at last falling forward, jerking to final stillness at an impossible angle, her abundance of hair spilling out of a plain white linen cap. Her lifeless body dangling at the end of a rope. Twisting in the wind.

The opening of the door had allowed a blast of freezing wintry air to invade the guard room. It swirled and dived around it, throwing a snowy chill over the warmth radiating out from the fire. Despite the sudden punishing drop in temperature, Catto felt a bead of sweat run down his spine. 'Twas her voice now that echoed around his head.

And what might they do to you? When they find out who the Jacobite agent is? Who is going to believe you did not allow him to escape?

Bone-deep, unease on his own account slid over the horror of the pictures in his head. He would have to answer the Sergeant's questions sooner rather than later. There would be others who would want to quiz him too, not least the Lord President. Knowing him and his history as well as he did, Duncan Forbes of Culloden would never believe Catto had allowed the Jacobite agent to escape. Would he? But others might. And if Catto's loyalty was called into question, where did that leave Christian Rankeillor?

'What is the problem with the prisoners up at the Assembly Rooms?'

Sergeant Livingstone drew in a breath deep enough to raise his powerful shoulders and took a run at it. 'They're no longer there, sir. We were obliged to allow them to return home.'

Catto swore a filthy oath. Livingstone glanced across at Christian Rankeillor.

'Dinna fash yourself on my account, Mr Livingstone,' she said. 'I've heard him swear before. Several times. Even though I've known him for but a week.'

Catto spared her the briefest of glances before he spoke again to Livingstone, his voice low and dangerous. 'Say that again, Sergeant.'

'We were obliged to let them go home, sir. Albeit under guard. Lieutenant Liddell and a detail of five men are even now escorting both prisoners to Mr Cosmo Liddell's town house. Where the Lieutenant says they will remain until he receives your further orders. The Liddell town house lies—'

'Thank you,' Catto said crisply. 'I know where the Liddell town house lies. May I ask on whose authority you and Lieutenant Liddell allowed the prisoners to go home, Livingstone? *Albeit under guard?*' He cloaked the last three words in withering sarcasm. God Almighty, how was he to get anything out of Cosmo Liddell and Arthur Menzies when they had been bloody escorted back to the sodding comfort and safety of the Liddell town house?

'Miss Charlotte Liddell sent for Mr Charles Paterson, writer to the signet.'

Catto narrowed his eyes. 'Since when does a lawyer wield any control over the Town Guard?' Especially that lawyer. The Lord President had supplied Catto with the names of a number of Edinburgh's citizens who might have Jacobite sympathies and were not under any circumstances to be trusted. Mr Charles Paterson was one of them.

'Miss Liddell also sent for Professor Monro, who was at the ball.'

'And from where does *he* get the authority to countermand my orders?'

'Professor Munro is a hard man to deny,' Christian Rankeillor put in. 'And Mr Charles Paterson can run rings around anyone with his lawyer's tongue.'

This time she got his full attention. 'I wasn't aware you were party to this discussion, Miss Rankeillor,' he snapped as he swung round to her. 'I am conversing with my Sergeant. We do not require any contribution from you.'

She looked at him for a moment. Then, with a stuttered, 'I b-beg your p-pardon,' she turned in a swaying of her bright skirts to face the guard-room fire, wrapping her arms about herself.

'Was there no way either of you could have stopped Miss Charlotte Liddell from sending for Professor Monro?' Catto demanded, wheeling back to face the Sergeant. 'I thought I could rely on you, Livingstone. And Archie Liddell.'

Livingstone didn't flinch. 'You can rely on us, sir. We made the best of a bad job. Miss Liddell was issuing a wheen of threats. Including towards yourself.'

Biting down hard on his anger, Catto managed a drawl. 'How very tiresome of the chit. What does she imagine she can do to me?'

'The Liddells are a powerful family, sir.'

He knew they were. He had made dangerous enemies tonight. Ones who now knew something about himself he never wanted anyone to know. Christ, he had kept this dangerous secret for so long—

And he was too rigorously honest with himself not to admit that he was shooting the messenger here. He should not have left Livingstone and Liddell for so long up at the Assembly Rooms. Nor could he blame the snow for his inaction. Nor entirely convince himself he had delayed so as to get information out of Kirsty Rankeillor while she was still shocked and vulnerable.

No, the truth was that he had been sitting here in some sort of a bubble with her. Indulging, despite everything, in a hopeless fantasy of what the future might hold for the two of them. The greatest idiocy had been in believing they could have any sort of a future together.

He was a fucking idiot, a poor hopeless sodding dolt. He had been lost in some ludicrous fool's paradise, not to mention neglecting his duty. Aye, and his own self-interest and self-preservation too. And for what? His mouth tightened. He had just mocked Jacobites for chasing after chimeras and wills o' the wisp.

She's made her own bed. The words leapt into his head. She had gone into this with her eyes wide open, knowing full well the risks she was running. God Almighty, she had chosen to involve herself in this hopeless bloody venture!

Rage ambushed him, reaction too, a delayed response to the events of this evening. Tonight he had found himself face-to-face with the past he tried so hard to forget, had stood here in the guard-room with the living embodiment of that past, the man he hated with a passion which seared his soul. Right at this moment, he wanted to run out into the snow, throw his head back and bay at the moon like a mad dog. As he wanted to be anywhere on Earth but here. As he wanted never to have met Christian bloody Rankeillor. Damn her to hell.

This girl who had met his cruelty and bullying with kindness and his biting sarcasm and foul language with calm good humour. This girl who had been so kind to him when he had been injured by that knock on the head a few days ago, this girl who against all the odds seemed to care for him, this girl who could never be his ... this girl who might hang for what she had done this week. Dear God in Heaven. 'Twas pity that ambushed him now.

8

No, not pity. Equal measures of paralysing fear and unwilling compassion, dragged out of him from some deep well of feeling. She had not exactly chosen the hellishly dangerous path she had trod this week. He had been a fool to allow her the opportunity of freeing Jamie Buchan and John Roy Stuart from their bonds. He could hardly have expected her not to take that chance. She'd been raised in the Cause, the damned, accursed Jacobite Cause which swallowed lives and energies and passion whole, demanded unquestioning commitment and gave nothing but blood and sorrow in return. God Almighty, he knew that better than anyone.

Catto studied Kirsty Rankeillor's rigid back and felt every drop of his blood urging him to put her safety and welfare first. Even before his duty. Shaken, he folded his arms in an apparently nonchalant gesture. Something else born of long practice. Never betray your true feelings to anyone. Especially not if — when — those feelings were churning away inside you, boiling like a stormy sea. 'Who else was the unpleasant Miss Charlotte Liddell threatening?'

'Lieutenant Liddell, Captain. Her own cousin,' Livingstone added in disbelieving tones. 'Told him she'd see to it he never gets taken on as an apprentice by any lawyer in Edinburgh or anywhere else unless he allowed Professor Monro to enter the room to attend to her brother and Mr Arthur Menzies of Edmonstone.'

'Bitch.' Catto pronounced the word with studied precision.

'Aye,' Livingstone sighed. 'I'm afraid that's the word. But you should know Lieutenant Liddell did not give way to Miss Liddell's threats. It was only when Professor Monro joined the discussion that the Lieutenant and I decided we needed to take action.'

The older man was giving him a very shrewd look. Catto had thought before that the Sergeant, with his shock of white hair, height, broad shoulders and imposing presence, bore something of a resemblance either to Old Father Time or a benign and kindly God. There was more than kindness in those piercing blue eyes now, though. There was a warning.

'It was all getting a wee touch noisy, young Captain Catto. What with Miss Liddell shouting her head off and being joined in that endeavour by Professor Monro. Who demanded to know why we were detaining Mr Cosmo Liddell and Mr Arthur Menzies, whose families have aye been such generous benefactors to the hospital.'

Livingstone raised his eyebrows. Like his hair, they were white and luxuriant. 'Professor Monro seemed intent on demanding that at some length. In addition to which, the learned medical gentleman has a voice that could carry from one side of Loch Linnhe to the other.' The Sergeant shook his head, as though to rid himself of a ringing in his ears. 'And when folk start shouting,' he added in his soft West Highland lilt, 'all manner of things are likely to be said. Many of which might well be better left unsaid.'

Catto looked at him. Was a silent message being transmitted here? *We'll keep your secret. Me and Archie Liddell both.* Yet the phrase *trust no one* was still echoing around his head.

'You might say Lieutenant Liddell struck a bargain with Professor Monro. Suggested he didn't want a shouting match at the Daft Friday Ball. Not good for the reputation of the Royal Infirmary.'

Catto nodded. Despite his anger, he could appreciate the strategy. 'Were Liddell and Menzies fit to be moved?'

'Only in chairs and with a strong arm to get them down the stairs to those, sir. Those two young gentlemen will not be walking easy for a wee while yet, I'm thinking.' The Sergeant's eyes gleamed with satisfaction. 'Professor Monro recommended cold compresses and the passage of time.'

'Good work, Livingstone.'

The older man returned his captain's further nod of approval. 'They deserved it. Begging your pardon that you had to witness such a sorry scene, Miss Rankeillor.'

Without turning from her contemplation of the guard-room fire, Christian Rankeillor raised a jerky hand in dismissal of the apology. 'After what they did to Geordie's sister, I think they deserved it too.'

Geordie's eyes widened. Catto threw him a glance. 'I'll tell you later, lad. Is the snow showing any signs of lessening, Livingstone?'

Livingstone tilted his impressive head to one side. 'Maybe.'

'Have the ball-goers left the Assembly Rooms?'

'They are doing so right about now, Captain. Professor Monro insisted. Said they were all the guests of the Royal Infirmary and he could not allow them to run the risk of being marooned at the Assembly Rooms overnight. Lieutenant Liddell persuaded him to wait ten minutes before alerting folk to the snow. Giving us a head start on getting the prisoners out of the Assembly Rooms and back to the Liddell house before anyone else noticed.'

'Probably got more than ten minutes,' Livingstone added wisely. 'It'll have taken longer than that for them all to see the snow and run about clucking like headless chickens afore they got into the chairs. The Lieutenant is a clever young man, sir. Good at the thinking ahead. Good at the diplomacy, forbye.'

'So it would appear. Ably assisted by yourself, I fancy.' Thank God for that. Calmer now, Catto remained very aware of Kirsty Rankeillor as she stood there with her back to him, Livingstone and Geordie. The boy had retreated to perch on one of the dark wooden settles, where he was carefully minding his own business. He always did step back from any argument. Catto suspected he'd learned the hard way that discretion was the better part of valour.

'What about the lawyer?'

'Wanted to go with the prisoners, sir. Although I am not too sure *wanted* was the right word. He looked gey relieved when Lieutenant Liddell said he could not allow him to as much as see them without first consulting you.'

'So the lawyer has not spoken with them at all tonight?' Catto confirmed.

'Not one word, sir. He did not seem too concerned about that. Asked me to present his compliments and request you to call on him tomorrow at an hour to suit yourself. Says he will be pleased to give you your breakfast, your meridian or your supper.'

'That sounds like a lawyer. Already seeking to soft-soap me into agreeing to some sort of a deal to the benefit of his clients,' Catto said, immensely relieved that Mr Charles Paterson at least had not learned his secret tonight. 'How did he deal with Miss Charlotte Liddell?'

'Told her to say nothing to anybody about what had transpired and to allow herself to be escorted back home. Then he took himself off to his own house. She wasn't best pleased about any o' that.'

'Brave man to go against her, then,' Catto observed.

'He is very canny, sir.'

'Aren't they all? Lawyers, I mean. Who is holding the fort now at the Assembly Rooms?'

'Sergeant Crichton, backed up by four guards who returned with him up there after dispersing the mob here. You've had an interesting evening, young Captain Catto.'

'You might say that,' came the dry response. 'Anything else to add to it?' Then, when Livingstone betrayed an uncharacteristic hesitation: 'Spit it out, man.'

'Professor Monro also presents his compliments. He requests that you present yourself at the Assembly Rooms forthwith.'

'I'm not going there now.'

'He was most insistent, young Captain Catto.'

'Ah. So he didn't exactly *request* my presence at the Assembly Rooms. Let me guess how he put it. He insists – no, he *demands* – that I return with you right now and *explain myself*. Something of that nature?'

'Exactly of that nature, Captain,' the Sergeant replied uncomfortably.

Catto hadn't yet met Monro but he knew his reputation. Well-respected but could be demanding in the extreme. Inclined to shout first and ask questions later. Influential man, too. Professor of Anatomy at Edinburgh University and one of the managers of the vast new Royal Infirmary, pet project of many of the city's *prominenti*.

He couldn't afford to make an enemy of Monro. If the snow was going to trap them all inside Edinburgh for the next days, with several other influential citizens absent, Catto might well need his support. At the very least, he needed him not to challenge his own authority as Captain of the Town Guard. Therefore he should do as he was bid. 'Twas foolish in the extreme not to.

Only he couldn't. He had to see Kirsty Rankeillor safely home, get her back inside her house, off the public stage and out of sight. He needed Livingstone's help to carry the chair to Infirmary Street. He would send Geordie with a message for Sergeant Crichton and Professor Monro. Although that wasn't going to go down too well. Crichton knew Geordie and would trust any message the lad brought. How might Monro react to such a young messenger, though, and to Catto's refusal to respond immediately to that peremptory summons to the Assembly Rooms?

Badly. How else? Thinking it through, Catto realized the Sergeant was bestowing an odd look upon him, inclining his white head towards Christian Rankeillor.

'The young lady has been here alone with you in the guard-room for some time now, young Captain Catto?'

'Geordie was here,' Catto responded, and immediately wished

the words unsaid. Shrewd blue eyes swept over Kirsty Rankeillor's shimmering rose-pink back, went to a now yawning Geordie, and from there returned to Catto.

'Just so, sir.'

One more complication to add to the bloody tally. He was worried about her neck. If it became common knowledge she'd spent time alone with him in the guard-house this evening, the first casualty would be her reputation, torn to shreds by the wagging tongues of Edinburgh society.

Geordie would not be counted as a chaperone. Boys like him were barely noticed by their so-called betters. They would leave him out of the story, relishing this juiciest of morsels, chewing it over for weeks and months, destroying Christian Rankeillor in the process. There had already been gossip about her, arising out of his raid on the Rankeillor house last week.

He had planned for that to happen, another way to frighten her and her father as suspected Jacobites, show them that actions have consequences. Catto had been there when Charlotte Liddell had followed up on the gossip, sweeping into the apothecary's shop and pretending to sympathize in the hope of hearing more. When she had spotted him, standing quietly watching her, she had switched from gossiping bitch to flirt. Not a pretty sight.

What he had done to Kirsty Rankeillor wasn't pretty, either. He knew what happened to women who lost their reputations. None better. The old sadness came rolling towards him, like a wave sweeping in from a stormy sea. Unstoppable. Uncaring. Giving no thought at all to the havoc it was about to wreak. In his mind's eye he saw a fleeting image of his mother, her face pale and stricken. The old rhyme said names could never hurt you but the old rhyme was wrong. Names could wound and lacerate, fester for years in someone's head. Catto pushed the painful memories away, knowing he wouldn't be able to put one foot in front of the other if he didn't.

'Professor Monro can insist all he likes,' he told Livingstone. 'My priority now is to get Miss Rankeillor safely and discreetly home to Infirmary Street. After a further brief delay to allow the ball-goers to go in front of us.'

Where they could be productively marooned in their own homes for the next few days, cut off from their friends and neighbours by the snow. Gathered round their own firesides, with their backs to the outside world. Even if they had noticed anything untoward at the Assembly Rooms this evening, they would be less able to exchange any gossip about it.

Christian Rankeillor turned at last from her study of the guard-room fire. 'You should get up the road before you escort me home.'

'I'll make the decisions, madam.'

Christ Almighty. He had thought her prolonged silence resulted not only from his own rebuke but from a realization of the danger of her situation. Did she have to be so bloody self-sacrificing? Or did she still have the arrogance — or naïvéte — that made her believe herself invulnerable? Did she still not realize the danger in which she stood?

Livingstone filled the spiky pause. 'Miss Rankeillor should replace her mask. You too, young Captain Catto. We cannot be sure there will not be someone watching us, despite the snow. If they see a gentleman escorting a lady they might think only that you're on your way home from the ball.'

Another possible pitfall occurred to Catto. 'Your uniform might draw attention, Livingstone. You're a well-kent enough figure without it.'

Geordie stepped forward. 'I'll can help you carry the chair to Miss Rankeillor's house, Captain.'

'Sure, Geordie?'

The boy nodded his bright head, sending the luxuriant waves of his tousled golden hair dancing. 'I'm stronger than I look, sir,' he said, adding a matter-of-fact confirmation of what Catto had just been thinking. 'And nobody ever notices me.'

Catto squeezed the boy's skinny shoulder. 'Good man. This is a much better solution. Go back up to the Assembly Rooms, Livingstone. My compliments and apologies to Professor Monro. I shall call on him at his house first thing tomorrow. Having further urgent business to attend to tonight, business which unfortunately cannot wait. Be as diplomatic as you can. Then dispatch two men down to the Netherbow Port. I have reason to believe it to be unmanned and possibly unlocked.'

'Indeed, young Captain Catto? That'll not do. Are you sure you and the lad can manage the chair?'

'We'll have to manage it. I need you to exercise your authority up the road in conveying my message to Professor Monro. He'll take it better from you. I trust I do not have to ask you to say nothing to him or anyone else about Miss Rankeillor having been here at the guard-house tonight, Livingstone. Or,' Catto added carefully, 'that I currently have her under arrest.'

'Indeed, no, Captain.'

He was once again on the receiving end of a very shrewd look. 'I shall brief you fully tomorrow, Sergeant.'

'You're going to have a busy day, Mr Catto. Shall you require me with you at any point?'

'I'll send a message if I do. Or I may call past *The White Horse* to give you that briefing. Possibly in the late afternoon or early evening.' *The White Horse* was the coaching inn at the foot of the Canongate Livingstone ran with his young wife, the mother of their three small children.

'We'll be there all day, Captain. Pleased to feed ye at any time, forbye.'

'Then I shall not starve tomorrow.' Catto drew his black velvet and satin mask from the pocket of his green and silver waistcoat. The bruise on the back of his hand was badly discoloured now. Beginning to hurt, too. He glanced at the Doune pistol, lying on the settle along from his white leather sword belt and empty scabbard.

Following his gaze, Livingstone lifted the firearm and went through to the press in the internal corridor of the building, returning a moment or two later with a sword. He was the only person apart from Catto who had a key to the small weapons store. The Town Guard's main armoury was kept up at Edinburgh Castle, safe behind its massive stone walls. An Edinburgh mob was enough of a threat without weapons. One led by men reckless enough to force entry to the guard-house and arm themselves didn't bear thinking about.

Catto gave Livingstone a murmured word of thanks. He fastened his mask and shrugged his shoulders into his dark-green satin evening coat before lifting the sword belt over his head and sliding it into place. Kirsty Rankeillor stood watching him, her eyes following every movement.

As he swung his grey military cloak around his shoulders, he was waiting for her characteristic little shake, the one she gave when she shifted from one subject or activity to another. That was another of her mannerisms he had observed this week. It had reminded him of a wee dog he had once known emerging from a lochan and shaking itself dry.

This time the little shake didn't come. Instead, she moved like a woman in a dream. No, not a dream. An old Scots word came back to him. She was in a *dwam*, a waking dream, her thoughts faraway from where she actually was. She lifted her cloak and drew out her own mask. More uncharacteristic behaviour. The young woman who so competently dispensed herbs, healing and physic had become all fingers and thumbs.

'Give it to me,' he said, holding out an impatient hand. 'I'll do it. Or we'll never get out of here.'

She turned away from him again, although not before he had seen tears spring to her eyes. After he had tied the strings, he allowed his fingers to linger for a few seconds on her shoulders. They felt stiff and tense under his hands.

I do not want to be harsh with you. But you have to realize the danger in which you stand and I do not think you do. Not yet.

She drew in a breath and lifted her head. Following suit, Catto found Sergeant Livingstone giving him that look again. 'What?' he demanded.

'Ach well, young Captain Catto,' said the sergeant, his accent soft with the cadences of his native West Highlands even after years of soldiering abroad, followed by years in Edinburgh as an innkeeper, 'if you dinna ken it'll not be me as will be telling you.'

9

Silent and withdrawn, Christian allowed herself and her gown to be tucked into the sedan chair. Working efficiently and quickly to bundle up her skirts and collapse the articulated hoops of the petticoat beneath them, Robert Catto shut her into the chair and warned her to be ready to be lifted. Outwardly as still as a statue even as he and Geordie raised the chair a few seconds later, inwardly she was rebuking herself for her stupidity. She should not have spoken to him as she had in front of his sergeant. It betrayed a familiarity which complicated an already complex situation.

'Twas a perilous situation too, as much for Robert Catto as for herself. She could well see the difficulties which confronted him. First and foremost came his connection to John Roy Stuart. As an officer in the British army, his allegiance sworn to German Geordie and the House of Hanover, he must have spent years doing his damnedest to keep that secret, never able to reveal who his father was. No wonder he was habitually so guarded, giving so little of his real self away. After tonight, here in Edinburgh, several people now knew his secret. Herself included. Some of those people, or the other people they might tell, would draw inferences from it, most of all that he had indeed allowed John Roy to escape.

She knew he hadn't. She could lie about that. Except she couldn't see how that would save her own skin. Except that she hated dishonesty with a passion. She never lied if she could help it, did so only when a patient needed kindness rather than the truth. She could never bring herself to lie about something like this, where the lie would hurt someone. Even an enemy. For he remained that. Despite the intimate interlude back at the guard-house, despite those kisses they had shared.

Others might lie, though. Or not care where the truth lay, as long as the story they told suited their book. He could be court-martialled, dishonourably dismissed from the army and the military service which clearly gave his life its meaning. Dear God, it could be worse even than that.

In her imagination the picture was clear: the shadow of the gallows casting the hideous shapes of scaffold and noose not only over her father, her friends, maybe even herself, but also over him. The British army was brutal on the minor misdemeanours of the common soldiers within its ranks, doling out brutal floggings. Lash after lash, until a man no longer had the strength to scream in pain but was reduced to slumping forward groaning out his agony, held upright only by the ropes which bound him, his back a bloodied mess.

She thanked God she had never witnessed such a scene but she had heard the stories. If the army thought a man or an officer guilty of treason, mercy was in even shorter supply. There would be no mercy from the other side, either. After tonight, she knew that for a fact. A bullet would dispatch the enemies of the Jacobites. No time to explain or try to justify or strike bargains, a ball of lead would whistle through the air and that would be it.

Hadn't John Roy Stuart himself had one of his pistols trained on her when she first entered the cell in the Infirmary where Jamie and her father had concealed him? She had thought then this must be what war was, driving men who had no personal quarrel to be prepared to kill each other. She shivered. As the chill spread throughout her body she tried with all her might to resist it. She could not freeze into fear and panic. She had to think. There had to be something she could do. There had to be.

❖

The only sound was the crunching of his and Geordie's feet. Not another living soul was moving up or down the High Street. No dogs trotting along as though they had an errand to run. No cats leaping up onto high walls or slinking in and out of dark closes. Like the humans, they too had sought shelter from the weather.

The Daft Friday ball-goers must have all been got safely home. The newly made tracks and footprints of the caddies who had conveyed them were there to be seen in the snow. That had finally stopped falling but Catto felt sure there was more to come. Looking up, he could discern heavy clouds, intensely dark grey against the blackness of the night sky.

Only an hour before, the High Street had been thronged with noisy, jostling revellers celebrating the start of Yuletide. Its emptiness now was unsettling. Or apparent emptiness. They were trudging past the yawning black mouths of too many dark closes. Any one of those might be concealing a silent watcher.

'Turning off the High Street and round this next corner now, Geordie,' Catto called softly. 'We'll take it slow.'

'Aye, Captain,' came the reply. Before the boy followed his lead in describing a careful arc as they changed direction to head for Infirmary Street, Catto sent a few more soft words back to Kirsty Rankeillor through the unglazed window in the side of the chair. 'Hold yourself steady in there.'

A burst of laughter rose loud enough to break out through the tightly shut windows of the tavern they were passing. The yellow light of candles spilled through the thick glass to warm the eerie blue whiteness of the snow. Freshly fallen as it was, with fewer footprints now they had left the High Street, there was purchase in it. They were making good progress.

There wasn't much moonlight but Catto's eyes had grown accustomed to the gloom. Geordie too seemed sure-footed in the dark.

The boy came from a long line of East Lothian coal miners. He was bound to have eyes more accustomed than most to dimly lit places—

A prickle of unease raised the fine hairs under the stiffened black ribbon bow at the back of Catto's neck. Someone was watching them. He could feel it. His brain began to race, calculating how long it would take him to shout to Geordie to set the chair safely down, whirl round and draw his sword from its scabbard. For a few intense seconds, the sound of his own breathing was louder in his ears than the crunch of his and the boy's feet.

He was on the point of calling out to Geordie to stop when the feeling of being watched quite suddenly faded, then passed, which was no guarantee unseen eyes weren't still trained on them. The sooner they got to Infirmary Street, the better. They had reached the top of the Horse Wynd. Catto threw a soft enquiry over his shoulder. 'All right, Geordie?'

'Fine, Captain. Forbye my hands are a wee bittie cold and sore.'

Catto swore under his breath. Another bloody delay, but a necessary one by the sound of it. Geordie was a stoical boy. *A wee bittie cold and sore* probably meant his hands were burning with pain.

'Set the chair down, lad. On three.' Catto counted out the numbers. 'Gently, now. We'll rest for a moment. Aye, that's it, rub your hands together to warm them up. We'll need to hold on even tighter going down the brae here.'

As he walked forward to stand next to her, their passenger pushed back the stiff pleated blind covering the window in the side of the chair. She'd had the sense to stay behind it on their previous journey from the Assembly Rooms down to the guard-house. Catto had glanced over at her conveyance often enough to be sure of that. Despite the bright evening gown, with a bit of luck she'd been well-shielded by a phalanx of guards when Catto had hustled her and his other prisoners in there earlier.

Geordie's face came into view as he leaned to one side and offered her a shy smile. 'Dinna worry, Miss Rankeillor. We'll no' tip ye oot into the snow.'

'Glad to hear it, Geordie.' The wan smile she'd given the boy in return for his own faded when she turned and looked up. Catto turned too, so that he had his back to Geordie. A yearning for what might have been swept over him. If only he were no more than a gentleman escorting a lady returning from the Daft Friday ball. The snow and the need to see her safely home would have allowed them this unusual moment alone together, with no chaperone save for the boy so studiously ignoring them: making this the time for a little dalliance. Some teasing, perhaps.

He could lean into the chair, wrap his chilly hands around her, seek out exposed flesh on her arms and around the neckline of her bodice, laugh as she yelped, keep his cold fingers on that soft skin till they were warm again. He could kiss her and murmur her name, press his lips against her creamy brow and smooth, silky hair. He knew the scent of that now, clean and sweet. Flowery but fresh. Probably some preparation she concocted herself in the apothecary's shop from where she and her father dispensed physic.

He wanted to do all that and more. He wanted to reassure her everything was going to be all right. He wanted to tell her he was sorry for speaking so harshly to her. He could do none of those things, could not even smile at her. They were standing close enough for her to be able to see him offer that small gesture of comfort, even in the gloom of the night.

Someone else might notice such a kindness, someone else watching from inside a tenement close or standing to one side of a darkened window. For both their sakes, he could not afford to give anything away. God, he hated this bloody game: and if he told Kirsty Rankeillor everything was going to be all right, he'd be lying through his sodding teeth. Although, by the look on her face, she wouldn't believe him anyway.

Frustrated beyond belief, Catto tipped his head back to gaze up at the dark heavens. The Jacobite agent couldn't be far away, no distance away out there under the snow-laden sky. Jamie Buchan of Balnamoon was probably guiding him to Leith. Or they might already have reached it. Risky, all too close to Edinburgh, but a good hiding place all the same, especially if the next stage of the journey was to head north by sea to the Highlands.

Nest of Jacobites down there on the Firth of Forth. Like Edinburgh, the busy port was full of tenement lands, closes and warehouses, all crammed together. Rabbit warrens and rat runs. Bloody needle in a haystack job trying to find anyone in those labyrinths. He had a handful of names of people the Lord President considered to be worth the watching but calling on any suspected Jacobite plotters in his official capacity would raise an immediate alert, sending out a warning to anyone else who might be involved.

In any case, the weather was against him. There was no way he could make his way to Leith tonight. By the looks of it, nor tomorrow or the next day either. The chances were high the road down there was going to be impassable for the next few days, maybe as long as a week. By which time the Jacobite agent would be long gone and the Lord President and the crucial people that gentleman needed to inform would still not know of the man's presence in Scotland and the danger he posed.

The man. The Jacobite agent. Aye, that was how he preferred to think of him. If he had to think of him at all. Right at this moment, standing there in the snow, Catto was finding it difficult to think about anything else. Even if there was some small satisfaction in reflecting that the weather was against his quarry too. Leith was less than three miles away but that was far enough in this snow, especially when you were nursing an injured leg. The man had been walking with a stick and clearly struggling. Catto wished him no respite. Let him be blinded by snow flurries. Let him freeze. Let his leg throb with pain. Let him fall off his horse and tumble arse over elbow into a fucking snow drift—

Deep in thought, he had lowered his guard enough that he did not sense any movement until the approaching assailant was nearly upon him.

10

'Stay back, Geordie!' Catto had barely time enough to utter that curt command as he whirled around, finding out exactly how long it took him to withdraw this unfamiliar sword from its scabbard. His assailant checked his headlong dash, skidded and almost fell, but quickly righted himself.

'Don't be a bloody fool,' Catto growled. One man. Dark clothes. A checked tweed plaid wrapped slantwise across his body, a fold or two pulled up to cover the bottom half of his face. A young man, judging by his slim build and by how quickly he had recovered his balance. One of Jamie Buchan of Balnamoon's friends and accomplices?

The would-be attacker drew a shaking hand from under his cloak. It held a pistol. Catto turned the naked steel in his own hand, allowing it to catch the light from the glow of a glass-enclosed lantern set above a door they had passed a few yards back along the street. The trembling hand grew even shakier.

'You know,' Catto drawled, 'this is becoming somewhat tedious. I've already had a pistol fired at me this evening. Before that someone was going to smother me with a cushion. I'm beginning to feel like a cat. Although by my reckoning I still have seven lives left. How about you? Do you think you can get your courage up to fire before I reach you with this blade?'

In one ear he heard a small exclamation of fear from inside the chair. The other was filled with the ragged breathing of the young man in front of him. The two of them stood facing each other in silence. In that moment of stillness, seeing out of the corner of his eye the flickering candle flame of the door lantern a few yards back along the road, an idea leapt like a flash of gunpowder into Catto's mind.

He rejected it as quickly as it had come to him. *No. Too dangerous. Potentially with far too many repercussions for me. Couldn't ever work, anyway. It's too late for it to work. Doesn't have a hope in hell of success.* Then, from one heartbeat to the next: *What else do I have? And maybe, just maybe, with a bit of luck and a following wind...*

'Go home.' He spoke softly but his heart was racing. 'Go home,' he said again. 'And I'd suggest you put that pistol away first before you shoot yourself in the foot.'

Strange how long a few seconds can stretch. Troubled eyes fixed on Catto's face. That shaking hand clutched and re-clutched the pistol. The man's palm must be damp with sweat. He was clearly an amateur. An amateur holding a gun with an unsteady hand could still dispatch you.

Maybe this was it, then. Maybe he was living through his final moments, would soon be flying backwards, falling onto the causeway, his arms flying out in reaction to the impact of the bullet tearing a jagged hole in his chest. He'd lie there dying on an Edinburgh street, his blood seeping out in a widening patch onto the fresh white snow, red showing black in the darkness of the night.

Kirsty Rankeillor and Geordie would be staring down at him, their eyes wide with shock. She'd crouch down and try to help him, of course. Her father was a medical man, a surgeon-apothecary. She was her father's apprentice when it came to healing herbs and potions. Whatever the circumstances, whoever the injured person might be, her first instinct was always to relieve pain, to cure and console.

Robert Catto was a soldier. His first instinct was to strike out, attack in defence of himself and others. He had taken other men's lives. He had looked his own death in the eye on more than one battlefield. On two or three of those occasions he'd been aware of what a captain from Saxony he'd fought alongside had called *Todeslust*, a desire for death. Yet even in his lowest moments, that had never been more than a fleeting thought. He wanted to live.

He wanted that even more now. Since he'd met her. However flimsy his plan might turn out to be. However much he knew there could be no possible future for Kirsty Rankeillor and himself. However much he knew, God help them both, that he was going to have to hand her over to justice sooner or later. Nor was he going to die lying on his back on the snow in sodding Edinburgh like some brawling fucking drunkard.

'Don't be a bloody fool,' he repeated, his eyes still locked with those of the other man. Once more he turned the sword to catch the light. Hold the line. Stay focussed. Face the bastard down. Hellfire, he'd done this times without number. The silence didn't stretch so far this time. With a grunt of despair, the attacker uncocked the pistol and turned away. He ran up the street and fell forward onto one knee before scrambling back to his feet in a frantic swirl of legs and flying snow. Wheeling to the right, he dodged down a close and was lost to view.

Catto stepped back and pushed the blind of the chair fully open. Her face was in shadow but he caught a flash from glittering eyes, saw her raise one hand to her mouth, slim fingers white in the gloom. 'He might have shot you dead!'

'So might you.'

'I didn't mean to.'

'Not sure he did either.'

Geordie was hovering at his shoulder. Catto swung round, sensing as much as seeing the boy's stunned reaction to what had happened. 'No harm done, Geordie. Back to the front of the chair, lad, and wait for my command. We'll be off shortly.'

Kirsty Rankeillor waited until Geordie had done that, kept her voice low. 'What if he tries again?'

'He won't,' Catto said, turning to face her. 'He's lost his nerve. Might never get it back again.'

'How can you be so sure?'

'Because I am.' Also because he had to be. The line he'd crossed in letting the man go was huge. He had no choice but to hope to hell it was worth it. A line? More like the bloody Rubicon in full fucking spate. There was no going back now.

'What do you think he wanted?'

'Maybe to rescue you. Or whoever he thought you were.'

'He might have thought you had … the Jacobite agent … in here in the chair?'

'Possibly. Or perhaps he sought to interrogate you as to exactly what happened at the guard-house an hour since.'

'You would not have permitted him to do that.'

'That might have been why he was pointing a pistol at me,' Catto said drily. 'To dispose of me in order to get to you.' He lowered his head, the better to safely return the sword to its scabbard. He'd prefer not to slice off a couple of fingertips in the process. He was answering her with one part of his brain. The rest of it was stitching together the plan that had so recently come to him. 'If he could have got his courage up, I daresay he might have shot Geordie too. Got rid of all the witnesses.' He too had lowered his voice so the lad could not hear him.

'No,' she breathed. 'He would never have done that!'

Transferring his attention from the scabbard to her, Catto tilted his head to one side in a gesture of interrogation. 'Do you have a particular *he* in mind?'

'Wh-whoever th-that w-was,' came a stuttered reply. 'No one would shoot a young boy. Murder him in cold blood? I cannot believe anyone would do that … *could* do that.'

'Believe it,' he said. 'Don't you know the old saying? Three men can keep a secret if two of them are dead. Men with a cause. Everything comes second to it. And their blood is seldom cold.'

Even in the gloom, he could see there was no longer any need for him to scare the living daylights out of her. Her teeth were beginning to chatter. He could quiz her further on the possible identity of the assailant while she was in this vulnerable state. Or he could do what he did next, reaching into the chair to grab one ice-cold hand, not quite knowing why he wasn't pressing her for a name while also taking such a foolhardy step. An unnecessary risk when he couldn't know if there were other watchers in the shadows. All at once that didn't seem to matter so much.

'I c-cannot let B-Betty see me l-like this.'

'Then hold on tight,' Catto said, folding his fingers around her own, feeling her grip tightly in return. 'I won't let you fall.'

'I think y-you have ch-chosen an unfortunate m-metaphor, sir.'

I won't let you fall. If she'd so quickly made the connection, she must be thinking about this too. The drop. Dancing the Tyburn jig. The Edinburgh mob at the Grassmarket, hooting and jeering as the condemned were launched into eternity. He did not want either of them to be thinking of any of that, although his gaffe had put some heart into her. He quashed the vile pictures in his head in favour of focussing on the little smile now curving her mouth, thrown into prominence by the velvet mask covering her eyes.

I won't let you fall. He wanted to say it again and again, promise her he would save her. How he was to do that he had no bloody idea. Nor how he might be going to save himself. Instead, he spoke with an air of apparent unconcern. 'I've always had a way with words.'

'I'd s-say so. Even if they are overwhelmingly of the sarcastic variety.'

His bluff, no-nonsense approach was working. The stutter was fading, as the trembling hand and mouth had stilled.

'Why did you let him go?'

'My hands are rather full at the moment. Don't you think?'

''Twas not because you want them to continue to doubt which side you are on?'

'You could relieve them of any doubts they might have about that.'

'Could I?'

Aye, and she knew that as well as he did. As he knew there was little chance of fooling her a second time as to his own motives and loyalties, especially not after their conversation this evening back at the guardhouse. A different weapon was required here. There were divisions and factions among the adherents of the Stuart Cause, also fears over the existence of *agents provocateurs* in the pay of the Government. *Beware the enemy who comes to you in the guise of a friend.* He stayed silent, allowing her to work it out for herself. Tried and tested technique.

'They might have doubts about me too,' she said. 'After the events of this evening. Especially if anyone sees us as we are now.'

'They might well have doubts about you,' he agreed. 'Which might well extend to your father. Therefore the longer we keep them in ignorance the better. Agreed?'

She nodded, giving him a momentary pang of shame for planting that thought in her head. She and her father were close. 'Twould not be long before she was imagining all manner of horrors that might befall Patrick Rankeillor if his loyalty to the Stuart Cause were called into question. 'Can you hazard a guess as to who our assailant might have been?'

'No.'

'And you would not tell me if you did,' he replied, and heard her take a quick little breath. Panic because she feared he might indeed press her on this? Which he would, although not tonight, a decision he was continuing to choose not to explain to himself. 'Do you know who they are? Those people who might have doubts about you, me and Professor Rankeillor?'

'You cannot expect me to tell you that either.' She blurted the words out, adding a hasty rider. 'Even if I did know.'

His heart sank. So there were more names to be got out of her. He needed each and every one he could find, from whatever source, all to be passed over to the Lord President. Most would probably be small fry but there was no way he could know for sure. He had to get as many as he could.

John Roy Stuart was definitely a major player in the Stuart Cause. Catto's failure to hold on to him was bitter as gall. He clamped down hard on the troubled memories that thought was already conjuring up. What he had to think about now was how he could continue to do his duty and carry out his mission, the one for which the Lord President had recalled him to Edinburgh from the war in Europe.

If John Roy Stuart headed north from Edinburgh by sea and Catto got a dispatch to Duncan Forbes by the same means of transport, Culloden could then sound the alert to the most trusted of his Scotland-wide network of agents and informants, especially those on the likely route such a high-ranking Jacobite agent would take through Buchan, Banffshire and the Highlands.

Armed with the knowledge and the names Catto gave him, the Lord President could also warn those who needed to know of this renewed threat from the Disaffected, convince the people he referred to as 'those buggers in London' that it was real. Perhaps yet more crucial, Duncan Forbes could also target those who might be tempted to nail their colours to the Stuart mast and turn them from that course.

Catto knew from his own experience how persuasive the Lord President could be. As a boy, he'd been convinced Duncan Forbes knew or was related to everybody from Gretna Green to John o' Groat's and beyond. Culloden made it his business to know people's secrets too, find out what their various Achilles' heels were. He would have no scruples about squeezing those hard. Persuasive was altogether too mild a word. Blackmail would be a more accurate one.

The weather wasn't going to make it easy to send a dispatch north. 'Twas frustrating beyond measure that the biggest obstacle was the handful of miles between Edinburgh and Leith. Not that any of the mail coaches or post riders were going to be able to get through this snow on any of the roads north. Although in another way the weather might prove to be Catto's ally.

Since he'd stepped ashore at Leith more than a month since, he'd been playing the role of a covert Jacobite. Making himself available in taverns, engaging in apparently casual conversations, dropping the odd word here, carefully withholding comment there. Fooling the genuine Jacobite plotters into trusting him. Raising smoke and tilting mirrors to conceal his true mission.

Sick of the whole bloody charade though he was, it had worked. He was by no means sure it still could. Yet the snow fast imprisoning Edinburgh gave him an opportunity he could not afford to lose. If the city were cut off for the next few days, maybe even a week, who among those people who thought he was at least ambivalent about the Stuart Cause was going to know any different? Mentally, he ran through those who would now be convinced of the truth, that Robert Catto was an implacable enemy to each and every miserable Jacobite who crawled the face of the earth. He glanced at Kirsty Rankeillor. With one possible exception.

Balnamoon knew and might possibly tell whoever was giving him shelter tonight. Would the man Jamie Buchan was protecting betray Catto too? Once more, he ejected that thought – and that treacherous word – from his head as quickly as both had jumped in there. In any case, if Edinburgh was cut off by this snow, Leith might as well be as far away as the moon.

Cosmo Liddell and Arthur Menzies of Edmonstone knew. Thanks to Livingstone and Archie Liddell, they were now under house arrest, although there was a potential problem there. Cosmo Liddell had too many friends in high places, the sort who could get him and his friend freed, give them the power to step back out into the world and tell other people what had happened at the Assembly Rooms tonight. Catto would have to try a different technique there. Back to the smoke and mirrors.

Archie Liddell and Livingstone knew. He had begun to think he might trust them both but only time would tell. For now he would continue to proceed with caution. The Rankeillors too had friends in high places but Catto was more confident of his ability to keep Kirsty Rankeillor confined to her house. Her fears for the father of whom she was so fond were a further encouragement to stay silent about the events of this evening. He spelled that out to her, all the same. 'You must say as little as possible about all of this. Including to your housekeeper.'

She relaxed enough for a tinge of amusement to once more colour her voice, sending Catto's emotions flying off in another direction. Even in the most trying of circumstances, 'twould seem her sense of humour was never very far below the surface.

'How do you think I'm going to get away with that?'

'You have to. The more she knows, the more dangerous it is for her. And they would be rougher on her than they would be on you.'

'My father said exactly that.'

'Bloody hell, woman,' he groaned, 'do you not realize how indiscreet that statement is?'

She bit her lip. 'I do now. I am not very good at this, am I? Being discreet.'

'You're hopeless. Fortunately it was only me who heard you. But you must learn to guard your tongue. Can Geordie stay at your house tonight?'

'As your spy? In any case, why are you asking me and not telling me?'

'Manners,' he said.

'Hah! That's rich, coming from you. If you're glaring at me, I cannot see it in this gloom.'

'I'm not glaring at you. Nor would I lay the burden of being my spy upon the lad. I'm asking you to let him stay overnight because once he goes in from the cold to a warm house he will very likely succumb to shock and weariness. Also because 'twould comfort him to be near his sister.'

'Also because 'twould be safer for him. Should whoever that was manage to get his courage up to try again.' She spoke in matter-of-fact tones, adding drily: 'Or perhaps someone else with malice in his heart towards you.'

'I imagine there might be a few who fit that description. I'm used to that. As I am well-used to taking care of myself.'

He might yet have to. Depending on how organized they were, how many of them there were and how much they knew. He suspected the botched attack had been made with one specific aim: to silence him before he could pass on the information about the Jacobite agent's presence in Edinburgh and departure for, in all likelihood, the North East and the Highlands.

Jamie Buchan of Balnamoon had wanted Kirsty Rankeillor to shoot him. Probably he had realized she wouldn't be capable of such an act and had asked someone else to do it in case she baulked at the task. Which added his assailant to the list of people who now knew Catto was no friend to the Jacobite Cause. By letting the man run away, Catto hoped he'd sent a message that would at least confuse him and any other plotters in Edinburgh, stay their hands. He had to hammer that message home. Tonight, for the sake of her safety and his own, which gave him an immediate dilemma.

'Twas too much to expect Geordie to guard her and the Rankeillor household. Catto could only be completely sure of her safety if he himself kept watch at Infirmary Street right through until the winter dawn. But who knew what machinations might be going on out in the town while he sat there at the foot of her stairs wrapped up in his cloak on the hard black and white squares of the floor with his back against the wall, trying not to doze off as the night wore on?

He had to get to Liddell and Edmonstone as soon as possible too, before the night was very much older. He had a seed to plant in Edmonstone's head and it was crucial that he did so quickly.

'Are you taking my measure … Kirsty?' he added, aware, despite the gloom of the night, that her eyes were focussed on his face. *Kirsty.*

Absurdly, like her with him, he was a little shy about using her first name. He'd have been better sticking to *madam* or *Miss Rankeillor*. But it was altogether too late for that. Enemies they might remain, yet they stood together in the midst of so much danger. Catto could very nearly feel it, a tangible presence circling around them like a marauding wolf, gathering its strength in the shadows.

Catching a snowflake on his bottom lip, he glanced heavenwards. 'Come on. It's starting up again. All right, Geordie?' he called softly to the boy. 'Once more on a count of three. Keep a tight grip as we go down the hill. I'll hold us back as much as I can.'

It took no more than a few steps for the backs of Catto's legs to grow tense from the strain of anchoring the chair. Halfway down the brae strain became aching pain. He gasped when it spiked up into his thigh. He had taken a French musket ball there at Dettingen back in June. Now and again the wound issued a vicious reminder that it had not yet fully healed. He followed the gasp with a few muttered curses directed at the misbegotten French bastard who had shot him. Poetic justice, he supposed. He still did not regret ill-wishing John Roy Stuart. Not for one fucking second.

He could have wept with relief when they reached the flatness of Infirmary Street and the snow became once again the only physical difficulty with which he and the boy had to contend. They had barely set the chair down in front of the Rankeillors' house when the ghost materialized at his side.

11

Every sense alert, Murdo Robertson slid through the shadows to let himself in by the unobtrusive side door which led directly into the apothecary's shop at Edinburgh Royal Infirmary. He turned to lock the door behind him, fingers fumbling as he transferred the key from one side of the lock to the other. His hands were shaking and his palms were moist.

He managed it at last, hung the key on its hook to the side of the door and wiped his damp hands on the thick tweed plaid wrapped around his body. Heart thumping with relief, he drew in one shaky breath before taking a cold metal key ring out of his pocket and repeating the procedure with the door leading out into the main lobby of the hospital.

The high-ceilinged space had never seemed so vast and echoing. Placing his feet as carefully as a cat on a midnight prowl, he stole up the stone stairs to the resident's room on the second floor. Small glass lanterns hung on each landing flickered, giving just enough light to see by. The hospital was eerily quiet.

Look confident. Have a plausible excuse ready as to why you are where you are. That had been Jamie's advice. Murdo straightened up and stood for a moment in the stairwell, catching his breath. He might legitimately have been up late tending to a patient and was now on his way back from one of the wards. He hoped all the same he wasn't going to meet the infirmary's lady governess gliding down the stairs on a similar errand. Agnes Moncur had a way of materializing out of nowhere. As she could look at you as though she knew all your secrets.

His luck held. He made the resident's room without meeting a single living soul. Selecting the second key from the ring he had slid over one finger, he unlocked the door and stepped inside. He remembered in the nick of time to catch the edge of the door, wrapping the fingers of his free hand around the wood to stop it from swinging shut. A door slamming on any of the landings echoed up and down the draughty stone stairs, the noise radiating out along the corridors to the wards.

He pushed the door to, closing and locking it as quietly as he could. Not easy when his hands were still not quite steady. Putting his back to the solid wood, he closed his eyes and sucked in a few more breaths. The air in the room was as cold as ice. In the winter it invariably was. He had swung the plaid around himself tonight not only for warmth while he was outside, but also to spread over the bed here as an extra blanket.

He drew the pistol from the deep folds of the cloth. With a small exclamation of disgust, he raised his arm and tossed the gun onto the narrow bed. He would find a hiding place for it in a moment. Professor Monro was strict about no weapons being brought into the hospital.

This is a place of healing. That's what he always said. *We will have no swords or guns here.* The professor's own weapon of choice was his booming voice and his sharp tongue. If you displeased him in any way, he never left you in any doubt about it. Nor did Murdo Robertson need to be in more hot water than he already was. Professor Monro would be incandescent with rage when he found out two of his junior doctors had swapped residency duties without first consulting him.

What else could they do? Jamie disappearing overnight and deserting his post was bad enough. They'd had to concoct a story that he'd received word his mother was very ill, up in Banffshire, and he had been obliged to head north before the snow made that impossible.

Murdo could only hope Professor Monro didn't know Jamie's mother was long dead.

His breathing less ragged, Murdo pushed himself off the door. He unwound the length of tweed, spread it over the bed and sat down on top of it. Bugger. This mattress was even lumpier than it had been the last time he'd slept on it. How long he was going to have put up with it now was anybody's guess. Jamie wasn't coming back to Edinburgh any time soon.

Oh dear God, but that was a thought to make a man feel lonely. Isolated. On his own. With nobody now to turn to for advice or guidance. For a moment, Murdo sat on the edge of the uncomfortable bed, thinking of his own mother. She worried about him, he knew. How much more anxiety would she have if she knew what he'd been up to tonight or what he had so very nearly done.

He sent her a heartfelt silent apology, leaned forward and slid out one of the boxes graciously allocated to the hospital's residents to store their meagre possessions. Jamie's bits and pieces were still in there. Placing the pistol next to them, Murdo slid the box back under the bed. Calmer but still shaken, he muttered an instruction to himself. 'Pull yourself together, man.' Easier said than done. The world he knew had turned into a bewildering place over the course of this last week. Bewildering ... and terrifying. Alone in this chilly and cheerless room, Murdo could admit that to himself.

I left Kirsty in the guard-house with a pistol trained on the Town Guard captain. Her father may well swing if she hasn't used it.

Kirsty's father. Professor Patrick Rankeillor. A teacher who actually seemed to like his students, one who drew the best out of them by helpful questions and smiling encouragement. A man who also seemed to remember what it was like to be young and poor and permanently tired and nothing like as sure of yourself as you tried to pretend.

We may all have to do things we would never have contemplated before this is all over. That was something else Jamie had said. He had said it again at the Netherbow Port, although not until Mr Fox was out into Leith Wynd and being helped up onto a horse by a man waiting there, on horseback, holding two other mounts. Murdo hadn't recognized him. As he hadn't recognized the other man who had played the caddy with him as they had carried the hospital's chair up to the Assembly Rooms with Mr Fox inside.

'Damn and bloody blast!' Murdo jumped at the sound of his own voice. The hospital's sedan chair was still up there. What the Devil was he going to do about that? He'd have to rouse one of the orderlies from his bed and persuade him to go up there with him in the freezing cold and darkness of the early morning, only a few short hours away. That wasn't going to make him very popular. Nor could he work out how to explain why the chair, used for transporting patients between the wards and floors of the hospital, had ended up at the other end of the town.

Murdo had waited outside the Assembly Rooms in the West Bow, not next to the hospital's chair, where some of the other waiting caddies might have engaged him in conversation, but standing freezing in the shadows of one of the closes opposite. Earlier in the day, Jamie had given him his instructions. *We shall leave about half past nine, giving us enough time to get down to the Netherbow before it closes at ten. You and I shall carry the chair.*

Seeing Jamie emerge from the Assembly Rooms, clearly under arrest, had given Murdo the fright of his life. For one awful moment, his brain as cold and numb as his feet, he had wished to be anywhere but the here and now. He had recovered himself, although he had remained terrified as he followed the little procession through the surging crowd of Daft Friday revellers to the guard-house. The Jacobite agent to whom Jamie had given the *nom-de-guerre* of Mr Fox had to be in one of the sedan chairs. Murdo had wondered who was in the other.

Later he had found out, or as near as dammit. If Jamie had left Kirsty Rankeillor pointing a pistol at the captain of the Town Guard, why on earth had that man been carrying her back home to Infirmary

79

Street an hour later? It had to have been her in there when Murdo had failed so abysmally in the task Jamie had set him.

Before Mr Fox had been helped out into the swirling snow he had insisted the boy Jamie had brought with him as a hostage should be freed. 'Away you go, lad!' That lad had wasted no time in taking to his heels. Another man who had been there, dressed in the uniform of the Town Guard, had called after the boy. 'Tell the Captain I'm sorry!' Then he too had disappeared into the snowy night, leaving Murdo and Jamie standing alone together in the guard-room of the Netherbow Port.

You still have the pistol?

Jamie's eyes had dropped to the weapon tucked into Murdo's belt before rising again to his face. He'd given him the gun this afternoon. God help him, Murdo had been excited by that. Now he felt sick to his stomach.

Use it, Murdo. You must use it. I'm depending on you. The Cause is depending on you.

There were other words ringing around Murdo Robertson's head. He had heard them too when he had pointed the pistol at the Town Guard captain. *First, do no harm.* The Hippocratic Oath. In which doctors swear to preserve life whenever and wherever they can. Then he had heard again what Jamie had said to him.

First do no harm. The Cause is depending on you.

What the Devil he was to do now he did not know. There were so many questions to which he had no answers. Most of all, why had the Town Guard captain let him go? He might easily have run him through or disabled him with a slash of that glittering sword to the arm or the leg and established who he was. Why had he not done so?

Murdo looked up and out of the window of his room. It had no curtains, offering a view of a sky above Edinburgh's rooftops and chimneys which was blue-black with the threat of more snow.

He was in uncharted waters now. They all were.

12

Catto's hand snapped to the hilt of his sword. It stayed there when a soft voice whispered in his ear. 'It's me, Captain.'

So much for his evening eye mask helping to conceal his identity. Although he supposed his height and Geordie being the second caddy might have been a bit of a giveaway.

William Angus Stewart was an Appin man and a kinsman of Sergeant Livingstone. His words were threaded through with the same musical West Highland lilt. 'I was heading back up to the guard-house when I spotted you coming along Infirmary Street, sir. Once I realized you were making for Professor Rankeillor's house I thought you might be needing me here.'

'I do,' Catto murmured. Thank God for one piece of luck on this disastrous evening. Or maybe it was naïve to believe this encounter was purely fortuitous. The sensation of being watched need not necessarily have come from his assailant. As other eyes might have been on him and Catto during their encounter, waiting to see who came off best. Scotland was a place of conflicting — and often shifting — loyalties.

Right now though, William Angus Stewart could give him the help he needed. The man was not only a member of the Town Guard and a caddie, but also one of the Lord President's informants and agents. Living between the Rankeillor house and the nearby Royal Infirmary, his wife, mother and brood of children had already been deployed this week in keeping watch on both buildings and any movements between them.

'Can you disappear but reinstate the watch on this house? Discreetly, as before.'

'Till the morning?'

'Till I tell you otherwise. Take note of anyone who leaves, anyone who arrives, anyone who so much as approaches the place. There may be no one but remain vigilant. My further orders to come. See this chair gets back to where it belongs before dawn tomorrow morning.'

'Consider it done, sir.'

'Can you enlist help from your family? I need the back of the house and the physic garden watched too. Just in case.'

'I'll get my two eldest laddies, Captain. If you'll give me a moment to juke back home and fetch them.'

'Quick as you can. I cannot bide here for long.'

'You're going back to the guard-house, Captain?'

'Briefly. If any of the men have returned thither, I shall dispatch two or three of them down here. Then your sons may stand down.'

Stewart had already disappeared into the shadows when the door of the house opened a crack. The Rankeillors' wee witch of a housekeeper opened it wider when she saw the sedan chair. She was well illuminated by the glass lantern hanging by a sturdy chain above the door. Fixed to the corner of the house, the oversized brass pestle and mortar signalling that this was an apothecary's shop gleamed in the light cast by the three tall white candles behind the glass.

The housekeeper was peering at him, trying to work out who he was behind the mask and under the white-powdered hair. He had fooled her at least. When he raised one finger to his lips, she obeyed the admonition to keep quiet. That was out of character. Her unusual caution had to be an indication that she already knew too much.

I ken everything that goes on in this hoose.

Good for you.

That was the interchange he'd had with the little busybody when he had last called at this house. When he had told Kirsty Rankeillor that Cosmo Liddell and his friends weren't going to get away with their brutal assault on Geordie's sister Alice. When he had allowed the young mistress of the house to think he was indeed on their side. Or, at the very least, sympathetic to the Jacobite Cause and ready to turn a blind eye. Not in a thousand years: but he was going to have to keep everyone else believing that. Both his own career and Kirsty Rankeillor's safety depended on it.

He turned his attention to opening the chair, offering her his assistance to step out. He had done this last week too, with a wordless but none-too-subtle mockery of her and her cumbersome evening gown. The look she gave him now left no doubt that she too was remembering the angry clash of their first meeting. Only a week ago. Only one short week since their very different worlds had collided.

'I can manage.'

'I don't think so. Take my hand.'

She did, clutching his fingers harder when she slipped on the snow. She was shod for dancing, wearing her evening shoes with no pattens beneath them to raise her feet and give her a better grip. They'd be wet through even after these mere couple of steps. He wasn't that well-shod for snow himself but his buckled black leather shoes were at least more solid.

'Maybe I should carry you in.'

'Throw me over your shoulder as you threatened to do a week since?'

'More like this.' He scooped her up and in a few long strides had her set back on her feet on the black and white chequerboard floor of her front lobby.

She blinked at him. 'How did you do that?'

'I'm an engineer,' he managed. After the brief respite of a flat Infirmary Street, the wound in his thigh was once more swooping in for the kill. The extravagant gesture of sweeping her into his arms, no doubt.

Damn bloody fool that he was. 'As I believe I have already demonstrated, I know where the weak points are in that contraption you choose to wear. Where they will give way.'

'But not where I shall give way?' she asked, her chin rising.

Oh, I know where your weak points are. Your father, your household, your friends, the patients you care for, your Cause. Me? Although not for much longer, if this works out as I want it to. Or as my duty demands.

He pulled his evening mask off. 'Ow!'

'Your hand?'

'My leg,' he said tersely.

'What's wrong with your leg?'

'Nothing.' He was fighting the urge to bend forward, slide one consoling hand down his aching thigh, give himself a moment before straightening up and dragging in a few recovering breaths. Since pride would not allow that in front of this audience, he'd have to ride out the shooting pains as best he could. Hopefully without any of them noticing.

He ought to be getting used to this. Pain has been his companion all week. This wound in his thigh from the musket ball he'd taken at Dettingen continuing to play up. Being knocked unconscious by Jamie Buchan of Balnamoon while he'd been examining the site where Jeannie Carmichael's body had been found. The resultant sore head. Having that steel pistol butt brought down hard onto the back of his hand. One part or other of his miserable cadaver hurting like buggery.

Cadaver. Bad choice of word. It made him think of Jeannie Carmichael, lying there so still and dead on the dissection slab, like a pitiful little broken doll cast aside by the careless children who'd been playing with her. Jamie Buchan of Balnamoon had carried out the dissection. Her murderer. Pretending he knew nothing of how she had died at his hands. Catto wondered how that must have felt.

Helping her mistress out of her cloak, the housekeeper remained unusually silent. Dressed for bed, her fair hair coiled in curling rags, she wore a plain brown wrapper with a colourful shawl decorated with fanciful birds draped about her skinny shoulders. She'd been wearing that when Catto had led the Town Guard raid on this house last Saturday.

She hadn't been so quiet then. He'd had to threaten to have her gagged to get her to shut up. When she'd continued to squawk like a belligerent sparrow, he'd had one of the men make good on the gag. No point in issuing threats if you weren't prepared to carry them out. Probably hadn't endeared him to the wee woman.

Her eyes landed on Geordie. 'Who,' she asked, at last finding her voice and her authority, 'is this laddie?'

'Geordie is Alice's brother, Betty,' Christian Rankeillor said as she removed her evening mask.

So hostile when they looked at Catto, the housekeeper's eyes softened when they focussed on the boy. 'Your sister is sleeping soundly, young man. I looked in on her a wee minute ago.' When her attention returned to Christian Rankeillor, her eyes narrowed. 'What have ye done tae your brow, miss?

'It's only a graze, Betty. I shall attend to it in a moment. Once I have attended to the Captain's injury.'

The housekeeper put her hands on her hips. 'Is it a fight ye were at, then, and no' the Daft Friday Ball?'

'Enough,' Catto growled. 'Are all the doors and windows shut and locked?'

'What's that to you?'

'Are they?'

'Aye.'

'Keep 'em that way. Keep the lantern at the front door lit overnight. Lock this door behind me when I go. Other than Geordie, no one is to leave this house tomorrow without my permission.'

The housekeeper bristled. 'Just who dae ye think ye are, young man?'

'Betty...' Christian Rankeillor began.

Robert Catto interrupted her. 'I'm the man who arrested your mistress earlier this evening. Which information is not to be passed on to another living soul. Miss Rankeillor, a final word with you. In private.' His gaze swept over the housekeeper. 'No arguments from you on that score, goodwife.'

Pale and visibly shocked, Betty Gilchrist gave him none.

❖

'He is not my spy in your house.'

'You've already told me that.'

'I thought I might need to tell you again.'

Christian turned to face Robert Catto where he stood with his back to the front door. The two of them had been watching Betty usher Geordie through the long narrow corridor that led to the kitchen at the back of the house, promising him a cup of warm milk with honey and a wee something to eat before he went upstairs to the room where his sister was sleeping. There was a truckle bed up there which could be pulled out from under the other one, so he could sleep close to her through the night to come.

'He would do anything for you.'

'I think we shall soon be able to say the same about you. Shall we therefore agree not to involve him in any way?'

'You would not have him wrestling with divided loyalties?'

'I would not wish that dilemma on anyone.'

'Because it's one that's familiar to you?' She studied him as he stood there, tall and rather pale, his face lit from above by the lantern over the door flickering through the fan light. 'Or having denied that earlier this evening, do you now wish me to believe it?'

'You think I'm plotting?'

'I think you're thinking on your feet.'

'Always. Not that I ever have much bloody choice. Are you not plotting too? Wondering how you can get a warning message to your father?'

'How can I?' She attempted a shrug but found she did not want to meet his steady gaze. 'You have made me a prisoner in my own house. Betty and the girls too.'

'It's for your own safety, Kirsty. For their safety too.'

'What if someone notices that we are confined to the house? 'Twill look somewhat odd if none of us are seen out and about and if I do not deliver physic to the Royal Infirmary on Monday as expected. Surely that will interfere with your plans to keep this as quiet as possible.'

'Our plans,' he corrected.

'You hold all the cards.'

'Not entirely,' he said drily. 'Few people will be stirring tomorrow and very probably for two or three days after that. Edinburgh is effectively cut off. Not even the post riders are going to be able to make it through. To Glasgow or anywhere else. Which might not stop you from trying to get a letter to the Post Office, to be dispatched as soon as the weather allows. Asking Geordie to take it for you. I'm sure the thought has already crossed your mind.'

Christian bit her lip, unable to deny it. 'We have just agreed not to involve Geordie in any way.'

'Aye. That we have. Bear in mind also that if you did find some way of warning your father, 'twould only land you in more trouble. As we have already agreed, nor is the Professor the kind of man to leave you and his household in the lurch. It would therefore be a wasted sacrifice. Am I not right?'

'You're right,' she managed.

'Look at me,' he said with soft command. 'I need your promise on this, Kirsty.'

She did not want to look at him — and that was a lie. She wanted not only to look at him but to drink him in, the way he looked, the way he looked at her, the way he stood so tall and strong, his reassuring presence. Reassuring? How could that be? He unnerved her, had the power of life and death over her and her father, yet he comforted her too. Soon he would be gone and she would be alone again, locked fast in her own house with no confidante to whom she could turn. She was cut off from her friends and she had to say as little as possible to Betty.

Struck by an acute pang of loneliness and isolation, she could do nothing except continue to gaze at Robert Catto. She saw him make a move towards her and check it, subsiding back against the door. Implacable and unyielding. In command of himself. Despite the powerful emotions she now knew to be not very far below the surface. Then, in the next instant, she saw his self-control desert him.

13

Grabbing her by the elbows, under the satin and lace of her sleeves, he pushed her back as well as he could in the full-skirted gown. 'Against the wall here,' he commanded. 'I will have your promise. Look me in the eye and tell me you will not try to warn your father or find anyone else to take a message. That you will run no more risks. That you will do nothing to put yourself in any more danger than you already stand in. That you will stay in this house until I tell you otherwise. Your word of honour on all of this, Kirsty. Now. Solemnly. Meaning it.'

'You do not need it. You have me under arrest. I have no freedom of movement. I am your prisoner.'

'Your promise,' he insisted, his long fingers digging painfully into the soft skin of her arms, his hands still freezing from the chill of the outside world. 'Your word of honour.'

'You cannot force a promise.'

He shook her. 'For God's sake, woman, have you no sense of self-preservation? Have you no idea how much I care for' He skidded to a halt, drew his breath in on a hiss and relaxed his grip on her.

She looked up into his face, as tongue-tied as he was, although it was she who spoke first, with a shy frankness which enchanted him, even in the midst of all this danger. 'How much you care for me, Robert? Is that what you cannot bring yourself to say?'

He shook his head. 'We both know it cannot be said. *Should* not be said. But I shall have your promise. And your word of honour.'

'I give you both,' she said, and felt her eyes brim with tears.

'Oh, come here!' Stepping forward, he pulled her into his embrace. 'Damn this daft gown. Damn hooped petticoats. I can't hold you close enough. Ow!' he added, as one of the cane hoops hit his shin. 'Daft and painful,' he grumbled, although when she would have pulled back, he issued a command. 'Stay where you are. 'Tis only one more war wound to add to the tally.' Despite the hoops, he succeeded in murmuring soft words into her hair. 'My promise in return for yours. I shall do my very best for your father. I shall do my very best for you.'

Christian swallowed back her tears. 'I know you will. You are a good man.'

'And you're a terrible judge of character.'

Giving him the smile he had earned, her mouth curved against his shoulder. For a moment they stood together in silence, until she murmured a few words. 'Dinna be kind to me. I think I can maybe stand anything except that.'

'I cannot be kind to you tomorrow. I must interrogate you, question you very closely as to the events of tonight and this week. You realize that, Kirsty?'

She raised her head and gave him a quick nod. 'I realize that. Do you have many war wounds?'

'One or two. You're wrong about one thing, Kirsty.'

'Probably many things.'

'I fear I must agree with you. But we'll talk about that tomorrow. I'm not a good man, Kirsty. What I did with Jeannie Carmichael...' He broke off, searching for the right words, finding none. Hard to talk about how he had coupled with a barefoot prostitute, pressing her slight body up against a wall in a dark close, paying her extra so she would let him squeeze her small white breasts in the frost of the winter's night, her nipples hard not from pleasure but from the cold. Not even asking her name. He had found that out only later. Christian Rankeillor already knew most of the story anyway. She had shown him sympathy after Jamie Buchan had knocked him on the head and he had blurted it out to her. He tried again. 'My morals...'

'Are reprehensible,' she said, regaining some of her crispness, as she had done when she had said the same thing back at the guard-house. 'I thought we were agreed on that.'

'Aye. For that reason among so many others I have no right to do this,' he said, and did it anyway. 'Close your eyes.' He pressed his lips gently to each of those in turn.

'You must go, Robert,' she said as he pulled back. 'You have delayed long enough. You will reassure my friends that I am all right?'

'Must you always think of other people before yourself?' He laughed, a soft rumble of sound in the shadows of the lobby. 'That was a question as daft as your gown, was it not? Yes, I shall reassure your friends.' She did not need to know he was going to do a lot more than that.

'Thank you.' Her eyes searched his face. 'Och, Robert, what are we going to do?'

He cupped her face in his two hands and studied her for a moment, intently, as though he was committing her face to memory. 'I am still to be Robert, then?'

'Aye,' she said, looking up at him. 'You are still to be Robert. Though I may yet come to regret that decision. We both may. Now go.'

'Not without a kiss goodnight,' he murmured. She turned her face up to his and gave him what he had asked for.

14

'Captain Catto. A word, if you please.' Anna Gordon birled round in a swirl of shimmering blue satin. She and Meg Wood stood now on the landing outside the ballroom of the Assembly Rooms. There were no other guests to be seen.

'We cannot wait much longer, young ladies,' Sergeant Livingstone was warning them. 'You have to leave now. You'll be spending the night here otherwise. Sergeant Crichton and myself will carry one of you. The other two caddies are threatening to leave at any minute. They have homes to go to, ye ken. Just like the rest of us!'

Livingstone wasn't a man who was quick to anger but it was clear he was growing ever more irritated. Catto had found a few of the men back at the guard-house, one with a message from the sergeant to say these two young ladies were refusing to leave the Assembly Rooms until he spoke to them and gave them news of their friend.

Glancing through the open double doors of the ballroom, Catto saw it was deserted except for a man walking around with a candle snuffer. Presumably an Assembly Rooms servant who lived on the premises, he looked to be in no great hurry. The other servants must have been dismissed. So too the musicians, allowed to scurry home carrying their precious instruments before any more snow fell. The man with the candle snuffer had already extinguished the wall sconces on one of the long sides of the room. The decrease in illumination was sending shadows spilling across the floor, as the warm smell of soft wax was drifting out here to the landing.

The snow had been getting back into its stride as Catto had reached the Assembly Rooms, swirling around him in a slow dance as the snowflakes fell to earth. His grey cloak glistened with white stars, twinkling now into tiny droplets of water as those stars melted under the heat of the building and the candles still burning brightly in their sconces out here on the landing.

A word, if it pleased him. Aye, and if it didn't please him, either. Bred to command, this one. Or so she thought. He took a moment, looking her up and down with deliberately insulting slowness. 'I should certainly like a word with you, Miss Gordon. But not tonight. For the moment you are free to go. Do so while you still can,' he added, backing up what Livingstone had told them by gesturing towards the long windows on the Assembly Rooms' staircase and the increasingly wintry weather.

The girl stood her ground. 'Aye, tonight, Mr Catto. Right now!'

He folded his arms and adopted a casual stance, extending one leg a little to the side and resting the heel of his black leather shoe on the floor. 'Strange,' he mused. 'I'm not aware of you and I having been introduced, madam. Yet we seem to know each other.'

'We ken each other fine, sir. Although you have had the advantage of myself and my friends these past few days. That much is now vastly clear.'

Catto raised his eyebrows, allowing himself to recognize the familiarity of her warm accent. There could be no doubting Anna Gordon was a Buchan quine, at home in Scotland's North East. As he himself had once been. She might know his mother's story. He might want her to. Need would be a better word. Oh, God.

Her father's Jacobite sympathies were well known. Catto knew she herself had been in on the plot to get the Jacobite agent up to the Assembly Rooms and then out of Edinburgh. He would be perfectly justified in putting her too under house arrest. He was deliberately taking another risk in not doing so. He might be able to explain that to the Lord President when the time came. If maybe not to anyone else.

He continued to study Anna Gordon, wondering if it was the arrogance which came from being a member of the wealthy and powerful Duff family or her passion for the Stuart Cause that blinded her to the realization of how she was incriminating herself by her admission of knowing he'd had them under surveillance over these past few days. She waded in yet more deeply.

'Miss Rankeillor did not do this alone!'

Ye gods, that reckless statement came with the toss of the head. Mayhap they'd had formal instruction on the deployment of that gesture at the academy for young ladies the three of them had attended, here in Edinburgh. That's how Kirsty Rankeillor, Anna Gordon and Meg Wood had met. Catto knew that courtesy of Duncan Forbes of Culloden and his encyclopaedic knowledge of the personalities and relationships of people and families throughout Scotland.

Catto supposed Kirsty Rankeillor and her friends had learned at their Edinburgh school what young ladies of their class were expected to know. Sketching and painting. The skills required to run a house and manage servants. With the imperious toss of the head coming in handy, how to manifest a crushing air of disdain, especially to those they perceived as their social inferiors. As Anna Gordon was doing now to him. With a long and difficult evening behind him, one that was far from over, his temper flared.

'Bloody hell,' he growled. 'You're in enough trouble as it is, miss. Don't incriminate yourself any further. I could arrest you right now!'

'Then why don't you?' she snapped back.

'Well now, there's a question.' His reward for swallowing his anger was to see her eyes narrow.

'Anna,' Meg Wood looked strained, her face pale above the glowing fabric of her sky-blue evening gown. 'Captain Catto is allowing us to go home. We must thank him for that and bid him goodnight. Now, Anna,' she added tightly. 'Or we shall indeed be marooned here in the Assembly Rooms.'

Observing the way she was looking at her friend, a mixture of sorrow and reproach, Catto felt the strangest feeling come over him. 'Twas as if the world around him and this girl had slowed down and come to a standstill. For a moment, he felt the hellish sensation of someone walking over his grave. Or hers. He blinked, and everything returned to how it had been before.

'Perhaps you will be kind enough to reassure us about our friend Miss Rankeillor before we leave you, sir.'

'Your friend is fine,' he told Meg Wood. 'Safely at home. If under house arrest.' Then, as the girl's eyes widened in dismay: 'You will help her best if you do not breathe a word about that. You too, Miss Gordon. You may also need to help yourself.'

'That sounds very like a threat, sir!'

'It is. Although it may also be good advice. Concerned advice.'

Her eyes searched his face. Hostile. Sceptical. Yet he thought he could also discern stirrings of the doubts he'd been trying to evoke.

'Home is also the safest place for you and Miss Wood to be, Miss Gordon. I shall call on you there at some point.'

'When?' she demanded.

'When I get there.'

'May we visit Miss Rankeillor tomorrow?' Meg Wood asked.

'No. I doubt the snow would permit that anyway. More is already falling, with yet more to come overnight, by the looks of it.'

'Then how shall we know she really is well and at home?' demanded Anna Gordon. 'That you do not have her confined in the Tolbooth?'

'Because you will take my word for it,' he responded, snapping back at her. God, this girl was infuriating. 'Also because 'twould be a very foolish thing for me to do when I am trying my utmost to keep the events of this evening quiet. Which is in all our interests.' He paused there. Anna Gordon said nothing in response. He had to hope she was indeed beginning to doubt her own certainties about him. 'Go home,' he said again. 'I have pressing matters to attend to before this evening is over.'

Meg Wood tugged on Anna Gordon's sleeve, pulling her away. 'Thank you, Captain Catto. Goodnight, sir.'

He stood at the top of the stairwell and watched them go. Of the three friends, Meg Wood was clearly the diplomat. Or perhaps the Glasgow girl was simply more clear-eyed, could see the terrible dangers which might be lying in wait for all of them around the next bend in the road. Was that the explanation for the odd sensation he had felt while talking to her a few moments earlier? 'Twas not only the feeling of life slowing down to a standstill but the sense of a pall of melancholy settling about her shoulders. Which was altogether too fey a thought to dwell upon when he still had work to do on this interminable evening. Especially when he needed all his wits about him for his next task.

15

The Liddell town house stood next to the one owned by the Duff family, with a narrow strip of garden in between. Judging by the clothes poles, that frosted strip served as a drying and bleaching green. There were earth borders where herbs or plants might flourish in the summer, as they would in the Physic Garden behind Christian Rankeillor's house.

The two town houses remained separate dwellings, unlike the high tenement lands and older houses split into smaller homes which lined the rest of the street. Following on foot behind Anna Gordon and Meg Wood after they left the Assembly Rooms in their hired sedan chairs, Catto made sure to hang back so there was no danger of them seeing him. Standing in the shadow of one of the tall tenements, he endeavoured to blow some warmth into his freezing fingers as he waited. He was almost too cold to be worried about the success or failure of what he was about to attempt. Almost.

Once the two young women had entered the Duff town house, he watched as the big front door swung shut behind them and the empty chairs were carried away. Sergeants Livingstone and Crichton and the other two caddies gave him a nod as they passed, as he returned the silent greetings. He'd exchanged a few words with them before they had left the Assembly Rooms and issued a few orders and instructions.

The night watch would keep a discreet eye on both the Duff and the Liddell houses on their patrols tonight and beyond, into first light.

After that, unless there were any further disorder, they would stand down for the day. Well aware that the watched also watched the watchers, he didn't want to be too obvious here.

For the time being and into tomorrow morning he thought he could take the risk. The snow and the sleeping off of tonight's over indulgence in alcohol would keep most people at home and render those who braved the outside world more obvious. Trudging through the snow, he walked up the steps of the Liddell house. Lifting the brass door knocker fashioned to look like a circle of ship's rope, he gave it three sharp raps. The door was immediately opened by Archie Liddell, standing in the front lobby with two of the Town Guard.

'Captain.' Archie Liddell nodded towards an open door off the opposite side of the lobby. 'They're in there. I've had the house searched, sent the servants to bed, and have two men on the kitchen door.'

'Good work, Lieutenant,' Catto said. 'Up at the Assembly Rooms too. You did the right thing. For which I am profoundly grateful.'

Archie dipped his head in embarrassed acknowledgement. 'Thank you, Captain. Glad to have been of service to you.'

Catto turned away from the guards and lowered his voice. 'I take it you did not find Mr Hector Grant of Soutra cowering in a cupboard. Or Mr Charles Paterson the lawyer lurking behind a curtain.'

'Afraid not, Captain. We conducted a thorough search. Behind every door and inside every closet. Behind all the curtains and bed hangings too. The same as you ordered last week at Infirmary Street.'

'Quite so,' Catto murmured, remembering how uncomfortable Archie Liddell had been about invading the Rankeillor house. Despite being a member of the Liddell family, if only the poor relation, he did not seem at all worried about the intrusion here. 'How much did you tell Professor Monro?'

'Only about the young girl. Nothing else.' Archie too spoke in low tones, his disgust as to what his Cosmo and his friends had done to Alice Smart written all over his face.

'You said nothing about the Jacobite agent? Or myself?' Catto added after a momentary hesitation.

'Not a thing. Nor shall I. To anyone. You may rely absolutely on my discretion, Captain. Absolutely.'

'That's good to know,' Catto said with grave courtesy.

Archie Liddell jabbed a thumb towards the open door. 'Do you want me to come in with you?'

'I'll spare you that, man. Where is your unpleasant cousin Charlotte?'

'Stomped off to her bedchamber with young Joshua and her lady's maid as soon as I had searched her room and closet. I have a guard on duty up on the landing too. Should I fetch her down?'

'I'll spare us both that pleasure. She can stew.' He walked into the room and closed the door behind him. He didn't want any witnesses to this meeting.

Worked in shades of yellow, green and ivory, a large square of carpet was set in the middle of the room. He stepped onto it as though he were walking onto a stage, hoping he looked as totally in command of himself as an actor might be, lines already written, actions already determined. In truth, he was back to balancing on the tightrope.

He had already crossed the Rubicon by letting his assailant and Anna Gordon go free and by what he had said to her. All he had to do now was keep heading in the same direction. In for a penny, in for a pound, albeit with creeping unease as to his strategy.

'Twould be all too easy to get irrevocably tangled up with these people. Like wool fankled by a playful kitten, it might be well-nigh impossible to separate out all the different coloured strands afterwards. What if William Angus Stewart had seen him allow the assailant to escape? Catto might be sure the Lord President knew where his loyalties lay but that one could be difficult to explain. He might compromise himself, his integrity and his military career beyond any hope of recovery. He had not only his own future to think about now. He held her safety too in his hands. Her very life. The thought sent a frisson of fear coursing through his veins: but he had to push all that to one side for the moment.

Cosmo Liddell sat on the edge of one of two armchairs covered in pale yellow and green silk to match the square of carpet in the centre of the room. The chairs were set to either side of a high marble fireplace, carved to resemble the front elevation of a villa in Ancient Rome. A huge mirror with an ornately gilded frame was fixed to the wall above it. A bit grandiose for Catto's taste, especially in this old Edinburgh house with its low smoke-blackened wooden ceilings. The miserable fire burning below the marble mantelpiece looked to have been but recently lit and was giving out neither much warmth nor a very impressive glow.

Liddell wore a fine linen nightshirt and a sumptuous bronze silk dressing gown. Pain was etched into every line of his face, the nightshirt flecked with blood stains at the crotch. Being kicked in the balls was never fun. Liddell's friend and acolyte Arthur Menzies of Edmonstone sat on another of the chairs and looked to be in much the same state. A dark blue banyan for him. Shiny at the folds, it had to be one of Cosmo's cast-offs.

Acolyte. The word had slid into Catto's head when he had first met this pair, not quite a week since at *The Sheep's Heid* in Duddingston. The wealthy young Mr Cosmo Liddell had been surrounded by acolytes, sycophants who hung on his every word. Although Catto had suspected since the middle of this eventful week and a low-voiced conversation in a dimly lit tavern there had to be more to Arthur Menzies of Edmonstone than that.

He was pretty sure Edmonstone was a member of the Association, otherwise known as the Concert of Gentlemen. Or was at least one of their go-betweens and messengers. This shadowy organization had as its purpose the restoration of the Stuarts to the throne of Britain. If so, Arthur Menzies must be more than the empty-headed fop he pretended to be.

He was also cruel, egging on his friends as all three of them had violated and ill-used Alice Smart. The girl had told Christian Rankeillor the story and she had relayed it to Catto. Edmonstone had given no thought to her youth, her innocence and the pain they were causing her. Clearly he had few scruples about damaging and destroying other people's lives, especially if it was for the sake of his precious Cause. Catto's mouth tightened. Damn the House of Stuart and the harm they had done to so many. They had to be stopped from doing more.

Groups like the Association made sure their adherents knew only what they needed to know. If one of them proved to be a weak link in the chain, or was discovered and interrogated, limited knowledge was one way of minimising the damage they might do by passing on information to the enemy, either to save their own skins or by having it forced out of them by torture or unrelenting interrogation. That said, Menzies had acted as a go-between for the Association, a maker of arrangements for John Roy Stuart's visit to Edinburgh and Scotland. He had to know at least one other link in the chain. Catto was determined to get it out of him.

Above the bronze banyan Cosmo Liddell's expression was a mixture of humiliation and fury. 'You'll pay for this, Catto, you bastard! You and those filthy rats you command!'

'Shut your bloody mouth, Liddell. You're in no position to make threats. You and Mr Menzies here are guilty of conspiring to foment rebellion and consorting with a known rebel, a man with a price on his head. I could throw you in the Tolbooth for that.'

Taking his time about it, he sat down on a sofa set between the two armchairs on which Menzies and Liddell were so awkwardly perched. He slid back over the smooth and cold yellow and green material, pretending an ease he didn't feel. The room was chilly in more ways than one. This pair made his flesh crawl.

'You are also guilty of the brutal rape of a young girl.'

'You'd never make that stick,' sneered Cosmo Liddell. 'Who'd accept the word of a trollop over mine?'

Somewhere behind Catto's head, a clock ticked.

'She's not a trollop.'

'She is now. What's she to you, anyway, Catto? Jealous because we got in there first?' Cosmo's sneer grew uglier. 'Quite literally. Every last little orifice.' He spelled that out, coarse and gloating. 'Tight little virgin, she was. Not any more. Gad, you should have heard her scream. Silly bitch. No one could hear her. We made sure of that.' Liddell's eyes narrowed. 'How did you even find out, anyway?'

No one could hear her. We made sure of that.

Catto had to stop himself from curling his right hand into a fist. He knew exactly what had befallen Geordie's sister Alice at the hands of Liddell and his cronies after they had spirited her away to an isolated hut by the sea on the Liddells' country estate near Prestonpans. Kirsty Rankeillor had told him after Alice had told her, waking screaming from a nightmare.

They violated her in every possible way. One after the other. Taking turns to restrain her. Then at the end, when she was exhausted and had no resistance left in her, all three of them at once... She keeps saying she'll never be clean again.

He wanted to shoot up off the sofa and smash his fist into Cosmo Liddell's face, wipe that sneering leer off his face. Christ, the bastard hadn't finished.

'Besides which, she's my property anyway. I can do what I like to her. Still can.'

'Oh, I don't think so,' Catto said, his voice a low growl.

'It's the law,' Liddell said contemptuously, as though explaining the obvious to an idiot. 'Her family are bound to the Liddells for life.'

No, one of them found the courage to run away. And he's worth ten of you. Make that a thousand—

Inside Catto's head, alarm bells began to ring. He'd learned of this from Alice Liddell and Kirsty Rankeillor, how Scotland's coal miners had the legal status of serfs, condemned to perpetual servitude. Paid slaves, although that payment was no more than a pittance. If they left, as Geordie had, they were guilty of desertion, as much as soldiers who went absent without leave. If a soldier who had deserted was caught he would be flogged to within an inch of his life. Runaway miners who were caught were also flogged but if they managed to remain at large for a year and a day they could claim their freedom. Geordie wouldn't reach that milestone until April next year. April was a long time away.

If they find out where I am, they'll take me back. Send me back doon the pit. Gie me a flogging afore they dae it.

They will do either of those things only over my dead body, Geordie.

He'd made that promise to the lad but he knew the law was on the side of the mine owners. Which meant he mustn't betray by the merest flicker of an eyelid that he knew Geordie or where he might be found. Uncurling his fist, he commanded his fingers to relax.

'I might yet dispatch you to the Tolbooth,' he said, outwardly calm. 'You're always seeking new experiences to alleviate the ennui of your idle life, are you not? I could offer you a prolonged stay among thieves and murderers, rats, puke and shite.'

'You wouldn't dare,' Cosmo breathed.

'Oh,' Catto said. 'I would. Be in no doubt about that.'

That statement silenced Liddell, if only for a moment.

'My man of business would have me out within hours! Where the Devil is that fool Paterson?' he demanded, looking around the room as though the lawyer might be lurking behind a piece of furniture. 'I demand to see him.'

'You're in no position to demand anything. Especially as we can also add attempted murder to the tally. Mine. So you'll forgive me for taking tonight's events a little personally.'

Edmonstone spoke. 'You seem to forget we now know something rather interesting about you, Catto.' He edged forward, winced, but recovered himself enough to pose a question. 'Isn't there another reason why tonight proved a little personal for you?'

'Your word against mine, Edmonstone.'

'What *have* you done with your father?' asked Cosmo Liddell, taking his lead from Edmonstone and smirking all over his face. 'Did you throw him into the Tolbooth?'

16

'The whereabouts of the Jacobite agent are none of your business. I should think you ought to be more concerned about your own situation.' Catto spoke in the coolest of voices. Inside his chest, his heart was thumping like a kettle drum. Inside his head, he was doggedly repeating a few words. *Not my father. Never my father.*

'I believe you have expectations, Mr Menzies. From your maiden aunt who lives out near Tranent. A wealthy and also a very religious lady, I believe. A practical Christian who adheres to her principles by helping the poor, especially young women and girls. What would she think if she knew what you had done to Alice Smart?'

Silently thanking the Lord President for yet another piece of useful information, with more in reserve up his sleeve, Catto raised an eyebrow. 'We both know the answer, do we not? She would be appalled. She would be unlikely to leave her money to you. Might well baulk at donating any of it to your precious Cause. You might, of course, think about marrying money. Although who would want you as a husband for their daughter I cannot imagine. Even without a charge of treason hanging over your head. As it does now,' he added carefully. 'I take it you are aware of the penalty for levying war against the King.'

He had to stay measured here, even as he was fighting the urge to leap to his feet and punch both men hard in the gut, send them sliding in two crumpled heaps to the floor. Drawing one foot back to power it as strongly as his fist, he would give Cosmo a kick or two in passing before hauling Edmonstone to his feet and grabbing him by the edges of the blue banyan. He would hold the bastard as close as possible, spit angry words into his face, spell out in disgusting detail the penalty for treason, tighten the screw till the man was whimpering with fear.

Listen to me, you stupid prick: even if you got a last-minute pardon, that would only commute your sentence to a living death in the sugar or tobacco plantations. Assuming you survived the roaring storms and the mountainous waves of the Atlantic Ocean and the stinking, overcrowded hold of the ship that would take you across it. 'Tis more likely you'll be hanged in front of a jeering, hostile crowd in London, no friends there to lock eyes with you, doing their utmost to ease your passing. You'll be cut down before you're dead. That's to ensure you suffer unimaginable agony when your cock and balls are cut off and your heart ripped out of your breast, all thrown into a bonfire built for that express purpose.

Murderers and thieves are dispatched with more mercy, hanged till they're dead. If they're lucky, their friends will surge forward and pull on their feet to spare them from being slowly strangled, bringing death more quickly to them.

Finally, and you'll be grateful for it, they'll slice your head off and place it on a spike on top of Temple Bar. It'll rot there for years, with the crows and the ravens pecking out your eyes. Assuming you're important enough, which I doubt. You and your head will probably be rolled without any ceremony into a pauper's grave, the location of your last resting place swiftly and forever forgotten. Is this the glory you seek?

Catto was locking eyes with Edmonstone now, though not to comfort him. The man had grown very pale. There was no need to say the words out loud. As Catto had not needed to when he had raided the Rankeillor house in Infirmary Street almost a week since.

I take it you are aware of the penalty for treason.

He had said that then too, seeing from the stricken faces of the Professor and his daughter that he had said enough. As he was seeing the same reaction in Arthur Menzies' face now.

'You have no title or money of your own. Your late father sold off much of your family's estate at Edmonstone to finance his ill-advised and unsuccessful business ventures. What remains is mortgaged up to the hilt. Add to that the stories of what you and your friends like to get up to in deserted places late at night, stories I shall be very happy to spread abroad… Well.'

'How do you know all this?' Edmonstone managed.

'I have my sources.'

'But they can't have given you anything with which you can threaten me,' Cosmo Liddell said, becoming once more the arrogant young buck. 'My parents are dead, my elder brother spends most of his time in London and my sister and I do as we please. No one in Edinburgh can gainsay Cosmo and Charlotte Liddell.'

God, now Catto was looking at a man who tossed his head, shaking up his powdered curls in the process.

'I am wealthy in my own right. Could buy and sell you a hundred times over.'

'No,' Catto said. 'You couldn't.'

Edmonstone had understood that response, while Cosmo Liddell was frowning in puzzlement. Money clearly hadn't bought him brains or understanding.

'I'm not for sale, Liddell. Nor can you buy my silence about any of this.'

Cosmo Liddell began to bluster. Arthur Menzies threw an arm out to stop him. 'Be quiet, Cosmo,' he said quietly. 'I rather think the boot is on the other foot.'

'Eh?' Cosmo queried. The expression on his face was almost comical. Being contradicted and told to hold his tongue by one of his acolytes was clearly a new experience for him.

'I think Captain Catto may be going to strike a bargain with us. One we have no choice but to accept.'

Edmonstone had given him the opportunity he needed. He was

going to have to take it, propose yet another Devil's bargain. He had struck the first with Duncan Forbes, the Lord President. When he had reluctantly agreed to appear at the very least ambivalent about the Stuart Cause.

He had also agreed not to adopt a different *nom-de-guerre*. The Lord President wanted him to keep using his mother's name, as he had done for years. That distinctive name might well muddy the waters, if some people recalled who had borne it.

'Twas a very long time since Robert Catto had been young Bob Stewart. Or Stuart. The man he refused to acknowledge as his father seemed to prefer the French spelling. As that man had always put Charles Edward Stuart before his own family and son. *Not my father. Never my father.* Christ, he didn't need these thoughts.

You're not here to help me, Bob?

I'm here to arrest you. And don't call me that.

Back of his mind. If he kept shoving it in there, that's where it would stay. He would think of the Lord President's words instead.

You must walk a tightrope, lad. Venture into a labyrinth where all is smoke and mirrors.

Catto stepped off the tightrope and headed into the labyrinth, metaphorically holding his breath, closing his eyes and hoping for the best. 'If you play your cards right, I may be inclined to spare you the humiliation of being publicly shamed. Or of spending tonight in the Tolbooth. Or as many nights as I can keep you in there.'

'Why would you spare us?' Edmonstone asked. 'In return for keeping your secret?'

Catto shrugged. 'Perhaps I shall keep *your* secret, Edmonstone. You never know.'

A charged silence settled upon the room. Even Cosmo Liddell seemed to feel it. Whether he understood the subtleties of what was going on here was debatable. Catto couldn't believe the man's support for the Stuart Cause had anything other than self-interest behind it.

He hoped for a title on his own account, grand enough to rival the one his elder brother had inherited and to match his overweening sense of his own importance. He doubtless saw himself being fawned over by the son of a king without a crown, a prince without a country.

Funny. Wrapped up as he was in himself and his appetites, Cosmo Liddell wasn't perceptive enough to work out Catto might once have known that prince, king and court-in-exile very well indeed. Not that he was going to tell the arrogant fucking sod anything about that. Definitely a step too far into the labyrinth.

Edmonstone might be able to work it out, though, and Catto might be going to have to let him do it. He was committed to this course of action now, had to keep going. One foot in front of the other. 'I might be prepared to turn a blind eye,' he said, adding, with the slightest emphasis on one word, 'as to with whom you have been *associating*.'

Once again he became aware of the ticking of the clock behind him.

Tick-tock. Tick-tock.

'Sometimes we all have to be careful about such things.'

Tick-tock. Tick-tock.

'Not show our hand, as it were.'

Arthur Menzies was watching him very intently. *Turn a blind eye.* 'Twas the phrase the man had used to him a few days before, taking the risk Catto was on their side, wrongly also assuming him to be drunk. In reality, he'd had very little alcohol, pouring away most of it to be absorbed into the sawdust of the tavern floor. He was stone cold sober tonight and he was watching Arthur Menzies as closely as he was watching him, passing on another silent message.

Watch your step. I might well be on your side. Do not tell this fool anything. Get him to keep his mouth shut about anything he already knows. Do this and who knows what I might be able to do for you. And your Cause. Which might be our Cause. For all you know.

'Where is he?' Arthur Menzies pronounced his next words very precisely. 'The Jacobite agent, I mean.'

'Safer for you not to know. At least at this stage.'

Edmonstone frowned. Yet there was also a tiny lightening of his grim expression. Catto could only hope the mirrors were tilted the right way and the smoke was thick enough to obscure the truth. This was all dependent on Menzies not finding out what had really happened tonight. Had he said enough to fool the man into believing he had indeed let the Jacobite agent escape?

'You have a proposal for us, Captain Catto?' There was something else in Edmonstone's face now. A dawning sense of relief.

'I have a *requirement* for you, Menzies. For the time being, you and your friend will stay here, confined to this house and discreetly guarded. If the snow clears before Yule Day, the two of you will proceed with equal discretion to Mr Liddell's house near Prestonpans, where you will lie low and receive no guests.'

'And after that?' Arthur Menzies asked.

'We shall cross that bridge when we come to it. These restrictions and conditions apply also to Miss Charlotte Liddell. Who is also to be told to keep her mouth firmly shut. Is all of this understood?'

'Well understood,' Arthur Menzies offered. 'Hold your tongue, Cosmo,' he added, cutting off a protest.

'I understand Miss Liddell has retired to her room. Which is all to the good. I imagine you might not want her present for what I require you to do now. Before I leave this house tonight the two of you will write and sign statements as to your involvement in the rape of Alice Smart and also as to your involvement with the Jacobite agent. After I have approved them, you will write out two fair copies of each. One set of your statements about the rape will be lodged with your lawyer, Mr Charles Paterson. I shall take charge of the other copies.'

'What, pray, will you do with those?' demanded Cosmo Liddell.

'Keep 'em safe,' Catto said. 'In case I might need to share them with someone else in the future. Lord Provost Coutts, for instance.

Professor Monro. Mr Edmonstone's aunt. Anyone who might have an interest in the story.'

'You cannot make us write these statements!' Cosmo blustered.

'If you don't write and sign the statements, I shall have you carried now to the Tolbooth. We'll have the gaoler let the other inmates know what you did to a young girl. Strange,' Catto mused. 'Thieves, cut-throats and murderers often take great exception to those who prey on the innocent. Several coves in there at the moment who're brutal with their fists. Their feet too.'

He was making that bit up. Well, it might be true. They weren't to know—

A pungent smell filled the air. Cosmo Liddell had filled his breeches.

17

'I'm confused.'

'We live in confusing times.' His arms behind him, Catto leaned against the door he had just closed. Now perched in obvious discomfort on an upright mahogany chair, Arthur Menzies of Edmonstone looked back at him. He and Catto were alone together in a small room off the lobby, next to the front door. In the room they had vacated, Cosmo Liddell's unfortunate valet, roused from his bed, was engaged in cleaning up his humiliated master.

Catto continued to hold Edmonstone's gaze, not giving anything away. Nor was he going to speak first. His well-practised strategy did not take long to work. The man was too anxious, too knocked off-kilter, too scared. As he himself had admitted, too confused.

'How do we know we can trust you?'

'You don't,' Catto responded. Outwardly nonchalant, inwardly he felt a spurt of elation. Somehow he knew Edmonstone wasn't referring to himself and Cosmo Liddell. If Catto handled this conversation carefully, it could take him several steps along the winding road leading him to the knowledge he sought: the information which would allow him to prove his own loyalty to the crown beyond any doubt.

Aye, and the same problem remained. By the very same actions, he could call that loyalty into question. As if the labyrinth wasn't enough, now he was back to balancing on the bloody tightrope. He had known this mission was going to make him dizzy. There was of course also the small matter of getting this information to the Lord President before someone else tried to smother him, shoot him or find some other inventive way of dispatching him.

'You're telling me we have to take you on face value?' Edmonstone grimaced. 'Or not the face you present to the world?'

'Pretty much.'

'I need some proofs. Some sort of a guarantee.'

Catto gave him a cool smile. 'There are no guarantees in our business. You must know that.'

'Our business?'

Catto threw him a bone. 'The business in which we gentlemen are associated.'

That word again. Edmonstone's expression changed in response to it. Bloody hell. Gullible and, like Christian Rankeillor, not very good at hiding his reactions. The man slid forward on the polished seat of the wooden chair, wincing again as he did so. 'And this?' he demanded breathlessly, gesturing with one hand towards his injured genitals.

Catto shrugged. 'Had to make it look authentic.'

'Authentic? *Authentic?*' Arthur Menzies' brows knitted together in fury. 'Your sergeant kicked the shit out of us!'

'You'll live,' Catto said drily. 'I might not have.'

'If your father had not saved you.'

'As you say,' Catto responded, letting that one go.

He watched the eyes once more narrow, saw the cogs turning, wondered if there was a hope in hell of getting away with this. Arthur Menzies had been there, heard the conversation between Catto and John Roy Stuart. The chances of him believing they had designed the whole scenario could be no more than a forlorn hope. Could it? Catto gestured with his head towards the room across the lobby. 'How much does he know? I would recommend as little as possible.'

'Very little. We need his money. He has to be given some sops, that's all.'

'Made to feel he's important?'

'Aye.'

'How much does his sister know?'

Edmonstone shook his head. 'Nothing.'

'But she shares your sympathies?' He could not bring himself to say *our* sympathies.

Edmondstone seemed not to notice, his mouth setting itself into a sneer. 'In a womanish way.'

'Although she has money too, I think, in her own right, and women can be curious.'

'The little bitch will hear nothing from me.'

'I wonder if she speaks as highly of you. Keep her in the dark. Until she is required to loosen the purse strings. The Cause always needs money,' he observed, and saw Edmonstone's eyes flicker. Surely to God it couldn't be this bloody easy to convince him, simply by continuing to use the right words?

'What happened tonight was all planned? To make it look like your loyalty is to the Elector?'

'I can be most useful that way.' Which wasn't a lie, simply a matter of interpretation.

'You cooked it up together? You and your fa—'

Catto interrupted him, pushing himself away from the door and raising one hand in warning. 'Mr Fox,' he said. 'It is always better not to use real names. Or allude to connections and relationships.'

'Catto being your own *nom-de-guerre*?'

He inclined his head, fancying he could hear a cock crow. Legally, he had never been Robert Stewart – or Stuart – anyway. Catto *was* his name. His beloved mother's name. His beloved grandfather's name. He would bear no other. Edmonstone's face showed no recognition of it.

'Listen,' Catto said. 'I cannot tarry here much longer. The plan is simple. You will tell Cosmo Liddell and his sister as little as possible. Only that I am a friend, not an enemy.'

Edmonstone frowned. 'I still do not have any real proof of that.'

'Mr Fox has escaped.'

'You let him go?'

'Of course not. I am the Captain of the Town Guard of Edinburgh. I could not let a known rebel, a man with a price on his head, escape. Could I now?'

Edmonstone studied him for a moment. Oh God. He had hoped it would not come to this but the man clearly needed more convincing.

'Lest you should need further evidence of my good faith...' Reaching inside one of the pockets in his waistcoat, Catto drew out a soft leather pouch. Pushing it open, he withdrew what looked like a small silver coin, laid it on his palm, and presented it to Edmonstone.

Arthur Menzies studied the object, drew in a breath, and gazed up at Catto. 'Who gave you this?'

'I had it from the hand of the Young Gentleman's father.'

'You have met him?' Menzies asked, his voice suffused with reverence.

'I have met all three of them. The Young Gentleman – I mean of course the elder of the two brothers – and I spent some time together when we were both boys.'

Those summers in Rome and that other week in Paris when they were both somewhat older – and he would rather walk across hot coals than meet Charles Edward Stuart again. Although if this thing could not be nipped in the bud, they might once again come face-to-face. That Catto knew what Charles looked like from real life rather than a potentially unreliable miniature painting had been one major reason why the Lord President had chosen him for this assignment.

'You've met him,' Edmonstone said again. He looked enthralled. Christ, any minute now he was going to ask Catto for a paean of praise. That he knew he could not bring himself to provide.

'We need to sort out the current situation. About the girl,' he added, seeing Edmonstone was still away with the fairies, lost in the shabby glamour of the Stuart Cause. It seemed that was strong enough to banish at least temporarily the horror of the penalty for rising in armed rebellion. Nor had the man asked for whom this silver token had been got. 'Twas enough for him to know it had been turned in the fingers of the man he considered to be his rightful king.

'What does the girl matter? It's the Cause that's important.'

'Aye,' Catto managed, reminding himself that in a few moments' time he would walk out of this house, back into the cleansing cold of the snowy night, reminding himself too that he would lose all the ground he had so recently gained if he did punch this bastard hard in the gut and send him slumping to the floor. 'Although you must expect a period of confinement. As I described earlier. Which means you will be unavailable to certain people. Who may need to know what has happened tonight. Is there a person or persons to whom I should be taking a message?'

18

Catto woke to a dark and chilly bedchamber. With Geordie absent overnight, the fire in his room had long since expired through lack of fuel. Muttering a curse, he yanked the rough sheet and scratchy army blankets up from his chest to his neck. He hadn't slept well and he hadn't slept for nearly long enough, stripping down to his small clothes and falling into bed sometime in the early hours. He'd been at the Liddell house for a good hour and a half after his private conversation with Arthur Menzies of Edmonstone.

The writing, approval and copying out of the statements had taken what seemed like an age. He'd expected objections. Instead, there had been a relish which had turned his stomach as they had described what they had done to Alice Smart. They had re-lived it, and wallowed in the memory. Drawing in a deep breath, he stretched out his legs, drawing them swiftly up again as his bare feet made contact with a patch of sheet as cold as a block of ice.

Like an arrow speeding to the centre of a target, his thoughts flew to Christian Rankeillor. She'd be waking up in a warm bedroom, lying down there in Infirmary Street in her fairy tale four-poster bed. He'd seen that when he'd led that Town Guard raiding party on the Rankeillor house a week ago. The posts of her bed were adorned with woodland animals: a long-eared hare, a bushy-tailed squirrel, a surprised deer. The gleaming wood into which they were carved smelled deliciously of beeswax polish. He fancied he had the scent of it in his nostrils now.

He wished he was lying there next to her, cocooned together within the bed's closed blue velvet curtains. He'd tug them back a little so he could watch her, a shaft of light from the room's window falling on her face soft with sleep, her glorious hair, dark as mahogany, loose about her shoulders. He imagined sliding his arm around her waist, bunching up the folds of her fine cambric night dress to touch warm skin, his fingers beginning to explore her luscious body...

His hand drifted down his own body to where his cock was already straining through his small clothes. As his fingers hovered there, he thought first of Alice Smart and then of Kirsty Rankeillor and of how distressed she had been last night. She was going to be much more so today, now she'd had time to absorb it all. He couldn't imagine she'd had very much sleep last night either. Or that her first thoughts when she woke up this morning would be of wanting to lie with him. He threw the blankets back. With the freezing air in the room putting paid to his arousal, he got out of bed and dressed as quickly as he could. He had more to do today than lust after Kirsty Rankeillor.

He'd written up his log and started compiling his list of names as soon as he had returned to the guard-house. The sooner he had the information written down in black and white the better. He had it under lock and key, safe in the secure cupboard in this room, along with Liddell's and Edmonstone's statements. It might be wise to give Livingstone the second key to the cupboard. In case his precarious plan failed or someone made another attempt to silence him. That was a happy thought with which to start the day.

Before he gave Livingstone the spare key to the secure cupboard he had to remove something from it. He unlocked and opened it, lifted out several pieces of paper and laid them on his desk. He scanned his list of names.

Professor Patrick Rankeillor

James Buchan of Balnamoon (Professor Rankeillor's apprentice and (until now) resident at Edinburgh Royal Infirmary.)

Arthur Menzies of Edmonstone

The Honourable Cosmo Liddell

Hector Grant of Soutra (?)

James Nicholson, coffee house keeper in Leith

Unbelievably, Arthur Menzies had given Nicholson's name to Catto last night, confirming his own inexperience as a plotter. Ludicrous how easily the man's name had fallen from Menzies' lips.

'They are there tonight? In the coffee house?' he had asked.

'I do not know for certain,' Menzies had replied.

Believing the man — he really was not hard to read — Catto had considered that in coffee houses everywhere, men met to conduct business. The business of the port of Leith was trade and ships. That Balnamoon and the Jacobite agent had spent last night at James Nicholson's coffee house had to be a strong possibility, their passage north already negotiated with a local ship's captain, putting in and sailing out again from the Shore, the harbour of Leith. By the time the snow would allow Catto to get down there they would undoubtedly be long gone, but it was a start. He swore softly. They might still be in Leith now, about to embark, but completely beyond reach because of the wintry weather.

All too aware he had not added Christian Rankeillor or Anna Gordon's name to his list, he put it with Edmonstone's and Cosmo Liddell's statements of their involvement in the Jacobite plot. He added one copy apiece of their statements about the rape of Alice Smart and put those papers back into the cupboard. Sliding the other two sheets of paper across his desk, he folded and sealed them, ready to take with him when he left the guard-house. Then he drew the other object he had put in the cupboard last night towards him, fishing it out of its little wash-leather pouch. Placing it in the palm of his hand, he gazed down at it, raised his shoulders and blew out a breath.

This medal the size of a silver sixpence with a small round hole punched in the top of it showed on one side a three-masted ship in full sail. The reverse showed St Michael, the warrior archangel, slaying a dragon. It was a touch-piece, struck for the Stuart court-in-exile for distribution to the followers of the man they called James VIII & III and whom his foes knew as the Old Pretender. 'Twas a criminal offence merely to own one of these, not to mention the dangerous implication that possession of such a token demonstrated loyalty to the Stuart Cause.

Catto had taken it to the Daft Friday ball last night, snug in one of the little pockets of his green and silver satin waistcoat, with the idea it might give him an entrée, should he need it, to the presence of the Jacobite agent. Ironic that he had once known this particular object very well indeed. Christ, the man had believed in the supposed magic and superstition that went with these touch-pieces.

So called because they had been touched by the king, these little pieces of metal were supposed to help cure the sick. A century before, kings had touched the sick directly, those suffering from scrofula, the malady also known as the King's Evil. Catto supposed the Stuarts believed their divine right to rule gave them a direct connection to God and thus to healing powers. Pathetic. Stupid. Illogical. Based on mediaeval superstition which modern men could only laugh at. Or weep over.

This little disc lying in the palm of his hand hadn't helped Catto's mother, dying in that damp and dingy room in Paris, her lungs weakened by years of racketing around Europe, living in too many other damp and dingy rooms. A picture from the past flashed in front of his eyes. He could see her smiling wearily as John Roy Stuart threaded a narrow white satin ribbon through the hole in the touch-piece he and Catto had brought home from one of those summer trips to Rome and fastened it around her neck. That had been a year before Mary Catto's death.

His father not there to stop him after she died, Mary Catto's son had thrown the touch-piece and the ribbon into a midden out in the street. Angry and distraught, he had immediately regretted letting go of the touch-piece. He'd retrieved it, fighting off another boy who had spotted the flash of silver. Catto had kept it ever since, as a memory and physical memento of his lost mother. That was also pathetic, stupid and illogical. She was gone. Although this talisman she had worn during the last year of her too short life had helped him last night. Edmonstone had been star-struck when Catto had told him he knew Charles Edward Stuart and the Old Pretender personally, so dazzled he had swallowed the pack of lies he was being told. Hook, line and sinker. Sodding bloody idiot.

Thinking about the past, for a moment Catto was transported back to the warmth and abundant sunshine of Italy and the summers he had spent there. There had been one year in particular, when he had been growing from a boy into a man, gorging himself on Italian girls and Italian peaches. Charles had been his companion on some of their amorous adventures, although not on the earliest one Catto had undertaken.

He smiled, remembering the first girl he had ever lain with: the landlord's daughter, a good five years older than him, and experienced. She had been kind to the awkward boy he had been when he had shyly accepted her teasing invitation to come to her bed, tucked away in a tiny attic room nestled under the red pantiles of her father's sprawling tavern in Rome. She'd been playful too, putting a ripe peach to his lips and then her own, laughing as the juice ran down over her breasts and nipples. He hadn't needed to be told twice to lick the peach juice off those. Catto sighed. Life had been a lot simpler back then.

19

Mr Charles Paterson, Writer to the Signet, looked a lot younger than Catto had expected. He had been anticipating a man well into middle age. Standing in front of him now as the lawyer leapt to his feet to greet him, Paterson looked to be somewhere in his middle thirties. He was still in his dishabilly when his pretty wife showed Catto into the room. Also in her dressing gown and clearly with child, she seemed to be about the same age as her husband.

Relaxed at home in the morning, Paterson was without the short legal tie-wig which presumably normally sat upon his learned head. His own brown hair cut short, he wore a red banyan over black breeches and a shirt unrestricted by a cravat, casually open at the neck. There was something rakish about his appearance, an air of devil-may-care.

'Come in, man, come in, and let me pour you a cup of coffee. The snow's gey thick, I'm thinking. You'll have had a cold walk here.' He stood up and ushered Catto into one of the armchairs by the fire, guiding him by the elbow. Another surprise. Paterson was tall and lean, yet his grip was firm. This was a strong and vigorous man.

'There's a clean cup to you for your visitor,' his wife said, lifting one down from the glass-fronted cabinet on the wall above the table set for breakfast and handing it to her husband.

'Thanks, Elspeth, lass. Close the door behind you. Mr Catto and I have serious matters to discuss.'

'I'm very happy to leave you to them,' she said with an impish smile.

Paterson responded in kind, his brown eyes warm as he followed her exit from the room. Turning, he went to the table, lifted a tall silver pot and poured coffee into the two fine china cups. Handing one to Catto, he sat down opposite him and raised his own in a toast. 'I fancy we shall be able to deal very well with each other, Captain Catto. To our mutual benefit, forbye.'

'Indeed, sir? Let us hope that to be the case.'

He took a sip of coffee. Nectar, after the sketchy breakfast he'd had this morning. A hunk of bread and a few gulps of water. The guard-house had been a cold and gloomy place without Geordie to put the porridge on and tend to the fires.

'A wee bite to eat to go with your coffee? I could ask our lassie to do you a couple o' drappit eggs?'

Catto raised a hand in refusal. 'The coffee is very fine on its own, thank you. Do you know why I arrested your clients?'

'Not until you tell me.' Paterson spoke cheerfully but there was an undercurrent there. Catto could feel it. He took another swig of coffee from the small white cup.

'As reported to me, you seemed last night to be not very curious. I am wondering why that was.' He paused again before offering a suggestion. 'Could it be you have some inkling of what they've been up to?'

'An inkling?'

'Aye,' Catto responded, and let the silence lengthen.

Paterson's face broke into a smile. Again, it was cheerful, yet it was also guarded. 'You're a canny chiel.'

'Takes one to know one.'

The cautious smile stayed in position. 'I'm a lawyer, sir. I measure my words carefully.'

'That's wise. But it's not moving us any further forward.'

'So you require a crumb from me if not from my breakfast table?' After the briefest of pauses, Paterson leaned forward. 'All right, then.

I thought Cosmo and Arthur might have got themselves in trouble over a lassie.'

'Not for the first time?' Catto would play this game, even if he was pretty damn sure the lawyer had been on the point of saying something else but had thought better of it.

'That could be a logical assumption. Although I cannot imagine you really expect me to answer you one way or the other.'

'No, I don't suppose I can. They have indeed got themselves in trouble over a lassie. They and their friend Mr Hector Grant of Soutra raped a young girl.'

Paterson's face clouded. 'They have confessed to this?'

'I made them write and sign confessions last night.' Catto pulled those papers out of the breast pocket of his coat. 'These copies are for you. I thought you might find them useful. Would you know where Mr Hector Grant of Soutra is, by the way? I believe he called here last night.'

'Aye. To tell me my presence was required at the Assembly Rooms. He's not still here, if that's what you're thinking. You're welcome to have a look around if you dinna believe me.'

'I'll take your word for it, Mr Paterson.'

'I understand he usually stays with Cosmo when he's in Edinburgh,' the lawyer volunteered.

'He's not there now. Nor was he last night.'

'Not surprising, given what you have just told me,' Paterson said, looking at the papers Catto had handed him. 'You have kept copies of these for yourself?'

'Of course.' Catto waited as the lawyer read further, his growing distaste clear to see. Whatever else he might have been expecting, there was no dissembling here. There could be no doubt Paterson's disgusted reaction was entirely genuine.

'A sorry story. They seem almost proud of themselves for what they did to the poor girl. But well done on getting them to write these. It can be hard to make those young gentlemen do anything. They have a very good conceit of themselves, especially Cosmo.'

'You say the words *young gentlemen* with some distaste, Mr Paterson. I think you do not much care for these clients of yours.'

'I inherited the Liddells from my father. Now regrettably deceased,' the lawyer added, laying the statements on the breakfast table. 'My esteemed parent, that is. I might perhaps not have chosen the Liddells as clients myself.'

'I imagine they are lucrative ones.'

'Indeed, sir.' Paterson sighed. 'Therein lies the problem. They help support others of my clients for whom I lower my fees. Although I work hard for my fee when it comes to Cosmo and Charlotte Liddell. This girl,' he said, tapping his index fingers on the papers. 'The one who has apparently suffered at the hands of Cosmo and his friends.'

'Apparently?'

The lawyer gave another little sigh. 'You do not then believe she was willing but cried rape afterwards? It does happen.'

Catto lowered his coffee cup from his lips and shook his head. 'Not in this case. She is an innocent. Was an innocent,' he corrected himself. 'Until those savages got hold of her.'

'You know the circumstances?'

Catto did. Alice Smart had worked as a maidservant at Eastfield House, the Liddell country seat near Prestonpans, where she had caught Cosmo Liddell's eye. Getting her on her own one day not long after she had started working there, he had indicated the paintings of nudes hung on the walls of the salon where he had waylaid her, told her the female form was beautiful and so was she. If she would agree to appear before him and his friends naked, he would give her five shillings. They would look and admire, but not touch her. Other girls had done it before her, as part of a club to which Cosmo and his friends belonged, the Beggar's Bennison, and no harm had befallen them.

Alice Smart had wrestled with her modesty and her conscience for a few weeks but in the end the money had been too tempting. Five shillings had been an enormous sum to a maidservant from a collier's family, enough to allow her to run away from Eastfield and go looking for her younger brother in Edinburgh. It had been Arthur Menzies of Edmonstone who had made the arrangements, spiriting her away from the kitchen door at Eastfield. After the rape, bound and gagged in the back of a cart, she had been taken to a brothel in Edinburgh, told she would work there from now on as a prostitute. Violated, bruised and bleeding, she had somehow found the physical and mental strength to escape and go in search of Geordie.

'She was tricked into meeting Cosmo and his friends?' the lawyer asked, his eyes shrewd. 'Not suspecting what they really wanted?'

'Aye. Three grown men against one young girl. And their attack was brutal.' He waved a hand towards the statements. 'As you have just read.'

Paterson's face clouded. 'They are sad examples of young manhood, sir. That I know.'

'They have done something like this before?'

'I cannot comment on that.'

'And thereby just did.'

'Perhaps,' Paterson conceded, with a little nod of the head which put Catto in mind of a watchful heron by a river bank. Alert. Very, very alert.

'I take it that's why you were able to ignore Cosmo Liddell's summons last night. Because you know rather a lot of about him and his friends. None of which is to their credit. You may therefore dictate the terms on which you remain man of business for the Liddells.'

He needed no response to that and he didn't get one, Paterson leading the conversation back to Alice Smart. 'You must know as well as I do the girl will find no redress in law. I will get some compensation out of Cosmo, though. Where is she now?'

Catto drained his coffee cup. 'Nice try, Mr Paterson.'

'You're a close one, eh? I dinna mean the lass any harm, sir.' He shook his head, his expression grim. 'Any further harm, that is. But I'll be needing her to make her mark on an undertaking she'll tell no one what happened.'

'Of course you will.'

'I'm a lawyer, sir. We like everything in writing. Signed, sealed and delivered.'

'Sometimes what's in writing can prove hazardous, sir. Have you never found that?'

Paterson's eyes narrowed. 'Are we still talking about this young lass, Captain?'

'What else might we be talking about?' Catto asked, and felt the atmosphere tighten. He was once again balancing on the tightrope of which the Lord President had spoken, wondering if he was going to make it to the other side of the canyon over which the rope was stretched so taut. 'Might I have some more coffee?'

'But of course,' Paterson said, bounding up out his seat.

'Tell me, sir,' Catto said as he took the cup from the lawyer, 'are you also the man of business for Arthur Menzies of Edmonstone?'

'I am.'

'Another connection that goes back to your father's time?'

'Aye. We are the family lawyers for his aunt and thus came to her brother, Arthur's father.'

'His aunt who lives out at Tranent?'

'You are acquent with the lady, sir?'

'I know of her. And,' Catto added carefully, 'her sympathies.'

'Ach weel,' the lawyer said after a tiny pause, 'I'd jalouse we all have our sympathies, sir. Maybe even yourself.'

'You think so, sir?'

The lawyer looked at him over his coffee cup. 'Ye're a grand man for answering one question wi' another.'

'I wasn't aware you were asking me a question.'

'Och, I think you were. I'm no' an awful lot older than you, Captain,' the lawyer went on. 'Ten years or so, I'm thinking. May I nevertheless presume to give you a wee piece o' advice?'

'By all means,' Catto murmured.

'You are an engineer, Captain.'

'How do you know that?'

'I understand you have been seconded here to Edinburgh from Guise's. Who are a regiment of engineers.'

Catto inclined his head in agreement, although he was still wondering how Paterson knew his regiment. Made him wonder what else the lawyer might know about him.

'I'm thinking that, as an engineer, you're a man who kens how to build bridges.'

'Has been known.'

'I might therefore suggest it's as well not to burn any bridges which may be in place. You never ken when you might need them. Same goes for all of us. And we remember our friends.'

We remember our friends.

Jamie Buchan of Balnamoon had said exactly those words to him the night before, at the Daft Friday ball.

20

'You remember your friends? That's reassuring to know. Or maybe that depends on who your friends are.'

'Och, I think ye ken that fine, Captain Catto,' Paterson said softly.

Another revealing comment. They were hovering on a knife edge here. Caution, Catto thought. *Stay cautious*. He put the coffee cup back in its saucer.

'Such dainty little pieces of porcelain,' he observed. 'So strong in one way, so very easily broken in another.' He went on without waiting for the lawyer, now looking faintly puzzled, to respond to those comments. 'Seems to me you might have been steering clear of some of your friends last night. As a prominent and esteemed citizen of Edinburgh, one might have expected to see you at the Daft Friday ball in aid of the Royal Infirmary.'

'Ach, weel,' Paterson said with a grin, 'I might just no' be as esteemed as I surely should be by some o' my fellow citizens. For some reason, there's a wheen o' folk who dinna like lawyers very much.' Amusement fading from his face, he turned his hands palms upward. 'The real reason for my absence being, as you cannot have failed to notice, that my wife is in an interesting condition. Since she was unable to go to the ball, I chose not to go either.'

'You're a considerate husband.'

'I love my wife.'

'As you naturally wish to protect her and the impending arrival. Against all the dangers life can bring.'

Something flashed across Paterson's face. Swiftly dismissed though it was, to Catto it looked like fear, more too than the fear any man might have at the prospect of a beloved wife about to undergo the rigours and risks of childbirth. Had he been exercising caution last night, choosing not to meet the Jacobite agent? Although he could not know if Paterson might have met the man earlier in the week at his hiding place in the Royal Infirmary. The building had several entrances. Despite the watchers in place at different times, Paterson might have managed to slip in there without being seen. Or could have claimed to have legitimate business in the hospital.

Catto was conscious of another emotion hanging in the air. He had been aware of something very similar a week since, when Patrick Rankeillor and Jamie Buchan of Balnamoon had been trying to convince him they were innocent of any plotting. He had felt their suppressed excitement all the same. It had been well-nigh tangible. Men with a cause. They carried an aura with them. And if he'd been trying to issue a warning here – had he? – he suspected it had fallen on stony ground.

'You're not a married man, Captain Catto?'

'I'm a soldier, Mr Paterson. 'Tis not a profession which sits well with matrimony.'

'Yet we have all heard tell of the captain's lady, have we not? Some women do follow the drum.'

'A few,' Catto allowed, impatient with what seemed like a meaningless diversion of the conversation. 'Might I ask how you know my regiment, Mr Paterson?'

The lawyer shrugged. 'I canna quite call to mind who told me.'

'Well, that's not good, especially after you've told me you remember your friends. Could make a man doubt the validity of such a statement.'

Paterson laughed. 'Very good, sir. Very good indeed. When may I visit my clients?'

'Not yet awhile.' Catto lifted his cup again and drank what remained in it. If he did allow the lawyer to see his clients he would have to tell him they had also been arrested for high treason and plotting rebellion. He wasn't ready to give Paterson that information yet, even if he suspected the man might already be pretty damn sure of it. 'I'll let you know if and when you may call on them. Thank you again for this very fine coffee.'

❖

Charles Paterson closed the door behind his visitor. His wife Elspeth stepped out into the lobby. He raised a finger to his lips, only speaking after he had glanced out of one of the windows which flanked the front door and seen the tall figure of Robert Catto trudge away from the house along the snowy street. 'Wanted to make sure he was gone.'

'Do we need to be worried, Charlie?'

He came towards her, took her hand and led her back into the room he had just left. 'What we need is for you to sit down here by the fire, put your feet up on the stool and rest.'

Her fair brows knitted. 'I can still worry in that position.'

'I ken that fine,' he said, placing the footstool under her feet and sliding a small cushion to nest snugly in the small of her back. 'But you dinna need to.'

'Really? When I'm very well aware something's going on and you're not telling me what it is?' She watched as he poked the fire, redded it up and added more coal. 'Charlie?' she said. 'We made a pact. When we wed. That we would aye be honest with each other.'

'Aye, we did.' He replaced the fire irons on their stand on the brown and cream Dutch tiles tiles of the hearth, seemingly transfixed for a moment by the windmills, canals and figures of men and women in hats, caps and clogs that adorned them. 'But you did say you were happy to leave me to discuss weighty matters with yon one.'

'That was for his benefit.' She shivered. 'There's something about him that scares me.' Her face grew thoughtful. 'Yet he carries some sadness with him too, I think.'

Her husband looked up from his scrutiny of the hearth. 'Gey perceptive. Even though you only met him for a moment or two. You've aye been a bittie fey.'

Elspeth made a face at him. 'I am a rational human being, Charles Paterson, and I have a brain.'

'A very fine one, too. Although I like your fey side as well. Shift these fairy feet.'

'A galumphing fairy,' Elspeth responded with a wry twist of the lips. 'Have you no' seen how swollen my ankles are?'

He gave her the sweetest of smiles. 'Your feet still look dainty to me.'

'Dinna change the subject. What did that man say to you?'

'We had a somewhat odd conversation. Hard to tell which side he's on.' Charles lifted her feet, sat down on the space vacated on the footstool, removed her slippers and began gently massaging her toes. 'Especially when he gave me what sounded very like a warning.'

'We stand in need of one, I take it. Charlie,' she urged when again he gave her no answer, 'I'll worry even more if I suspect but dinna ken for certain.'

'Aye,' he said, his fingers stilling. 'We may stand in need of a warning.'

She lowered her voice. 'There is to be a rising?'

He looked up at her, his expression a mixture of fear and excitement. 'It's in the planning.'

'Oh...' Elspeth breathed. 'Och, Charlie. Are you sure?'

'Certain sure. We have had a visitor in Edinburgh this week. An influential Jacobite agent.' He gave her toes a gentle squeeze. 'I canna tell you his name. For your own safety, Elspeth lass.'

'What about your safety?'

'I am being very cautious,' he assured her.

'You met this Jacobite agent?'

'Aye. Where our friends have been hiding him this week past.'

'That does not sound very safe.'

'Nobody saw me. Apart from the person who took me to where he was. We can trust her implicitly.'

'Her?' Elspeth pounced on the revealing word. 'Kirsty Rankeillor?'

'No.' He shook his head. 'Not her.'

'But Kirsty is involved in this, is she not?'

'You have no reason to think that. We have no reason to think that.'

'So it's—'

Charles raised his free hand. 'No more names, Elspeth. They can be dangerous when spoken in the wrong hearing. No more questions.' He transferred his hand from her lips to her stomach. 'Try not to worry. 'Tis not good for this long-awaited wee one, is that not so?'

He laughed when a melting look was swiftly followed by a glower. 'I have merely hinted, said nothing to Captain Catto to give him any firm proofs of our sympathies. It may be that he shares them, which could be very advantageous to us. Highly advantageous,' he said. 'But I am not ready to trust him yet. Not until I know exactly what happened at the Assembly Rooms last night.'

'Something was supposed to happen? Other than Cosmo and Arthur being arrested, I mean,' she added drily. For he had told her that much last night as she had lain awake in their big comfortable bed waiting for him to return home.

Charles Paterson nodded. 'Aye. I need to speak to Arthur Menzies. Although Captain Catto has not yet given me permission to do so.'

'If he is on our side, would he not have given you that permission, here and now?'

'Not necessarily. People are constrained to take certain courses of action for fear of who might be observing what they are up to. Captain Catto has to watch his step. I did not press the point about seeing Cosmo and Arthur, thought it was best for me to seem to be co-operative.'

'Why did he arrest them? On what charge?' For Hector Grant of Soutra had not communicated that information, delivering his message and leaving the Paterson house within moments of arriving there. 'Did the Town Guard Captain tell you?'

'He told me one of the charges, although I dinna think you will care to hear it. It seems they have ravished a young girl.'

'Both of them?'

'All three of them,' Charlie said unhappily. 'Hector Grant too.'

Elspeth paled and straightened up from the relaxed posture in which she'd been sitting, her hands flying to her mouth. 'Och, that's horrible! Where is the poor lass now?'

'That I do not know. Although I suspect she is being cared for.'

'The Town Guard Captain said as much?'

'There was that implication.'

Elspeth's face took on a grim expression. 'They've done something like this before, haven't they?'

'Elspeth,' he said, 'whatever they've done, they're still my clients.'

'More's the pity. They're still supporters of the Cause, too. Which is an even greater pity.'

'I do not disagree with you. Politics makes for odd bedfellows.'

'An unfortunate turn of phrase, Charlie. Considering the circumstances.'

He pulled his mouth down, acknowledging the hit. 'As I have told Captain Catto, I will get some money out of Cosmo to give to the girl. I know nothing will compensate for what they have subjected her to, still less the innocence they have so brutally stolen from her, but 'twill give her something.'

'She was an untouched maid before this happened?'

'Aye. So Captain Catto says.'

Elspeth's voice shook. 'How awful,' she said. 'How awful for a young girl to have that happen to her.'

'Aye,' Charlie said. 'Awful.'

'The Town Guard Captain knows where she is?'

'It would seem so. He has also put something into my hands which may help hold Cosmo and his cronies back from doing whatever the Devil they feel like doing in the future to some other unfortunate lassie.' He told Elspeth about the signed confessions.

'So he is a good man,' she said slowly, weighing her words.

'Yet may also be a dangerous one. As I said, I need to know more about what happened last night at the Daft Friday ball.'

'Where they more than likely met the Jacobite agent,' Elspeth said flatly. 'Which means yon Captain probably also arrested them on a count of treason. By their lights,' she added, shrugging her shoulders in dismissal of the rule of the House of Hanover, whose laws and loyalties her husband was duty bound to uphold. In theory. 'I dinna want you taking risks, Charlie.'

'We all must play our part, my love. If we want this, which we do, we cannot ask other people to take all the risks for us. I promise you this,' he said, lifting each of her hands in turn and softly kissing her palms, 'I shall be as careful as I possibly can. My love?' he queried, responding to her troubled look.

'I am remembering what I have heard is a Chinese curse, given in the form of a blessing. '*May you live in interesting times.*'

Charles Paterson nodded. 'Aye. We are most certainly living in interesting times.'

'I'm very sorry, sir,' said the woman Catto assumed was Professor Monro's wife. 'My husband has been called across to the Royal Infirmary. Some emergency which requires his immediate attendance.' She smiled, albeit somewhat wearily. 'Even in this snow. Would you care to wait here or will you follow him across?'

'I'll follow him across,' Catto said, not wanting to delay his interview with Monro. On the way to the man's house, he'd been rehearsing what he was going to tell him. Or how much he was going to tell him.

Professor Monro was not on the Lord President's list of suspected Jacobites but Duncan Forbes wanted him to be cautious with everyone. As Catto understood it, Monro took little interest in politics. He was devoted to his wife and family and equally devoted to the Royal Infirmary. The magnificent new hospital was dependent on donations, particularly from those wealthy enough to make substantial financial gifts. People like the Liddells.

Catto was prepared to believe many people donated money to the Infirmary out of the goodness of their hearts. Not that lot, though. On his first and so far only meeting with the unpleasant Miss Charlotte Liddell at the Rankeillors' shop, she had tripped in with money she had collected for the tickets for the Daft Friday ball from among her friends. Catto couldn't imagine she had many real ones but people like the Liddells always attracted sycophants and hangers-on.

Her young black manservant had been carrying the heavy bag of coins, of course, and Charlotte Liddell had obviously expected Kirsty Rankeillor to express more gratitude than she had. She couldn't know the other girl very well. The surgeon-apothecary's daughter wasn't one to defer to people unless and until they had earned her respect. He might have known her for only a week but Catto was sure of that. The thought made him smile.

He stepped in under the hospital portico, relieved to have his feet on flat stone rather than uneven snow, much of it beginning to freeze into slippery ice. Someone must have cleared what had blown in under the portico. Inside the austere but impressive entrance hall, a rough hessian rug had been laid to allow the wiping and drying of shoes and boots. His eyes went to the inscriptions carved into stone plaques on the walls at eye level.

I was a stranger and ye took Me in.

I was sick and ye visited Me.

He'd noticed them last week when Kirsty Rankeillor had walked him to the portico after he'd been called to the Infirmary and found himself confronted by the dead body of Jeannie Carmichael. Seeing her lying there so stiff and cold had been a shock. He had coupled with the girl the night before, rutting in the street like a wild dog.

Reading those texts from the Bible, he felt shame wash over him. What would his mother have thought if she had known about him and Jeannie Carmichael? What would Mary Catto have thought if she had heard how roughly he had spoken to Christian Rankeillor, the girl who had been so kind to him, the girl with whom he was fast falling in love, the girl against whose friends he was now gathering evidence? He thought too of the Patersons, warm and affectionate and looking forward to the birth of their child. If the lawyer was involved in the Jacobite plot, their loving home would be ripped apart. Paterson too might meet his end on the scaffold. Catto could tell himself none of that was his fault. He could not deny this was dirty work he was engaged on here.

Despite the signs of activity, the cleared snow and the makeshift rug, the entrance hall was deserted. He could hear voices, though. They were coming from the apothecary's shop. He had reason to know that corner of the ground floor of the hospital. Jamie Buchan had stitched up the wound in his head there, the one Balnamoon himself had inflicted while Catto had been investigating the spot outside the infirmary where Jeannie Carmichael's body had been found. Jamie Buchan must have dumped her lifeless body there so he could pretend to find it later.

Walking towards the voices, pushing those uncomfortable and disturbing thoughts about his mother and the Patersons to the back of his mind, Catto mused that it was probably time to get his stitches removed. He could do that himself. Probably. He'd done it before. Or he could ask Christian Rankeillor to do it. Maybe.

Pushing open the door to the apothecary's shop, he saw there were three people already in there. A woman in a plain blue gown he knew to be the lady governess, a handsome fair-complexioned man in his forties he assumed must be Professor Monro and a miserable looking young doctor or medical student. Monro and the lady governess seemed to be haranguing him for some misdemeanour. He looked up and met Catto's eyes.

Well, well, well. He had suspected his assailant of the previous evening had to be one of Jamie Buchan's friends and accomplices. He hadn't expected finding him to be quite this easy.

21

Christian woke with a start, knowing she had slept late, knowing too she was opening her eyes on a new world and a new reality. Everything looked the same but everything had changed. It had taken her ages to get to sleep last night, her head overflowing with the events of the evening, joy, sadness, disbelief and fear fighting for supremacy. It had been an hour before she had even got to her bed, delayed by the need to calm Betty down.

'Arrested?' The housekeeper had whispered the word. She had only uttered it at all after she had closed Christian's bedroom door behind her once Geordie had been seen off to his truckle bed on the floor next to his sister and the rest of the Rankeillor household was safely asleep. '*Arrested?*'

'Help me get undressed first, Betty. I need to get out of these clothes.'

Getting her out of her evening clothes and into her nightdress and wrapper took some time. As she had hoped, the familiar routine helped put Betty back onto an even keel. Taking her by the hand, Christian led her over to the bedroom fire, insisting she sit down in one of the armchairs while she sat on a stool at her feet. Holding the older woman's hands between her own, she endeavoured to reassure her. Gey hard when she stood in sore need of reassurance herself. Although it helped that she had to stay strong for Betty's sake.

'Tomorrow,' she'd promised, knowing she would still be guarding her tongue then, telling Betty only what she absolutely needed to know.

'We can talk more about it tomorrow. Only when we're on our own, though.'

'Aye,' Betty had said, nodding her head in agreement. 'Nae need for the rest o' them tae ken onything aboot all o' this.'

'Geordie kens,' Christian said, 'but he will keep his own counsel.'

'Aye,' Betty had said again. 'Yon one has an auld heid on young shoulders.'

Now tomorrow had arrived, a thin sliver of grey sky visible through the narrow gap between the heavy blue velvet bedroom curtains. Betty had told Christian last night she'd been watching for her from here. The housekeeper had hurried downstairs when she'd spotted the sedan chair coming along Infirmary Street and must have forgotten to draw the curtains fully closed before she went down to meet the chair.

Movement flickered in the gap. It was snowing again. Sharp as glass, the memory of the night before came swooping in. Despite her wonderment at what she and Robert Catto had found in each other last night, one quite different thought dominated. Jamie had murdered that girl. Swamped by distress, Christian sat up and swung her legs over the side of her four-poster bed. Jamie, who had dedicated his life to healing the sick and mending the injured, had committed cold-blooded murder. He must have got Jeannie Carmichael drunk – the smell of alcohol had been overpowering when he had cut her body open on the dissecting slab, Christian acting as his note-taker – and then he must have smothered her. As he had been going to smother Robert Catto.

Jamie Buchan of Balnamoon had taken one life and been prepared to take a second one. All for the sake of the Cause. All to allow Mr Fox to escape undetected from Edinburgh. Her breathing coming fast and shallow, Christian wrapped one arm around the tall bedpost to her right, anchoring herself. She had failed the Cause last night, had aimed to miss, some half-formed thought in her head that Jamie would think she had at least tried.

She could no more have shot Robert Catto than fly in the air. Not even for the sake of the Cause. Not even for the sake of her beloved father, miles away in Glasgow, unaware of what was going on here. Jamie had known that, had asked someone else to do the deed because he knew she would baulk at it. She was pretty certain she knew who that other person was. Murdo Robertson. She had heard his voice last night at the guard-house, when he had called out, roughening his soft Perthshire accent in an attempt to sound like one of the raucous Edinburgh mob. Murdo hadn't been able to bring himself to shoot Robert Catto either.

She thought again of her father. Even if she hadn't bound herself to inaction by her promise and her word of honour, there was no way to get a warning through to him in this weather. When the snow did finally clear, he would ride blithely back into danger and Robert Catto would arrest him on a charge of giving aid and succour to an enemy of the King. As he had arrested her last night. On the same charge. Treason. A hanging offence.

The bedroom door creaked open. Betty put her head around the solid wood, opening the door wider when she saw her young mistress sitting with her nightdress puddled around her knees and her legs dangling over the edge of the high bed. 'Cover your legs,' she scolded, 'you'll catch your death.'

Christian looked across at her and gave an odd little laugh. 'Not from having bare legs, Betty. It takes more than that.'

'Aye ready with the smart answer, that's you. You must be wide awake. I looked in on ye an hour since and ye were dead tae the world.'

You'll catch your death. Dead to the world. The words and phrases people used so casually held a multitude of traps. Fighting to keep the anguish and fear at bay, it took Christian all her strength to answer Betty calmly. 'What time is it?'

'Ten o' the clock. I've brought your porridge. Let's get you into your wrapper and ower tae the fire. I'll redd it up a wee bit first and gie it some mair coal.' Betty kicked the door shut with her foot and bustled across the room. Laying the tray she carried on the small high table set to one side of the mantelpiece, she lifted the poker and got to work. Kept in all night during the winter, it took only a moment for little orange flames to flicker up through the blanket of dross.

Betty swapped the poker for its companion tongs and placed a few lumps of coal on the fire. Tears prickled behind Christian's eyes. *Are you warm enough?* That was one of Betty's favourite questions. The housekeeper was making sure of that now, looking after Christian's comfort and well-being as she always had done. The fire revived, Betty pushed the hinged brass shelf and matching kettle closer to the heat.

Christian forced the tears back. She had to remain calm. She had to not blurt any of this out to Betty, or at least tell her as little of it as possible. *The more she knows, the more dangerous it will be for her.* She had told her last night that Jamie had fled Edinburgh with a Jacobite agent. Nothing more. Nothing about Jamie and Jeannie Carmichael. Nothing about him having wanted Robert Catto dead. Like Christian, the older woman had known Jamie since he was a young lad, when he had first become Patrick Rankeillor's apprentice, a motherless boy whom she had taken under her wing. She would be distraught if she knew what he had done.

'Up ye get, lass,' Betty said, plucking the quilted cambric dressing gown from the foot of the bed and urging Christian into it. 'Come and sit by the fire and tell me this, if you please. Did onything else happen last night I'm needin' tae worry aboot?'

It took Christian until she had sat down by the fire to realize what Betty meant. She was concerned about her reputation. She let out a sound halfway between a laugh and a sob. 'We have so much to worry about, Betty. Far too much!'

In an instant she was in the skinny arms where she had so often sought comfort as a child, her own arms wrapped around Betty's trim waist. She had never known her mother, who had died a few days after she had been born, but Betty had always been there. As she was now.

'There, there, ma wee sugar dumpling. You cry it oot.'

She laughed at that old endearment before bursting into a storm of weeping. Betty wrapped her arms more tightly about her and murmured soothing words above her head. After a few moments Christian pulled back and straightened up, giving the housekeeper a shaky smile. 'I was so determined I wasn't going to worry you.'

'Ye think I'm no' already worried, pet?' Betty's familiar face was lined with concern. 'We could dae wi' your faither hame, eh?'

'Oh aye, Betty, we could! But he needs to stay away too! There's no way we can warn him about what's happened. Not when we're confined to the house. Not with this snow either.'

Betty snorted. 'Wouldna dae ony good anyway. He'd still come hame even if we could get word to him.' She lifted her apron and wiped Christian's eyes dry. 'Eat your porridge.'

Christian took a few spoonfuls before she spoke again. 'Captain Catto says he will do his best for us. He also says we have to keep everything as quiet as possible.'

'I might just agree wi' him there,' Betty said grudgingly.

'Tea. I need some tea. Have a cup with me, Betty.'

'Ye ken fine I dinna hold wi' yon foreign muck. I'll bide here while ye drink a cup if that's what you want. Efter that, I'm going back downstairs. I'm still needing an answer tae ma question, in ony case.'

'Nothing happened last night that you need worry about, Betty. Not in the way you mean, anyway.'

'So that's why you're blushing,' Betty said flatly, and made Christian colour up all the more.

'You have feelings for yon man,' Betty continued. 'Dinna try tae deny it.'

She'd be wasting her breath if she did. She knew Betty's keen eyes had spotted this last night when Robert Catto had delivered her home. Silver-blue like a bolt of lightning, some sort of a thread shooting between her and him. Binding them together. As fine as a spider's web, as strong as tempered steel.

She had hoped and dreamt of love. Over the years, she and her friends had spoken of it, sometimes in jest and sometimes with longing. She had never expected it to feel like this, as though she were permanently on the verge of being sick, as though she was going to need all her courage to withstand it, and him. He aroused so many conflicting emotions in her breast.

'Feelings I ken fine can go nowhere,' she told Betty now, thinking that was what Robert Catto had said last night.

'Those can be the maist dangerous sort o' feelings.'

'Betty?' Christian narrowed her eyes, bounced out of her anxiety about the here and now by the way the housekeeper had said those words. Funny, she'd never thought of Betty as once having been a young woman, maybe once having had a sweetheart.

'Make your tea,' Betty said, indicating the kettle, steam beginning to puff out of its spout. 'I canna bide here all day. This house doesna run itself, ye ken.'

'Aye, Betty,' Christian said gently. 'I ken that fine. How would it run at all if we didn't have you at the helm?'

22

Catto placed his right hand over his heart and made the older man a bow. 'Professor Monro? I am Robert Catto, Captain of the Town Guard. Good morning, sir. At your service.'

'Better late than never,' the Professor observed, not returning the bow. Unless you were clearly a senior officer, many people didn't, even when you were in uniform. Soldiers were never the most popular of men and junior officers were seldom seem as gentlemen. Some did see themselves as such, especially those whose grand relatives had bought them a commission, insisting others did too. Catto never had. The lack of basic good manners could be irritating, all the same.

Monro turned to the woman at his side, although Catto suspected the polite introduction was for her benefit, not his own. 'Mrs Moncur,' he said. 'Lady governess and mainstay of the Infirmary. We would be lost without her.'

The lady governess bobbed a curtsey. Minding his own manners, which seemed advisable, Catto responded with another bow. He'd seen her last week when he had stumbled into the hospital after Balnamoon had knocked him on the head when he'd been investigating the spot where Jeannie Carmichael's body had been found. This Mrs Moncur and Christian Rankeillor had been standing talking together in the entrance hall.

'Here,' the professor said in weary tones, 'we have Murdo Robertson. Who was just explaining himself to me.'

'I think Mr Robertson and I may have met before.' Catto tapped one finger against his lips, as though he were turning the possibility over in his mind.

The nervousness in Murdo Robertson's eyes deepened into a flash of what could only be blind panic. Confirmation, if Catto had needed it, that he was indeed looking at his assailant of the night before: the young fool who might have killed him. Or got himself killed.

'You think the two of you are acquainted, young Captain Catto?' Professor Monro queried, looking expectantly at him.

Another constant irritation was how so many older people here in Edinburgh prefaced his name with that adjective. He was damn sure none of them knew an old Captain Catto. It seemed also to call his authority and military experience into question. For a few brief seconds, as the previous night with Arthur Menzies of Edmonstone, he indulged himself with the fantasy of backing the professor up against a wall and firing a volley of words at him: 'Listen! You may be a sawbones of several decades' experience but I bet you haven't seen some of the things I have! Want to hear a few of my more gruesome war stories? I don't think so!'

Murdo Robertson was a much easier target. Like a cat torturing an unfortunate mouse before finally dispatching it, Catto decided to spin this out. The bloody fool deserved to suffer.

'Let me see now,' he mused. 'I have met so many people since I came to Edinburgh. Yet somehow you look very familiar to me, Mr Robertson. Of course, in my capacity as Captain of the Town Guard I am required to *associate* with many people from all walks of life.'

He let the words hang in the air for a moment, saw that the one to which he had given a slight emphasis had hit home, as it had with Edmonstone last night. Hellfire, this was too easy. At this rate, he'd soon know every adherent of *The Association* in Edinburgh, even if some of them were mere foot soldiers in what could only be a ramshackle army, as he suspected Robertson was.

Menzies had not given him Robertson's name. Since he had been so free with the name of the coffee house keeper Catto suspected Jamie Buchan had not passed Robertson's name on to Arthur Menzies. They must be unaware of each other's involvement.

The trapped mouse looked not only panicked now but also confused. He opened his mouth but before he could stutter out an answer, Catto cut across him. 'No,' he said. 'I'm wrong. I have not had the pleasure of making Mr Robertson's acquaintance until now.' He swung round to address Professor Monro. 'But I fear I interrupt hospital business, sir.'

'Not at all, Captain. We are finished here. You may return to your duties, Mr Robertson. Forthwith.' He flicked his fingers at his student in a gesture of dismissal. 'Get on with it, laddie. The physic won't prepare itself.'

'I shall take my leave, Professor Monro,' the lady governess said. She glided out of the room, as though she were hovering above the floor rather than walking on it.

'A formidable woman,' Professor Monro said. 'Who knows everything that goes on under the roof of this hospital.'

'Indeed, sir?' Catto responded, mentally filing that observation away. Might Agnes Moncur potentially be another name for his list?

'Aye. It was she who alerted me to the fact that two of my residents have taken it upon themselves to exchange duties. There is an established roster. As they know very well.' The professor glared at the bowed head of Murdo Robertson. He was busy over a pestle and mortar, small brass weighing scales on the table in front of him.

Catto was reminded of Kirsty Rankeillor last week, sitting at the same table grinding up willow bark to make into a potion to relieve the pain in his head after Jamie Buchan had knocked him unconscious. Only her cool fingers had been steady. There was a definite tremor in Murdo Robertson's.

'Will you accompany me to the hospital library, young Captain Catto?'

Catto followed the Professor out into the corridor and across it. He waited until Monro had sat down at the head of a large table surrounded by bookshelves. The older man did not ask him to sit down and spoke without preamble.

'An explanation,' he said. 'Of the events of yesterday evening at the Daft Friday ball. If you please.'

Not yet entirely sure how much he was going to tell him, Catto's restless gaze was caught by an inbuilt lectern running down the centre and full length of the library table. It held a series of prints in card mounts, drawings and sketches. 'The plans to which the hospital was built?' he queried, scanning each one in turn. 'Very fine pieces of work in themselves,' he added.

'Examine them more closely if you will.' The stern expression on Monro's face relaxed as he swept one hand through the air in invitation. 'Take a seat to do it. You have an interest in such matters, young sir?'

'I'm an engineer, Professor. I appreciate a finely-drawn and detailed plan.' Despite his current unease, he was speaking nothing but the truth. 'May I?' he queried after he had pulled out a chair and sat down, indicating the print directly in front of him.

'Please do.'

Catto lifted it from the lectern with both hands and studied it more closely, immediately spotting something of more particular interest here. As the legend told him, he was looking at *The General Plan of the Ground Storey of the Royal Infirmary.* He commented on two or three aspects of it before coming to what really interested him.

'These cells indicated here, at the back of the building, marked *For the Safe Custody of Lunaticks.*'

Monro nodded. 'Those among that unhappy group who might be a danger to themselves or others, hence the need to keep them confined. Although the cells have no occupants at the moment.'

'They remain unused? Or can you adapt them to other purposes?'

'We have enough space elsewhere that we do not need to, which is just as well. Many of those who work here do not care to be in that corridor.'

'Why is that, sir?'

Alexander Monro hesitated. 'They claim to feel an atmosphere, a sense of sadness, even despair. We had one patient there last year. A young man, much troubled. He took his own life. Hanged himself.' He made a fist and tapped it hard on the table. 'Damn it. He should not have been left alone and with the means to do away with himself. We failed him and his family.'

'A sad story, sir,' Catto said gently, seeing how much the man cared. 'You are very proud of the Infirmary, I think.'

'Indeed I am. I cherish its good name. Which brings us to the matter in hand.'

'I believe Lieutenant Liddell told you something of the story, sir.'

'He did. It is indeed a regrettable one. I have a daughter of my own, young sir. But you should not have ordered such summary justice as you did.'

'We both know the girl will get no other kind.'

'Aye, we do, and that's not right. But your actions were not right either.'

You know something, sir? I would do exactly the same thing again. Swallowing that retort, Catto took the rebuke. 'Twas a somewhat long-winded one. Funny how older men in positions of authority assumed people would listen to them for as long as they chose to speak.

'I trust we can count on your discretion in this matter,' Monro said at last. 'So that, other than those directly involved, the wider world need never find out about this unfortunate incident.'

Sweep it all under the carpet. Oh, that's an excellent solution. That'll really help Alice Smart and all those other girls who fall foul of young so-called gentlemen. Poor girls with no one to look out for them, not cherished and protected girls like your daughter. Or Kirsty Rankeillor and her friends.

Then he remembered his fears for Kirsty Rankeillor if she should be interrogated by someone other than himself. Thought too of how she and those friends wanted to shout from the rooftops what Cosmo Liddell and his cronies had done to a defenceless young girl. Thought also how distressed Geordie was, the boy blaming himself because he had not been there to protect his sister. Catto knew how that felt.

'You can rely absolutely on my discretion, Professor Monro. I give you my word that no one shall hear of this … unfortunate incident … from me or my men.'

Christ, he was a two-faced hypocrite, repeating that bland description of the horror to which Alice Smart had been subjected. Nor would he put it past Sergeant Livingstone to have a quiet word with one or two folk. Catto would have no problem with that.

'Good,' Monro said. 'One more thing. What do you propose to do now with Cosmo Liddell and Arthur Menzies?'

'I have them under house arrest. When the snow clears I shall have them escorted to Eastfield, the Liddell house near Prestonpans. Where I have told them they are to lie low for a time.'

'Until all this blows over? And Miss Charlotte Liddell?'

'For the moment I have her too confined to the Liddell house. She will accompany her brother and his friend to Eastfield.'

Monro frowned. 'Yet she is not a guilty party here.'

Guilty of being a complete bitch. Yet another thought Catto could not express out loud.

Monro was still frowning. 'I would ask you to release her forthwith. Allow her freedom of movement.' The professor raised his head, looking at one of the windows set high up in the wall of the library and the snow-laden clouds visible through the panes of glass. 'Not that anyone will be moving anywhere for a few days yet but once travel is again possible, I would ask you to give Miss Charlotte the choice of biding in Edinburgh or going to Eastfield.'

'Professor, I cannot do that.'

'Why not?' Monro demanded.

Because Charlotte Liddell was a loose cannon, because she had witnessed too much at the Assembly Rooms last night, because she might well find out about the Jacobite agent, because she was a spiteful gossip who could prove dangerous to Kirsty Rankeillor, especially if Charlotte chose to remain in Edinburgh with free access to her usual social circle. She more than likely would, prizing the entertainments of the town over those of the country.

'Sir, I understand you do not wish to offend Miss Liddell—'

'I cannot afford to offend her. The hospital cannot afford to offend her. Not only has her family always donated generously to us, they have an influence over other wealthy and regular donors.' Monro shot him a sharp look. 'It's easy to sit on one's high horse when one does not have the constant need for funds.'

Catto raised his hands in a placatory gesture. 'I am not judging, Professor Monro, I assure you. What worries me is that she might speak to others about what happened. I understand she was very vocal last night at the Assembly Rooms.'

'I shall talk to her.'

'I cannot allow you or anyone else to call at the Liddell house, sir. Not while I have Cosmo Liddell and Arthur Menzies confined there as my prisoners.' Bracing himself for an explosion of anger and his necessary resistance to that, Catto was relieved when he didn't get it, only an abrupt question.

'Are they guilty of more than this rape?'

'Isn't that enough?' Catto met the Professor's eyes. Like Sergeant Livingstone, the man had a piercing and intelligent gaze. 'Although might I ask why you pose that question, Professor?'

'Straws in the wind.' Monro replied, each word carefully pronounced.

'Aye,' Catto said after a brief pause. 'There may well be some straws in the wind. There may well be more which we hope will also blow over.'

God send it would do that and not roar up into the storm the Lord President so feared could be unleashed. Ferocious. Violent. Bloody. Causing that bitterness and those divisions which would last for years. That was why Catto was engaged on this dirty work, to prevent something even dirtier and uglier. If a few people had to suffer now, it was to save thousands from suffering later. He shifted in his chair and did not feel any more comfortable.

The piercing eyes narrowed. 'Do you answer to Provost Coutts, young man? Or Lord President Forbes?'

'I'm not sure which is the correct answer here, Professor.' As the Lord President had told him, Provost Coutts was suspected of holding Jacobite sympathies and was not under any circumstances to be trusted.

'The honest one.'

'As the Captain of the Town Guard of Edinburgh, I am answerable to the Lord Provost. He is not here at the moment. Marooned outside the town by the snow, I believe.'

'In any case, I think you report to Lord President Forbes rather than Provost Coutts.'

Catto gave a little dip of his head, in agreement and acknowledgement of that statement. He could hardly do otherwise. 'I aim to keep the peace, sir. That is my duty.'

'That's what yon other young man said to me last night. The law student. Archie Liddell? He is related to Cosmo and Charlotte Liddell, I believe.'

'They are cousins.'

'You seem to know a lot for someone who is a stranger to Edinburgh.'

'It is also my duty to know as much as I can.'

'Whilst sharing as little of the intelligence you gather with others? Except perhaps for one other, the Lord President. But I shall not pester you with further questions. Only one last one. Do you aim to keep the peace in Edinburgh or in Scotland as a whole?'

'For both Edinburgh and Scotland.'

'Mmm,' Munro said, but it seemed Catto had given him the answer he wanted. The professor might not take much interest in politics but he clearly took a lot of interest in keeping the peace. An unexpected ally, even if it didn't look as if much practical help was going to be forthcoming, coupled with one definite hindrance. Munro raised that again now. 'The matter's settled, then? About Miss Charlotte Liddell?'

'Can we reach a compromise, sir? Perhaps Miss Liddell could stay somewhere else. Where she might be constrained by not being mistress of the house and where wiser heads might prevail as to what she says or, preferably, does not say.'

'Wiser heads?' Grasping Catto's point, Monro shook his own wiser head. Quite vehemently. 'Oh no, not with myself and Mrs Monro. My wife does not see eye-to-eye with Miss Liddell. Nor does my daughter.' The professor gave a thin smile. 'And I prefer my home not to be a battleground.'

'Another older friend or relative of Miss Liddell's perhaps?' Catto suggested.

Monro answered that in a soft, amused murmur. 'Several of those might have a similar point-of-view to my wife and daughter.'

Christ, there had to be someone. A name slid into his head. 'Lady Bruce of Kinross,' he said. 'Are she and Miss Liddell not also related to each other?'

'You are indeed well informed, Captain Catto.'

'I believe they have other things in common. Chiefly political sympathies.'

The only response he got to that statement was a further searching look. Lady Magdalen Bruce of Kinross was another name he had got from the Lord President. This older lady lived in Leith. So far, her advanced years and gentle birth had allowed her to make no secret of her Jacobite sympathies but she did so quietly, known for her discretion. With a bit of luck, she could keep the girl in check. There was a second possible advantage. If Arthur Menzies of Edmonstone knew it was Catto who had recommended Charlotte's temporary hostess, that would add credence to the idea of Catto himself being a covert Jacobite. So Catto would make sure Edmonstone did know.

'Perhaps, sir,' he suggested, 'you might like to write Miss Liddell a letter, telling her you have secured her freedom as long as she exercises it only to go to Lady Bruce's house in Leith, also strongly advising her to be discreet about what happened at the Assembly Rooms last night for the sake of her brother and her family's reputation. If you cared to write that now, I could arrange to have it delivered to her. Also of course a letter to Lady Bruce, making the request, which I shall have delivered as soon as the snow clears.'

'Excellent idea.'

Oh aye, especially if that's all I'm going to ask you to do. You're not giving me much help here, Professor.

'Of course, as an officer of the law, you could insist on Lady Bruce's agreement,' Monro said thoughtfully.

'I should prefer not to make demands of an elderly and well-respected lady, sir.'

The professorial eyebrows shot up. 'Indeed? I understand you to be somewhat forceful in the execution of your duty.'

So he knew about the raid on the Rankeillor house last week – but was not quite challenging Catto about that. Because he knew of Patrick Rankeillor's Jacobite sympathies and did not want to reinforce them by further discussion? What would he say if he knew Catto had Patrick Rankeillor's daughter under house arrest?

Plenty. Monro might dislike Rankeillor's politics but Catto felt sure he would be fiercely loyal to a medical colleague and fellow manager of Edinburgh Royal Infirmary. Which gave him even more of an impetus to get this matter resolved as quickly and as quietly as possible.

Monro glanced across at a small desk on which stood paper, ink and quills. 'I shall do that right away. After which I would offer you a tour of the Infirmary but my wife is waiting for me at home.' He smiled broadly and transformed himself. People were infinitely complex. 'She thinks I spend too much time here as it is.'

'Would you object if I took a look at these cells while you are writing your letter, sir? As an engineer, I am always interested in methods of construction. How plans translate into reality.'

'Be my guest, laddie. Get young Mr Robertson to give you a lantern and show you where the keys are.'

23

'Do you wish me to accompany you?'

'No,' Catto said, hoping he was further confusing this inept plotter by giving him a friendly smile. Or what he hoped passed for one. He'd rather have punched him in the nose and told him to come to his senses before it was too late, asked him if he was a complete fucking idiot, didn't realize what he stood to lose, what a Pandora's box he and his fellow plotters might be opening here.

'I'll manage fine by myself. The keys to the individual cells hang behind the door over there in the corner, you say?'

The solid door swung shut behind him, wood sliding smoothly over stone with a soft murmur of sound. He was immediately glad of the small lantern Murdo Robertson had given him. This corridor at the back of the Infirmary had little natural light, only some narrow windows set at intervals into the top of the wall. He could see why people might feel uncomfortable here, especially when they knew the story of the suicide. He wondered if Kirsty Rankeillor had been scared when she had walked along here. Carrying supplies to *him*: John Roy Stuart.

Unlocking the doors in turn, Catto found the evidence he was looking for in the third cell. Blankets and pillows were piled in tumbled disarray on a narrow bed fixed to the wall. Close by it, also secured to the wall, stood a small rough-hewn table. A brass lantern identical to the one Murdo Robertson had given Catto sat on the table, along with a couple of news-sheets, an inkwell, a quill and a few sheets of paper.

He picked one of those up before dropping it as though it had burned his fingers.

The first few lines of a half-composed poem, written in Gaelic. It was a long time since Catto had read that language but he found he could still understand most of the words, translating its title as *The Bonnie Dark Haired Lass*. That was followed by some sentimental twaddle about *eyes shining with compassion*. This was where she had exercised that compassion, bringing food, drink and physic to this cell. Hiding a known rebel. Endangering herself. The damn bloody little fool.

For a moment Robert Catto was so angry he could barely move. When he did, reaching for the lantern he had set down on the rough table, he found that his hands were trembling. Commanding his fingers to be steady, he opened the glass door of the lantern, curled the paper on which the lines were written and lit it, holding it upside down so the candle flame would catch. Only at the very last minute did he let it drop onto the stone floor of the cell, where he ground the fragments of paper into dust with the heel of his shoe.

Drawing a small notebook and the stub of a pencil from his waistcoat pocket, he placed himself at the door of the cell and made a sketch of it and its contents.

❖

Murdo Robertson jumped when Catto pushed open the door of the apothecary's shop.

'Thank you for the loan of the lantern. 'Twas most useful.'

'You found what you were seeking then, sir?' Murdo managed. He'd spent the last half hour in a state of abject misery, expecting at any moment to be denounced as a rebel and hauled off to the Tolbooth. He had the feeling Robert Catto was toying with him, stretching this out so as to torment him. He was already imagining dreadful scenes in his head, of his mother and sisters trying to see him and being refused the privilege but not so faraway he couldn't hear their pleas and tears. He was almost on the point of confession to this terrifying man, desperate to lance the tension building up inside him.

'I did find what I needed. A word to the wise.' Robert Catto tapped the side of his nose. 'Third cell down on the right. There are some bits and pieces in there that should be returned to their proper places or disposed of. They rather give the game away.'

'The g-game?' Murdo stuttered.

Robert Catto smiled. 'We both know which game I'm talking about, Mr Robertson. Good-day to you.'

Head bowed over his pestle and mortar, Murdo Robertson's hands were no longer trembling, although he remained ready to jump at the slightest sound. The day had started badly. Hurrying downstairs as quietly as possible before 5 o'clock this morning, well-wrapped up in anticipation of stepping out into the chilly morning, he'd had to stifle a gasp of astonishment. The hospital's sedan chair was back where it always was when not in use to carry patients up and down to the wards.

As though it were some kind of a mirage, he had walked forward and touched the wooden conveyance where it sat next to the main entrance doors to the hospital, laying his hand flat against it. Cold, but not freezing. It had clearly been carried back here a little while before. When he tried the main doors of the hospital he had found them locked, as they should be so early in the day. He'd spent the rest of the morning trying not to look sideways at everyone else in the building, wondering who might have brought the chair back.

Returning him to the here and now, his heart began to race. Someone was standing close behind him. He'd been so lost in thought he hadn't heard the opening of the door to the apothecary's shop. He swung round and found himself looking up at Mrs Moncur.

'Dinna look so worried,' she said, patting him on the shoulder. 'He's away. I watched him go. Tell me what he said when he came in here afore he left.'

'S-said about wh-what?' Murdo stuttered.

Annoyance crossed Agnes Moncur's face but her next words made it clear her anger was directed against herself. 'About what was left in the cell where our visitor was staying. I should have cleared away the evidence first thing this morning but there was an emergency in the women's ward and then yon Captain Catto arrived.'

'You ken about him? Our visitor, I mean?'

'I ken about him.'

'The sedan chair. You arranged for it to be brought back?'

Agnes Moncur didn't answer, only glided across the shop, lifting the key ring which hung at her waist, selecting a key and opened one of the cupboards that lined the walls. 'I'm thinking you need a restorative, Mr Robertson.' Bringing out a decanter, she set it on the table in front of Murdo, returning to the cupboard to fetch two glasses and a small wooden box. 'Here,' she said, opening the box, 'have a ginger biscuit. We'll both have a wee glass of madeira. It's been something of a tense morning.'

She poured those out and allowed a bemused Murdo to eat half his biscuit before she spoke again. 'Now. Tell me what he said.'

By the time he had finished speaking, Agnes Moncur was frowning. 'Do you think we can trust him?'

'I don't know. I've been wondering that myself.'

'He's a clever man, I'm thinking.'

Murdo nodded. 'Aye. Observant too. I dinna think much gets past him.'

'You're sure he was escorting Kirsty back to her house?'

Murdo nodded again. 'That's what it looked like.'

'You didn't follow them all the way to Infirmary Street?'

'No.' Despite the searching look she was giving him, he could not bring himself to tell her why he had been following Robert Catto. 'We need to speak to Kirsty.'

Agnes Moncur nodded. 'Aye. But I suspect he might be having her guarded, and her house watched. He's probably watching us here at the Infirmary too. We'll have to be gey careful.' She lifted her wine glass. 'Or at least lower our voices. May times mend,' she said, obeying her own suggestion.

'And down with the bloody Brunswickers,' Murdo responded in similarly low tones, raising his glass only far enough to gently clink with hers. 'If they're watching us, I take it we're watching them too. Might we hope to receive some intelligence about Captain Catto?'

'We might hope,' Agnes said. 'Although after last night, we are rather in disarray. Not to mention that 'tis harder to follow anyone with any discretion when so many people are biding at home because of the snow and the streets are well-nigh empty.'

Murdo nodded. 'We may have to play a waiting game?'

'Aye, well, we ought to be used to that by now.' Agnes Moncur gave him a surprisingly mischievous smile and took a healthy swig of her claret. Then her face grew serious again. 'But we must speak with Kirsty as soon as we safely can.'

24

It was half past eleven and Christian was in the shop, making a not very good job of assembling the physic she was due to deliver to the Royal Infirmary on Monday, not that she was going to be allowed to. In which case someone was going to have to come and fetch it. Who that was to be and how a collection was to be arranged in this snow she did not know.

She would have to ask Robert Catto. Maybe he would do it. No, that wouldn't work. To have the Captain of the Town Guard delivering physic on her behalf would look distinctly odd. They had to try to keep all of this quiet. They had both agreed on that. No doubt he would work something out. Thinking on his feet, as seemed to be his strong suit.

Unable to settle to the task, she walked over the floorboards to the half-glazed door and looked through its leaded window panes at Infirmary Street. The day was bright with winter sun, although more snow had fallen during the night. There was nobody to be seen out in the street to help her judge, but she thought the snow must now be knee-deep. 'Twas only a short walk from here to the hospital but if this hadn't cleared by Monday, 'twould be a difficult one, whoever was going to make it.

'Under arrest.' She said the words softly but out loud, scarcely able to believe them. 'I am under arrest.' She wondered when he might arrive to question her. It could be hours yet.

And I shall have answers. Believe me.

She believed him. He'd already got enough of those answers last night. Too many. She feared he would get more out of her. By hook or by crook. Or by her too expressive face. She'd been trying to rehearse both what he might ask and how she might respond but she wasn't getting very far.

Too upset and confused by the events of the previous evening to be able to think clearly, she turned and went back behind the counter. For a moment she gazed at the pestle and mortar, small brass weighing-scale and the assortment of glass phials and blue and white china jars and pots lying there waiting for her. Her deep wicker basket stood next to them, ready to be packed for Monday. She tried to calm herself by focussing again on these familiar tasks but kept being distracted by two questions among the many buzzing around inside her head. Was the Cause worth the death of Jeannie Carmichael? Was the Cause worth anyone's death?

She had never questioned this before. All her life the Stuart Cause had been an article of faith, the restoration of the rightful king something that had to happen because it was right and fair and just that it should. It had been a shining silken banner to lead them to a glorious destination, up to the top of hill from where they would gaze out at the promised land. It was inevitable. It was right. Yet none of this seemed right.

A shadow fell across the windows of the door and the bell on the back of it jangled. Christian jumped, hoping he hadn't seen her do so. Grabbing the ring of keys lying farther along the counter, she hurried to unlock the door and open it. As at the guard-house yesterday evening, a blast of wintry air hit her, rendering her momentarily breathless.

'Dinna bring any snow inside, if you please,' she managed.

'Oh, for God's sake. Do you not have more to bloody worry about than a bit of snow making a wet patch on the damn floor?'

He muttered a few more choice words. She felt her eyes widen in response. Last night when he had taken his leave of her, he had been kind, even tender. This morning foul-mouthed and bad-tempered Captain Catto was back in full measure. Although he did lift each foot in turn and, with an ill grace, draw them over the metal boot-scraper on the right hand side of the steps. You could still just about see the top edge of it showing above the snow piled up on those.

'I should clear the steps.'

'Why bother? Anyone who chooses to sally forth in this snow has to be a damn fool.'

She took a quick little breath. 'That makes you a damn fool.'

He looked up and glowered at her. 'I'm not choosing to be out here. I have a job to do.'

'Other people might have no choice, either. Those in desperate need of physic for themselves or a relative.'

He brushed snow off his grey woollen stockings, kicked the toes of his shoes against the underside of the threshold, and let out an exasperated sigh. 'Give me a shovel and a stiff broom and I'll do it.' With that, he stepped up and into the shop.

'Your hand looks as if it is still very sore.' Fighting the urge to step back and put some distance between them, she was concentrating on the badly discoloured bruise. The swelling had gone down a little from last night but remained obvious.

'It's nothing.'

'Really?' She reached out and touched it with two gentle fingers. Clearly they weren't gentle enough.

'Ow!' he exclaimed, jerking his hand back and bestowing another ferocious glower on her.

She should offer to apply some soothing salve. The thought of the necessary intimacy of that made her hesitate, and the moment passed. 'Am I to be permitted to admit any customers who might call this morning?'

'No,' he said tersely. He swung round and closed the shop door, his hand going to the heavy card sign hanging over the window in the top half of it. She had turned it earlier to show *Open*. Now he turned it back to *Closed*. Without so much as a by-your-leave.

Her own anger flaring, she whirled round and headed for the counter, putting herself behind it. She cut a compact figure today, clad in the simple dark blue dress, white linen apron and neat cap she customarily wore when she was working in the shop or helping out at the Royal Infirmary. She threw the ring of keys onto the counter, where they landed with a jangle and a crash.

His eyes went to those before travelling up to her face. 'I take it you are displeased about something, madam. How subtly you make your point.'

'Displeased about something? La, what could that be? Apart from being under arrest, confined to my home and having you storming in here this morning like a bear with a sore head, what on earth might I be displeased about?'

He stepped forward so he was standing in the middle of the shop, halfway between the door and the counter. She raised her eyebrows, struggling to play the haughty young miss, to keep him at arm's length, to hold her own confused and conflicted feelings towards him at bay. Fear was fighting attraction, overwhelming in its intensity. She longed to go to him and allow her body to melt into his, touch him and be touched by him in return... She wanted to feel his mouth on hers, his strong arms settling around her waist. How could she possibly feel this way about a man like him? He was her enemy, dangerous to everything and everyone she held dear.

That did not stop her eyes from fluttering shut, allowing her to travel back to yesterday evening in the guard-house, when he had spoken to her so movingly about his mother, when the two of them had kissed and embraced ... when he had so very nearly touched her in the most intimate of places. A wave of embarrassment washed over her. She had been scared of that but she had wanted it too.

'Are you ill?' he demanded.

'No,' she said, opening her eyes. 'I'm not ill. Nervous, but not ill.'

'You are right to be nervous. And if I'm like a *bear with a sore head*,' – his words were once again cloaked in sarcasm – 'it might be because of what I found when I visited the Royal Infirmary, some half-an-hour since. Is there no end to your foolishness?'

That question deprived her of speech, if only long enough for him to detail what he had found. 'You might at least have thought of clearing the detritus away.'

'I did think of that!' she burst out. 'I would have gone over there this morning.'

'Too late now,' he said grimly, patting one of the pockets of his coat. 'You're not the only person who can draw. I've made a sketch of what I found. Lying there in one of the cells in that corridor at the back of the building for anyone to find. As I found it. You do realize it gives me yet more damning evidence against you?'

'I may be foolish but I am not an idiot, sir. Of course I realize that.' Her voice shook.

He stood looking at her. It seemed important to hold his gaze, even if she was obliged to raise the back of one hand to still her trembling lower lip. It was very quiet inside the shop and there was no noise out in the street, any there might have been dampened by the snow.

'Maybe you were hoping the lady governess would have cleared out that cell. Mrs Moncur?'

'Agnes? How would she have even known there was anything to be cleared out?'

'You tell me.'

'There's nothing to tell,' she said, although her brain was racing. Agnes Moncur was in on the plot?

'Oh, I think there's a lot to tell,' he said softly. 'And are you not now wondering why you had to put yourself in danger when she could have tended to the Jacobite agent?'

That was exactly what she was thinking, even as she could see the justification for Jamie asking her to look after John Roy Stuart. He had said something about people being used to seeing her in the hospital, yet at the same time, not really noticing her, Professor Rankeillor's daughter who was so often there.

Agnes Moncur was there almost all of the time, with the trick of being able to materialize out of nowhere, coming silently up behind you. Yet see her from a distance and you always noticed her. She might have drawn unwanted attention to the supposedly deserted corridor at the back of the hospital.

That was why Jamie had used her instead. Used. Christian did not care for the word. She had been scared but she had been more than willing to help. Her father had not wanted her to be involved but Jamie had insisted. Everything for the Cause. That led her thoughts back to Jeannie Carmichael and the hideous reality of Jamie having taken the girl's life.

Watching her, Robert Catto posed a simple and surprisingly softly-spoken question: 'How are you?'

'How am I?' she demanded. '*How am I?* You come breenging in here and then ask me how I am? How the Devil do you think I am? I am sure it is not beyond your intelligence to make a guess. I'm tired. I'm frightened. I'm wondering what is happening over at the hospital without Jamie being there.' Her voice shook again on that name. 'I'm sad,' she managed. 'Finding it hard to believe he could do what he did to that girl and, oh God, that he was prepared to do the same to you!' Robert Catto took a step towards the counter. Christian held up a hand. 'No. Please. Do not come any closer.'

'I had promised myself I would not,' he muttered. 'Damn it, I do not *want* to come any closer! But you are distressed.'

'Oh, aye.' She laughed, a wild little sound. 'I am distressed. Not quite knowing what I am doing. Saying things I should not be saying to the Captain of the Town Guard.'

He was indeed the Captain of the Town Guard but he wasn't wearing his uniform today. 'Twas not a Redcoat officer who stood before her but a man in plain black breeches and a dark-blue topcoat, a soft black silk neckcloth knotted at his throat for extra warmth. He might have been a prosperous young tradesman. In a gesture of frustration she was beginning to see as characteristic, she saw one hand go up to his brow, poised to run his fingers through his hair. As last night, he stopped, giving a little grunt of disgust when he found he could not complete the action.

Yesterday evening he had been dressed in green and silver satin, his identity concealed behind a black velvet eye mask. All that remained of that elegant gentleman was his powdered hair. Tied back at the nape of his neck, it was secured today by a simple black ribbon. She could see he had brushed out some of the pomatum but it always took days to get rid of it completely.

'Damn it,' he said again. 'I am so bloody angry with you!'

She raised her chin. If he was expecting an answer to that statement, he was going to be disappointed. Then he once again took her by surprise. Deep within those impassive grey eyes, a light flared.

'Och, but Kirsty,' he said, adding her name with a diffidence, almost a shyness, that made her heart skip a beat, 'right at this moment, it's only Robert standing here in front of you. There's only you and me here. No one else is listening. You're safe to say anything you want to me. We may have to toughen you up for questions someone else might put to you later. But,' he repeated, 'right here and right now, you are safe with me.'

'Safe with you? *Safe with you?*' she repeated, the pitch of her voice rising in disbelief. 'That's the last word I would use. I knew you were dangerous from the moment I first set eyes on you. And you are not *only Robert* today. You are the Captain of the Town Guard and you have me under arrest!'

'Kirsty...'

'Don't,' she said, once more putting up a hand to stop him stepping further forward. 'Please don't come any closer.'

Dangerous and perceptive. She saw him relax his posture, doing what he could to put her at her ease. Oh God, why did he have to act in such bewildering ways?

'As to what is happening over at the hospital,' he offered, 'when I got there I found Professor Monro berating someone called Murdo Robertson, who has changed places with Balnamoon to become the resident. Allegedly they arranged this yesterday on account of Balnamoon having to travel north to Banffshire to be with his sick mother. Strange, that. I had understood she died several years ago, when he was but a boy.'

'Is there nothing you do not know?' she asked after a tiny pause.

'Well, I do not know for an absolute fact that the assailant of last night was Murdo Robertson but I'm pretty sure he was. Wondering if you might agree with me.'

She wanted to lower her eyes, busy herself with the paraphernalia in front of her, knew that would give her away. Not only herself. 'Murdo Robertson is the most peaceable of men. It could not have been Murdo.'

'It was him.'

'He would never do such a thing.'

'He didn't do such a thing. Which rather proves your point. Besides which, did you not think the same about Jamie Buchan until last night? Men with a cause,' he said. 'Nothing matters more. Not friend, not lover. Not wife, not children. Not their life, not anyone else's life.' He was repeating what he had said to her in the guard-house last night, when Christian had been fighting the realization of Jamie having ended Jeannie Carmichael's life. 'Murdo Robertson played the caddie last night. Carried the Jacobite agent up to the Assembly Rooms.'

'Did he?'

'I'm pretty sure of it.'

'Have you arrested him?'

'No.'

'Not yet, you mean.'

'Aye. Not yet.'

Another little pause. 'So you will cut us off from one another and allow those who do not know to continue to believe you are on our side.'

'With the help of the snow, yes.'

'You are very frank with me, sir.'

'I am trying to be honest with you … Kirsty. As much as I possibly can be.'

Honest. Sarcastic. Angry. With the power of life and death over her, her father and their friends. Her eyes filled with tears.

25

'Kirsty,' he murmured. He took a couple of side-steps towards the end of the counter, his left hand already sliding along the smooth dark wood towards the flap. He had promised himself he would not touch her. He had promised himself there would be no more kisses. He had thought he was too angry with her for that. When he had found the evidence of John Roy Stuart's stay in the Royal Infirmary, the red mist had risen, filling him with unreasoning fury. The stupid little fool really did have no sense of self-preservation. Why was he risking his own career, his very future, potentially even his bloody life, to try to save her when she had chosen to put herself in such danger?

Always rigorously honest with himself, it had not taken long to admit his anger had another source. He was jealous of what she had done for the man. Food and drink. Medical attention. News-sheets. Paper, pen and ink. Sympathy for his plight. Admiration for the risks he was running for their Cause. Robert Catto despised himself for caring so much about all that. Behind him, a door opened. He swung round and saw the wee housekeeper come bustling in from the lobby of the house.

'Whit are you daein' here?'

Muttering a curse, Catto gave her a look that would have withered a lesser woman. 'I am here to talk to Miss Rankeillor, goodwife. In my capacity as Captain of the Town Guard.'

'You'll talk tae her in front o' me.'

'No,' he said. 'I won't.'

'Good morning, Captain,' piped a voice from behind the housekeeper.

'Geordie,' Catto said, looking round the little woman at him. 'How does your sister?'

'She had a good sleep, sir. So did I. You're looking a wee bittie tired, though.'

'He's a wee bittie pale too,' Betty Gilchrist observed. Like gun carriages being swivelled to aim at a single target, three pairs of eyes now focussed on him. Christian Rankeillor's were dry. She must have taken the opportunity to wipe away her tears while he'd been concentrating on Geordie and the housekeeper. Never upset other people if you can possibly avoid it. Another tenet of the credo by which she lived.

'When did you last sit doon and eat a proper meal?' demanded the little woman.

'I don't remember. Does it matter?'

'Sometimes he does that,' Geordie supplied. 'Forgets tae eat, I mean. When he's busy with his letters and papers or he's been out on an important mission—'

'You hold your tongue, Geordie Smart. And kindly all stop studying me!'

Feeding his exasperated irritation, none of his observers paid any heed to that command. Domesticity. He'd been away from it for so long. Women scolding men. Men allowing themselves to be scolded. People who had nothing more to worry about than the running of their houses and the minutiae of the safe little lives they led within those houses.

'Of course it matters,' said the wee wifie. 'Guid sakes, some folk dinna hae the sense they were born with. Ye'd better bide and tak your meridian wi' us.'

'For God's sake,' Catto howled. 'I am here as an officer of the law. This is not a social call!'

'Even officers of the law have to eat,' Kirsty Rankeillor observed, and sent Catto's emotions tumbling off in another direction. Once again, even in the midst of her distress, she had somehow managed to find something to laugh at, his current discomfiture. Tiny but there, an imp of mischief danced in her green eyes.

Catching himself on, he managed to divide a black look between her and her housekeeper. She must be one of those women who felt the need to feed everyone who came within range of her little empire. Even him. Sod it, now he came to think about it, he was bloody hungry. The woman had left the internal door open, allowing tempting smells to waft through from the kitchen at the back of the house. Soup. Freshly-baked bread. Something sweet. Smelled like gingerbread. He loved gingerbread. His mouth watered at the thought of it.

'Out of here,' he barked, impatient with his own weakness. He'd stay here to eat only sometime after hell froze over. 'Right now. You too, Geordie. I require to speak with Miss Rankeillor. In private.'

'It's warmer in the library,' Geordie offered. 'I did the fire for Mrs Betty an hour since.'

'Aye,' Betty Gilchrist said. 'He's cleared the ashes frae the kitchen range forbye. And brought the coal in for all the fires, upstairs and downstairs, and filled the bunker in the kitchen so we willna need tae ging oot in the snow for another day or twa. The lad's been a big help this morning.'

Catto and Christian Rankeillor exchanged a look. He caught the silent message. This belligerent little sparrow of a housekeeper might hate his guts and irritate him beyond measure but she'd been doing her best for Geordie, finding wee jobs for him to do, keeping his mind off what had happened to his sister.

'By all means let us go through to the library,' Catto said. 'Miss Rankeillor, will you please lock the shop door again before we do? The one to the street, I mean.'

She lifted her chin. 'Do you not wish to do that yourself, Captain?'

Once again she was taking them back to their first meeting, when he had demanded she hand over the keys to him before he took them from her.

With as much force as you oblige me to use. That was what he had said to her. If he'd had to, he'd have followed through on that.

'I do not know which is the correct key,' he said crisply. 'You do.'

Wordlessly, she lifted the keys, selected the right one and handed the dangling ring to him, holding the key by its business end. Another reminder of last Saturday. She had done the same then. He had quite deliberately not taken the key by its shank but had closed his fingers over hers. It had been another way of knocking her off-balance, touching her in an invasion of her person, as he had invaded her house. Today he avoided any contact. By the time he'd locked the shop door and turned around again, she had glided out from behind the shop counter.

'We'll leave the library doors open a wee bit, Betty. Ajar.'

'No, we won't. People can eavesdrop more easily from behind a cracked-open door than they can through a wide open one.'

That provoked the fishwife stance from the housekeeper, hands on her skinny hips. 'I hae better things tae dae wi' ma time than listen at doors, young man!'

He threw the little woman another black look. He chose not to waste his breath by pointing out he was hardly likely to tumble Christian Rankeillor in front of the library fire in a house full of people. Or demand to know why she was so concerned about propriety when her young mistress's life might be at stake.

❖

'How does your father ever find anything in this mess?' Catto asked, gazing at the melée of papers, medical tomes and discarded quills lying on top of the big square table Patrick Rankeillor used as a desk. 'It looks like the relief map of a battlefield after a battery of canons has done its work.'

'You have stood on many battlefields?'

'A fair few. How long has Professor Rankeillor been a member of the Association?'

She hesitated for only a few seconds. Long enough.

'Ah. One question answered. You know the purpose of the Association?'

She did. Her father had told her of its existence before he had left for Glasgow. The Association was a secret organization which aimed to restore the House of Stuart to the British throne. Its head was James, the King-over-the water, who had been in exile in Rome for many a long year. Any rising in favour of the Stuarts was likely to be led by his elder son, Prince Charles Edward Stuart.

'The Association is also known as the Concert of Gentlemen,' Robert Catto supplied, folding his arms and propping one shoulder against the closed library doors.

'I know that—' She stopped dead, horrified by her own betraying mouth, swallowing hard before she spoke again. 'I am making this very easy for you, am I not?'

'Aye,' he said. 'You are. Sit down, Kirsty. If you please. In front of the fire.'

He unfolded his arms and followed her across the room, waiting for her to seat herself before he sat down opposite her.

'You were not so mannerly last Saturday.'

'I was making a point last Saturday.' When he had thrown himself down in this chair, leaving her standing, using outrageous rudeness as yet another weapon to knock her off-balance. 'I intend to make the same point today. Pointing out the dangers of armed rebellion.'

'I think I probably understand those.'

'I'm sure you don't.'

She sat like a nervous schoolgirl, bolt upright, her hands clasped on her lap, her feet in their little black leather shoes neatly placed together on the colourful red and green hearth rug.

'Don't look so worried,' he added, his voice gentling. 'I haven't brought the thumb screws with me.' She held his gaze but he had heard the sharp intake of breath. 'I see my attempt at a jest was ill-advised. I'm not going to hurt you, Kirsty.'

The mutinous chin rose again. 'But you might threaten me a little?'

'I don't think I need to. You said you were scared. You are right to be so. Politics fought on the battlefield is bloody enough. Politics fought within civil society is immeasurably worse. Running battles through streets and houses and villages. Maybe you can imagine a little of what that is like. Who suffers as a result. More than soldiers, Kirsty. Boys as well as men, women and children too. Dumb and defenceless animals.'

He turned his head away to gaze into the flames of the fires, remembering once again the farmhouse in Saxony. Strangely silent as they had approached it. No cattle lowing or dogs barking or hens clucking or women talking and laughing as they slapped clothes against a rock in the nearby stream. The horror of the slaughtered family he and his troop had found within the farmhouse had never left him.

The hideous, tortured pictures had stayed in his head ever since. The mutilated bodies of an old man, a young boy, a woman and her daughters, all of them bearing the marks and lacerations of brutal abuse and violent rape inflicted before they had been murdered. Sick-making smells. The stink of fear and terror.

'You do not need to imagine it?'

'No. I have witnessed it at first hand.' He looked away from the fire and back at her. 'Such rebellions and insurrections spare no one and there are always reprisals afterwards. I wonder if you think your Cause is worth that. I wonder if you want to see Scotland plunged into bloodshed.'

She did not immediately answer him, her brow creasing. He hoped she was thinking about what he had just said, that her imagination could indeed encompass the horror.

*Do you know what can happen to girls and women in times of war,
sir?*

That was the question he had put to her father last Saturday in this
very room and in front of her. He had seen her reaction to it.

'There does not…' She coughed and started again. 'There does not
necessarily have to be bloodshed.'

'Ah,' he said again, tapping one long finger against his lips. 'The plan
must then be to seize power by stealth. Perhaps an occupation of
London under cover of darkness, using French troops. They might
land in Kent and sail up the Thames during the night. Then, when they
have seized London, home-grown Jacobites around the country will
rise, declare themselves and take power in their own cities and towns.
Is that it?'

She looked at him in horror, once again realizing too late her over-
expressive face was telling him what he needed to know.

'I believe this attempt is to take place in spring next year, even
earlier if the weather allows. I further believe John Roy Stuart has been
dispatched to Scotland to acquaint people with the plan and to enlist
support, ask them to hold themselves in readiness for a rising in
Scotland once London has been seized. He was here in Edinburgh at
the behest of Menzies of Edmonstone, who is assuredly much more
than the empty-headed fop he pretends to be, in the hope of persuading
Cosmo Liddell to be one of those who might loosen his purse strings to
help finance the military operation. You have gone rather pale, Kirsty.
Can I take that as meaning I am correct in my surmises?'

She stared at him for a moment. Then, for the second time that
morning, she buried her face in her hands. In the next instant she
uncovered her face and straightened up from the slouch into which she
had slumped. 'No,' she said, 'I shall not weep. I'd cried enough this
morning even before you got here. You shall not make me cry again!'

26

He reached her before she could achieve her clear intention of standing up. A couple of long strides and he was down on one knee in front of her chair. He was still angry with her, but he was once again feeling compassion too. How much choice had she ever really had about this, this unreasoning allegiance to the Stuarts and their bloody cause?

'Get out of my way. I need to stand up.' She spoke now through gritted teeth. 'I need to *move*!'

'In a moment. What I need is to tell you something.'

'I dinna want to hear it.' She shook her head, setting her neat white cap askew and uncovering a thick strand of her dark hair. 'I don't want to hear anything from you!'

'You need to hear it.' He grabbed her hands before she could resist, held them securely in his. 'There is no need to look so stricken. It really is not so difficult to work it out. There are only so many possible options. You have not told me anything of which I was not already pretty sure. You have not betrayed anyone's secrets.'

'Och, you are so clever, are you not? You look and you listen and you watch how everyone else looks and reacts and you work it all out!'

'More or less,' he agreed. 'I am a gatherer of intelligence, Kirsty. That is my role here in Edinburgh.' Then, surprising himself, he laughed. 'If your housekeeper were to look in on us now she would think I was proposing marriage rather than interrogating you.'

'Dinna be ridiculous,' she snapped, and succeeded in sliding her hands from his grip. 'We have known each other for but a week.'

'Have you never heard of love at first sight?'

'Do not remind me of last night. 'Twas all false! And get out of my way!'

He rose to his feet and stepped back. She stood up and brushed past him, putting some distance between them, but did not turn around. He contemplated her rigid back, thinking about what he had just said to her. She was absolutely right. It had been a ridiculous thing to say. Given the circumstances, completely ludicrous. Yet somehow the words had slipped out: and he did not regret them.

'Turn around.'

'Stop ordering me about.'

'I'm asking you to turn around, not ordering you to do it.'

'With you, it can be hard to tell the difference. You do have me under arrest, do you not?'

'Aye,' he agreed. 'I do. You might do well to remember that, Kirsty. Also that I am trying to do my best for you and your father. So face me and sit down again. If you please.'

That brought her whirling round. 'And if I don't please?'

'Then I shall sit and you shall stand and it won't be me who's lacking in manners.'

He was already in the armchair she'd only recently vacated. 'I didn't think I was that bad a prospect,' he murmured, resting his elbows on the arms of the chair and making a steeple of his fingers. 'For matrimony, I mean,' he added when she gave him no reply, his lips twitching.

'It's not funny. Not at all funny!' She began pacing the floor, a few steps in one direction, wheeling round to retrace her steps to where she'd started from. 'Besides which, I could never marry someone like you! I *would* never marry someone like you!'

'Thanks,' he said mildly. 'I'm glad we've got that settled.'

She stopped pacing and stood with her hands at her waist, her elbows crooked and jutting out. 'Do you think my father would ever let me marry someone like you? A soldier? A Redcoat? A man who rackets about Europe in the service of the Elector of Hanover?'

'Mind your words,' he growled. 'And sit down. Why were you weeping before I got here this morning? Because of what Balnamoon did to Jeannie Carmichael?'

She looked at him for a moment before her hands and the belligerent posture relaxed. 'Aye,' she said, her voice thick with emotion. 'Because of that.'

'Sit down, Kirsty,' he said again. 'If you please.'

She moved back, sinking down into the chair opposite his, the embodiment of misery. 'Because of that,' she repeated. 'Also because I am worried about my father and my friends. Have you already questioned them?'

'Not yet. I thought perhaps you might want to write a letter for me to carry to reassure them that you are well.' He threw a glance over his shoulder, to the open doors into the shop and the outside world beyond. 'Although,' he muttered, thinking aloud, 'it might be better for me not to leave here today until darkness falls.'

'To make it less likely you will be seen leaving this house or calling on them?' she queried, adding when he nodded his agreement: 'You are still having this house watched and guarded, I take it.'

'Night and day. The Royal Infirmary too.' He had reinforced his orders on that this morning, calling in on William Angus Stewart on his way here, although he had decided there was no longer any need to have the back of the house watched. 'Now,' he said crisply. 'My conditions. They should not to be too difficult to adhere to if the snow continues to fall and if it continues to lie. No one will expect you to deliver physic to the hospital in this weather.'

'It is still our turn,' she protested. 'For almost another week. Until Christmas Eve.'

'Then you will pack two full baskets of physic and I shall get one of my men to deliver them on Monday. I presume you have more than one basket?' Then, when she gave him a reluctant nod: 'That should surely see the dispensary at the Infirmary through for the following week. I shall ask one of the guards who is also a caddy, so it will look as though you have bespoken his services.'

'Some physic cannot be prepared too far in advance.'

'Presumably it can if the necessary raw materials are available to someone with the necessary skills. You will write a letter to Murdo Robertson to go with the physic, saying you're sure he will understand your unwillingness to brave the snow. I shall of course read this letter before it is dispatched.'

'And if the snow clears before the end of this coming week?'

'We shall cross that bridge when we come to it. If you wish to receive a visit from your friends once the causeways are less hazardous underfoot, you must agree the day and time with me in advance and I must be present.'

'What if I receive them without your knowledge? If they turn up at the front door I'm not going to leave them standing there.'

'I'll come to that. You may continue to work in the shop from this coming Monday. If people find you there, 'twill seem all is as normal. You will speak to no one about the events of yesterday evening. Absolutely no one. Is that understood?'

'What if I do tell someone?'

'Then you will be putting your father and yourself in more danger. Do we understand each other?'

'Yes,' she managed. 'We understand each other. *I may continue to work in the shop,*' she repeated. 'If you wish to be present while I do that you will not have time to do much else.'

'I shall know who calls when I am not there. As I shall know who calls at the house. I have the ability to prevent and detain anyone who seeks to enter. Including your friends.'

'So I might as well be in the Tolbooth!'

'You would not find it very comfortable there.' Fear flashed across her face. That defiant statement had been bravado, her trying to find her courage. He did not want to think that if someone else had been in his position, she might already be in the Tolbooth, isolated and fearful in Edinburgh's unforgiving prison. 'Do you agree to my conditions?'

'I do not seem to have any choice.'

'Neither do I.'

She sent him a searching look at that, then when he did not respond: 'How long are these conditions of yours to prevail?'

'Until I decide otherwise. Until this situation is resolved.'

'When will that be?'

'You tell me.'

She held his gaze. 'In the lap of the gods?'

'That's not quite what I meant.'

She did not drop her eyes but the fear was still there, lurking in their depths. He hoped that meant he wasn't going to have to frighten her any more, that she had finally realized the danger in which she and her father stood. He was reluctant to employ the most vicious weapon in his armoury, did not want to put those pictures from the farmhouse in Saxony into her head. He'd never been able to get them out of his own.

'I hope I do not have to ask you again for your word of honour that you will not attempt to get a message to your father. That is one reason why I have to be present when you see your friends. To make sure you do not try to send a message via them. Either verbally or perhaps by means of a little sketch rather than anything as obvious as a letter.'

When she gave him a guilty look, he pressed his advantage. 'Even if you did contrive to get a message to the Professor, we have already agreed he would never think of his own safety before your own or the other members of his household.'

Her mouth twisted in a wry grimace. 'You do not fight fair, Robert.'

'This is too important for that. And I fight to win. Always. But in this case I'm telling you nothing but the truth. You're not any different.

You refused to leave when Balnamoon asked you to go with him. *I cannot leave Betty and the girls.* That's what you said, Kirsty. The apple does not fall far from the tree, it seems.' Then, when she sent him another searching look: 'There's no need to look at me like that. There's always the exception which proves the rule.'

For a moment there was silence in the room, the only sound the crackling of the fire in the grate. He thought back to last night at the Liddell house and the ticking of the grandfather clock in the corner of the room, wondered yet again if he had a hope in hell of getting away with any of this, of getting her and himself safely out of it and through to the other side. Whatever lay over there on that other shore.

'I do not like these times in which we are living,' she said at last. 'I cannot believe what Jamie did to Jeannie Carmichael. Or what he was going to do to you.'

'It's a war, Kirsty.'

She shuddered. 'Don't say that!'

'It's the truth. I had not thought you to be a woman who shied away from facing the facts. War is like a storm. Once the fury is unleashed, it acquires its own speed and force. All any of us can do then is move our feet faster and faster, strive to keep ahead of its destructive power.'

'Dance to the storm?'

'Aye,' he agreed, his mouth tightening. 'Dance to the storm. Not an easy undertaking when none of us knows what the steps should be or into what danger and grief they might lead us. I ask again. Do you agree to my conditions?'

She drew in a breath. 'Yes. I agree to your conditions.'

'Your friends,' he said.

'What about them?'

'I do not think Miss Wood is involved in any of this.'

'No.' She gave her head a decisive shake. 'Meg is no Jacobite.'

'Miss Gordon is, though. She was in on your plot to get the Jacobite agent out of Edinburgh.'

This time she was more ready for him, the mutinous chin rising. 'Are you asking me or telling me, Captain Catto?'

'I'm telling you,' he replied, pulling a face at her return to that formal form of address. 'I know all about her father the banker and his Jacobite sympathies.'

'Is it the Lord President who has made you so well informed? I'm beginning to wonder if he has always been a friend of your family. Perhaps he is even a relative.' She tilted her head to one side, considering. 'There is something too in your manner of speaking. Mostly you sound like an Englishman. Sometimes there is a hint of somewhere else. Where did you grow up?'

'In the army. And I'm asking the questions, Kirsty. Did you know what the map was for?'

'Not until you pointed it out last Saturday. Not until I found out someone had added details of the military garrisons.'

'That will be a point in your favour. That you were ignorant of its true purpose.' He had found the map of Scotland when he had mounted the raid on Surgeons' Hall a week since. Rolled up and protected in a leather cylinder, he had it safe now at the guard-house. Meticulously drawn, it had shown the main towns, ports, roads and ferries, just the sort of information an invasion force would need. Putting two and two together later, he had realized that she had been the cartographer. She was a gifted artist and draughtswoman.

'Apart from your father and Balnamoon, do you know anyone else to be a member of the Association?'

'No.'

He thought he could probably believe her. For her own safety, Patrick Rankeillor and Jamie Buchan would have told her as little as possible.

'I have asked you this before but I feel I have to keep asking you. Tell me you realize how serious this is.'

'Oh, I realize that very well. You have made it abundantly clear that I am your prisoner.'

No, you've got that wrong. It's the other way around. For a few wild, despairing seconds, all he wanted was to throw himself at her feet and blurt out those words.

'What?' she asked, a tiny frown creasing her creamy forehead.

'Nothing,' he said, and schooled his features back into the mask she had accused him of wearing. Those words had to be left unspoken. He didn't have the right to say them to her. He never would have, whatever the consequences of this current adventure. He made a jerky gesture with his hand and bumped it against the arm of the chair.

'Ow,' he muttered.

Her eyes dropped again to the bruise. 'Will you let me apply some salve to that?'

'Maybe. I think Geordie will be going between this house and the guard-house for the next few days. Despite the snow.'

'I had already thought that. He is very welcome to come here for his Yule Day dinner. May I know what is to happen to Cosmo Liddell and Arthur Menzies? So that, if required, I may reassure Alice she is in no further danger from them.'

'She isn't,' Catto said drily. 'Now they have had their way with her she is of no further interest to them.'

Her eyes flashed. 'So, having forced themselves upon her and stolen her innocence, they now discard her as though she is a worthless piece of rubbish.'

'I'm afraid that is how they think. I have them under house arrest too. As soon as the weather permits, they will be at the Liddell country house near Prestonpans. Where they will stay until I tell them otherwise.'

'Eastfield,' she said.

'Aye. You know it?'

'I have been there once or twice. Always reluctantly. Will it not be harder to guard and keep them there?'

'I think the confessions I made them write and sign last night will make them think twice about doing anything else.'

'Confessions?'

'In respect of Geordie's sister. I have also given copies of their statements to Mr Charles Paterson, their lawyer. He says he will get some compensation out of Cosmo Liddell.'

She sat up straighter in the chair. 'I do not think Alice will want money from Cosmo Liddell! I would not want a brass farthing from that brute if it was me he had wronged!'

Catto raised one hand, palm upwards, indicating their surroundings. 'You have all this. Alice has nothing.'

'She will have my support for as long as she needs it. Or as long as I am in a position to give it.' She looked at him. 'Yes. To save you asking again, I do realize what I might stand to lose here. Everything.'

'Yet still you did it.'

'Aye. Yet still I did it.'

'Clearly this line of questioning will get me nowhere.' He slid forward, placing his hands on his knees in readiness to stand up. 'I cannot think me eating with you will be very comfortable for the rest of your household, Geordie's sister and that little maid of yours. They are both now scared of all men, are they not?'

For Alice Smart and young Tibby shared an unfortunate bond. Tibby had been raped by the son of the house in which she had first worked. His parents had thrown her out into the street when they had found out, blaming her rather than him. Finding her sitting sobbing on the stone steps of St Giles, the High Kirk, Betty Gilchrist had brought Tibby back to Infirmary Street and the Rankeillor household had taken her in.

'I shall bring you a tray of food in here. You have to eat. Och, that is rather a weary smile, sir.'

'I was thinking that you sound like your housekeeper.'

'It is indeed a female preoccupation. Making sure everyone is fed.' She looked past him, gazing out in the direction of Infirmary Street and the world beyond the house. 'Warm too. Women always wish everyone should be warm. And safe,' she added.

'You are thinking of Balnamoon and the Jacobite agent.'

Her gaze came back to Catto's face. 'I am wondering if they found shelter last night, yes. Have you not been wondering the same?'

'Only insofar as I hope they found such shelter in a house whose occupants will tell me about any travellers abroad on such a snowy night. Once I am able to get on their trail,' he added, thinking of the coffee house in Leith. Once again he felt the frustration of being defeated by the weather.

'You truly wish to capture your father?'

'He is not that. Almost never was.'

'*Almost* never was?'

'Save your breath, Kirsty. This line of questioning will get *you* nowhere.'

'It must have been a terrible shock coming face-to-face with him like that. After how many years?'

He rose to his feet without answering her. 'You may write your letter to your friends now.'

He followed her across to the table, stood and watched as she did that, sanded the paper and pushed it onto the scant amount of free space to be found on her father's untidy desk. 'You said you wished to read it.'

Standing at her shoulder, he scanned the letter, and nodded. 'You may fold and address it now.'

When she did that and proffered it to him, he tucked it into the inside pocket of his waistcoat. 'I regret having to read your letters.'

She shrugged. ' 'Tis your duty to do so, is it not?' She glanced at the long-case clock in the corner of the room. 'Nearly noon. Betty will be getting ready to serve the meal.'

'I shall not stay. There's so much snow lying. Hardly anyone will be out and about.'

'Then where will you eat?' she demanded. 'Few of the taverns will be open in this weather and Geordie is here.'

He had that invitation from Livingstone to eat at *The White Horse*, whatever time he called past. The Sergeant and his wife more than likely had hungry and temporarily stranded travellers staying over with them. Even if they didn't, Catto had no doubt they would set another place at their own table for him.

Spending more time with Kirsty Rankeillor wasn't going to help either her or him. Yet he allowed himself to be persuaded to stay here at Infirmary Street.

27

He cleared the steps to the shop before he ate. Job done, the bruise on the back of his hand aching only a little more than it had before, he walked through to the library. Finding her making some more space on the corner of the table and setting two places, he raised a questioning eyebrow.

'You are a guest in this house. Even if you do have me under arrest. We do not leave guests to eat alone. Please sit here.'

'So we shall break bread together,' he said as he obeyed that instruction. She joined him, the two of them sitting at right angles to each other.

'Aye,' she said, darting him a quick little look which left him in no doubt she understood the significance of that as well as he did. Once you have shared a meal with someone the two of you cannot then be enemies. Aye well, that was how it was supposed to work. The turbulent history of Scotland showed it didn't always happen that way. Hadn't King Kenneth MacAlpine, first king of the Scots, invited his Pictish rivals to the throne of Scotland to dine with him and promptly cut their heads off?

The bread was already broken, a few slices arranged on a white plate. Pats of butter sat in a smaller porcelain dish with sloping and fluted edges, a small round-bladed spreading knife laid neatly next to it. She lifted the lid off a soup tureen and reached for the ladle lying beside it.

'Smells good,' he said, breathing in the aroma.

'Cock-a-leekie.' She spooned them both out a plateful.

'Your keys,' he said, laying them next to her place.

'You must be the only gaoler who hands your prisoner the keys.'

'Very droll. How did you persuade your housekeeper that you and I should eat here alone together?'

'Betty is not quite herself today. Not that any of us are. Including you.'

'Me? I'm fine.' He gestured with the spoon he had lifted to tackle the soup. 'What would your father say if he knew you had moved his papers?'

'He'll never know. I'll put them back to exactly how they were.'

'An art at which you've become adept over the years, I take it,' he said before applying himself to his soup. 'Tastes as good as it smells,' he said after two or three mouthfuls. 'Did you make it?'

'Betty and me between us.'

'The gingerbread as well?' He nodded towards the two shallow dishes each holding a thick slice of that. Beside them, a sturdy blue-ringed pottery jug held yellow cream so thick it looked as if you might be able to dance on top of it.

'Mary and Tibby. They're learning how to cook and bake.'

'Looks and smells as if they're learning well.'

'You like your food?'

'One of the pleasures of life.'

'Yet sometimes you forget to eat. Or so Geordie says.'

Catto shrugged. 'When there's work to be done it takes priority. Would you sit down to eat if you had a patient waiting to consult you or for you to prepare physic for them or their sick wife or child?'

She answered him with a quick smile. 'More soup?' she asked when he had emptied the plate in front of him.

'If you please.'

She did not give herself a second plate. Aware after a few spoonfuls that she was watching him, he glanced up. 'What?'

'Nothing. There's pleasure in seeing someone enjoy food, that's all.'

'Even me?'

'Even you. Even under these very peculiar circumstances. And I now know that you like cock-a-leekie soup, gingerbread and tablet.'

'I like all food. Well, almost all. Not too keen on cheese. What?' he asked again, wondering why that innocuous statement had evoked such an uncomfortable look.

'He said that too. Your father. *A man can get tired of cheese.* That's what he said.'

Catto laid his spoon in his now empty plate. The tinkle of steel against china sounded too loud in the silence that had fallen between them.

'A convenient food to carry with you, I suppose. Although potentially rather monotonous.' She tapped one index finger against her lips. Then, when he didn't say anything: 'You're going to have to face up to it sometime.'

He looked at her. 'I faced up to it a long time ago.'

'But did not come to terms with it, I think. Last night must have brought it all back. This must be very painful for you.'

'Leave it,' he said. 'Please just leave this subject where it fell.'

After another little pause, she served them both gingerbread and cream. When they had finished and he had once again expressed his appreciation, she stood up. 'I shall fetch some salve for your hand.'

He too rose to his feet. 'I shall come with you.'

She threw him a challenging look from under her dark eyebrows. 'I'm not going to try to escape.'

'I didn't think you were,' he said as he followed her through to the shop. 'I just thought it would take a little longer for your housekeeper to find us if she comes looking. She probably wouldn't approve of you ministering to my injuries.'

'A patient is a patient and everything must be done to relieve whatever ails them. That is the rule in this house. Which Betty understands perfectly, as we all do.' She pointed to a high stool set in front of the counter. 'Sit there.'

'Now who's doing the ordering about?' he asked, although he obeyed her as she went behind the counter and lifted down a blue and white pottery jar from the multiplicity of those neatly arranged on the shelves behind it. He had noticed the shelves last week too, registering they were painted the light colour he'd heard described as apple green.

She turned, took the cork stopper from the top of the jar and set both items down on the counter between them. 'Put your hand out, please. I shall be as gentle as I can. You should start to feel the soothing effects of the salve very soon.'

He wasn't feeling at all soothed. Far from it. The stirrings in his breeches had already started. Bloody hell, he didn't want a repeat of what had happened last week, when his damn fool body had reacted all too enthusiastically to her touch. He had been in the Infirmary after Balnamoon had rendered him insensible by that knock on the head.

Coming round some time later, Catto had found himself lying on a couch in the hospital's dispensary, as he had sarcastically observed, at Christian Rankeillor's mercy. When she had straightened the blanket under which he was lying her fingertips had accidentally brushed his thighs, with the inevitable and instantaneous result. She had noticed too, damn her eyes.

She had lovely eyes. Green as a summer meadow. He raised his own to look but hers were downcast as she concentrated on applying the salve to his hand. Her eyelashes were as dark as her hair, that beautiful hair the colour of mahogany... Bloody hell, he was waxing lyrical here. He was a practical man, not a poet. Yet maybe there was something of the latter in him too— An unwelcome thought, given the piece of paper he had burned over at the Infirmary earlier this morning. 'That'll do,' he said, pulling his hand away.

The apple doesn't fall far from the tree. He'd said that about her. He refused to believe it about himself. He had nothing in common with John Roy Stuart other than the accident of his birth. An occasional tendency to flowery language, extravagant description and a mutual dislike of cheese meant nothing. That particular antipathy came from travelling in hostile country and not wanting to alert your enemy to where you were by the smell of food cooking. Therefore you ate bread and cheese and got heartily sick of them, especially as the latter was often on the point of going mouldy and the former was frequently stale.

He muttered a belated *thank you* for the application of the salve, followed by a question. 'Should my stitches come out?'

Sod it. That was a bloody brilliant thing to ask. She was bound to touch them now. Even with the counter in the way, that would bring them closer together, her fingers on his brow, her face close to his. He wanted to jerk back as though he'd been stung when she did exactly that. Oh, and dear God, he wanted to lean forward and kiss her.

The world shrank. There was nothing in it but her and him. The sweet fragrance of gingerbread on her breath. The clean smell of her skin. The warmth of her body. The awareness of her luscious breasts, so close to his chest. The other hidden places and curves of her womanly body under the plain gown and businesslike apron.

This was torture. Exquisite torture. Hurry up, he thought. Make a decision. Before I leap over this counter and put my arms about your waist and my mouth over yours.

'Not yet awhile, I don't think,' she said at last. 'We should leave them in for a few more days. To be sure we're on the safe side.'

'Why do medical people always say *we*?' he grumbled, feeling relieved but bereft when she pulled back and went to wash her hands and put the salve away. 'It's me who's got the stitches.'

❖

'You and Arthur arrested? Me also confined to the house until the two of you are escorted back to Eastfield, with me obliged to go and stay with that old biddy Lady Bruce in Leith? Who the devil does this Robert Catto think that he is?'

'We have no choice, Charlotte. He has us over a barrel.'

'Because you were a fool,' Charlotte retorted.

'I will not hear any criticism from you of my behaviour.' Tight-lipped, Cosmo glared at his sister. With Arthur Menzies of Edmonstone, they were sitting around the grandiose fireplace in the front room. The blaze was a lot warmer than it had been the previous night. The atmosphere remained chilly. 'When it comes to morals, you don't have a leg to stand on.'

Over the last few minutes, once she had read her letter from Professor Monro, she had got the story of what they had done to Alice Smart out of him. Cosmo's leering gaze swept over his sister and his friend. Arthur Menzies and Charlotte Liddell were occasional bed partners. They did not like each other very much but sometimes lust overtook them. Cosmo had heard them at it, grunting and groaning like farmyard animals. Sometimes he pleasured himself as he listened. Nor was Arthur her only lover, as her brother knew.

'In fact,' he went on, labouring the metaphor, 'seems to me your legs often won't hold you up very well. Especially if there's a bed in the room and someone in breeches standing in front of you.'

She snapped back at him. 'I do not judge your behaviour, Cosmo. The girl is worthless. A collier's daughter. They are lower than beasts. But you might have had the sense to give her some money in return for having used her. That would have kept her mouth shut. The Smart girl, you say. That little slut with the yellow hair? Sister of the wee brat who ran away?' Realization dawned in Charlotte Liddell's blue eyes. 'So that's why you got her a job as a skivvy in the house. Felt an itch when you saw her and planned it all out, did you?'

'Yes, Charlotte,' Cosmo said smugly. 'I did. The little bitch didn't suspect a thing.' His sneer grew gloating. 'Thought I was being kind to her, getting her a job in the house.' His eyes gleamed. 'Until it was too late for her to do anything about it.'

His sister looked at him with contempt. 'But you failed to plan for the Town Guard Captain having something to hold over you. Something to hold over the Liddells. That is intolerable. What?' she demanded, as Arthur Menzies and Cosmo Liddell exchanged glances. 'Is something else going on here?'

'Nothing,' Edmonstone said hurriedly. 'Nothing else. The girl is hardly going to take us to court.'

'She can tell her story all round Edinburgh.' Charlotte's eyes narrowed. 'If we cannot find a way of silencing her. Where is she now?'

'Not where she was taken by the sounds of it. 'Twould appear someone has taken her in and given her refuge.'

'Refuge? She has no right to claim refuge. She is our property, along with her brat of a brother. Wherever he might be.'

'I do not see how we can know where either of them are. Or who might be shielding them. Except that in the case of the girl, her protector must know Robert Catto.'

Something changed in Charlotte Liddell's face.

'Charlotte,' Arthur Menzies warned. 'You must leave this alone. You must go to Lady Magdalen's house and not speak of any of this. None of us must do anything rash when it comes to Robert Catto.'

'Why?' she demanded.

Edmonstone tilted his head back. 'There may be other things going on here. Do not pester me to elaborate further. I'm not sure I could even do so,' he added, almost to himself, a puzzled frown creasing his brow.

Charlotte opened her mouth to speak again, then closed it again. A moment before, it had suddenly occurred to her who might be shielding Alice Smart. A spurt of malicious pleasure coursed through her. If she was right, Kirsty Rankeillor was going to pay for it. However long it took to wreak that revenge.

28

Bloody hell. He must have dozed off in front of the library fire. The room had darkened. Kirsty Rankeillor was sitting at her father's desk, watching him. She had one tall pewter candlestick beside her, its light framing her in a glowing circle. Reminding him of Mr Charles Paterson the lawyer, she looked too alert: aware and watchful. Catto stood up in one fluid movement and walked across to her through the shadows of the room. The dishes from their meal had been cleared away but she had not yet reinstated her father's papers to spill once more across the area of the table she had cleared earlier.

'Hand it over. And don't ask me what I mean. You slid something under these papers just as I woke up.'

'It's nothing. I was drawing, that's all. A wee sketch.'

'Give it to me.' He held out his hand.

With obvious reluctance, she pulled a small sketch pad out from under the papers and flipped it open.

'Oh,' he said, balancing himself on the surface of the table with the heel of one hand as he stood looking down at the sketch. 'You were drawing me.'

'Aye. I was drawing you.'

Him asleep by the fire here in the library, long legs stretched out in front of him, his head to one side, supported by one wing of the armchair. He looked remarkably peaceful. Off guard. 'You could see me by the light of the fire?' He wheeled round, answered his own question,

195

and turned back to the sketch. 'You've caught my likeness very well,' he said, lifting his gaze from the drawing to her. 'Although I don't understand why you would choose me as a subject.'

'You were here.' She shrugged. 'You make a change from cadavers.'

'Damned with faint praise,' he murmured. 'If that was indeed a compliment. I suppose I should be glad you did not think to murder me in my sleep. Ow!'

She looked up at him. 'Which one of your various war wounds is now reminding you of its existence?'

'None of 'em. My scalp is infernally itchy. If you weren't here I'd be scratching myself like a dog with fleas.'

'What a lovely picture you put into my head. I shall give you a preparation with which to wash your hair. 'Twill help get rid of the powder and soothe your scalp forbye. You will know to put a splash of vinegar in the water with which you rinse your hair?'

'No. I didn't know that.'

''Twill also help restore the natural shine of your locks. Restore their chestnut gleam.'

'My *locks*?' he queried, mischief curving his mouth. '*Their chestnut gleam*?'

A faint blush stained her cheeks. He could see it clearly, even by the light of one candle.

'I should light the sconces. Or we could go through to the kitchen. How is the bruise on your hand?'

'Less painful. Measurably soothed. Don't light the sconces yet. Or have us move through to the kitchen.' Reinforcing those statements, he pulled out the chair next to her and sat down at the table. 'Will you give me some of the salve to take away with me too?'

'Of course.' Then, as though she were casting around for some innocent topic of conversation: 'You do look somewhat older than your years with your hair still white from the pomatum.'

'I don't care how I look.'

'Oh, but you do. You are a man who is fastidious in his dress.'

'I like to look clean and decent.'

'You look a lot more than that.'

'To you, you mean? I'm still thinking about your description of my *gleaming chestnut locks*. Sounds almost as though you've made a study of them.' As his lips twitched, his eyes dropped to her mouth … and amusement was swiftly overtaken by a quite different emotion.

'Don't,' she said. 'Robert, please don't…' she began, but he leaned forward and stayed her words with his fingertips.

He shouldn't be doing this and they both knew it. Yet he could not stop himself. There was something about being in this shadowy room with her, with the warmth of the fire on his back, watching her lovely face lit up by the glow of the candle.

'If only we could stop time. Or wind it back.'

'An impossibility,' she said sadly. 'Can't be done. We would know if we could, is that not so?' She raised her arm, curling her fingers around his wrist, under his shirt cuff.

'I like your touch,' he murmured. 'I think you like mine, too.' With exquisite gentleness, he drew the tips of his long fingers down the side of her face, saw her eyes flutter shut. 'Am I right?' When she opened her eyes again and nodded, his voice grew softer still, even as he knew he shouldn't be asking her this, either. 'Do you know what I want to do right now?'

'No,' she breathed. 'I cannot imagine what you want to do right now. Or maybe I can…' Her words trailed off till they were almost inaudible.

'Do you want to hear?'

She turned her head away. Seconds later, as though a decision had been made and a barrier crossed, she looked back at him. 'Yes,' she said, 'I want to hear.'

'Sure?'

She nodded. 'Certain sure.'

'Know this, then. What I want to do now is to make love to you. I want to carry you upstairs to your bedroom and undress you.' His voice was as soft as a caress. 'I want to lay you down on your fairy tale bed and make love to you, watch your lovely face and see your beautiful hair spread out across your snowy-white pillows. I want to see you throw your hands back on either side of your head and see you curl and uncurl your fingers as you surrender yourself to pleasure.' Then, as she reacted to that statement with a quick little breath which mingled panic with desire: 'Don't look so scared. We both know it can never happen. We both know we have to keep our hands off each other.'

Her fingers flexed on his wrist. 'We are doing a grand job of that.'

'So honest,' he said. 'Always so honest.'

'I do not know what other way to be. Och, Robert, what are we going to do?'

'I think,' he said, 'that I shall never grow tired of hearing you say my name. As to what we are going to do, we are going to put one foot in front of the other and keep going until we get through this.'

'If you like,' she said unsteadily, 'I can give you this drawing.' She lifted her chin, gesturing towards it. 'Only not until I have made a copy of it. I wish to keep one.'

'I cannot believe you want a remembrance of me,' he said sadly. 'I have brought you nothing but trouble.'

She bit her lip and took her hand from his wrist. 'I must put my father's papers back to where they were,' she muttered, fingers already moving to perform that task.

Catto laid his hands over both of hers. 'Be still,' he said. 'For a moment.'

She raised her eyes once more to his face.

'Aye. I know how hard that is. Your thoughts are racing, are they not? You're thinking about you and me. You're thinking about your father. About Balnamoon. About Jeannie Carmichael. About Alice Smart.'

'All that and more. It is very hard not to think about all of it.'

'I know. But thoughts that cannot be translated into action lead only to frustration. Dwell on them and you will soon find yourself sliding down into a vortex of despair.'

'I am not sure I can see how not to slide down into that vortex.'

'Distraction. Occupying yourself with something else.' He gave her the most rueful of smiles. 'Since we cannot allow ourselves one form of distraction, we need to find others.' Now it was he who indicated the drawing. 'Like that.'

'What do you do?' she asked. 'When you find yourself in despair?'

'I tend to drink more claret and brandy than is good for me and tumble—' He caught himself on.

'Tumble an obliging woman?' she suggested, and now it was she who had the imp of mischief dancing along her lips.

He released her hands and straightened up in his chair. 'Forgive me. I should not be having this conversation with a respectable young lady.'

'After what you have just told me you want to do? Knowing as we both do how you are a person of such high moral standards?'

Feeling the beginnings of a blush in his own cheeks, the second time she'd had that remarkable effect upon him, he reached inside the smallest of his waistcoat pockets. 'Here is something I think will distract you. Hold out your hand, if you please. Do you know what it is?' he asked, as she looked down at the little silver disc he had placed on her palm.

'Oh,' she said, taking it closer to the light of the candle. 'Is it a touch-piece? I have heard of them but never seen one.'

He nodded. 'Aye, it is a touch-piece. It belonged to my mother. Mary,' he added. 'Her name was Mary Catto.'

Kirsty Rankeillor looked up from the little silver disc. 'Mary Catto?' she asked, looking faintly puzzled. 'That was her maiden name?'

'That was her name,' Catto said, his voice grown husky. 'The only one she ever bore. She was never lawfully married to him, they were only hand-fasted. Under the light of the moon with only the two of them there. He would have persuaded her that was romantic. Always did have a silver tongue,' he added, ice in his voice. 'Inside a druidical circle at a place called Rothiemay. Not that you'll know where that is.'

'I do know where it is. I've been there.'

'You've been there?' He looked surprised.

'On a visit to Anna Gordon two years since. She has relatives who live at Rothiemay House. Dinna tell me I've actually told you something you don't know. And Jamie—'

'Comes from Balnamoon,' he supplied as she caught herself on. 'Which is also not too far from Rothiemay.'

She raised her eyebrows. 'I see you know Banffshire. Is that where you come from?'

'I know that James Buchan styles himself of Balnamoon.'

'But how do you know where Balnamoon is?' She thought back to what Anna Gordon had said about Jamie's sensitivity about his social status. His forebears' loyalty to the Stuart Cause had cost him and his family dear, the family home burned down in reprisal for Jamie's grandfather's and father's participation in the Rising of 1715. Anna Gordon had described what had once been Mains of Balnamoon as *now no more than a pile of stones in a field.*

Robert Catto ignored that question. 'Did you hear what I just said, Kirsty? My parents were never lawfully married. Which makes me a bastard.'

She winced. ''Tis a harsh word. I have always thought it unfair that the child bears the stigma. When in no way is it the child's fault.'

He shrugged. 'It's the way of the world.'

'Which we are all obliged to accept? Even when the way of the world is patently unfair, as it so often is?'

'I do not think any discussion on how the world needs to change will lead us anywhere fruitful. Shall I tell you about this touch-piece? I accepted it on behalf of my mother. In Rome. From the hands of the man you call King James.'

Her eyes widened. 'You have met him?'

'More than once.'

'His sons too? I think you are much of an age with Prince— with the Young Gentleman.'

Catto nodded. 'Aye. We are much of an age.'

'You were friends when you were boys?'

He made a balancing gesture with one hand, reminding her, with a sudden pang, of Jamie. That was one of his characteristic mannerisms. 'Unless you are a prince yourself, it is hard to be friends with one. They are inclined to tell you to treat them as an equal, then pull rank when you do something which offends their sense of their lofty status in this world.'

'What is he like? As a person?'

'Like the rest of us. He has good qualities and not so good ones. But I was telling you about this touch-piece.'

'Your mother was ill with the scrofula?'

'Something of that nature. The man you call King James said a prayer, held this little disc between his palms and handed it to me to take back to my mother in Paris. It had a white satin ribbon threaded through it and she wore it round her neck until she died a year later. I had no faith in the superstition. I took it off after she died and threw it onto a midden out in the street.'

'You thought the cold, damp room and that noisy, smelly street in Paris had more of an impact upon her health?' For he had told her last night of his mother's death and where it had occurred.

'Aye. That's what I thought.' His fingers tightened on the touch-piece. 'Yet still we hoped.'

'You and your now long-lost sister?'

He nodded, tight-lipped.

'Of course you hoped,' she said gently. 'And after your mother died, you discarded the touch-piece but then retrieved it from the midden. Because she had worn it. Because, perhaps, she'd had faith in it.'

She saw him swallow hard. 'Or pretended to. To please him.'

'You can see no good in him.'

'No. I cannot. I had to fight another boy for the touch-piece. He'd spotted the gleam of silver in the muck. A few punches were exchanged.' He caught his chin between his thumb and forefinger, moved it from side to side and gave her a very boyish smile. 'They all hurt.'

'Although you won the fight.'

'Aye.' The smile became a grin. 'The ribbon slithered back into the midden but I kept hold of the touch-piece. Went back inside, rinsed it with clean water and have kept it ever since. Stupid, isn't it?'

'Not stupid at all,' she protested.

'The hope it embodied for that year before my mother died didn't work. Hope never works. Not on its own.'

'There you are wrong. Hope can move mountains. I have seen it do so.'

'You and I should hope, then?'

'Aye,' she said. 'You and I should hope.'

'Then give me an undertaking which will allow me to hope. One that will allow me to trust you, as I trusted you enough to fall asleep in your company. As I have trusted you enough to be honest with you as to my intentions.'

'I think I have already given you that undertaking.'

'I need you to mean it,' he said, once more taking her two hands between his. 'If not for your own sake, then for mine. No more risks, Kirsty. No more risks. I fear I must also remind you that danger might threaten you and your father from your friends as well as your enemies.'

'So I should keep your secret?'

'Aye. And your own.'

❖

'Twas half-an-hour later, the world outside growing ever darker as the winter's day drew to a close. Robert Catto was about to leave Infirmary Street, exiting via the back of the house. As they stood together in the kitchen doorway, Christian cast him a doubtful look.

'You'll have to climb over the wall of the physic garden there.' She pointed to the left. The wall was still distinguishable, if only as a chest-high shadowy bulk.

'I scaled a higher wall when I first visited this house.'

'So you did,' she said. That was how he and the Town Guard raiding party had first approached the Rankeillor house. Her home and the physic garden lay tucked in behind a long length of the city's Flodden wall as it ran up towards the Pleasance. The wall was named for the disastrous battle that had caused it to be built. When an English army had inflicted a crushing defeat on the Scots at Flodden in Northumberland, two hundred years and more before, there had been panic in Edinburgh at the prospect of an invasion by the Auld Enemy.

Jamie had commented on the manner of approach Robert Catto had chosen, clambering over the Flodden Wall at the head of his men. It had made Christian shiver at the time. As it did now, bringing with it the possibility of violence and the clash of arms, not safely wrapped up inside the history books but now, in the present, in their peaceful, modern Edinburgh. She repeated Jamie's comment now. 'When you were testing the strength of Edinburgh's defences?'

'You mean the walls that have been deliberately weakened by covert Jacobites within the city, acting the part of the Horse of Troy? Stones knocked out. No repairs sanctioned or carried out for a good few years?'

'Flodden was a long time ago. Maybe no one thinks city walls necessary in this day and age.'

'Aye,' Robert Catto said. 'Right. I'm sure you know the story that after Flodden the Scottish parliament passed a law banning women from weeping in the street. They were spreading a pall of melancholy over the whole town as they grieved so publicly for lost fathers, husbands, sons, brothers and lovers. The flowers o' the forest,' he went on, 'that's the name history has given those menfolk. Cut down in the prime of their manhood. Leaving their families bereft for ever more.'

'Two hundred years ago,' she managed.

'During which mankind has not given up going to war,' he said drily, although he did not labour the point. 'I must go. Lock this door behind me and keep the shop door locked too. The door from the shop through to the house also.'

Thank God for irritation and the tendency of the male of the species to tell you what was blindingly obvious. She rolled her eyes at him. 'It's a winter's afternoon with night-time approaching. I would normally lock all the doors. Especially when tomorrow is the Sabbath.'

'People don't need physic on a Sunday?'

'They tend to go to the Infirmary if they do. Do you think we are in any danger of someone trying one of the doors in the middle of the night? Are we not also being guarded by your men, night and day?'

'The front of the house, yes. I need to know you're as safe as possible.'

'Also locked fast inside the house.'

'That too.'

She looked out at the snowy garden. The coal shed, one or two other outhouses and the drying and small bleaching green a few steps away from the back door gave onto the bigger physic garden. Dormant now, its pathways, neat drills, vegetable patches, flower and herb beds lay under a thick white blanket of snow. The little summer house in the shape of a pagoda stood at its centre, a hazy shape in the freezing mist of the late afternoon.

'You do not want the light at the front door to stay lit tonight, as you did last night?'

'No. Because what we must do now is not draw undue attention to your home. Or the Rankeillor household.' Hands behind his back as he leaned against the door frame, he looked down at her. 'Which is one reason why I shall not call on you tomorrow. In case some people make the effort to go to church and might spot me in the vicinity of Infirmary Street. Whether I am leaping over a wall or not. I shall probably not call on you on Monday either.'

'Because you have many other things you must do or because the snow may have started to clear and people will be going about their weekly business again?'

'Both. You have plenty to keep yourself occupied with, inside the house?'

'Always,' she said. 'Even without Alice Smart to care for.'

'It is good of you to take her in. To keep her in your care.'

She shrugged. 'It is my duty to help anyone in need of help. You said you had to go.' She hesitated but only for a moment. 'You are welcome to eat your Yule Day meal here too, as well as Geordie.'

'Thank you.' He reached for her hand, raised it to his lips and kissed it, keeping his eyes locked with hers. It felt as intimate as a kiss on the lips. He did not seek that, said only, 'Goodnight, Kirsty. I shall wait until I hear you turn the key in the lock and shoot the bolts, top and bottom.'

He stood for a moment, thinking of the things he wanted to say to her and hadn't dared to. *Don't entice and enchant me, make me feel alive again in a way I haven't been for so long. Don't make me think there might be more to life than soldiering and duty, food, drink and a warm and willing woman whenever I want one. Bought and paid for. Women who call me* Captain *or* sir, *never* Robert. *Don't make me want to sweep you up and carry you off somewhere safe.*

'You have made it abundantly clear that I am your prisoner.' Aye, she definitely had that wrong: and he would do everything in his power and whatever his duty allowed to keep her safe. Everything. Even if it meant she was going to hate him for it.

❖

On the other side of the locked door, she listened too, heard only the muffled sounds of a handful of departing footsteps before those were lost in the snow. His footprints would leave their mark, become frozen in place overnight, but she supposed he would not worry about that. 'Twas only his men, guarding the house, who might notice them. She stood with the big key to the back door in one hand, the other resting on the softness of the cloaks and an old leather riding coat of her father's that hung there. They were all there to be hastily slung over shoulders before rescuing the washing from a sudden summer downpour or a chilly visit to the coal and woodshed in the winter.

She wondered how long he was going to keep his men on guard. If he was wary about drawing attention to the house he was going to have to stand them down at some point. Discreet though she imagined they must be, the longer they stayed, the more likely they were to be noticed by someone taking an interest in this house and the Rankeillor family.

The men of the Town Guard did not serve in a full-time militia. They had their own jobs, businesses and trades to attend to and, at this time of year, their social duties to their families. Robert Catto's resources had to be stretched. He would want the men on his side too, well-affected towards him, not grumbling at having to keep watch outside in the winter's cold for hours on end.

Christian took a moment, composing herself before she went through to speak to Betty, thinking of the solemn promises Robert Catto had once again exacted from her, that she would run no more risks, do nothing to put herself in any more danger than that in which she already stood, stay in this house until he told her otherwise. She had given him both her promise and her word of honour. 'Twas not something she took lightly. She was also becoming increasingly aware of what else he had said, that danger might threaten her and her father from their friends as well as their enemies. If she left the house she was likely to meet the former, who would want explanations.

She tilted her head back against the cloaks and the old riding coat. Despite all that, if an opportunity to leave the house without being seen were to arise, she did not see how she could not take it. Her love for her father outweighed everything else. Yet if she were called upon by their friends to give those explanations, she would be putting Robert Catto in mortal danger. Christian shivered.

29

'Good God, man, how did you make it up from Leith through this snow and ice?'

'I am used to winter in the Highlands, sir. This is nothing in comparison. I'm here now and ready to take any letter or message you may have for the Lord President.'

Catto stared at the man, hardly able to believe his luck. Fergus Chisholm tugged off his knitted bonnet and stood in the guard room, passing his headgear from one hand to the other. That probably wasn't so much a nervous gesture as one of profound discomfort, most likely at having to string a few sentences together.

Catto was faintly surprised Duncan Forbes' manservant could speak at all. When he had dined with the Lord President shortly after his arrival in Edinburgh five weeks before Chisholm had been a somewhat unnerving presence, silently sliding plates in front of them and refilling claret glasses. Not that the man's devotion had been in any doubt. Catto's mother had told him a long time ago all the Lord President's servants felt the same about their master.

It was midday on Monday and although the sun was shining as brightly as it had done yesterday, a second overnight frost had only made the snow more treacherous and tricky to negotiate. Catto had discovered that the hard way when he had stepped outside the guard-house for a moment, glad no one was there to witness him falling arse over elbow, apart from a superior looking ginger tomcat sitting on a windowsill opposite. Catto could swear it had a smirk on its furry face.

Chisholm must have taken a tumble or two on the way here this morning. Crusty snow and crystals of ice adorned his dark clothes at the elbows and the knees. That clearly hadn't put him off from undertaking the journey up from Leith this morning. No doubt the honour of the Highlands had been at stake, proving its inhabitants to be a lot tougher than soft Lowlanders.

'I haven't written the letter yet,' Catto admitted. 'I did not expect you here today. Are you still hoping to embark for Inverness tomorrow, as was the original plan?'

'Aye,' Chisholm said in his deep, slow voice. 'The ships have not stopped sailing.'

'There is less snow and ice by the Firth?'

'Aye.'

'But did the snow fall heavily down there on Friday night too, as it did in Edinburgh?'

'Aye.'

''Tis beginning to thaw now? More quickly than up here?'

'Aye.'

This was like pulling teeth but it told Catto what he needed to know. John Roy Stuart and Jamie Buchan of Balnamoon had likely sailed north on Saturday morning. They were gone. He felt crushing disappointment but also an odd sense of relief. He still had to get down there but he could leave the trip for another day or two.

'The letter, sir?' Chisholm said, stirred into the further extravagant expenditure of three more words at once.

Yes, the letter. The Lord President would then be alerted to the situation. 'Let us get you some warm ale and something to eat while I write the letter. Geordie, see to Mr Chisholm.'

'Aye, Captain. Will you come on ben to the kitchen, Mr Chisholm?' The boy had appeared at the guard-house earlier this morning, insisting he resume his duties. 'We canna have ye going hungry, sir. Or the fires no' being tended to.'

'What about your sister?' Catto had asked.

'She says I need to come back to my work. Miss Kirsty and Mrs Betty are looking after her. Mary and Tibby, too. I'll maybe can go back down to Infirmary Street the morn's afternoon and see how she is. If you can spare me, sir?'

Striding on through ahead of Geordie and Fergus Chisholm, Catto heard the boy advise the man to take off his coat. 'Then you'll feel the benefit of it when ye ging back oot, sir. Right cold and skitey today, eh? I landed on my erse a few times this morning. Forbye I had some fine slides too.'

Catto smiled wryly, glad Geordie had found some amusement today. Closing the door of his bedchamber, he walked over to his desk, sat down and pulled a sheet of paper from the neat pile on a narrow shelf above the desk. He reached for quill and ink and considered what wording he should use.

One decision was already made. He and Duncan Forbes of Culloden had agreed they should not use codes or ciphers. Often they sufficed only to alert your enemies to the fact that you had something to hide. Catto didn't doubt Fergus Chisholm would guard this letter with his life but there could be no guarantee he or it might not be intercepted. He was going to have to balance discretion with ensuring the message was crystal clear.

Sir, he began, *You will recall our Conversation of a Month since. I must advise You that what You posited on that Occasion looks very much as though it is coming to pass. Much sooner than we might have expected. I have Proofs of this.*

The map of Scotland Christian Rankeillor had drawn, for one. Catto glanced at the green leather cylinder which still held it, lying on its long edge along the back of his desk. He had thought to pin the chart it held up on the wall above the desk, next to his map of Edinburgh, but had decided against it. His own side might need it in the best possible condition for reprinting several times over. He hoped to God that wouldn't be necessary but it was as well to be prepared. It showed the main cities and towns, ports and military garrisons.

He would not tell the Lord President about the map in this letter. Time enough when Duncan Forbes returned to Edinburgh in January, when he would also have to know Christian Rankeillor had been the cartographer. Unthinkable not to tell him. As he had thought before, lying to the Lord President would be like lying to God. For the umpteenth time, Catto wished she had not involved herself in any of this. He resumed his letter writing. Chisholm would want to get back down to Leith before the end of the short winter's day and another overnight drop in temperature.

The Agent of the Plan is a Person known to Both of us, most reluctantly on my Part. I believe him now to be heading for the North and would advise You to be on the Lookout for him.

He paused for a moment, wondering if he was giving too much away. *Most reluctantly on my Part.* Knowing his history as he did, the Lord President would know immediately who he meant. If this letter were to fall into the hands of Jamie Buchan of Balnamoon, or be shown to him or the Jacobite agent by a third party, they too would know Catto was giving the Lord President a very specific warning.

Yet he had to give it. Duncan Forbes of Culloden would immediately understand the gravity of the threat. Nor could Catto see a better way to word it. What he would not do was set down his list of names in writing. He would pass that on via a verbal message to Fergus Chisholm. Dipping his quill once more in the pewter inkwell, he completed the missive.

I remain, Sir, Yr. most humble & obedient Servant,

Robert Catto, Acting Capn., Edinburgh Town Guard.

He sanded the paper, waited a moment before folding it and sealing it with the official seal of the Town Guard. Lifting another letter from his desk, the one Professor Monro had written to Lady Magdalen Bruce of Kinross, he rose to his feet and took both missives through to the kitchen, where Geordie wasn't getting much conversation out of Fergus Chisholm, who was concentrating on the soup and bread the boy had set in front of him.

'Give us a moment, Geordie.'

Once the boy had taken himself off to the guard-room, Catto sat down opposite Fergus Chisholm, sliding the two letters across the table to him. 'Will you oblige me by delivering this letter to Lady Bruce of Kinross at her house inside the Citadel of Leith?'

Spoon in hand, Chisholm nodded. Catto tapped his own letter to Duncan Forbes.

'I have a further message not committed to this paper. Tell the Lord President I hope to have several names for him when he returns to Edinburgh in the New Year. That I already have a few.'

Chisholm nodded again and dug deep. 'Should he return earlier?'

Catto shook his head. 'No. Although 'twould be best if he returns no later than he originally planned, what is in this letter may give him reason to be busy where he is. He may well wish to ascertain the whereabouts of a certain person, alluded to in here. Who I believe, even as we speak, to be sailing north.'

'To Inverness?'

'That I do not know. Maybe Banff or one of the other ports. Although I am pretty sure this person will want to meet with certain other persons, all of them known to the Lord President. Lord Lovat would be worth the watching.'

Chisholm dug even deeper. 'The Old Fox is aye worth the watching.'

'Indeed he is. I am now going to give you a few names, to be passed on to the Lord President: Professor Patrick Rankeillor. James Buchan of Balnamoon. Arthur Menzies of Edmonstone. The Honourable Cosmo Liddell. Hector Grant of Soutra. James Nicholson, coffee house keeper at Leith.' He stopped there, telling himself he was giving Chisholm the names in smaller batches. Easier for the man to remember them that way. 'Repeat those names back to me, if you please.'

Chisholm did so and looked expectantly at him.

Murdo Robertson. Agnes Moncur. Charles Paterson. Anna Gordon. Christian Rankeillor. Those were the names Catto should give Chisholm now. Only he didn't. Later. The Lord President could get these names later. *Would* get those names later.

'I have one more commission for you, Mr Chisholm. I believe the packet for Banff sails on Wednesdays. I require you to bespeak a berth for a lady and her serving woman. I shall give you the money before you leave. Eat up, man,' Catto said, standing up. 'I'll send Geordie back through to serve you another bowl of broth.'

He stood at one of the guard-room casements, watching Chisholm leave the guard-house. You could see a fair way up and down the High Street from this vantage point. Even on this first day of the working week, normally full of hustle and bustle, most folk were not venturing forth unless they had to.

Catto had taken the precaution of not standing outside the guard-house with Chisholm as he left. He could not know if anyone was watching, curious as to who the man was and why he had called at the guard-house. He saw nothing obvious. There were no changes in the light cast from any of the windows or tenement closes opposite as someone moved to one side to get a better view as the sure-footed Highlander went off down the street.

In this weather there were no idlers who might be pushing themselves with staged casualness off the corners of buildings. 'Twas also much harder to follow someone when so few people were going about their daily business. He had asked Chisholm if he thought anyone had followed him up from Leith. The man had been sure no one had.

Catto didn't need the confirmation of the slippy going underfoot to take his word for it. As a Highlander, Chisholm would have an innate sixth sense about such things.

As satisfied as he could be, Catto turned his thoughts to the next problem: Kirsty Rankeillor's two friends. He had handed in her letter to them late on Saturday afternoon, along with a message that he would call on them in due course. His own sixth sense was telling him to leave it for one more day. That way he might not have so much persuading to do to get Anna Gordon and Meg Wood to step off the overcrowded stage.

30

It was 10 o'clock on Tuesday morning and Catto had just arrived at the Duff town house. The winter sun was blazing down on Edinburgh and the thaw was at last setting in, water dripping off the low roofs of outhouses, as the ice on the ground was beginning to recede. Walking down the centre of the causeway hadn't proved too hazardous. There was ice in this room, though.

Meg Wood sat in a chair set back against the wall, her hands clasped so tightly in her lap her knuckles had turned white. Anna Gordon stood in front of the fire, the fingers of one hand resting on the high wooden mantelpiece. She too looked pale and anxious. The tension between the two young women on Friday night at the Assembly Rooms had been palpable. It had clearly festered and grown since then. Wasn't that why he had left them for another day, to unsettle them and knock them off balance?

Meg Wood rose to her feet and crossed the room to stand in front of him. 'Captain Catto, I may be in no position to put this request to you – or indeed any request – but I should like to ask you a favour.'

'Meg,' Anna Gordon burst out, 'there's no need for this!'

'There is every need.' The Glasgow girl spoke without turning to look at her friend. 'Every need.'

'Miss Wood?' Catto asked, pretty sure he knew what was coming next. It seemed his strategy had worked. Pity his success was lowering his spirits so much.

'I wonder if you might recommend a respectable inn where I could stay until the mail coaches to Glasgow start running again. If I am free to go.'

'I know one very respectable inn. It is run by my Sergeant Livingstone and his wife at the foot of the Canongate. *The White Horse*. You are perfectly free to go. Although the weather remains not exactly conducive to travel.'

'Meg, you need not stay at an inn! Nor travel back to Glasgow through the snow and ice so close to Yule Day! You know you are always welcome here! However much you and I disagree about'

'Anna, for God's sake!' Meg Wood implored, finally swinging round to directly address the other girl.

'Politics?' Catto suggested into the jagged silence that had fallen. 'Is that what the two of you disagree about?'

When Meg Wood cast her friend a despairing look, a pang of pity pierced him. This was such a pleasant room, much more welcoming than the corresponding cold and austere one in the nearby Liddell house. Here the fire burned brightly, drawing glints from the rust-red tiles of the hearth in front of it and the gleaming, well-polished brass tea kettle on a matching stand on top of those.

The furnishings were of colourful red and blue tapestry and the cushioned chairs looked comfortable. These two girls and Kirsty Rankeillor must have spent many happy hours here, sipping their honey-sweetened tea and talking about anything and everything. They might have been friends since they were laughing, carefree girls but he did not see how their friendship could survive this crisis. Especially not when he was currently in the process of helping to destroy it.

'Miss Wood, may I suggest you collect your things and I shall then escort you to *The White Horse*?'

'I have already packed my portmanteau. I need only fetch it.'

'Give me ten minutes,' Catto said. 'I wish to have a few words with

Miss Gordon first.' He held the door open for Meg Wood, closed it behind her and walked over to the fireplace.

Anna Gordon wasted no time. 'Mary Catto,' she said. 'You are Mary Catto's son.'

❖

Christian Rankeillor swung the front door wide, a smile of welcome and relief spreading across her face. 'Och Meg, I'm right glad to see you!' She looked along the street, craning her neck to see beyond her friend and Catto, standing side by side on the steps at the front door. The path he had cleared up the centre of those was still clear. The sparkle of overnight frost had long since melted and dried out. Behind Meg Wood and Catto two caddies waited by a sedan chair. 'Coming through the snow wasn't too difficult for the chairmen?'

'It's hard-packed,' Catto said. 'Also starting to clear from the centre of the causeway.' He made a face. 'If still slippy in places. Not the best of surfaces but needs must.'

'Is that why Anna has not come?'

'Anna's not coming because I asked her not to.' Pale and drawn, the Glasgow girl had not returned her friend's smile.

'Meg?' Christian Rankeillor asked, a little frown between her brows.

'Let us go into the house,' Catto suggested, thinking this would be better done without an audience. 'It's cold out here.'

'Oh aye, of course it is. Come in, come in,' Kirsty Rankeillor urged, standing back so the two of them could step into the lobby. 'Come upstairs and take a cup of tea with me, Meg. That will warm you up.'

Catto intervened again. 'Not upstairs. We shall go to the library, if you please. I shall just set this portmanteau down in the lobby first.' He slid the leather bag under the tall table that stood against the back wall of the hall and straightened up to find Kirsty Rankeillor looking fixedly at it before raising her eyes to look at him.

'You're going somewhere?'

'No,' Meg Wood said. 'I am. Captain Catto tells me it is hoped the coach to Glasgow will start running again on Thursday or Friday. If there are no more snowfalls between now and then.'

Kirsty Rankeillor's frown had deepened. 'You're going home early, Meg? Not staying here to spend Yule with us, as planned?'

'Aye.' Meg briefly closed her eyes, then opened them again, like a woman in pain who does not know for how much longer she can bear the agony. 'I am going home early.'

'You have brought your portmanteau because you want to stay here with us instead of with Anna at the Duff house?'

'No. Captain Catto tells me there is a respectable inn at the foot of the Canongate. He is kindly escorting me there now.'

'Oh,' Christian Rankeillor said. 'Let me run upstairs and bring down the kettle and the cups. You'll need some nice hot tea, Meg, after being out in the cold. Especially if you're going back into it.'

'There is no need. Not on my account.' Meg Wood's voice was flat, her face sombre.

'But you must have a cup of tea,' Kirsty Rankeillor said, and now there was no mistaking the pleading note in her voice. 'You look gey cold, Meg. I could ask Betty to warm you some ale?'

'I don't want a cup of tea.' Once again, Meg Wood briefly closed her eyes. 'Or warmed ale.' 'Twas clearly an effort for her to utter each word.

'A glass of wine and a biscuit, then. A wee sit down by the library fire to go with them. I've been working in there this morning, sorting out some sketches for my father's next classes when they resume in January, it's fine and warm.' She moved forward, clearly intending to take her friend by the arm. Meg Wood stepped back. Her hostess bit her lip.

Catto gestured towards the double doors of the library. 'Let us go through.'

Hastening ahead, Kirsty Rankeillor made for the claret and brandy decanters and the wine glasses which stood next to them.

'Not for me,' Meg Wood said.

Her hostess whirled round. She was wearing her sensible dark blue gown again today, a neat cap on her head and a freshly laundered, starched and ironed white apron tied around her waist as usual. 'Nothing, Meg? Nothing at all?'

'No.' Meg Wood moved over towards the fire but did not sit down, simply stood there with her back to them.

'Captain Catto?' Kirsty Rankeillor asked.

He shook his head at her. 'Sit down,' he said, consciously softening his voice. 'Over there by the fire. I shall bring one of these chairs for myself.' As he swung the upright carved wooden chair into position between the two armchairs that flanked the library fire, Meg Wood still made no move to sit down.

Kirsty Rankeillor was looking more and more upset. Torn between demanding of her why she was so surprised by her friend's attitude and pity for both girls' distress, Catto came down on the side of the latter. 'Please sit down, Miss Wood. Then I may do likewise.'

She came a little alive at that. 'I beg your pardon, sir. I had not considered I was obliging you to keep standing.'

For a moment the three of them sat in silence, until she spoke again, with a restraint that told of the effort behind it. 'What of Andrew, Kirsty? Don't you care into God knows what danger he might be led? You know what's he's like, how passionate he is!'

'Of course I care! You cannot think I do not care about your brother!' She raised both arms and sliced them through the air in a gesture of frustration that was abruptly checked as she pointed one shaking finger at Catto. 'And you've just given him another name, Meg!'

Both girls turned to look at him then, their faces pale and stricken. For once in his life, Robert Catto was lost for words. He could usually come up with a sarcastic comment. Hellfire, he could always come up with a sarcastic comment.

I'll forget I heard that name.

He couldn't say that. He had to scoop up every morsel of intelligence that came his way. That was both a crucial part of his plan and his bounden duty, to gather together as many names as possible. Andrew Wood, then. Brother to Meg Wood. He had intercepted mail between her and Kirsty Rankeillor and he knew she lived in the High Street of Glasgow and that her brother was a shoemaker. Andrew Wood, who might willingly be led into danger of the Jacobite sort, would not be hard to find.

Meg Wood hunched her shoulders. Her next words were expelled on a breath of incomprehension. 'Did you not realize the risks you were running, Kirsty? You and Anna?'

Illogically, he intervened at that. He did not need any more evidence of Kirsty Rankeillor's guilt. 'Say no more,' he warned. 'Say no more, Miss Wood.'

Christian Rankeillor did not speak, only gazed beseechingly at her friend, who looked sadly back at her.

'No, I shall say no more. I want to leave now.'

'As you wish,' Catto said, rising to his feet. The sooner this painful conversation was over, the better. For both girls.

'Meg,' Kirsty Rankeillor said. 'There's no need for this!'

'There's every need,' Meg Wood said quietly. 'Good-bye, Kirsty.'

'Meg,' Christian Rankeillor said urgently. 'Don't go. Not like this.'

'I have to,' Meg Wood said, and walked in front of Catto out of the room.

Hurrying through into the shop, Christian stood looking out of the window set into the top half of the door, willing Meg to turn around and give her even the swiftest wave of farewell. That would be something to hang onto, the slender hope the two of them could put this right and become once again the close and loving friends they always had been.

She saw Robert Catto offer Meg a choice between taking his arm or getting back into the chair. Meg looked up, said a few words, gave him a brave little smile and put her arm through his. He dismissed the chairmen. The caddies went one way and he and Meg the other.

Christian watched the two of them walk along Infirmary Street until they went round the corner and disappeared from view. Only then did she turn away. Leaning back against the door of the shop, she wondered if she had ever felt as miserable as she did now. Jeannie Carmichael. Alice Smart. Now this. One other thought was swirling around her head.

If Meg and Patrick Rankeillor passed on the road between here and Glasgow, would she alert him to what had been going on here in Edinburgh? She was fond of Christian's father, as he was of her. Like Anna, they were on the easy and friendly terms of an uncle and niece who had long been comfortable in each other's company.

'Only they're not going to be comfortable with each other now.' Christian said the words out loud, raised one hand to her mouth and bit down on her knuckles. 'Especially if he's been talking to Andrew Wood about the planned rising.' For her father had told her he was going to Glasgow not only to give his yearly anatomy lectures but also to discreetly sound out what support there might be for that in Glasgow and the west.

A trill alerted her to the presence of Lucy the little black and white cat, walking daintily towards her. She stooped and picked her up. 'Oh Lucy,' she whispered as she held the warm little body close, 'surely Meg would still warn my father of the danger he's coming back to.'

All sorts of answers came flying back at her. There was no guarantee Meg would reach Glasgow before Patrick Rankeillor returned to Edinburgh, nor that they might meet each other on the road. He was on horseback. She was in the mail coach. A coachman and a lone or small group of riders might raise their arms in greeting but did not necessarily stop and talk to one another. If the road was wide enough at that point and unless there was a hazard or obstruction to which attention needed to be drawn, there was no need.

Christian's pulse quickened. The lying snow was a hazard, especially going down the long brae into Glasgow. The resumption of travel after the snow was a hazard. Advice might be sought from those travelling westward or eastward. Everyone would want to hear what lay up ahead, would want to contribute their tuppence worth. If Meg leant out of the mail coach to see what was happening and spotted Patrick Rankeillor, what would she do then?

Distressed as she was after what had happened over the past few days, Meg might well draw her head back in and pretend she hadn't seen him. 'Twas not that she would not want to warn Patrick but 'twould not be the thought that was uppermost in her mind. She would be too worried about her brother Andrew. Christian could not hope, far less count on her father being warned to be on his guard.

She drew in a deep breath. As his daughter, she had been raised in the Cause. He had brought her up to believe the restoration of King James and the House of Stuart had to happen if Scotland were to prosper and once more become a free and independent nation. She did not want to see bloodshed but if that goal could only be achieved by an armed uprising, then so be it. She would not fight with sword or gun but she would play her part.

When she had found out about Mr Fox and his mission, she had been reminded of the words of William Wallace. He had led the struggle to free Scotland from the rule of Edward I of England, Longshanks, the Hammer of the Scots. Scotland's guardian and hero had paid the ultimate penalty, betrayed by a fellow Scot, tried and hideously executed in London. It was said the prolonged cruelty of hanging, drawing and quartering had been specially designed for him. The humiliation had been brutally emphasized by the execution taking place at Smithfield in London, the market where the butchers plied their trade.

Long before then, Wallace's uncle had given him the words he had passed on to his men before the Battle of Falkirk. *I have brought you to the ring. Dance according to your skill.* William Wallace had died but he had inspired King Robert the Bruce, who defeated an English army and reinforced Scotland's independence at the Battle of Bannockburn. William Wallace and King Robert had inspired a nation. Jacobites raised their claret glasses in several favoured toasts.

May times mend – and down with the bloody Brunswickers!
Prosperity to Scotland – and no Union!
To the memory of Bruce and Wallace!

This was something quite different from dancing to the storm, not knowing where the steps of the dance were going to take you. However small the actions she might be able to take, there was a glimmer of hope here, intention and purpose. She had been brought to the ring. She would dance according to her skill. There was only one way she could be sure her father would be warned. If she sent that warning herself.

31

'You're sure this is the best thing for me to do, sir?'

'I'm sure,' Catto said, standing with Anna Gordon on the quay at Leith. He had escorted her and her serving woman down here this Wednesday morning, Anna Gordon and himself on horseback – she had chosen that option herself – and the older woman bracing her feet against the boards of the small cart which carried their baggage, anchoring herself. The frozen snow and ice had retreated somewhat, but only enough to allow a careful descent down a narrowed Leith Walk, the horses picking their way through the centre of the causeway. Catto had been glad of that. It allowed little opportunity for conversation between him and Anna Gordon. He could feel the prickle of her unease as she rode behind him.

As the baggage was being transferred to the boat, a stable boy came out of a nearby change-house. 'Need some lodgings for the cuddies, sir?'

'Aye. I'll come back for this one in about an hour,' he said, pointing at Tam. 'Can you arrange for someone to ride the other horse up to Edinburgh today or tomorrow? To Mr Livingstone at *The White Horse* at the foot of the Canongate?' He knew the Sergeant and the keeper of this change-house had a reciprocal arrangement.

'I'll dae it myself. Likely be tomorrow, mind.'

'That'll be fine,' Catto replied. 'For your trouble,' he added, digging out a florin and flipping it between his thumb and index finger. The boy caught it and grinned.

As he and Anna Gordon stood here on the cobbled quayside of the

Shore he sensed her unease again as she asked him if she was doing the right thing. He hardly knew her but he could tell she was a forceful woman and not an indecisive one. It was loyalty to her friend that made her ask the question for a second time. One thing was sure. Christian Rankeillor's friends were worthy matches for her, brave as well as loyal, unwilling to accept anything but the evidence of their own eyes and ears, unwilling to make a decision till they had weighed the evidence and were convinced by it.

'I feel I am deserting my friend.'

'No,' he said firmly. 'This is how you may help Miss Rankeillor the most. We must make everything as simple as we can. Have fewer players on the stage.'

'I wish you would have permitted me to bid her farewell.'

He shook his head. 'Too many people are watching other people. Making assumptions from what they observe.'

Her eyes searched his face. 'I am not sure why I should trust you.'

Catto wasn't sure why she should, either. He wanted her out of the way for his own reasons, so she would have no opportunity to interfere with his plans. Yet she did seem to trust him. Or had done back at her house, yesterday morning, when she had agreed to take his advice and head home by sea to Banff before Yule. He hadn't needed to produce the magic touch-piece, either.

He had agreed he was his mother's son and Anna Gordon had told him what she knew of the story. Thank God, without him having to fill in any gaps other than that Mary Catto had died in Paris over ten years before. Her running away with John Roy Stuart, returning after a few years with two children before leaving again six months later, had clearly been something of a nine days' wonder in Banff and Buchan. It had been a juicy scandal for the gossips to get their teeth into back then, now and again to be remembered, raked over and enjoyed anew. His name must have triggered the memory in Anna Gordon's head. As he had wanted. Or needed.

She had summoned the woman who now stood on the Shore, a few yards away from them. About the same age as Kirsty Rankeillor's housekeeper and clearly cut from the same cloth, she had looked him up and down and declared he had aye been 'a happy wee loon. Ye're handsome enough, but it disna look as if ye crack your face much in a smile these days.'

Wondering why servants in Scotland had to be so damned unlike servants anywhere else, he had looked from the older woman to the younger one.

Anna Gordon had shrugged. 'She wanted to see how you had turned out.'

'And you wanted to make sure I am who you think I am.'

'Just so,' she had agreed, her chin rising very much in the way Christian Rankeillor's did. 'We cannot be too careful, can we? What about me?' she asked now.

'What about you?'

'On Friday night you threatened to arrest me.'

'Aye,' he agreed. 'I did.'

'Are you not therefore making trouble for yourself by not arresting me?'

'Very possibly,' he said. 'But that's for me to worry about.' Then, ignoring her searching look: 'You must go aboard. I have paid the captain for your berths.'

'For which you must allow me to recompense you.'

'No need,' he said. 'No time.'

Most of the boats tied up at the Shore looked deserted. On the *Helen,* the sailors were beginning to move over the deck and the rigging. The day was chilly but calm where they stood here. The ebbing tide would bear them out of the harbour where they would find the wind they needed, away from the shelter of the land out in Leith Roads as they headed further into the Firth of Forth and the open sea beyond.

'You will do your best for Miss Rankeillor?'

'You have had my promise on that. You have it again.' On this subject at least he could give this girl an honest answer. He would do his best for Anna Gordon too, insofar as that would be in his power. For she might well be arrested later, although probably not by him.

She turned towards him. 'You care for Kirsty, I think. I believe she cares for you too.'

He looked over her shoulder to the *Helen,* spotted the signs of a captain and a crew making ready to cast off. 'You must go aboard now. They are anxious to catch the tide.'

She stood on the deck as the gangway was pulled up, the ropes untied and the ship glided away from the quay. Catto waited a few moments, watching as the boat and Anna Gordon grew smaller, until he could no longer see the worried expression on her face. Raising a hand in farewell, he turned on his heel.

Brave and loyal. He might not have arrested her. Yet it remained his duty to put her name on the list. Along with that of Meg Wood's brother Andrew, Mr Charles Paterson the lawyer, Murdo Robertson the medical student and the other names he had listed and given to Fergus Chisholm. He stopped in his tracks, earning himself a curse from a porter pushing a handcart of wooden crates who had to swerve to avoid crashing into him.

Catto threw his head back and looked up at the sky. It was grey and unremarkable. Empty, like himself at this moment. Empty and aching and numb. Not for the first time, he asked himself what in the name of God he was doing here in Edinburgh. The answer came immediately back at him. He was doing his duty. To the best of his ability. Without fear or favour. And his duty demanded he become the angel of death and destroyer of worlds.

He was a soldier. He had killed his fellow man, on too many occasions. He regretted every one. Given the choice, often he had let others turn and run. But there were times on the battlefield when there was no choice. It was either kill or be killed and both parties understood the rules and risks of the game. Here in Edinburgh it was quite different. The people he sought to flush out from these closes, tenement houses and lands thought they were master plotters but they were curiously innocent, like babes lost in the wood. They thought they knew the risks but they did not understand the brutal reality. They had no idea how swiftly the mailed fist might emerge from the velvet glove, no idea how hard that fist might strike, leaving them reeling, bloody and broken.

He thought of Elspeth Paterson, waiting for her baby to arrive. Of Charles Paterson, so protective of his wife but about to risk everything for the sake of restoring the Stuarts to the throne. The actions Catto was duty-bound to take would destroy their world, there could be little doubt about it. He thought of Murdo Robertson, miserably out of his depth. He thought of Meg Wood, desperately worried about her impulsive Jacobite brother. Likely torturing herself mentally because she had blurted out his name in front of Catto.

He thought of Christian Rankeillor, committed like her father to the Jacobite Cause but devastated by what Jamie Buchan of Balnamoon had done to Jeannie Carmichael for the sake of that cause. On top of all that, now the surgeon-apothecary's daughter was mourning the loss of her friendship with Meg Wood. Adding layers of trouble to the whole situation was the attraction sparking between Kirsty Rankeillor and himself. *Attraction.* It was a lot more than that. Yet there was no hope for them, none at all. Nor could there ever be, when they both stood where they did. Despite what she had said about hope moving mountains.

Empty and aching, he took a deep breath and starting walking again. Putting one foot in front of the other.

❖

His first call was to the house of Lizzie Gibson's mother. Lizzie had spoken of it, so he knew roughly where it was, one of a group of fishermen's cottages half a mile from the Shore. He asked an old woman who, despite the cold day, was sitting at her front door puffing on a clay pipe turned a quite disgusting shade he could only describe as shit-brown, and found he was nearly there. Stooping as he entered the low doorway the old woman opened for him, taking him straight into an earthen-floored room, he saw Lizzie dandling a child on her knee. She raised her head, her face lighting up. 'Captain Catto, sir, it's grand tae see you!'

'You too, Lizzie,' he responded. 'I had business in Leith today so I thought I would call past.' He stood there, feeling too big in the tiny room, like a giant among the fairy folk, only then noticing the other person sitting in a shadowy corner of it. One small window punched into the thick wall next to the door did not cast much light into the interior of the house.

'Ye'll tak a warmed ale, sir.' Lizzie's mother brushed past him, heading for the small brazier burning against another of the walls.

He swung round to her. 'Thank you. I'll have a word in private with Lizzie first.'

'Sit doon here, Captain,' Lizzie said, standing up to give him her chair. Her mother disappeared off with the wee boy. God knows where. Catto could only presume this humble dwelling did have another room. 'Friday night?' Lizzie asked, sitting down on a low, three-legged stool.

'No harm done.' Which wasn't remotely true, but Lizzie didn't need to know about any of that. She had warned him not to turn his back on Jamie Buchan of Balnamoon.

'I'm right glad to hear it. I was that worried aboot ye.'

'Nice to know someone was.' He managed a laugh, easy as he always was with girls and women like her. He had lain with her several times since he had come to Edinburgh, finding her in a directory of ladies of pleasure of Edinburgh. Planning on working his way through them – as it were – he had found Lizzie on his first foray and liked her. She normally worked in a house on the High Street but was spending Yule and the Daft Days with her mother and son.

'The person of whom you warned me,' he asked now. 'Have you heard aught of him while you've been here in Leith?'

She shook her head. 'No. Was that to be expected?' She looked alarmed, and Catto cursed himself for asking the question. That Jamie Forbes of Balnamoon had threatened her was not in any doubt. She wasn't a woman who frightened easily, so it must have been something really bad. Her child, he thought. The bastard must have threatened the boy.

She might not know who had fathered her son but she loved the boy beyond anything, had high hopes for him as he grew up. She wanted him to have an education, a steady job and a respectable life, saved as much of the money she earned as she could to achieve that dream. As she had told Catto, offering her a sympathetic ear as they lay together after they had coupled.

'I am pretty sure you are in no danger of seeing him now,' he hastened to reassure her. 'I think he was here on Friday night but left on Saturday morning. He will be in no hurry to return, either to Leith or Edinburgh. Could you bear to tell me what you know of him?'

Lizzie hesitated. 'I dinna like tae talk aboot my gentlemen. Have aye prided myself on that.'

'Is he one of your gentlemen?'

'Nae really,' Lizzie said, sliding her hands under her knees and the folds of her skirt. His eyes adjusted to the gloom, he could see now that it was dark blue, worn under a black laced bodice.

'He treated you for the pox?'

She nodded, the stool on which she sat creaking as she shifted on it. 'Aye. But a long time ago, Captain. Ye dinna need tae worry aboot that.'

'I'm not,' he said. 'Besides which...'

'Besides which...' Lizzie repeated, tilting her head to one side in mockery of himself and her, and leaving the sentence unfinished. When he lay with her he always wore a sheath. The madam of the house insisted upon it. They had shared other pleasures which didn't require protection. Lizzie Gibson was very good with her hands. And her mouth. His eyes dropped from her mouth to her breasts, landing on the generous curves pushing out the laced black bodice and the frill of the white shift she wore beneath it.

'Ooh,' she said, her voice warm and teasing, 'what are ye thinking aboot noo?'

Returning the mocking look, he wondered if she would be offering herself to him if her mother and son weren't here. He wondered if he would be accepting. The thought that he might turn down a willing woman was a startling one. Reminding himself that he was here on business, he posed another question. 'Did he threaten to tell some of your other gentlemen friends about having treated you for the pox?'

'Aye. Said he would keep his mouth shut if I agreed to meet three o' his particular friends. Gentlemen of quality, he said.' Her mouth twisted. 'Gentlemen of no quality at all, that's what I'd call them.'

'They were rough with you?'

'Aye. Very rough.' She hesitated before continuing. 'Disgusting, too.' Her voice was a whisper. 'They did disgusting things tae me.'

'Did you catch any names?'

She had, repeating them to him now: Cosmo, Arthur and Hector. She got the names out and turned her head to gaze into the fire, the cheeky glint gone from her eyes. Funny how the victim bore the shame. Wrong. So very, very wrong.

'Not your fault, Lizzie,' Catto said gently. 'Not your fault at all. I'm pretty sure these same gentlemen of no quality at all did much the same thing to a young girl. A maid still before they got hold of her.'

That brought Lizzie's head back round. 'Is she badly hurt?'

'Perhaps even more so in her head and her heart than her body.'

'Poor lass. Is anyone caring for her?'

'Aye. A very kind person. A Miss Christian Rankeillor.'

'I ken Miss Rankeillor,' Lizzie said, perking up. 'A skilled young lady too, good at the healing. One wha doesna judge other folk, forbye.

If this young maid is being cared for by her, there is hope that she will heal and recover. Will ye take that warmed ale now, Captain?'

On an impulse, he stood up, walked over to her, lifted one of her hands and kissed it. 'I will. You can introduce me to the rest of the family too.' As he straightened up, he saw that Lizzie was looking up at him, bemused but pleased.

'Ye're a fine gentleman, Captain.'

'I don't know about that,' he murmured, kissed her hand once more, turned and sat down again.

❖

After he left Lizzie, having admired her boy, ruffled his hair and placed a coin into his chubby little hand, Catto headed back to the Shore, walking into Nicholson's coffee house. A man looked at him across the solid wooden counter as he walked into the warmth and fragrance.

'A dish of coffee, sir?'

'Aye. Most welcome on this chilly day. May I also look at your register of ship movements for the last few days?'

The man gestured towards a narrow table that ran along under the leaded window of the coffee shop. 'You'll find the ledgers over there. Although I'll ask you to kindly leave your coffee here while you peruse them.'

'Of course,' Catto replied. 'A wise precaution against spillages. You'll be Mr Nicholson?'

'I am. You hae the advantage o' me, sir.'

'Robert Catto. Acting captain of the Town Guard of Edinburgh. At your service.'

'Or your own,' Nicholson said. 'I take it you have urgent business in Leith today. No' exactly a good day for riding doon here. Will you take your coffee first, Captain? Or have that look at the lists?'

'Coffee, if you please.'

Nicholson swung round, lifted down a plain china bowl, set it on the counter and lifted the coffee pot from the metal plate next to him. As he poured out the steaming brew, Catto dug into his pocket for his purse, found a penny and handed it over.

'Had to see a young lady off to Banff. Miss Anna Gordon,' he volunteered, as though he were simply making conversation while he waited for the coffee to cool a little. 'Cousin to the Duffs of Banff.'

Nicholson did not react to either name, only observed that the young lady would be at sea on Yule Day.

'Urgent family matter, I understand. Hence the haste.' The lie coming easily to his lips, Catto lifted the bowl of coffee in his two hands, blew on it, and looked at his host over it. 'Did our guests get away all right? Saturday morning, wasn't it?'

The hesitation was minimal, but it was there, closely followed by a denial. 'Which guests would those be, sir? I have no letting rooms.'

Catto took a sip of coffee and set the bowl down again. 'Indeed? Then I must be mistaken. Although I would wish Godspeed to any travellers, especially at this time of year.'

'Godspeed?' Nicholson queried.

'Aye,' Catto said firmly, mentally gritting his teeth. 'Godspeed.'

He walked away from the coffee house twenty minutes later, pretty certain he had one more name for his list: and totally cast down by the discovery.

32

She felt sick. Today was Yule E'en, the final day for physic to be delivered to the Infirmary by the Rankeillors. On the day after Yule Day another apothecary would take over. Christian laid a hand flat on her stomach, trying to calm her nerves. It was now or never. She had laid her plans yesterday, when Geordie had delivered a letter from his master. He had produced it the day before with an air of quiet but enormous pride at having been entrusted with it.

The folded paper was not sealed, nor had Robert Catto signed it. His message was brief. *Madam, You may make your final Delivery personally on Christmas Eve. I trust you will remember our Agreement.*

After going to so much trouble to keep her away from the hospital, he was now allowing her to go there? She could only think he had decided it would look odd were she not to deliver the final batch of physic as normal, now that the rapid thaw on Tuesday afternoon, followed by two days of bright winter sunshine, had made getting around so much easier. The snow and ice had retreated to the very edges of causeways and paths, whose surfaces had been given enough hours of sunshine to dry out and not freeze up again.

She had not spotted any Town Guards keeping watch on the house but she knew it was their job to watch without being watched themselves. She did not know if they would know how long she might be expected to spend at the Infirmary. 'Twould surely not excite their interest as long as she wasn't away from the house for much longer than an hour. One hour before they might notice she had not yet left the hospital and taken the short walk home.

I trust you will remember our agreement. She could hardly forget it. For her father's sake, she had to say as little as possible to anyone, especially Murdo Robertson and Agnes Moncur. For her own sake, too, and for Robert Catto's. Yet for the sake of the Cause she should tell Murdo and Agnes everything she knew. If she came face-to-face with either of them, it wasn't going to be easy not to blurt it all out.

I trust you will remember our Agreement. God in heaven, she was between the Devil and the deep blue sea.

Looking quickly up from her weighing and measuring at the sound of a youthful step, Christian saw Geordie coming through into the shop. On his now regular visits to Infirmary Street, he always came the back way, using the shelter of the physic garden, making sure no one spotted him. Robert Catto had decided it was safer for the boy not to be seen heading for the Rankeillor house.

'You're early today, Geordie.'

'Aye. The Captain said I could come down once my work for the morning was done. There's no' going tae be many tae feed at dinner time today. I've left a pot of beef ragoût on the edge of the range for any as might be there tae heat up if they want it.'

'Including your Captain?' she asked, an image popping into her head of Robert Catto standing stirring a pot of beef stew. She didn't doubt he'd be capable of it. He was capable of many things.

As he could die as easily as any other man. The nightmare that had evaporated on waking slid back into her head. In this version, Murdo Robertson succeeded in firing the fatal shot. With a cry of shock Robert Catto staggered backwards, arms flung wide. He seemed to hover there between life and death for an eternity of seconds. Then he fell, dark blood pouring out of his chest to seep into the freshly fallen bed of snow on which he lay. Dead. Silenced. Gone.

Murdo had not shot Robert Catto dead. Neither had she. Someone else might be prepared to. Especially if she told others what she knew. She could not see Agnes Moncur raising a pistol. Or maybe she could. The hospital lady governess was a warm and witty woman but she could be formidable too. There was a core of steel in Agnes Moncur. If Christian didn't tell her, Murdo or anyone else not to trust Robert Catto, she would be betraying the Cause. If she did tell them, she might be signing his death warrant.

'Are you all right, Miss Kirsty? Ye're looking a bit no' weel.'

She blinked. 'I'm fine, Geordie. Where's your Captain now?'

'He's gone off somewhere. Told me not to expect him back at the guard-house until later this afternoon. He's maybe gone back doon tae Leith again.'

'He's been there already this week?' she asked, hoping the question sounded casual. Difficult to gauge when her heart had begun to pound with excitement. If Robert Catto was out of Edinburgh for the next few hours, her opportunity to get to the post office was now. She could not know when another one might present itself.

She glanced at the clock that hung in a wooden case on the opposite wall of the shop. It wanted five minutes to eleven. Almost time for the ward round to start over at the Infirmary, for which Professor Monro would require the presence and full attention of his resident and the lady governess, tying them up for the next hour and more. There was no time to lose.

Geordie's bright young eyes drifted to the jar of tablet on the counter. Christian lifted it, pulled off the lid and proffered the jar to him. 'Take two. Or four. One for each of you. Make sure you eat them before Mrs Betty catches you eating sweeties at this time of the morning. She'll say they'll put you off your dinner.'

Geordie grinned. 'Nothing puts me off my dinner, Miss Kirsty.'

'Put the tablet in this wee twist of paper,' she said, wrapping the sweet squares up in it before handing the little package back to him. 'Will you ask Mrs Betty to come through and take over the counter here while I go to the Infirmary? Tell her I've gone to deliver the last batch of physic.'

'I'll can take it for you, Miss,' he said eagerly. 'Save ye going oot into the cold.'

'Och, no,' she said, wondering how much faster a human heart could beat. 'I'm fair in need of a wee bittie of fresh air after so many days in the house. On you go through,' she said again. She watched him obey that instruction, took a deep breath, lifted her basket, and set off before Betty arrived and also offered to deliver the physic. The unlocked shop would come to no harm in the few moments it would take the housekeeper to get here.

'Mrs Betty must have gone upstairs,' Geordie announced to the empty shop a moment or two later. 'I dinna see her in the kitchen. Or onybody else for that matter.' Breaking off from where he stood in the doorway, he took a few cautious steps forward, putting himself behind the counter. 'Naebody minding the store either,' he observed. As he stood there pondering what to do about that, the shop door opened.

It was the black boy about the same age as himself who stepped in. As he saw the light of recognition dawn in his eyes, now it was Geordie's heart that was beating too fast.

❖

Betty would definitely have offered to take the physic. Nor would the older woman have baulked at taking the letter concealed within the basket to the post office. Christian had worded that carefully, writing it in the library and hastily sliding it under her father's mass of papers each time the housekeeper had come bustling into the room on some task or other. Aye, if she knew about it, she would insist on taking the letter for her. Christian was not going to let her run that risk. *They would be rougher on her than they would be on you.*

Walking under the portico and into the Infirmary it was Jamie's words that were echoing around her head. *Look confident. Walk as though you have every right to be where you are and where you are going.* She felt as she had done when she had come into the Royal Infirmary last week carrying food and drink for John Roy Stuart, concealed beneath the physic in her basket. She'd had the fancy the wicker had turned to glass, displaying to everyone what she was doing. She had her own keys to the hospital's apothecary's shop. She unpacked her basket, putting the physic on the small table so Murdo would immediately see it had been delivered, re-locked the door and walked through the entrance hall to the back of the building.

As before, when she had made her covert visits here before the Daft Friday ball to bring food and medical attention, she fumbled with stone and flint to strike a light for the lantern she had picked up, both concealed in her now empty basket. She had been scared when she had made her first visit to this corridor, had to admit some of that fear came from the thought of the unhappy young man who had taken his own life here. Although she'd been more scared by the knowledge that she was helping a man with a price on his head. At least then John Roy had been on hand to reassure her.

He'd done so in full measure. He was a charming man, with a wry sense of humour. Like his son, when that son relaxed enough to allow his sense of humour and his other good qualities to show. She remembered now how John Roy had seemed distracted when she had mentioned Robert Catto's name to him. Now she knew why. Had he dreaded coming face-to-face with his long-lost son or had he longed to see him again? He cared for him, that much was obvious. As was the fact that his son could see no good in him.

That was so sad. She thought about how she felt about her father, who had brought her up and taught her not only about physic and how to care for patients but about life. She thought about how she was running this risk to warn Patrick Rankeillor he was travelling back home into danger and knew she would not have had it any other way.

She tried not to think that she should have written another letter and left it with the physic she had just delivered to the apothecary's shop. *He is not on our side.* Those few words would have sufficed. But she had not been able to bring herself to write them.

33

The first time he had seen her here in Edinburgh, not long after he himself had arrived, Geordie had immediately recognized Miss Charlotte Liddell. Her family owned the mine and the nearby miners' cottages where he had been born and raised. Now and again he had seen her from afar. It had been a moment of sheer terror when he had first spotted her in Edinburgh only a foot or two away from him.

He had feared that was it, the end of his all-too-short freedom. She would shout out and he would be seized and taken back to the pit and everything he'd run away from. When her blue eyes swept over him without betraying any interest or sign of recognition the relief had been huge, so much so he had stumbled right into her path.

'Dolt!' she said, giving him a vicious push. He ended up out in the causeway, colliding painfully with the large iron-rimmed wheel of a heavy cart. She laughed at that, as she did when the carter gave him a mouthful of foul-tongued abuse. As a bewildered Geordie turned, rubbing his sore hip, she was already sweeping off, her young black manservant following on behind.

This morning the black boy was on his own. Geordie looked through the window in the door, just to make sure. The other boy gave him a tentative smile. His teeth were very white against his dark skin. Geordie thought about it, decided the smile looked genuine enough, and offered one of his own. 'Geordie,' he said, pointing to himself before pointing at the boy. 'You?'

The boy laughed. 'I have a guid Scots tongue in ma heid the same as you do. My name's Joshua.'

Geordie laughed in return. 'Ye aye look ower well dressed tae speak like maist o' us dae here in Edinburgh.'

'Och, she likes me to talk like a wee English billy. But when she's no' around I can talk how I like.'

'Miss Liddell?' Geordie asked, disliking the very taste of that name in his mouth. Wondering if it was a mistake to admit he knew it.

'Miss Charlotte, aye. Who,' the black boy continued, affecting the voice he'd said she preferred, 'is currently confined to the house.'

'Not well?' Geordie asked. 'In need o' some physic?'

'Not allowed out. By orders of your captain.'

Geordie had begun to relax. Now he tensed again. 'My captain?'

'I've seen you coming out o' the guard-house. Saw you at Eastfield too. You ran away. Wish I could.'

'No' so easy for you tae hide,' Geordie said sympathetically.

'No,' the boy agreed. He seemed more resigned about that than anything else.

'Are they looking for me?'

'You and your sister.'

'What sister?'

Joshua threw him a pitying look. 'I saw the baith o' you at Eastfield. More than once. First time I saw you I thought you were black like me. You had just come up oot o' the pit. Then you shook your heid and I saw the colour o' your hair gleaming through the coal dust. Your sister had come tae meet ye at the end o' your day's work. Same colour o' hair. She's here, is she?' Joshua lifted his head in a gesture that encompassed the rest of the house.

Geordie looked back at him. Both his wits and his usual power to turn dangerous questions aside seemed to have deserted him.

The other boy's expression softened. 'Dinna worry. I'll no' tell a soul. Ye'll have tae pay me a forfeit, mind.' Like Geordie earlier, his eyes went to one of the glass jars on the counter. 'I could fair go a wee piece o' tablet.'

❖

Retrieving the spare set of clothes which belonged to the young man who had taken his own life, Christian quickly changed into them, twisting her hair up to fit into his tricorne hat. By some oversight none of this apparel had been returned to his grieving parents. Disguising herself had seemed like a brilliant idea when she had first thought of it: but, oh God, what if they were out and about today and recognized their son's clothes? She straightened up and lifted her chin. 'Twas too late to worry about that now.

She slid the letter she had written to her father into one of the pockets of the topcoat. There were no mirrors here, so she could only squint down and hope she passed muster as a young man. Nor was she going to dwell on how much she was trying to conceal her identity not only from Robert Catto's watchers but also from Agnes Moncur and Murdo should she have the bad luck to run into them.

She wrapped the plaid she had brought from the house around her neck, pulling it up over her mouth and chin. If anyone spoke to her, she would plead the toothache or a heavy cold and hope she could make her voice deep enough to pass as a young man. Then she drew in a breath to steady herself, walked along the corridor and went out into the entrance hall.

She was in luck. Several people were entering and leaving the building at that moment. Reminding herself once again to look as though she had every right to be there, she headed for the main door. Two caddies were waiting outside, leaning on their sedan chair. She didn't like the appraising glance one of them swept over her. Was he another of Robert Catto's watchers? Be that as it may, whatever he saw seemed to satisfy him. He looked away again. Christian passed him and his comrade and walked out into the quadrangle. If only she could have hired the caddies. Chairs attracted attention, though. People were always nosy about who was in them.

She stepped out into an Edinburgh which seemed too bright by half. Surely everyone she passed must see she was not the young man she was pretending to be. *Lengthen your stride. Try to make yourself look taller.* Despite the longer stride, the ten minutes it took her to reach the post office in the High Street seemed more like ten hours. Her heart was thumping as she pushed open the door and the brass bell on a spring at the top of it jangled. She only just managed not to jump when it did.

'A letter to post,' she said from behind the folds of tartan wrapped around her neck and pulled up to the point of her chin. 'To Glasgow. How much will that be, please?'

The clerk looked up at her. 'Got a cold? Dinna gie it tae me.' He took the letter, laid it on small brass scales on the counter in front of him, and told her the cost. 'I canna say when it'll go, mind. No' in this weather. There's a wheen o' letters backed up frae a' the snowy days.'

'This is an urgent letter. Can I pay more for it to go early?'

'Aye, if ye want tae throw your money aboot like a man wi' no arms.'

She muttered her agreement, opened her purse, found the sum he asked for, and handed the coins over. Terrified and elated in equal measure, she stood for a moment outside the post office. She had done it. Her father would still return to Edinburgh but at least now he would know something was amiss. Whatever Robert Catto said, forewarned was forearmed. As she went down and back up Horse Wynd, avoiding patches of ice, a little seed of confidence began to flower. So far so good, she thought, and promptly hit a patch of ice she hadn't spotted.

'Hang on to me,' said a voice she recognized as she flailed her arms like the sails of a windmill in a frantic attempt to keep her balance. 'There,' said Mr Charles Paterson the lawyer as he grabbed her by the arm and righted her. 'No harm done.'

'Thank you,' Christian managed. Oh God, her voice didn't sound nearly low enough. He had recognized her, anyway, his brown eyes narrowing as he looked into her face.

'Miss Kirsty? What the Devil are you doing, lass? And why are you dressed as you are? Daft Friday is past and gone.'

'I h-had to post a l-letter to my f-father,' she stuttered, answering one question and not the other. 'He's through in Glasgow.'

'But the post won't be going anywhere in this snow,' he protested, his brow wrinkling in a frown. 'For the sake of not braving it, would you not have been better to have waited a day or two?'

'Aye,' she agreed, 'very probably,' and thought she must sound like a halfwit. He was still looking very quizzically at her. She knew where his and his wife's political sympathies lay. She knew he was the man of business for the Liddells. For the sake of the first of those considerations, she should at least warn him about Robert Catto, even if she only hinted at the need for caution – but she couldn't seem to get the words out. Others took their place, tumbling over one another in her haste to get away. 'You must be keen to get back to your wife, Mr Paterson. Please give her my best regards.'

With that she was off, knowing she had left him standing there staring after her as she moved away as quickly as she could without once more slipping on the ice. Once she was safely out of sight, she paused for a moment, considering calling on Anna Gordon at the Duff town house. She longed to see her friend, missing her and Meg Wood so much: but it would take too long, someone might see and recognize her and the same argument held good about not endangering Robert Catto. She knew she would not be able to hide anything from Anna's shrewd gaze.

She reached the Royal Infirmary and made it through the quadrangle, into the building and on through to the back corridor without incident. As she pushed open the door to the cell where she had left her own clothes, relief flooded through her. She had done it. Thinking she could relax now, she felt herself quite literally go weak at the knees. Until she saw who was standing there waiting for her. Her whole body snapped to attention.

34

One shoulder propped against the wall, arms folded across his chest, the stance appeared casual. Until Christian registered that Robert Catto's face was clouded with cold fury.

'Care to explain this?' She looked at the open and unfolded piece of paper he held in his right hand. Her letter to her father. The one she had posted less than twenty minutes ago. Or thought she had. Crushing disappointment flooded through her.

'Well?' he demanded. His voice was harsh, his grey eyes hard as slate. 'I'm waiting for your explanation. With bated breath,' he added with biting sarcasm. 'And don't try and spin me some cock and bull story. I was at the Post Office when you called.'

He looked her up and down. Despite his obvious anger, he took his time about it. His gaze lingered on her hips, clearly outlined in the borrowed breeches, rose to her breasts and then up to her blushing face. He was wielding his sexually charged scrutiny of her as a weapon, one designed to embarrass and humiliate her. 'Your attempted disguise did not fool me for one moment.'

'What do you think I was doing?' she yelled back, her temper flaring. How dare he treat her like this? *How dare he?* Especially after she had tied herself in knots over him, all that soul-searching over whether or not to warn her friends about him. She had also failed in her mission. That was the worst thing. 'I was trying to warn my father, of course. I suppose it's too much to expect you to be able to understand why I would want to do that!'

He raised one derisive eyebrow. ''Twould seem it's too much on my part to expect you to apply some logic to the perilous situation to which your own folly has led you. Bloody hell, woman, have you no sense of self-preservation? Did you really not realize what a risk you were running in taking this letter to the post office and attempting to dispatch it?' Then, when Christian looked at him in despair: 'For God's sake! You know I intercepted your mail before.'

'I did not expect you to manage to be everywhere at once! Geordie thought you had gone to Leith!'

'Geordie thought wrong. Bad luck, Kirsty.'

Her chin went up. 'I would prefer you to address me as Miss Rankeillor, sir.'

He snorted. 'Get off your high horse. We are long past that stage. I repeat, did you really not see the risk to yourself? For God's sake!' he said again. 'You knew I was having your house and the hospital watched!'

'I did not expect your watchers either to manage to be everywhere at once! Of course I saw the risk to myself. But love has no logic!'

'Keep your voice down,' he growled.

'Nobody can hear us. Not in here.' Yet she had lowered her voice and for a moment a charged silence sparked between them, until he fired out a question.

'Did you say anything to the lawyer?'

'You followed me from the Post Office?' Her eyes widened.

'Of course I did. When I realized you were heading here, I overtook you by a different route. I repeat. Did you say anything to the lawyer?'

'Nothing about any of this. I made you a promise. Nor did I call on Anna Gordon, as you must know if you were following me.'

'You would not have found her in. I saw her off on the packet from Leith to Banff on Wednesday morning.'

'You did what?'

'You heard me. I thought it would be better for both you and her that she should be out of the way.'

'And she agreed with you?' Her voice rose in incredulity, hurt too that Anna should have agreed to leave without trying to see her. He must have heard that in her voice, casting her a glance which combined sympathy with impatience.

'I persuaded her. She did not want to go. Certainly not without seeing you.'

'But you did not allow either of us that consolation. Presumably because you have some sort of a plan for her as well as me.' She lifted her chin. 'What if someone saw you coming into the Infirmary?'

'I came in by one of the side doors.'

'How do you even know where there is one? Och, I forget,' she said angrily, slicing one hand down through the air in a gesture of frustration, 'you know everything!'

'Not everything,' he said quietly. 'There are lots of things I don't know. So many things. You speak of your love for your father. The love he has for you will see him return to Edinburgh anyway. That's one thing I know. As you do better than anyone, Kirsty.'

'I still had to try to warn him. I had to.'

'The risk you took was in vain. I shall burn this letter as soon as I find a fire to do it in. Aye, and you should be grateful to me for doing so.' He brandished the sheet of paper at her. 'I don't need any more evidence to prove your guilt, Kirsty. I can already show you to have been guilty of rendering aid and succour to an enemy of the King. Up to your bloody neck in a conspiracy to foment armed rebellion. God Almighty, it beggars belief that you have chosen to take this further risk!'

'*Up to my bloody neck*,' she repeated. 'A very apt metaphor, sir. We seem to keep coming back to it!'

'Aye!' he yelled at her. 'I have enough evidence to hang you, your father and Jamie Buchan of Balnamoon!'

'If you can catch him!' she flung back.

He closed the distance between them in two long strides, grabbed her by the arm, whirled them both round and backed her up against the wall of the cell. The movement dislodged the tricorne hat so that it tilted and slid down the wall to the floor. It bounced once before it came to rest. Her hair tumbled free to swing loose around her face. 'This is not a bloody game, miss!'

'I know that!'

He shook her. 'I see no evidence of it! I see a reckless little fool. I see a stupid little bitch. What if your letter had fallen into hands other than mine?'

'I'm not stupid. I was careful not to write anything incriminating!'

'You think so?' One hand still holding her arm in a punishing grip, he flipped her letter open and began reading it out. '*Dear Father, This is to let you know we are all fine here. We are missing you greatly but do not wish you to try to get back from Glasgow through the snow. We worry about your health and think it would be best for you to stay on in the West until it is quite safe for you to return here to Edinburgh. By the way, our visitor managed to get away before the snow fell. However, his departure did not go unnoticed.*'

He looked up from the letter and glowered at her. 'For God's sake, Kirsty! You are no conspirator!'

'I had to try!' she yelled, her face flaming at his mockery of her letter.

'No, you damn well did not,' he said hotly. 'We struck a bargain.'

'I did not know if I could trust you!'

'That,' he said grimly, 'is unworthy of you. And of me. I have promised I will do my best for your father and for you.'

'You yourself said matters might be taken out of your hands! How can we know?'

'Aye,' he said, his mouth settling into a grim line. 'Matters might well be taken out of my hands. Which is all the more reason for you to do as we agreed while I am still in control of the situation. To not hobble me by acting with such damned stupidity and unbelievable bloody arrogance. You think nothing can touch you. You think your safe little world will go on turning and being safe no matter what inane things you do and what fucking risks you take. It seems I seriously over-estimated your intelligence.'

'How dare you?' she breathed. 'How dare you speak to me like this? Swear at me and insult me?' Losing all control of her temper, she found common sense going with it. Twisting her arm painfully out of his grip, she raised both hands, trying to snatch the letter from him. He raised his hand and lifted it above his head and hers. 'Give it to me! You have no right to intercept my mail. No right at all!'

'God Almighty,' he muttered, tossing the letter onto the bunk on which her clothes lay. Seizing both her wrists, he pinned her once more against the wall of the cell.

'You're hurting me!'

'Good,' he said. Leaning forward, he covered her mouth with his own.

35

A kiss to punish her. A kiss to silence her. A kiss to keep her where she was. A spitting, snarling wildcat but a safe one, with only him aware of her folly. He expected resistance and he got it. As she struggled against him, he felt the inevitable result as his body reacted to hers. Expecting even fiercer resistance as his arousal pressed against her belly, he heard her instead utter a little moan of desire that fired his blood. She relaxed against him and the resistance was no longer there.

She was kissing him back now, as hungry for him as he was for her. He released her wrists and her hands came to his chest before sliding up around his neck, under his tied-back hair. The bunk. He would lay her down on the bunk and take her. Breaking the contact, he pulled back, and saw her face. Wide green eyes framed by gloriously tousled dark hair. Desire. But fear too.

That stopped him in his tracks. She deserved more than to lose her innocence like this, taken in anger on a hard wooden bed. He froze for a moment before carefully moving back. One step. Another one. Putting some space between them. He raised his hands, palms outwards, signalling that he would not touch her again. 'Listen to me, you damn stupid little fool.'

She looked dazed, her breathing fast and shallow. She could still snarl. 'No! I shall not listen to you. You cannot make me!'

'Oh yes, I can.' Then he told her what had happened at the farm in Saxony.

❖

She was very pale, and when she lifted one hand to her face he saw that it was shaking. He did not wonder at that, after what he had just told her. He had recounted the story of the farmhouse he and Fred Scott had come upon, the one which held the bodies of a whole family. A mother, her three daughters and son. The grandfather of the family. All murdered, the women and girls brutally violated first. He had spared Christian Rankeillor none of the details.

'You tell me this to frighten me?' she asked after a moment.

'I think any woman would be frightened by what I have just told you. By the horror of what can happen when war spills over into fighting and violence against the innocent.'

'You think I am a woman who frightens easily?'

'I think you are a woman who does not realize what may be the consequences of the path she is treading.'

She raised her face towards him, her eyes glittering with unshed tears. 'The story you have told me is a truly terrible one. It must have been an awful scene for you to come upon. It must have affected you deeply.'

He shrugged, as though to dismiss that, and knew he had fooled neither of them.

'I do not think such an awful thing could happen here. Not in Scotland. Not in our day.'

'What happened in Saxony happened in our day.'

'In the middle of a war.'

'What do you think it will be if your Prince comes to Scotland? Once the dogs of war are unleashed there's no stopping them, Kirsty. Do you remember what I said to you about it being like a storm, that it has to run its course? Or like a dance where no one knows where the steps will take them?'

'I remember. But what if the Prince were to come and there were to be a peaceful transferral of power? As there was back in '88?'

'Do you think those who hold power now would simply stand aside? People do not willingly cede control of the reins. Let me tell you something the Lord President said to me. Scotland has been a thorn in the flesh of England for centuries. Give the powers that be the excuse and they will pluck that thorn out and tramp it into the mud. That's what he said, Kirsty. If this happens — and I pray to God it does not — there will be a bloody reckoning.'

One tear slid down her smooth cheek. He reached out a hand and wiped it away. 'Come,' he said gently, 'I shall escort you home. Where you shall bide until I say otherwise. I shall wait out in the corridor until you have changed into your own clothes and we shall leave by the door I came in by. With a bit of luck no one will see us. I relieve you of the responsibility to feed Geordie and myself tomorrow.'

She lifted her chin. 'I invited you both to share our Yule Day meal. I shall not withdraw the invitation. Whether you choose to come or not is up to you.'

❖

'Nothing? You found out nothing?'

'Miss Rankeillor wasn't there! There was nobody to ask!'

Charlotte Liddell took Joshua by the shoulders and shook him hard. 'You'd better not be lying to me, you little black slug!'

'Why would I lie to you, Miss Charlotte?'

'How many times do I have to tell you not to answer me back?' Charlotte Liddell straightened up, drew her hand back and slapped the boy hard across the face. The blow sent Joshua staggering back, stopped only by one of the armchairs in front of the hearth. As he made painful contact with it, gasping for breath, she was on him again, seizing his arm to haul him upright and making him yell in pain.

'Don't!' he pleaded. 'That hurts!'

'I'll rip your arm off if I want to! And I can do anything I want to you! Remember that!'

Joshua looked up at her as she loomed over him. There were men who thought she was pretty, men with whom she played the coquette, giving them simpering smiles and flirtatious looks from under fluttering eyelashes. She was ugly now, her face contorted with rage. He knew fine well she could do what she wanted to him. She often had.

The only power he had was to withdraw, retreat inside his own head where he could be who he wanted to be and where he wanted to be. Anywhere in the whole wide world as long as he was a thousand miles away from Charlotte Liddell. Anywhere in the whole wide world as long as he was free. She looked triumphant now, pulling him with one hand and dragging him to the tapestry bell pull to the right of the fireplace. He knew what was coming now and it terrified him. His chin began to tremble.

'The coal hole,' she said to the liveried footman who knocked, entering the room only when their mistress bellowed out permission to do so. 'Throw the wee black brat into the coal hole and lock him in. Till the morning,' she said.

❖

'Kirsty has been?' Agnes Moncur asked, looking at the physic Murdo Robertson was sorting through.

'Been and gone,' Murdo said. 'It must have been during the ward round.'

'She hasn't left a note?'

'No,' he confirmed, looking troubled. 'So we are none the wiser. What are we to do, Mrs Moncur?'

Agnes Moncur drew in a breath. 'Watch our step, young Mr Robertson.' She narrowed her eyes and spoke thoughtfully, almost as though to herself. 'It seems we shall also have to watch Kirsty's steps.'

36

The Captain was swearing again. He did that a lot. Geordie didn't much like it but he had grown accustomed to it. Even for the Captain, though, the filthy words tumbling out of his mouth seemed a bit strong for what had provoked them. Looked like he was having difficulty with his neckcloth. Geordie's own was simply tied but the captain was going for that fancy soldiers' knot, the Steinkirk.

Well, it wasn't meant to look fancy. It was meant to look as though you'd just stepped off a battlefield, ridden hell for leather to bring news of a victory and hadn't had time to secure your cravat more neatly. Mr Catto had explained to him that was how the Steinkirk had originated.

'What?' he demanded now, throwing a black look at Geordie.

'I didna say a word, Captain,' Geordie protested.

'You don't have to,' Robert Catto growled. 'You have a way of looking at people that speaks volumes.'

Mischievous words skipped onto Geordie's lips. 'Are ye a wee bittie nervous, sir? Because we're going to Miss Rankeillor's hoose to keep Christmas?'

'Why the Devil would I be nervous about that?' the Captain demanded, patting the neckcloth into a position which seemed at last to satisfy him. 'I've been to her house several times now. Though why I'm getting myself titivated up to go there today I do not know.'

Wise beyond his years, Geordie did not respond to those muttered words, only watched as Catto studied his reflection in the shaving mirror propped up on the big dresser. He had brushed his hair with such viciousness this morning it had made Geordie wince. He supposed he was getting as much pomatum out as possible before washing it, demanding a splash of vinegar in the water with which he had rinsed it. Even though he had seemed to do all that with some reluctance.

The Captain was not a vain man but Geordie knew he liked to look smart, when he was in his dark red Town Guard uniform and when he was off duty too. Not that he ever really was off duty. Mr Catto was a busy man, with heavy responsibilities. There were times when he looked gey weary, even sad. Grateful to him beyond words for how he and Miss Kirsty had helped Alice and himself, Geordie was resolved on doing whatever he could to make his life easier.

With everyone wanting laundry done before Christmas and Hogmanay — neither you nor your clothes could go dirty into the New Year — Geordie had charmed the washerwoman into having their own ready for collection earlier in the week. Both the neckcloth and the shirt were snowy white. Geordie approved of the wee frill at each wrist. Mr Catto was a soldier and an engineer but he was also a gentleman, so his clothes should have some little furbelows. The boy reached for the little knapsack he had laid on the dresser and began unbuckling its fastenings.

'What's that?' asked the Captain, indicating what Geordie was now gingerly lowering into the knapsack. 'Some sprigs of holly?'

'Aye, Captain. From the bush out in our courtyard. We canna go and eat at Miss Rankeillor's hoose without taking her a wee gift. No' on Yule Day. I've tied it up wi' some red ribbon.' Geordie hoisted the prickly green leaves out of the knapsack a little way to show Catto. 'Thought that would look bonnie. The red against the green.'

'Is that the ribbon Miss Rankeillor put round the tablet she brought us last week?'

'Aye. I never throw away anything that might come in useful, Captain.' Geordie lifted his chin to indicate the dresser. 'Keep it all in the middle drawer. Big lumps o' small stuff. That's what my father used to call it. Are you taking Miss Rankeillor a wee gift as well?'

'Why would I do that?' Even as he asked the question, Catto patted one of the pockets of the brown waistcoat he was buttoning.

'What have you got for her?' Geordie asked eagerly. 'Can I see?'

Catto hesitated. 'I'm not so sure it's a good idea for me to give her a present, Geordie.'

'Dae ye ken why we gie gifts at Yuletide, Captain?' Geordie grinned. 'As long as the ministers dinna see us doing it. That's why I'm putting the holly in a knapsack.'

'Everyone knows that, Geordie. Because the Three Wise Men brought gifts to Christ when he was born.'

Geordie shook his head. The movement shifted his abundance of fair hair, cut short but very thick and wavy. He too was smartly dressed today. On top of his own snowy linen and simply tied neckcloth, he wore a dark blue waistcoat and topcoat above black breeches. One of the men had brought those in for him. His son had taken a growth spurt and there was a lot of wear left in the clothes. As Sergeant Crichton had said with a friendly laugh, Geordie the ragamuffin had been transformed into a young gentleman.

'There's another reason, Captain. It's tae bring good luck. And I'm thinking we could all be doing wi' some o' that.'

The guard-house kitchen had one narrow casement, set into the corner of the room. Winter sunlight chose that moment to stream through it, warming the back of Geordie's head. The Captain was looking at him a little oddly.

'Luck,' he said. 'Aye, some luck would be good.' He patted the front of his waistcoat again. 'I'll give Miss Rankeillor this wee gift, then. I think she might like it.'

'Those are the best kind of gifts, sir.'

'Very droll. It's a little book I bought in Berlin a year or two ago.' He took it out of the pocket of the waistcoat. 'A list of words and phrases in the German language. Ones that might come in handy for travellers. Or is that a daft idea?'

'I reckon Miss Rankeillor would like that fine, sir. She's a lady wha likes to learn new things, I'm thinking.'

'Like you do. Here, take a look.' He slid the book across the table. 'They print everything in a very fancy script over there. Takes a wee while to get used to it.'

A wee while. After years away from Scotland, he was sounding more Scottish by the day. That gave him a pang. When he had arrived here a month and more ago, all he had wanted was to complete his assignment and return to the continent, kicking the dust of Scotland from his feet forever as he sailed away. And now … but he chose not to follow that thought through.

Geordie was studying the book of useful words and phrases. 'I see whit ye mean, sir. But I'd like fine to have a go at it. It would be like that deciphering we did, eh? Maybe Miss Rankeillor will let me see it after she's had a good look at it. You've still to wrap it, sir.'

'Do I need to wrap it?'

'A present's best if it's a surprise.'

'What would I wrap it in?'

'Brown paper and string.'

'Do we have any?'

'Middle drawer of the dresser.'

'Some of your big lumps of small stuff?'

Geordie nodded. 'I'll fetch them for you, Captain.'

'I'll get 'em myself. You need to put some carrots and apples into that knapsack. Wouldn't want any killjoy ministers to see us with those gifts either.'

Geordie's face lit up. 'We're going to the stables, sir?'

'Didn't I say I'd take you there to see Tam and the other horses?'

'So that's your Yuletide gift tae me, sir,' Geordie said happily.

'Let's get on with it,' Catto said gruffly. 'Sergeant Livingstone is expecting us at eleven of the clock.'

37

'Dinna look at me like that, Betty.'

'A cat may look at a king.'

Christian rolled her eyes at their combined reflections in the big cheval glass in her bedroom. Shaken by the events of yesterday, she was doing her utmost not to show it in front of Betty. They had enough to worry about as it was. 'I know you disapprove of me inviting them here today.'

'You're the mistress o' the hoose,' Betty responded. She put down the hairbrush, pulled back two strands of Christian's hair from her brow and secured them at the back of her head with a narrow ribbon. 'Mind and be careful when you put your wee cap on. So ye dinna mess your hair up.'

'I'll be careful, Betty. I've been able to put a cap on my head without messing my hair up for quite a few years now.'

The housekeeper didn't dignify that long-suffering comment with an answer. Instead, she began making her way around the bedroom looking for things to tidy up. Since she'd done exactly the same the night before, there weren't any. She was forced to turn, pursing her lips. 'You're the mistress o' the hoose,' she repeated, 'and may do as ye please.'

'I still like to have your approval.'

Dressed simply for a morning in the kitchen, Christian stood up and shook out the dark blue skirts of her workaday gown. She would change later into an afternoon dress. She wasn't in a festive mood but you had to make an effort on Yule Day. There was something talismanic about that, even more so now.

Right at this moment, everything was all right. Right at this moment, they were all safe. She had to hold on to that, not think how precarious that feeling of safety might be. She managed to throw the housekeeper a teasing smile. 'As for me being the mistress of the house, well, I'm not so sure about that.'

Betty snorted.

'It is the season of goodwill, Betty. Time to show hospitality to friends and strangers alike.'

Enemies too. Doesn't the Bible tell us to love our enemies? And was he my friend or my enemy yesterday when he told me that dreadful story about the farmhouse in Saxony? Or when he kissed me and I kissed him back? Or when I decided not to pass on what I know about him and where his loyalties lie?

'Och, but that's another gey fearsome look,' she said, trying not to think about either the story, the kiss or the warning she had failed to give. Either to Agnes Moncur, Murdo Robertson or Charles Paterson. She didn't want to dwell on what they must be thinking about her now, especially Agnes and Murdo. Murdo knew Robert Catto had accompanied her back to Infirmary Street on Daft Friday. If Agnes had also been in on the plot to conceal John Roy Stuart, 'twas only to be expected that Murdo would have told the lady governess what he had seen. Christian managing to avoid speaking to either of them yesterday might well have aroused suspicions in their minds and who knew where such suspicions might lead?

'I'm no' objecting to the boy,' Betty said. 'He's a fine lad and it'll bring a smile tae his sister's face tae see him.'

'How do you think Alice is this morning? I'm not sure. She's so quiet.' Christian grimaced. 'When she's not waking up screaming from her nightmares.'

'Aye. Poor lass. Whit is it your faither aye says aboot the patients — as well as can be expected?'

Christian nodded. 'Aye. What she went through… I can't imagine how awful it must have been. How Cosmo Liddell and those vile, disgusting friends of his could have done what they did to an innocent young girl.' Her voice shook. 'I said *friends*. I should have said *fiends*…' She lifted a hand to still the trembling of her mouth

Betty was beside her in an instant, sliding one skinny yet comforting arm around her young mistress's shoulders. 'There, there, lass. She's safe here wi' us noo.'

Christian took a moment, soothed by the solace she had always found in Betty's arms. When she spoke again her voice was husky. 'Because Captain Catto rescued her and brought her to safety.' She had to give him that. Complex. He was a very complex man.

'Aye,' Betty agreed reluctantly. 'He did dae that.'

'Does that mean you will welcome him here today?' Christian lifted her head. 'To our house and our table?'

'I've fed him already, have I no'?'

'Aye. On sufferance.'

The housekeeper straightened up. Her face was troubled. 'Ye ken fine why I dinna want the Redcoat captain here. I'm no' blind.'

'Nothing can come of it, Betty. Nothing will.' Especially not after yesterday. However strong their mutual attraction, however much desire they felt for each other, they had met at the wrong time and in the wrong place, stood on different sides of a yawning and unforgiving divide.

Betty frowned. 'Would your faither welcome him intae the hoose?'

'You know my father welcomes everyone.'

'Yet yon young man will arrest your faither as soon as he comes hame.' Now it was Betty's voice that trembled. 'As much as we're wanting the Professor back, I could wish he would stay away until a' this blows over!'

Christian shook her head. 'He won't stay away, Betty.' She'd known that even as she'd written the warning letter. Robert Catto was absolutely right. Patrick Rankeillor would never leave his daughter and his household to face this trouble without him. She'd had to try all the same. 'What are you thinking now?' For a very odd expression was stealing across the older woman's face. Wary. Concerned. Fearful.

'Lass, ye're no' thinking o' trying tae … soften the Redcoat's heart, are ye?'

Christian went very still. 'Do you mean what I think you mean, Betty?'

There was a little voice inside her head. *En garde.* That's what it was saying. Hadn't Robert Catto told her everything she thought showed on her face, warned her she had to learn to hide her feelings? Although he hadn't hidden his yesterday. As he hadn't on Daft Friday, when he had told her about his childhood. He had told her about his father too, the man he claimed he hated. He had told her why, coming out with a heartbreaking statement.

I never had a father who cared about me as much as yours does about you.

'I'm not thinking of trying to … *soften his heart* … Betty.' *Don't blush. Don't blush, Kirsty Rankeillor.* Don't let Betty guess that even after yesterday you would lie with Robert Catto for no other reason than because you want to. That you lay awake last night wondering how it would feel to have him touch you, to feel his hands on your body. To feel him move inside you. That his very anger called forth a response from you.

'He has already said he will do his best for my father.' Christian lifted her chin. 'He does not ask any price in return for that.'

'D'ye believe he will dae his best?' Betty had given her a very cynical look but the question she asked wasn't put in a belligerent tone. She really wanted to know the answer.

'I believe Captain Catto will do everything it is in his power to do.'

Everything that is in his power to do when her father was deemed by the state in which they lived to be guilty of treason. She knew what the penalty for treason was. It took all of her strength to push the horror of that knowledge away and force herself to speak in matter-of-fact tones. 'We'd best get started, Betty. I'll be down directly.'

As soon as the departing housekeeper had closed the bedroom door behind her, Christian sank down into the armchair by the fire. Lucrezia Borgia advanced towards her, stretching out her front paws in turn in greeting.

'Only a moment or two up here, baudrons,' Christian said as she lifted the little creature onto her lap. 'I'm sure you'll be happy in the kitchen today. Who knows what tasty morsels might drop into your wee mouth?' She tickled the cat under her chin. An outbreak of purring ensued.

Impossible to have told Betty how she had reacted to that question about softening Robert Catto's heart. She would do anything to keep her beloved father from harm. Even that. Impossible also to have told Betty about the quite different sensations and emotions aroused by the thought of lying with Robert Catto. She only had to close her eyes to transport herself back to yesterday. Him backing her up against the wall. Feeling his body reacting to hers. She had been scared and excited all at the same time. Her body had reacted to his too.

'I'm blushing now, Lucy.' Christian rubbed her knuckles over the small bony head. 'Dinna tell Betty, will you?'

Robert Catto aroused desires she hadn't known she possessed. There had been young men to whom she had taken a fancy. The odd kiss. A clumsy touch or two. Nothing that had left her breathless and trembling as the merest brush of his fingers did. Or those kisses in the guard-house on Daft Friday. The kiss which had followed his tirade yesterday had been different. Passionate. Searching. Despairing. He had described the situation in which the two of them now found themselves as a bloody mess. Now it was an even bigger mess.

Until all this blows over. That's what Betty had said.

Christian shivered. This wasn't going to blow over. The scudding clouds, rising wind and driving rain were only beginning to gather their strength.

38

'A pipe, Captain?'

Catto shook his head. He'd always thought it was a filthy habit, not one he'd ever understood.

'But you will be taking some warm ale?' Livingstone asked.

'I will, Sergeant. With thanks. 'Tis chilly outside. Fine to sit here by your fire for a wee while.' Surprising himself by meaning that, he stretched his legs out to the warm glow of the tavern fire. The wooden chair creaked as he sat back into it, before it settled onto the flagstones of the floor. He surprised himself again by giving a soft laugh. 'That'll give Geordie more time to wish a good Yule to each and every one of your horses.'

Livingstone laughed in response. 'Aye, and my bairns more time to make the introductions. I like to see the wee ones enjoying themselves together. A sociable life refines the soul.'

The two men had just walked through a stone corridor from the stables of *The White Horse,* the coaching inn at the foot of the Canongate run by Livingstone and his wife. Horses, wooden stalls and hay were kept a safe distance from the tavern fire. The stable itself was fine and warm all the same. Some heat passed through the rough-hewn stones of the wall that separated it from the inn. The horses gave out warmth too. As Geordie had previously observed, stables were fine cosy places. Aye, it had been heart-warming to see the lad making friends with Livingstone's children and the horses.

With everything that was going wrong in Robert Catto's world right now, it was good to be reminded of life's simpler pleasures. He was glad now he hadn't decided to stay at the guard-house today, a possibility which had crossed his mind several times since he'd had that angry confrontation with Christian Rankeillor yesterday. He had finally decided to go to Infirmary Street because he didn't want to disappoint Geordie. That decision had led to an unexpected development. As he and the boy walked down the High Street from the guard-house to *The White Horse*, he had felt his mood lightening as they went. He wasn't sure what had wrought this change in him. Maybe because it was Christmas Day. Maybe because somewhere deep inside him, a spark of hope still flared.

The Sergeant's striking blue eyes twinkled. 'I'm thinking it was yourself I saw and heard wishing at least one of my cuddies a good Yuletide, young Captain Catto.' *Cuddies.* The Lowland word sounded funny in Livingstone's Highland accent. 'That was a fine juicy apple you gave Tam.'

Catto pulled a face, mocking himself. 'Ach well, the beast has been a good companion on my Sunday jaunts out of Edinburgh these six weeks past.'

'Here's the ale for you and the Captain, husband.'

Catto looked up from watching Livingstone slide a clean and gleaming steel poker into the fire and greeted the Sergeant's wife. Marjorie Livingstone was bonnie, buxom, the mother of their three young children and thirty years younger than their father. She winked at Catto as she set two pewter tankards down on the scrubbed grey stones of the hearth. All for show. She was as devoted to Livingstone as he was to her.

She turned and went back to her duties behind the long wooden counter of the tavern. 'Twas almost empty at this hour of Christmas morning but there would be plenty of customers later. In theory Christmas Day was a working day like any other. The Kirk disapproved of celebrating Christmas as it had been done in days gone by, seeking to distance modern Protestant Scotland from its Catholic past. In practice plenty of people managed to get their work done early.

Livingstone's eyes followed his wife all the way back to the bar, soft with love and lingering desire. Over sixty the Sergeant might be but he was a strong and vigorous man. Finally tearing his gaze away from her, the older man bent forward and removed the poker from the fire. He put it in turn into each of the tankards, raising an almighty hiss and a cloud of bubbles. 'We'll leave them for a wee minute. Allow the handles to cool.'

'Aye,' Catto agreed. He was feeling some lingering desire himself. Must be good to have a lover who was also your friend and companion. 'Twas only a week or so since he had last tumbled Lizzie Gibson. Seemed like months. He could hardly have availed himself of her bounteous charms when he had been down in Leith the other day.

Besides which, there was only one woman he wanted to lie with now. Which made him even more of a poor bloody fool than he already was. That could never happen. He thought back to yesterday's kiss. That could never happen again either. He and Kirsty Rankeillor had to keep each other at arm's length. For both their sakes. Aye, and if he kept telling himself that he might eventually believe it.

Livingstone laid the poker back on the hearth, sat back and raised his head. As ever, his shock of white hair was clean and neatly trimmed. Brushed back from his high forehead, it curled on his shoulders. The white beard that followed his jawline was equally well groomed.

Catto reached for his ale and raised the tankard in a toast. 'I wish you and yours all the best this Yule Day, Sergeant.'

'Likewise, young Captain Catto,' Livingstone said, lifting his tankard and taking a healthy swig.

'Do we have any more intelligence on the state of the road between here and Glasgow, Livingstone? 'Twould be good to know the mail coach made it through and didn't get stuck in a snow drift somewhere outside Kilsyth.'

'All we know is that the mail coach made it as *far* as Kilsyth, Captain. I've heard no further news. As yet there have been no journeys in the opposite direction. Or mail, of course.' He frowned in concern. 'I could wish the young lady from Glasgow had not been so determined on travelling home in such difficult weather.'

'She was not to be gainsayed.' Thinking again how well-matched Kirsty Rankeillor and her friends were, Catto's mouth twisted with regret. 'I did try to talk her out of it.'

'As did Marjorie and myself,' sighed Livingstone.

Probably with a lot more force than Catto had. He might feel slightly guilty about Meg Wood getting stuck in a snow drift or Anna Gordon spending today at sea. He might feel a lot more guilty about how he had intervened in the friendship between Meg Wood and the other two, probably to its eternal detriment, but it suited him that both girls had left Edinburgh.

'Where do we go from here, Captain?'

Catto met the shrewd blue eyes. 'We wait for Professor Rankeillor's return. If you see him before me, I wish you to apprehend him.'

'Confining him to the Tolbooth or his house?'

'The latter. Our aim remains to keep what happened on Daft Friday as quiet as possible.'

'Aye,' Livingstone said, nodding his majestic head in agreement. 'Although that will not be easy once the snow clears completely, the Daft Days are over, and life gets back to normal.' He hesitated.

'Spit it out, Livingstone.'

Catto might not be certain where the Sergeant stood in this Scotland of divided and conflicted loyalties. He did know the man was an old soldier, a veteran of Malplaquet, that bloodiest of battles. Livingstone too knew what happened when politics spilled over onto the battlefield, had seen with his own eyes how ugly and brutal life could become for the civilian population when soldiers swept through their villages and farms.

'Do you think there is a real threat, Captain?'

'I do, Sergeant. I fear there are people among us who seek to bring war here to Scotland. Who would welcome that to achieve their ambitions.'

Livingstone glanced once more over to where his wife stood, then back in the direction of the stables. For a moment there was silence between the two men. Catto thought of Geordie and the Sergeant's children, laughing and talking together while clapping the horses on their warm necks under their rough manes in the warm, hay-scented stable. Cosy. Safe. Settled.

'You are thinking of those whom you hold dear.'

'Aye, young Captain Catto. That I am.'

'We must do our utmost to protect them. Whatever the cost. The first requirement is that we remain vigilant at all times.'

'Aye. Will you have another?' he asked as Catto drained his tankard.

'I thank you, but no. Geordie and I must be off.' He got his feet, Livingstone looking up at him.

'You and the lad are very welcome to stay and eat with us on this Yule Day.'

'I appreciate the invitation. But we are promised elsewhere.'

'At Miss Rankeillor's house?'

'Geordie wishes to see his sister. On this day of all days. 'Tis a natural desire.'

A natural desire. For a moment the words seemed to hang in the air, taking on a very different meaning. Livingstone was reminding Catto even more of God now. He felt as though those piercing blue eyes were looking deep into his very soul.

'Tread carefully, sir.' Livingstone rose to his feet.

'Are we speaking of my duties as Captain of the Town Guard, Sergeant? Or our current difficulties?'

'We are speaking of life, young Captain Catto. Tread carefully.'

39

Glancing out of one of the long narrow windows which flanked the front door, Christian saw Robert Catto and Geordie standing there. The boy still had his hand on the tirling pin. She had come through from the kitchen before the brass wire attached to it had danced its way along its housing high up on the wall to jangle the bell in the kitchen.

She'd been waiting here for the last ten minutes, walking backwards and forwards on the chequered black and white squares of the lobby floor. Waiting for them. Wondering if they were coming or not. Wondering what she would say to Betty if they did not. Taking refuge from not knowing what to do about the domestic drama currently playing out in the kitchen.

Plastering a smile on her face, she flung the door open. Robert Catto looked startled. No wonder. She must resemble a poor simple-minded creature, especially when you considered how they had parted yesterday. Her smile to the boy could be genuine, though. He flashed her one of his dazzling grins in response.

'I wish ye a Happy Yule, Miss Rankeillor. Are we your first visitors this morning?'

She nodded, and he went rattling on. 'That means you've let in Yule. Should bring ye good fortune, Miss. Mr Catto said it would be fine for me to come by the front door today,' he confided. 'Seeing as how we've just come from the other direction than I usually do.' He shrugged his way out of the small knapsack he wore on his back and lifted it towards her. 'We've brought ye a wee present.'

'Come in out of the cold first.' Hoping she sounded a lot more cheerful than she felt, she ushered the boy into the lobby. There was no reason why he should have to be upset by the tension between her and Robert Catto. Who could fend for himself. He hadn't stood on ceremony when he'd first entered this house. He'd invaded it, bringing a troop of the Town Guard in with him, tramping dirt and ice all over the floor and the rugs. It had taken her and Betty and the girls the whole of the next day to clean everything.

Why she hadn't withdrawn the invitation to eat with them today she did not know. She was clearly not in her right mind. Out of the corner of her eye, she was aware of him swinging shut the big front door which gave out onto Infirmary Street.

'We've just been to see the horses at Mr Livingstone's stables, miss,' the boy said excitedly. 'It was grand.'

She managed another smile for him. 'Put your knapsack on the hall table, Geordie. Then it'll be easier for you to undo the buckle.'

The boy obeyed her, lifting his head as he reached the narrow high table set against the wood panelling of the back wall of the lobby. 'Och, but those are grand smells coming from your kitchen, Miss Rankeillor!'

'Goose pie,' she managed. 'With plum porridge to follow. And... and...'

She raised a hand to her chest. The little brown velvet bows running down the centre of the stomacher of her afternoon gown were quivering under the force of her emotions. God in Heaven, she was behaving like the worst kind of simpering miss!

Lifting a bunch of holly out of the knapsack, Geordie presented it to her. Red ribbon was tied in a bow around the stalks of the prickly green leaves. That must surely be one of the ribbons she had used for the two little boxes of tablet she had taken to the guard-house before

Daft Friday. On the last occasion when she'd thought she wasn't right in the head. Obeying an impulse. Making an offering to the gods. Praying Robert Catto might be on their side.

She looked at the bunch of holly. She looked at Geordie behind it. As her tears welled up, his bright young face fell. 'Och, Miss Rankeillor, d'ye not like my wee present?'

'I love your wee present, Geordie! But the back door's stuck open and we can't get it closed! We've tried all leaning against it at once but it won't shut!'

She saw Robert Catto step forward before her vision blurred behind the waterfall of tears.

'Geordie, on you go through to the kitchen and scout out the situation with the door for me. Miss Rankeillor and I will be there in a moment. Take the holly with you.'

'Come here.' Catto murmured the words as soon as Geordie had disappeared down the corridor and through the door that led into the kitchen and scullery.

'No.' She raised both hands to his chest, trying to fend him off. She wasn't trying very hard. 'We can't do this,' she said breathlessly. 'We mustn't do this!'

'I know that as well as you do. But desperate situations call for desperate remedies.' He pulled her into his arms, holding her close.

She made a fist of one hand, struck it twice against his chest. 'I wasn't going to do this. I was going to keep you at arm's length today. Oh, and I have cried so much since I met you! And I am not the sort of useless female who has fits of the vapours at the drop of a hat!'

'I can tell that. And I made the very same decision about you less than half an hour since. But you don't want to upset them through in the kitchen, do you? You're not made that way. Therefore I am the only comforter available to you.'

'You said that on Daft Friday too. That's what got us into this mess.'

'Wheesht. No hoops under this pretty gown,' he observed. 'Feels rather nice. Apart from your stays.'

'A gentleman would not mention such things.' She hit him again, provoking a soft laugh.

'I'm guessing the door sticking was the final straw. On top of everything else you have to contend with.'

She nodded, her face and her fist against his chest. 'Daft Friday. Jamie. Jeannie Carmichael. Alice. My father. Meg. You,' she added. 'Yesterday.'

'And Geordie completed your downfall.'

'Yes. He has so little, is so distressed by what happened to his sister. I fear he blames himself for not being there to protect her. Yet he contrived to find some brightness and joy and share it with the rest of us.'

Catto spared a hand to run it down the silky softness of her hair. 'Mahogany,' he said. 'Your hair is the colour of mahogany.'

'And my head is as dense as mahogany. That's what you think.'

'Sometimes. I think you do not always see where your own best interests lie. But I'm sorry I was so rough with you yesterday.'

'You were very angry with me yesterday.'

'My anger was born of fear.' Jealousy too, he thought, jealousy of *him*. 'Twas pathetic in the extreme that the man still had the power to wound him. He threaded his fingers through her hair. 'I fear for you, Kirsty. I shall do everything I can for you and your father but I cannot make it all right. I cannot fix everything that is wrong.'

'No more can I.' She said the words into his chest. 'When my father's not here, they all look to me. They think I can fix everything. I can't do that either.'

'Well,' Catto said easily, 'I expect I can fix a stuck door. I am an engineer. Now, raise your head and kiss me. Quickly, before your wee witch of a housekeeper flies through here on her broomstick to stop me ravishing you on the lobby floor.'

'Robert Catto!' But he had shocked her into pulling back, looking up at him and laughing.

He spared one hand to wipe her tears, told her she had a smudge of flour on her nose, and wiped that away too. He dropped a kiss on the tip of that nose. 'I have a present for you too. By way of a peace offering as well as for Yule. I hope 'twill not make you start crying again.'

40

Geordie turned eagerly towards them as they came into the kitchen. Alice Smart and the two maidservants shrank back. Given that on his first visit here Catto had swept into the house at the head of a troop of the Town Guard and threatened to have the housekeeper and the girls gagged if they didn't keep quiet, following one of those threats through, he could hardly blame them. Alice's sister and the younger of the two maids — Tibby? — had another reason to be scared of men. The bond they shared was an unfortunate one.

'I'm thinking you might need to take a wee bittie off the door, sir,' Geordie volunteered. 'On the side here where it willna fit into the frame.'

'Let's take a look. Aye,' Catto said, after cautiously pushing the door as far into the frame as it would go, opening it again and running his hand down its side. 'It wants chamfering. Here on the leading edge.'

'I think it must have got damp from the snow.'

'Aye. Looks like that's been sliding down the door during the day and collecting here as it melts. Then night falls early as it does in the winter and it freezes up, staying in this spot. Well assessed, Geordie.'

'Chamfering.' The boy repeated the word, his nose wrinkling as it always did when he was absorbing a word or a piece of information new to him.

'You will need a file, Captain Catto?'

'Along with a sharp knife, Miss Rankeillor. Fortunately I have one such in my pocket.' He unbuttoned his tan leather horseman's coat and found she was easing it from his shoulders. The private playhouse in his brain immediately presented him with a mental image of the two of them undressing each other. They were standing by her fairy tale bed, that four-poster on the first floor of this house whose well-polished uprights were carved with images of woodland animals and draped with soft blue velvet curtains. She was shyly loosening his neckcloth. More than happy to sacrifice his Steinkirk knot, he was peeling each item of clothing away from her peaches and cream skin... Bugger. He really was a hopeless case.

Think about doors, Catto. Doors and fixing them. Think about the fearsome expression on the housekeeper's face. If looks could kill you'd be lying dead on the floor. That should dampen your ardour. He was thankful when the little woman took his coat from Christian Rankeillor and went off with it. Hopefully she was going to hang it up somewhere rather than tossing it over a wall into the nearest pigsty.

He unfastened his cuffs at the wrist and rolled back his sleeves, looking up from the task to find it was now the young mistress who was watching him very intently. Her eyes were on his bare forearms with their dusting of fine coppery hairs. She raised her head and their eyes met. She blushed and looked away. Funny what men and women found arousing about each other.

'Are ye needing ony help, Captain?'

He heard Geordie through a haze of mingled pleasure, desire and regret. He might rouse Kirsty Rankeillor's passions as much as she did his but that could lead them no farther, least of all to her fairy tale bed. Doors. Chamfering. He had to think about chamfering the door. 'Aye. You hold the door steady, Geordie. Here,' he said. 'Where you indicated. We need to trim back a very little down these few inches here on the edge.' He scored the door and began slicing.

'I'll fetch the file.' She sounded a little breathless. Catto hoped she was thinking about doors too. The housekeeper would soon be back and watching them both like a hawk in her self-appointed role as guardian of Christian Rankeillor's virtue. Damn the wee woman to hell and back again.

'I'll have that now,' he said a few moments later.

When she put the file into his hand their fingers touched. Bloody hell. This was torture. Exquisite torture. He wondered how the Devil he was to stop himself from grabbing her hand, running upstairs with her and throwing her onto her bed. That would shock the assembled company.

'Something amusing you, young man?'

'My mouth is watering,' Catto said, turning on the charm. He was capable of it, if somewhat out of practice. 'The goose pie smells wonderful. And the plum porridge.' He hoped he wasn't fooling himself that the grim expression relaxed. If only by the merest smidgeon.

41

Catto raised one hand in protest. 'Have mercy, Mistress Gilchrist. I have no room left for any more food!'

'I think I might burst,' Geordie said happily. 'I'm stuffed as full as the goose was!'

'Havers,' Betty replied as everyone laughed and she divided what was left of the plum porridge between boy and man.

Christian watched from the top of the table. She didn't believe Betty liked or trusted Robert Catto any more than she had before. What she had noticed was how much the housekeeper had enjoyed his appreciation of the food set in front of him. He'd even been persuaded to try potatoes. Christian had told him sternly that not only were they a perfectly edible and nutritious vegetable, they had a very fine taste too.

'Try them with a little butter and salt,' she'd suggested.

He'd gone along with it, although he had put the first piece of salted and buttery potato into his mouth with the air of a man conducting a dangerous experiment.

'A very fine taste,' he'd pronounced a moment later, looking surprised. 'Very fine indeed.'

After the savouries there had been a multitude of sweet things to eat: syllabub, mince pies, nuts, fruit, biscuits and the plum porridge. Christian and Robert Catto had drunk two or three glasses of claret each. Betty had sipped a port at the end of the meal.

Everyone had enjoyed the food. Everyone had relaxed over the meal, even Alice Smart. Since she'd arrived at Infirmary Street she had spent her waking hours sitting in the corner of the kitchen like a pale, golden-haired ghost, doing her utmost not to draw attention to herself. You might hardly have registered her presence in the house at all were it not for the nightmares which woke her and everyone else in the early hours of the morning. There had been no nightmare last night. Alice had eaten well today. A few shy smiles had crossed her face. There was hope. She could heal, begin to put her terrible experience behind her.

Something happened inside Christian's head, then. 'Twas as though a small candle had been lit, a tiny flame in the midst of the darkness. Throughout the meal she had felt her mood shifting and lifting. Maybe she was in a fool's paradise. Or maybe she should accept this lightening of her spirits for as long as it lasted. What was done was done.

'Who's going to give us a song?' she asked. 'It's Yule Day. We must have music.'

'You wouldn't want to hear me sing,' Robert Catto said, giving her a disarming smile. 'But Geordie warbles sometimes as he goes about his work.'

'Geordie has a real bonnie voice.'

Sitting to Christian's left, Robert Catto looked down the table at Alice and spoke very gently. 'Aye. That he does. Give us something appropriate to the season, lad.'

Amused, Christian watched as Geordie pretended he needed to be coaxed. 'Come and stand over here,' she said, rising to her feet and beckoning him out from behind the table. 'Where we can all see you as well as hear you. What will you sing?'

'*Balulalow*.' Alice had spoken again. 'Sing *Balulalow*, Geordie. I remember our mother singing it to you.'

Balulalow: the lovely old lullaby to the Christ child. Geordie opened his mouth and began to sing.

I come frae Heaven here to tell
The best nowells that e'er befell
To you their tidings true I bring
And I will of them say and sing.
To you this day is born a child
Of Mary meek and Virgin mild
That blessed bairn benign and kind
Shall you rejoice baith heart and mind.

Alice Smart had spoken no more than the truth. Geordie did have a real bonnie voice. As Christian listened to him, she felt herself fill up with emotion. A lullaby for the Christ child. Sung to a baby boy born into the poverty and serfdom of the coal miners of East Lothian. Requested by a sister who might herself be with child, not as the result of love but of brutal rape. Dear God in Heaven, what were they going to do if Alice had conceived? They would never know which of those monsters was the father. Who would rejoice over such a child? Geordie continued to sing.

O my dear heart, young Jesus sweet,
Prepare thy cradle in my spirit!
And I shall rock thee in my heart
And never mair frae thee depart.
But I shall praise thee evermore
With songs sweet unto thy glore
The knee of my heart shall I bow
And sing that richt Balulalow.

All children should be welcomed into the world. The circumstances of their conception were not their fault. All children should be rocked in loving arms and hearts, have lullabies sung to them. That was what should happen. In this cruel and heartless world, it so often didn't.

With that thought, Christian made a silent promise. If Alice was with child, that baby would be welcomed into the Rankeillor household. No matter what the wagging tongues of the gossips said.

When Geordie finished singing silence descended on the kitchen. It was Robert Catto who broke it. 'Bravo, Geordie. Bravo.' He started clapping and everyone joined in.

❖

Catto looked around the kitchen before turning to Christian Rankeillor, back in her position at the top of the table. 'They're all asleep,' he murmured.

Her gaze too swept the big room. The two maids, Geordie and his sister sat companionably on the long pine settle in one corner of the kitchen. 'Twas comical to see how they had all relaxed against one another. They were like a row of slumbering rag dolls.

Geordie had sung two more carols. The little maidservants had genuinely needed some coaxing but had joined in with him on two more, growing in confidence as they went on. A few rounds of *The Minister's Cat* had been played. Catto had given Kirsty Rankeillor and Geordie an impromptu German lesson, using the little book of useful words and phrases as a basis. Should they ever need to, they could now bespeak a room and supper at an inn in Frankfurt or Berlin.

Betty was sleeping in an armchair by the range. Kirsty Rankeillor and the two maids had led her there, laughing and over-riding her protests. They would clear the table and put any leftovers from the Yuletide meal into the pantry. And yes, they had said with a communal rolling of eyes, of course they would cover everything that needed covering.

A footstool had been fetched. The belligerent sparrow lay now stretched out with her feet up and snoring gently. Full of scraps from the table, Lucy the cat lay on Betty's lap, also sound asleep and snoring gently. Catto could hear both of them. He couldn't quite see them.

From where he sat, his chair turned around from the table to face the room, he could only glimpse the side of the armchair. It occurred to him that its position offered one great advantage. It had its back to the doorway without a door which led into the scullery off the kitchen. As Geordie had earlier scouted out what the problem was with the back door, so Catto had scouted out the lie of the land. A good soldier always did.

'Come in there with me,' he said, keeping his voice low. He inclined his head to indicate where he meant. 'Even when they all wake up, they won't be able to see us. We'll hear them stir anyway. Besides which, the wee witch is going to need a ladder to climb down off that footstool and chair.' He expected an argument. He didn't get one, only the smile he'd been angling for and an observation after they had moved through.

''Tis cooler in here.'

'Refreshing after the warmth of the kitchen.'

The scullery had a stone floor, its walls whitewashed. Painted apple green like those out in the shop, four rows of shelves ran around three of its walls. There were gaps in the neat rows of gleaming copper pans, white pottery crocks, ashets and plates of varying depths and sizes. The crockery and cookware used to prepare and serve the meal stood stacked on one of the lower, broader shelves, waiting to be washed in two round wooden tubs.

Catto folded his arms across his brown waistcoat and surveyed Christian Rankeillor. It occurred to him that their clothes complemented each other in colour today. Her light-coloured gown was decorated with small brown velvet bows. He was wearing his long brown waistcoat over his spotless fine linen shirt with the little ruffles at the wrists. They stood opposite each other in the small amount of free space in the middle of the scullery.

'What were you thinking about when Geordie sang that first carol?'

'The future and what it might hold. For Alice, I mean. That if she is with child, we shall care for it and her.'

'I thought it might be something like that. You looked sad and then as though you had resolved on a course of action.'

She raised both hands to her face and drew them down over her eyes and cheeks, steepling her fingers against her chin. 'Right now I'm wondering if I will be in a position to follow any course of action nine months from now. Or if the Rankeillor household will be either.' She spoke calmly enough, although her voice had faltered a little.

'Will you sit down with me?' he asked. 'Please?'

When she nodded, he took her by the hand and led her to the window seat set into the one wall of the scullery that was clear of shelves. It had no cushions but its soft yellow pine was smooth and polished. He guided her so they sat on it half-turned, facing each other. Holding both her hands in his, he clasped them on top of her knees and the folds of her gown which was, he'd decided, the colour of creamy buttermilk.

Her voice was steady. 'I shall spare you the necessity of asking me yet again if I am aware of the danger in which I stand. Yes. I am.' She gave him another little smile. 'Reality has always had a way of catching up with me. Usually somewhat later than it should.'

Catto squeezed the hands he held. Her fingers felt cool. Cool and competent, that was her. She was used to administering physic and laying a soothing hand against someone's forehead, bringing healing and comfort wherever she could. Yet she was passionate too, so very passionate about the people she loved and the Cause she espoused. She had shown him a different kind of passion yesterday, when she had responded so eagerly to his mouth and his hands. 'We have some time. The snow and the season have been our allies.'

'*Our* allies? We are on opposite sides, Robert.'

He shook his head. 'Not in this. I'm going to lie for you, Kirsty.'

Her eyes widened. 'But you always do your duty.'

'Because my duty is all I've ever had to hold onto,' he supplied, quoting her. 'But now I have something else. Some*one* else.'

283

'And I am that someone else?'

'You know you are. It seems to me we are getting nowhere in trying to fight our feelings for each other. Other than me, only your father, Balnamoon and the Jacobite agent know that you took food and medical assistance to him. That you hid him within the Royal Infirmary.'

'The Jacobite agent,' she repeated. 'Is that still really the only way you can bring yourself to think of him?'

'Do not look at me with sadness in your eyes. There is no need. I am not sad. Are you cold?' he asked, seeing her give a little shiver.

'A wee bit.'

'There are things I need to say to you. Here, where there is no chance of anyone else hearing us.'

'Go on.'

He raised her hands to his lips and kissed her knuckles. 'A few people saw me arrest you at the Assembly Rooms. I can deal with them.' He hunched his shoulders, thinking about that. 'Have already dealt with most of them. No one else need know about the Royal Infirmary and your involvement there. As long as you play no further role in any Jacobite plots. Ever.'

Her face grew troubled. 'You cannot ask me that, Robert. How can any of us know what we shall do when the moment comes? How can any of us know what the future holds?'

'We can make plans. Do our damnedest to follow them through.' Livingstone's words came back to him. 'We can tread carefully.'

'Learn the steps to this dance of which you have spoken?'

'Try not to take them. Learn a different dance.' He doubted Livingstone would think he was treading very carefully here, sitting alone with Christian Rankeillor in the scullery of her house. Offering to exchange his integrity for her safety. He was reminded of words spoken by another wise and shrewd man: Duncan Forbes of Culloden, Lord President of the Court of Session of Scotland.

You will have to walk a tightrope, Bob, enter a labyrinth, a place of smoke and mirrors.

Catto was deep within that labyrinth now. He should have tied a length of Geordie's string round a tree or a stone at its entrance so he could find his way back out. Too late for that now.

'You and your father have friends in high places. Do not forget that. Chief among them is the Lord President. He is a friend of you and your father, is he not?'

'The Lord President is your friend too, I think.'

'He has known me since I was a boy.'

'He has known me since I was a girl. Where do you come from?' She cast him a challenging look, daring him to evade the question. 'Other than the army, I mean.'

'The back of the north wind. That's where I'm from. You're shivering again. Swing your feet up onto the window seat and permit me to do this.' He put his arm around her shoulders, turning her and drawing her back to lean against him. The smooth stuff of her dress slid along the well-polished wood of the window seat.

'Bumfle your gown up around your ankles.' He was already helping her do that. 'Then you'll be warmer.'

'*Bumfle*,' she repeated with a little laugh. 'You remember that day in the Infirmary?'

'How could I forget? I still blush when I think of it.'

He had stumbled into the hospital after taking that blow to the head from an unseen assailant, knew now it had been Jamie Buchan of Balnamoon who had struck him. Losing consciousness, Catto had come to lying on a couch under a blanket. She had remarked that the cover was *all bumfled up.* When she had straightened it, he had reacted to her touch. In the most embarrassing way possible. He was reacting now. He adjusted his position so she would not be aware of that. More exquisite torture.

'Every moment we sit here we're making things worse for ourselves.'

He drew the back of his index finger down the curve of her cheek and chin. 'Yes. We are. Even though you did tell me on Daft Friday that we would find a way.'

Her eyes fluttered shut. A tremble ran through her. This time he knew that wasn't because she was feeling the cold. 'I think I was a little delirious on Daft Friday. I had aimed a pistol at you and fired.'

'You missed.'

'I meant to.'

'So you said at the time. I'm still not entirely convinced. Don't frown.' He transferred his finger to her brow, smoothing out the lines of concern. 'Right at this moment you are safe and well. We are safe and well.' He laughed. 'Also very well fed.'

She tilted her head back to look at him. 'I had not thought you to be so sanguine about what lies in front of us. You do not strike me as a man who looks at life from an optimistic point of view.'

He was still smiling, giving the lie to that statement. 'You said *us*.'

'What of it?'

'You said *us*. I said *we*. Every time you say that it makes me happy. Us. We. The two of us.'

'You're havering and we've had this conversation before— What are you doing?' For his fingertips were dancing now along the neckline of her dress, tracing the outline of its bodice.

'Trying to take your mind off what the future might hold. Physical … eh … intimacy can often achieve that desirable effect.'

'You would know… Oh,' she breathed. 'Ah…'

'*Oh*?' he queried, laughter bubbling through his voice. '*Ah*?'

'Be quiet. Let us just … be here … in this moment out of time …'

'I think my strategy is working. Wouldn't you agree?'

She said nothing, only took his hand and pulled it down inside her bodice.

'Hoyden,' he murmured against her ear.

'That's the pot calling the kettle black if ever I heard it. Oh,' she said again, arching her back, filling his hand with her breast, meeting his caressing fingers.

He sighed, an expression of pure pleasure. 'Been dreaming about doing this since the moment we met.'

'I don't believe you. You hated me on sight.'

'Not exactly. While Miss Hoity-Toity Rankeillor was looking so condescendingly down her nose at the Captain of the Town Guard, I was looking down the front of her gown.'

She raised her free arm and slapped him in the chest. 'Do you ever stop talking? Is there any means by which one can silence that sarcastic mouth of yours?'

'Possibly. Do you know something?'

'Not unless you tell me.'

'Whatever lies before us, I don't think I've ever been as happy as I have been today, as I am at this moment. Which makes very little sense but there you are.' He raised his eyebrows, thinking about what he had just said. He kept his hand where it was, cupping her breast. ''Tis a somewhat novel experience for me. Being happy, I mean.'

'How can we be happy when we may only have this moment?'

'Because we do only have this moment, this Yule Day, these Daft Days. We have to seize these fleeting hours and days, catch them before they slip out of our grasp.'

'Oh, I had not realized that you number philosophy among your many talents.'

'Jade,' he said. 'Impertinent baggage. Have you not been happy today? Are you not happy now?'

'Until Betty catches us like this.'

'She won't.' He looked past her drawn-up knees to her feet, flat on the window seat. She wore neat little evening slippers, embroidered in circles and whirls of red, yellow and green. 'I remember those. You were wearing them when we first met, tapping your foot and wishing me gone. I like your feet,' he added.

'You like my feet?' She wrinkled her nose. 'Men are very strange.'

'You speak from vast experience?'

'Of patients only. I have very little experience of men like you.'

'I shall not ask for a definition of *men like you*. I don't dare. You didn't answer my question. Are you not happy now, in this moment, sitting here with me?'

'Aye,' she said slowly. 'I am. Though I think we must both be disordered in our wits to feel this way.'

'Well, these are the Daft Days. We're allowed to be daft.'

She stared at him for a moment, seeing amusement lend a sparkle to his grey eyes and a curve to his well-shaped mouth. Then she began to laugh and made him laugh too. She clapped her hands against her own mouth. 'We dinna want Betty to hear!'

He lifted her fingers away from her face, using his spare hand. 'If you're interested, I know one sure way of silencing our betraying mouths and my sarcastic one.'

'Then kindly demonstrate it. Forthwith, in fact.' She giggled. 'Immediately.'

'Do you ever stop talking?' he replied, and did as he was bid.

42

C atto was woken by a clap of thunder. Startled out of sleep, he came swiftly upright as lightning cracked and flashed. Shooting through the narrow gap between the wooden shutters, it lit up his bedchamber, turning everything around him blue and silver. The storm must be directly overhead.

Wrists resting on his drawn-up knees, he sat up in his bed waiting for it to pass, counting the lengthening delay between the rumble of the thunder and the lightning that followed it. His grandfather had taught him how to do that. He supposed Kirsty Rankeillor would know about counting the seconds too, wondered if she might still be scared as mother nature vented her fury above Edinburgh.

Fear would not stop her from being up out of her bed reassuring everyone else spending tonight in the Rankeillor house down in Infirmary Street. That included Geordie. Catto hadn't had the heart to take the boy away from the kitchen fire when he had left the house last night. He and his sister and the two little maidservants had been taking turns pulling a length of wool across the hearth rug for the cat to chase.

'No, no, Geordie,' he'd said when the lad had said he should come back here to the guard-house with him so he could bank up the fires, steep the oatmeal for the following morning's porridge and be up to cook that for his captain and any other guards on early duty. 'You stay here and sleep off your Yuletide dinner.'

Catto doubted if Geordie would be sleeping now. It was some time before the storm moved away, heading out over the Firth of Forth by the sounds of it. He remembered how he had wanted a storm when he had sailed up the firth, more than a month since. It had seemed the right kind of weather to accompany his unwilling return to Scotland after so many years away, matching his growing sense of foreboding as the boat drew ever closer to Leith.

Well, he had got a storm tonight. Long before, if he counted not the seconds between rumbles of thunder and flashes of lightning but the events of this past week and more. They too had matched his sense of foreboding. How he wished they had not. Yet there was one thing he could not regret. Meeting Kirsty Rankeillor.

Yesterday at Infirmary Street, he had been happier than he had ever thought he could be again. Being with her was enough, vastly more than enough, but 'twas more even than that. Absurd though it might be, he had felt part of a family again. That had been her Yuletide gift to him. Good food, a warm kitchen, singing and laughter. The almost forgotten sensations of comfort and care wrapping themselves around everyone in the Rankeillor household. Even Geordie's sister Alice had seemed to take solace from it.

The storm was farther away now, its rumbles and crackles disappearing into the distance. As though a tap had been turned on, it was replaced by rain, drumming down onto the causeway outside. Catto fell back onto his pillows. With a bit of luck the rain would wash away the snow.

❖

'Well,' Christian said, standing in the kitchen with Geordie, 'that was spectacular.'

'Spectacular,' the boy repeated, rolling the word around his mouth. 'That's a grand word.'

She turned from gazing out of the window at the rain that had taken over from the storm and looked at him. 'You like words, don't you?'

'Aye, Miss Kirsty, I do.'

The noise of the storm had woken everybody. Surprising Christian, although she had been careful not to show it, Alice Smart had been the least frightened of the girls. She had comforted Tibby and Mary while Christian, Betty and Geordie had gone down to the kitchen to heat cups of warm milk to soothe everyone and help them get back to sleep. Betty had carried those upstairs on a tray while Christian and Geordie had stayed downstairs to drink their own. Christian had assured her they wouldn't tarry too long. Yet with the fire in the range kept in all night, the kitchen was fine and cosy. She wasn't ready to go back to bed quite yet.

'And you can read?' she asked, continuing the conversation. Then, when Geordie nodded. 'We have a lot of books in this house. Why don't you have a look in the library in the morning and see if there's anything you fancy? You could take it back to the guard-house with you. I might recommend one for you to start with, by Mr Daniel Defoe. It's about the adventures of a shipwrecked sailor called Robinson Crusoe. It's a great story. Although,' she added, 'I'm not so keen on Mr Defoe himself.'

'I'd like that fine, miss,' he said shyly. 'I'd take real good care of it and bring it back to you as soon as I'd read it. Why don't you like the man who wrote it?'

'It's a long story. I'll tell you another time. And I know you would look after the book. After you've read it and brought it back you can borrow another one if you like. Have you finished your milk?'

'Aye, miss.'

'Then away to your bed, I'm going to stay downstairs for a wee while longer.' She took his cup from him, exchanging it for a lit candlestick from one of the two on the table. 'Mind and blow that out before you get into bed. Goodnight, Geordie.'

Leaving her own candlestick on the table, she took her and Geordie's empty cups through to the kitchen's scullery, setting them down beside one of the washing bowls. For a moment she stood looking out through the window at the rain. That was still coming down, hitting the flagstones of the path outside with such force the raindrops as long as darning needles were bouncing back up again. With the light from the candle out on the kitchen table casting flickering shadows around the scullery, she transferred her gaze to the window seat.

She laid a hand on her breast, experiencing again the sensations his hand had aroused when he had caressed her. Sighing, she remembered the pleasure his long fingers had given her, how her nipple had stiffened under his touch. Robert Catto had woken something within her, something which had no logic but its own: which was no logic at all. She should not have let it go as far as it had. She should not want it to go even farther. Only she did. She longed for more, to know him completely and to let him know her completely in return.

She knew what happened when a man and a woman lay together. Embarrassed but determined not to let his daughter and only child remain in ignorance, her father Patrick had explained the mechanics to her a long time ago. Although her father had not told her this, she knew too how a man and woman managed to not make a baby. The man pulled out before spilling his seed. Or wore a thin protective sheath. She was pretty sure Robert Catto would know where to get one of those.

So a man and a woman might lie together without being married and no one need ever know. Until the woman did marry and her husband found out on their wedding night that she wasn't a virgin … but there were things a woman could do to stop him finding that out, however dishonourable that might be.

Men are easily fooled. Especially when they want to be. A girl who had come to the shop seeking ointment for a rash on her hand had confided that to her in the course of an eye-opening conversation.

Giving Christian a shy yet knowing smile, she'd left her in no doubt as to how she earned her daily bread. Pity the memory of that conversation brought back to mind how Robert Catto had coupled in the street with a prostitute. He had told her so himself. In a weak moment. And she was seriously considering lying with him? She really must be disordered in her wits.

A pang of yearning for her friends struck her. She wished she could talk all this over with them. She knew Anna Gordon would have plenty to say. She and her sweetheart Alick had not yet lain with each other but, as Anna had put it, a mischievous glint in her eye, *we've taken a few steps along the road*. Her family did not see him as a suitable suitor. Virtually penniless, nor did he see himself as such, despite how hard Anna worked to try to convince him. Christian felt sure Anna's determination would win him and her family over, which made her situation different. Vastly different.

Marriage was never going to be an option for Christian and Robert Catto. Not that he had offered it. Although he had made that strange comment about it looking like he was proposing when he had knelt in front of her the other day. When she had angrily rejected the very idea of it. Absurd in the extreme to even think of marriage when they had known each other for such a short time. Quite apart from everything else which stood in their way.

So an illicit liaison might be all they could ever have. A passionate but short-lived love affair which would end forever when he left Edinburgh and returned to his regiment in Europe. Another treacherous thought crept into her head. What if she gave herself to him and he was disappointed? He had lain with many women, that was obvious. She did not know if she could hope to please him in that way. In any case, she could not see how they would be able to conduct a liaison under Betty's watchful eye or once her father came home.

The desire remained overwhelming. Her brain had filled up with the remembered sensations of yesterday afternoon here in the scullery.

Now it began to offer her a tableau of pictures of herself and Robert Catto in her bedchamber. They were kneeling on the rug in front of the fire. His broad shoulders were barely covered by the sumptuous silk banyan he'd been wearing over his nightshirt when she had called at the guard-house a week or so since and got him out of his bed. It was a gorgeous garment, decorated with red and turquoise dragons rearing up out of a yellow background.

He wore nothing beneath the dressing gown, exposing the light dusting of coppery hairs on his chest. Below that, she was aware of his arousal, growing and stiffening as they knelt there, beginning to brush against her belly. She wore her cambric wrapper, its ribbons untied so that the slightest movement exposed her breasts. Focussed though he was on her face, every so often his eyes dropped appreciatively to those. He had already loosened her hair and was running his fingers through her dark waves. He brought strands of those forward to rest on her breasts, sighing in satisfaction as he drew his thumbs over her nipples. As they sprang into life, she rose to her knees and reached round behind his head to untie his hair ribbon.

In her imagination he took immediate advantage of their positions, kissing one breast and taking a nipple into his mouth, raking it gently with his teeth. For a moment she froze. Where had that rogue thought come from? Other than those few stolen kisses and clumsy brushes of a hand over her clothes, no man had ever made love to her. Yet this imagined lovemaking felt very real, as it was real pleasure which flooded through her at the thought of his mouth on her naked breast. It made her lower her hands, throw her head back and arch her back. 'My other breast too,' she murmured, seeing herself coming forward again and burying her fingers in his own abundance of hair. Glorious gleaming chestnut locks, like silk sliding over her fingers.

She could hear him give a low, full-throated laugh. 'So you won't fall over due to lack of balance? Happy to oblige,' he said, and did.

'I want you above me,' she murmured, her voice slurring.

'Then I'd better take you to bed, hadn't I?' In an instant he had scooped her up, setting her on her feet by the side of the bed only long enough to push her wrapper off her shoulders and discard his own banyan, both garments puddling onto the floor. Lifting her up onto the bed, he climbed in after her and pulled the blue curtains around them. Straddling her, he leaned forward so that his loosened hair trailed over her breasts and down over what lay between her legs. 'Is this what you want?'

'Yes,' she murmured, once more saying the words out loud and feeling herself begin to drift away on a haze of pleasure, feeling his hair glide over her skin. 'Oh, yes … this is what I want…'

And then there would be more kissing and caressing and touching as they gave each other ever more pleasure. They would both grow breathless and then he would enter her—

Her eyes flew open. What was she doing? *What was she doing?* This could never be. She was standing here alone in the scullery, thinking thoughts that could never come true. Ridiculous thoughts. Shameless thoughts. She stared out at the rain. No longer warm, she felt chilled to the bone. She pulled the greeney-blue plaid she wore over her wrapper more tightly around her body.

Robert Catto wore the red coat of the British army. He was an enemy, implacable opponent of the Jacobite Cause. His allegiance was sworn to German Geordie. He was the man who was going to arrest her father for conspiracy to commit treason, the man who was making a list of their friends and fellow supporters of the Cause, gathering evidence against them all. He was the man who had made her promise she would not warn them of the danger he posed … and that last thought wasn't fair. She hadn't withheld a warning because he had coerced her into doing so. She had told them nothing because she wanted to protect him, because of how she felt about him. She had put that in front of trying to protect them. Dear God in Heaven.

Deeply troubled, she stepped back into the kitchen and found Betty bustling into it from the passageway which led from the lobby of the house. Her own personal sheepdog, always checking her lamb was safe from the wolf. Too late for that now. The wolf had more than one form, not least her own awakened desire. It was a good job the older woman couldn't see inside her head.

The hands went to the skinny hips. Betty was all angles. 'Why are not back in your bed, miss?'

'I'm heading there now.' Christian picked up her candlestick. 'Come on, we'll go back upstairs together.'

It had been a long night, one full of terror. Times without number, Joshua imagined the shadows in the coal hole forming themselves into monsters and looming out of the darkness. It was ages after he'd been thrust in here before he'd got his courage up enough to feel his way around. At the expense of a twisted ankle, caught in the frayed edges of an empty sack, he found one small corner free of coal, where he could sit on the hard floor. It was cold under his bottom and legs, so very cold. The air was chilly too, coming in from the outside through the barred and padlocked gate set up at street level through which the coal was delivered. He drew the rough sack he'd tripped over across his body in an attempt to give himself some warmth.

A small bundle of misery, he trembled as he waited for the next monster to take shape out of the shadows. He flinched so many times, sure they were springing forward to attack him, on the point of digging their claws into his skin before throttling the life out of him. Then the thunder and lightning started and the monsters became a hundred times worse. He cried out loud, chewing on his knuckles, tears running down his cheeks. Sobbing, he heard the storm move away and the rain start falling outside, raindrops bouncing into the coal hole. At last, exhausted, he fell asleep.

When he woke, he thanked God. The long and stormy winter's night was over. Daylight showed through the grilled gate and he could see a patch of blue sky. There were no more monsters. Apart from his mistress. A small seed of determination grew within his breast. She would love to hear how scared he had been last night. She would relish it as greedily as she ate sweetmeats, wanting to know every detail, giggling and laughing and smiling her nasty smile.

Joshua threw the coal sack aside, rose to his feet and limped a few steps to relieve himself. He would tell her nothing. Whatever she did to him.

43

Catto's second waking was to a quiet bedchamber and an awareness that the world beyond the shutters felt, if not warm, then considerably milder. Getting out of bed, he slipped on his dressing gown and walked through the small internal courtyard of the building to the guard-room kitchen.

'Captain,' said one of the men sitting eating porridge at the big table. His eyes travelled up and down the extravagant yellow banyan. A seamstress in Antwerp had made it for Catto a couple of years before. For a long while it had seemed too good to wear but he had brought it to Scotland with him all the same. Helping him unpack, Geordie had been very taken by it, asking with boyish directness why he'd brought it with him if he wasn't going to use it. Seeing his point, Catto had shaken out its folds and started wearing it.

'A better day, is it?'

'Much,' replied another man, leaping up and heading for the large pot where the fragrant oatmeal was being kept warm. 'We'll be doing wee Geordie out of a job here. Shall I put you out a bowl, Captain?'

'Not yet. I've a letter to write to be delivered as soon as possible, if you please. I'll just stick my nose out of the door first.'

The snow was almost completely washed away, lingering only in narrow strips close in to the bases of tenement lands. Good. That meant he could get rid of Charlotte Liddell today. He'd dispatched her brother Cosmo and Arthur Menzies to Eastfield on Christmas Eve, on horseback

298

and under escort. Not wanting to give Charlotte anything else to complain about, he'd decided to wait till the road was clear enough to allow the passage of the Liddell coach from Edinburgh to Leith. Catto's eyes lit on Geordie, walking up the High Street through the lightening morning.

'Good morning, Captain. I thought I'd come back and make the porridge.'

'Good morning to you, Geordie. The porridge is already made and being eaten. Have you had your own porridge?'

'Mrs Betty wouldna let me out of the house without eating a big bowl o' it,' Geordie said with a grin. 'The storm was gey spectacular, eh?'

'Indeed,' Catto responded, amused. 'Definitely gey spectacular. Is that what Miss Rankeillor called it?' Then, when Geordie nodded: 'What's that you've got in your pocket?'

Geordie brought out *The Adventures of Robinson Crusoe*. 'Miss Kirsty says I can borrow this,' he said proudly, holding the book out to Catto. 'Once I've read it and taken it back, I can borrow another of her books.'

'I've read this.' Catto turned the book over in his hand. 'It's very good.'

'That's what she says. Although she doesna like Mr Defoe very much.'

'Did she say why?' Catto queried, even more amused. He wouldn't have expected her to like Daniel Defoe, who had been an undercover agent of the English government gathering information in Scotland and influencing Scottish opinion in favour of the Union of the Parliaments almost forty years before.

'Only that it was a long story and she would tell me another time.'

'Well, that's something for you to look forward to. As for today, you can go back to Infirmary Street and let ... eh, Mrs Betty ... give you your dinner and supper too and stay over down there again tonight. I don't expect there to be much going on here today. Do you want to leave the book here? I'll put it in a safe place.'

'That would be grand, Captain. Nothing I can do for you before I go back to Infirmary Street?'

'Not today, lad,' Catto said. 'Off you go.'

He went back into the guard-house, put the book on a shelf above his desk and wrote his letter, handing it over to one of the guards for immediate delivery to the Liddell town house. He could not have asked Geordie to take it on his way back to Infirmary Street for fear Charlotte Liddell might see and recognize the boy. The letter instructed the unpleasant Miss Liddell to make herself ready to leave Edinburgh today, informing her that he would call at half past twelve of the clock to personally accompany her down to Leith. Which was more than she deserved but that way he would know she had definitely gone. He had chosen the timing carefully, to make her departure from Edinburgh at a time when most people would still be sleeping off the excesses of Yule Day or indoors lingering over their meridian.

❖

Geordie was a wee bit disappointed by the rise in temperature. There were no more patches of ice for him to slide along, only chilly puddles. He was taking a different way back to Infirmary Street than he normally did, hoping to find some more ice. There wasn't much, so he was playing a game of his own devising which involved stepping on and off the plainstanes with a certain rhythm onto the causeway. His head snapped up when he heard a voice calling to him.

'Geordie!'

It seemed to be coming from between two big houses. Curious, he crossed over the causeway and walked along the narrow strip of grass between them. The call came again, seemingly from beneath his feet. 'Geordie!'

❖

Catto stood on the front doorstep of the Liddell house, perplexed. The house was locked, the shutters closed. It was shortly before half past twelve. He tirled the pin, heard the bell jangling through what sounded unnervingly like an empty house. There were certainly no footsteps walking towards him on the other side of the door. He rang the bell again, waited. A third attempt produced the same result as the previous two. Nothing.

He walked round to the kitchen door and hammered on the solid wood with his fist. No reply there either. He tried again. Silence from inside the house. He stepped back and looked up at the windows on the ground floor and the one above it. They too were shuttered. Had Charlotte Liddell gone off to Leith on her own, taking her entire household with her, exercising what power she had by not waiting for him to escort her there? His mouth tightened. 'Twas the sort of petty revenge he might have expected her to take. Petty, but for some reason he was finding her absence unsettling.

There was a coach house and stable off to one side. The doors of both were closed and padlocked but he put his eye to a gap in the wooden slats of each in turn and saw no coach and no horses. The plan had been for him to travel in the Liddell coach only as far as *The White Horse,* where Sergeant Livingstone would have Tam tacked up and saddled for Catto to ride beside the coach on the way down to Leith. He had no desire to spend any more time in close proximity to Charlotte Liddell than he absolutely had to.

He stood for a moment, pondering his next move. He could still head for *The White Horse* and then Leith but it occurred to him that Charlotte Liddell might have decided to go instead to Eastfield, the Liddell country house beyond Musselburgh and Prestonpans. Her arrogance would allow her to think she need not obey his orders that she should go to Lady Bruce's house in Leith. Mentally kicking himself for not having realized this before, he considered his options.

It would take him an hour to get to Leith and about the same amount of time again to reach Eastfield. He might not find her in either place. She could have taken herself off somewhere else entirely. Even as he stood here, she could be spreading malicious gossip about Christian Rankeillor. Even as he stood here, she could be doing worse than that—

Out of nowhere, panic seized him. Like some mythical and malevolent bird, it seemed to be spreading huge black wings above his head. For a moment he was paralysed with fear. Then he turned on his heel and headed as quickly as he dared to Infirmary Street. Even with the streets as empty as they were, he had to remind himself not to break into a run. That might draw attention from inside a house or close.

As soon as the opportunity presented itself, he vaulted over a stone wall and ran through gardens and courtyards until he reached the wall of the Physic Garden. Scaling that, he ran along the paths through the herb and vegetable beds, dormant at this time of year. Christian Rankeillor opened the kitchen door to him.

'You're all right,' he blurted out, relief flooding through him. 'You're all right!'

'And you're out of breath. Have you been running? Why wouldn't I be all right? What's wrong?'

'There's nothing wrong. Not now.' For he would not tell her of his unreasoning fear that some evil had befallen her at Charlotte Liddell's hands. Ridiculous to even think such a thing. 'Something wrong here, though?' he queried archly, catching his breath and registering her uncertain look. 'Another stuck door? Your housekeeper's broomstick snapped in two by the lightning last night and her distraught over the loss?'

She didn't laugh. He glanced in the direction of the scullery before looking back at her, his eyes narrowing. 'Second thoughts?' he asked. 'About you and me?'

'Yes. No. Maybe. I'm confused about it all. Oh, and I do not want to hurt you!'

She already had. He came into the back lobby, closed the door and leaned back against it, winded. She might as well have punched him in the gut. 'And yesterday? I rather thought you were enjoying yourself as much as I was.'

'I was. Too much. I can't stop thinking about it. Or you. Shameless thoughts.' Her hands flew up to her mouth, as though to stop the words. 'Och, and I wasn't going to tell you about those!' She cast a swift glance over her shoulder.

'They can't see us from where they are.' Lifting his chin, he indicated the kitchen beyond the small back lobby.

'No,' she agreed, her voice soft and low, 'but Betty has ears like a hare.'

Proving her point, the housekeeper called out. 'Who's that at the back door? I'm just putting out our meal. We're no' wanting it to get cold.'

Christian Rankeillor half-turned and called back. 'It's Captain Catto, Betty. We're just coming through.'

He grabbed her arm before she could move. 'We need to talk about this.'

She looked up at him with sorrowful eyes. 'I don't know what there is to say. You're going to arrest my father and you're gathering evidence against our friends. Are you and I not unsuited to each other in every possible way?'

'Where's Geordie got to?' Catto asked as he looked at the kitchen table around which everyone but the boy was gathered. There was a large platter holding slices of the meat left over from the day before, plus serving bowls piled high with hot vegetables, steam rising off them. 'Not like him to be late for a meal.' Unsettled though he was by the brief conversation he'd had with Kirsty Rankeillor, he tried a smile at Alice Smart, Geordie's sister. She dropped her eyes.

Kirsty Rankeillor looked surprised. 'Geordie left after breakfast.

Insisted on going back up to the guard-house as soon as he'd had his porridge this morning. Said you might be needing him to cook or see to the fires or run some errands for you.'

Catto swung round to her, away from the table at which everyone had so abruptly gone so very quiet. 'Aye, and I sent him back down here for the day. Told him he could stay over again here tonight. That was hours ago.'

'He's not here,' Christian Rankeillor said. 'He hasn't come back. Betty, Tibby, Alice,' she asked in turn, 'have you seen Geordie since he left this morning?'

They all shook their heads.

'Then,' Catto asked, 'where the Devil is he?'

Alice Smart raised her eyes to his face. They were full of terror. For the second time that morning, fear clutched at Catto's heart. It took a huge effort of will to soften his voice. 'Alice,' he said, addressing the girl as gently as he could, 'what do you fear has happened to Geordie?'

❖

Geordie was in the Liddell coach, kneeling painfully in the footwell between the cushioned seats on either side of it. Joshua was in the same position, facing away from him. There was barely space enough for the two boys. Both were gagged. Charlotte Liddell's footman had done that, grabbing Geordie as he approached the grille of the coal hole where Joshua was imprisoned, Charlotte Liddell at his heels. The man had grabbed Geordie with one beefy arm crooked around his neck, pulling off the boy's little knitted cap in the process. When his golden waves were revealed, Charlotte Liddell laughed out loud.

The footman had gagged Joshua too and shoved both boys roughly into the coach. While they knelt on the hard floor, Charlotte sat comfortably on the cushions, her legs propped up on the long-cushioned seat facing her. Geordie's cramped position was giving him pins and needles in his legs and feet. The sensation was well-nigh unbearable, only he had no choice but to bear it. Each time he tried to move even as little as he could to ease the pain, Charlotte gave him a thump in the back with her heels. He thought Joshua must have the same problem. He was getting the heel thumps too.

Terrified though Geordie was, it was a huge relief when the rocking coach finally came to a stop and they were dragged out of it as roughly as they'd been thrown in, their gags pulled off. Both boys staggered to their feet, only to stumble and fall down again. 'Cramp in my leg,' Geordie managed, again hardly able to bear the sensation. 'Me too,' said Joshua, lying on the hard ground next to him. 'I'm sorry, Geordie, I'm so sorry you're back here because of me!'

That earned him a cuff round the ear. He was dragged off by a couple of men, while Geordie was left where he was. He struggled up onto his elbows, the ground achingly cold beneath his hands, recognizing he was at the pithead of the Eastfield mine. The row of miners' cottage where he'd grown up were somewhere behind him. The big house lay in the other direction, a few hundred yards away. The footman who had grabbed him at the Liddell town house was hurrying towards it. He and Charlotte's lady's maid had been travelling behind the coach in a second coach.

Behind Eastfield House, another few hundred yards again, the sea glittered in the winter sun. The light bouncing back up from the dark blue waves was dazzling. A tall shadow fell across his face, temporarily blinding him. Someone kicked him in the side. 'On your feet, you wee shite,' growled a rough voice. 'No' much o' a man, are ye? Despite your fancy clothes. Did ye steal those?'

'No,' Geordie protested, realizing with horror that he was looking up at one of the cruellest overseers in the mine. 'No! They were a present!'

He was hauled to his feet, feeling as if his arm was being wrenched out of its socket. This overseer was a strong man, broad-shouldered as well as tall. 'Who would give a wee shite like you a present?'

he demanded, spitting the words into the boy's face. 'You're worth nothing tae naebody.'

Swaying, but determined on staying upright, Geordie blinked up at his tormentor. There were two other men standing behind him. In vain, Geordie scanned their faces. There were miners here who had shown him kindness in the past, but not these three. He looked at Charlotte, standing watching this happen, and saw he could not expect any mercy from her. She was relishing it all.

Confusing him, the overseer smiled at him. 'Those clothes might be worth a bob or two, eh?' The smile grew broader. 'Strip the wee bastard, lads. As naked as the day he had the misfortune to be born at Eastfield. And then bind him tight. Over there.'

Geordie moaned. He couldn't help it. He knew without having to look what was over there. Maybe if he didn't look this wouldn't be happening. He couldn't shut out the picture in his mind's eye. Two solid upright posts, around six feet tall. A crossbar linking them, from near the top of one post to the other. Ropes hanging down to bind his wrists. He had seen men being flogged there.

Now it was his turn.

44

Christian was crouching beside Alice Smart, holding one small and trembling hand. The attention of everyone in the kitchen was focussed on Geordie's sister. She raised her eyes to Christian's face, her voice an agonised whisper. 'I'm feart they've found him, Miss Kirsty. I'm feart they've found him and taken him back to Eastfield.'

Robert Catto sat down on the chair Christian had recently vacated. Concentrated though she was on Geordie's sister, a stray thought flitted through her brain. Sensitive. He's sensitive, knows it won't help Alice for him to stand there towering over us all.

'Why do you think that, Alice?' she probed gently. 'Why do you think they might have found him?'

'I just have this feeling, miss. This horrible feeling. In here,' she added, laying her free hand against her small breasts, then all but jumped out of her skin as one of the brass bells high up on the kitchen wall jangled.

'Noo there's someone at the front door,' Betty said. 'I'll go and see who's disturbing oor peace this time.' Despite the comment, the look she cast Robert Catto wasn't entirely hostile. Rising to her feet, she gave Christian's shoulder an encouraging little pat. She was back a few moments later with the announcement that she had shown Mr Charles Paterson into the library.

'Tell him I'll be with him shortly,' Christian said without looking up.

'It's no' you he wants to see. It's this one,' Betty replied, jerking a thumb towards Robert Catto. That statement had both Christian and Robert Catto spinning round to look at the housekeeper. The expression on Betty's face was guarded. 'I'm thinking maybe the two o' you should go through and see him. We'll look after Alice.'

❖

He wanted to scream. He wanted to throw his head back and yell for help to the heavens. But he would not. No one who would help him was able to hear him. He blinked again and when he opened his eyes saw that the overseer was now holding a cat o' nine tails, strips of leather knotted at their end. The tails were tangled and the man was concentrated on straightening each one out.

Geordie did not think what was about to happen to happen to him could get any worse. Until, stumbling out of the big house in the wake of the footman, fou' as puggies in the middle of the day, Cosmo Liddell and Arthur Menzies of Edmonstone whooped and came running towards Geordie and their sister. 'We're not too late to see the fun, are we?' Cosmo asked.

'Just in time,' Charlotte said. 'You can join in, if you like. I'd lay a few strokes on myself but I don't have the strength to hurt him enough. You might, Arthur.'

'Happy to watch,' Edmonstone said, giving Charlotte a leering look. 'More than happy. But why don't you give it a go, Cosmo?'

'Don't mind if I do.'

Bound now to the frame, shivering naked in the cold, Geordie's bare feet were on the cold hard ground. When they'd stripped him they'd taken his shoes and knee-length knitted stockings too. Closing his eyes tight, he prayed he wouldn't wet himself. Or worse. He didn't, but he bit down hard on his lip when Cosmo Liddell lashed him. Once. Twice. Three times. He was catapulted into agony.

'Somewhat fatiguing.' Cosmo Liddell's drawling voice seemed to be coming from a long way off. 'Take over, would you?'

Lashed then by a man used to hard physical labour, the pain grew indescribably worse, the rough ropes searing his wrists. Geordie lost count of how many times he was struck. Twenty, maybe more, he wasn't entirely sure. He was aware only that someone close by was sobbing, and knew it was Joshua.

'His turn now!' Charlotte Liddell shrieked. 'His turn!' Seeing her through a blur of pain, Geordie thought she looked like she was dancing with joy.

'Just a wee minutie, mistress.' Cold water hit him. It was freezing cold, making him draw in his breath on a hiss. The pain raging in the welts rising on his back shot up to a new intensity. The ropes fastening his wrists were untied but there was no mercy in the action. It was done roughly and without care. As Charlotte Liddell had made Joshua watch his punishment, now he was to be forced to watch whatever she had in store for his friend. One of the men held Geordie by his skinny and aching shoulders and smacked the side of his face when he tried to turn his head away.

'More water!' yelled Charlotte. 'We're going to need a few buckets!' In a moment or two they were standing ready, five wooden buckets, filled up and set down so hastily some of the water was spilling over their edges. What she wants, she gets, Geordie thought hazily. He hated her voice. So shrill. The opposite of Miss Kirsty's soft tones and kind manner.

'Not that it'll turn the little black slug white!' Charlotte cried, watching gleefully as Joshua was stripped naked and the first bucket of water thrown over him. She clasped her hands together in delight. 'Go on, he's not clean enough yet! Can't let him into the big house till all the dust from the coal hole is washed off! More water!'

That was the moment Geordie felt something die inside him. He knew what it was. Hope.

❖

'I'm wondering how you knew I was here, Mr Paterson.'

Christian looked at Robert Catto where he stood with one shoulder propped against the corner of the high mantelpiece of the library fireplace, his arms folded. He sounded so haughty. Not so long ago she had thought that was all he was. Arrogant. Always in control of himself and the situation. Now she knew better. He still sounded haughty. He had walked into the library as though he owned the place. Standing warming his hands in front of the fire, Charles Paterson had been obliged to move to accommodate him and stood now somewhat awkwardly in the middle of the hearth rug. The lawyer might be a clever talker but he was a nice man too. Whatever had brought him here today, he didn't deserve to be greeted by this haughtiness from Robert Catto.

'Perhaps,' she said, 'we should be more concerned as to why Mr Paterson is here. Would you care to sit down, sir? And may I offer you some refreshment?'

'I'm fine, Miss Kirsty. Are you?' The question was phrased a little abruptly. Yet it might still be mere politeness. Somehow she knew it wasn't.

'I'm well,' she told him. 'I trust Mrs Paterson is also well?'

'Elspeth is fine,' he said. Worried though he looked, a smile lit up his brown eyes as he said his wife's name.

'Now that we have the pleasantries out of the way,' came a sarcastic voice, 'I'd appreciate an answer to my question, Mr Paterson. I repeat, how did you know you would find me here?'

'Och, stop growling at people,' Christian muttered, swinging round to glare at him, her hands going to her hips. She must have learned that from Betty. Someone laughed. It wasn't Robert Catto. She turned back and saw that Charles Paterson looked amused, albeit somewhat puzzled.

'Won't you sit down, Mr Paterson?' she asked again, gesturing towards one of the two armchairs which flanked the fireplace. 'And may I pour you a wee glass of something? Brandy, perhaps, to arm you against the cold when you go back out?' She gestured towards the decanters and upturned glasses which sat on a tall high table to the right of the armchair in which she had invited him to sit.

'Thank you,' he said. 'That would be most acceptable.'

She poured the brandy, lifting the decanter in a silent question to Robert Catto, who shook his head. Christian handed Charles Paterson his glass, sat down in one of the armchairs and gestured to the lawyer to sit opposite her. She was very aware of the brooding presence beside her. It felt like Robert Catto was standing guard over her. Although whether he was her protector or her jailer she wasn't sure.

Sweeping back the folds of his cloak, Charles Paterson took a swig of brandy and set the glass down on the high table next to him. He dug into the pocket of the frock coat he wore beneath the cloak and brought out a letter. 'I received this missive this morning. From Miss Charlotte Liddell. It concerns a boy by the name of George Smart.'

Christian and Robert Catto spoke at the same time. 'Geordie?'

'You both know him?' Charles Paterson looked from Catto to Christian.

'Aye,' she said, 'we both know him.'

The lawyer made an indeterminate sound in his throat before directing his next words to Robert Catto. 'I'm afraid Miss Liddell has taken agin you, Captain. Is accusing you of harbouring two fugitives, to wit, a brother and sister by the names of Alice and Geordie Smart. I'm guessing the former is the girl about whom you recently spoke to me.'

'Are you indeed?' Robert Catto raised his russet eyebrows.

Charles Paterson responded with a weary look. 'Miss Liddell says the Smarts are both the lawful property of the Liddell family, bound from birth to perpetual servitude, and that in harbouring them – that is the word she uses – you have broken the law and thus shown yourself unfit to be Captain of the Town Guard.'

Christian was aware that the man standing beside her had gone very still.

'The law is with her,' Charles Paterson said into the silence which had settled on the room.

Christian glanced up at Robert Catto and saw him draw in a breath. 'And you are a lawyer.'

'Indeed.' Paterson lifted the letter he held. 'One who has been officially informed of this allegation against you.'

Robert Catto threw his head back. 'If you intend to try to enforce the law, I would have to point out there's a bit of an obstacle in your way, Mr Paterson. Me. As the chief enforcer in Edinburgh of said law.' He jabbed his thumb into his chest to reinforce his point.

'Which is all well and good now,' Paterson responded quietly. 'But what happens when Provost Coutts returns to Edinburgh and when Charlotte Liddell starts shouting even louder about this to other prominent citizens? You might be risking not only your captaincy of the Town Guard but your whole military career over this.'

'Sometimes we all have to take risks, Mr Paterson. As I think you know only too well.'

Paterson's eyes narrowed. 'And have you been taking risks since the Daft Friday ball?' He looked at Christian. 'You too, Miss Kirsty? I'm still puzzled as to why you felt you had to don male apparel before you took a letter to the post office. I do not think you were indulging in some revelry associated with the Daft Days. You're too serious-minded a girl for that. I'd also like fine to ken what's been going on in this house over the last few days.' He looked at Catto and then at Christian again. 'Even if I'm not entirely sure to which one of you I should be directing my questions. I ask again, are you all right, lass?'

'I'm fine, Mr Paterson,' Christian began, leaning forward in her chair. 'Truly. The situation is however somewhat complicated.'

'And at the same time very simple,' Robert Catto said. 'I'm just trying to...' He paused, clearly searching for the right word. 'I'm just trying to *rescue* a young lad and lass, a brother and sister, who deserve a better life than the one they've had up until now.' Unfolding his arms, he raised his hands, palms upwards. It was the gesture of a man whose patience and ability to dissemble had been stretched to the limit. 'And right at this moment, I've had enough of secrets and lies. Right at this moment, I'm sick of the whole damn thing. Please don't insult us both by asking me what I mean.'

'I have no intention of doing so.'

'I cannot strike any sort of a bargain with you.'

Charles Paterson could raise disdainful eyebrows too. 'I'm not asking you to.'

'Nor suggest a mutually beneficial arrangement?'

'I'm suggesting a truce, Mr Catto. In the interests of the greater good. In the interests of humanity. In the interests of this young lad and lass.'

Robert Catto studied him for a moment. 'What else does Charlotte Liddell say in that letter?' He spoke abruptly, without any of his usual poise. Strong feelings, Christian thought, such strong feelings raging below the surface.

'It would appear Miss Charlotte has taken the law into her own hands. She writes that she has reclaimed one half of Liddell property. And that she requires me to reclaim the second half.' Paterson's face was grim. 'That people can be regarded as property in our day and age is an abomination. I have always thought so. Whether they be African slaves or home-grown perpetual servants, no more than serfs.' He unfolded the letter and leaned forward, holding it out. 'Read it if you like.'

Catto stepped towards him, took it, scanned it, and handed it back. 'You are aware what might be going to happen to Geordie Smart, Mr Paterson?' He glanced over at the long-case clock which stood in one corner of the room. It was approaching one o'clock. 'What might already have happened to him?'

'I'm aware of the rights of the coal owners, aye. And I'm concerned to stop any harm befalling the boy.' Charles Paterson's mouth set in a grim line. 'Or any further harm. That's why I'm here right now. This letter was delivered to me a little over an hour ago. When I didn't find you at the guard-house, I told young Archie Liddell a little of what I was concerned about. He directed me to *The White Horse* where your Sergeant Livingstone told me I might find you here.' He too looked over at the clock. 'Time would seem to be of the essence.'

Robert Catto nodded grimly. 'Yet you are indeed a lawyer, Mr Paterson. You are duty bound to uphold the law.'

'So are you.'

'I'll take my chances.'

Charles Paterson gave him an odd little smile. 'As well as being a lawyer, I am also a husband. God willing, one who is soon to become a father.' He crumpled up the letter he held, leaned forward and threw the paper into the glowing coals. All three of them watched as it burned, its words consumed by a little spurt of flame. 'I shall deny it ever reached me. That should buy you some time. As for the other matter...'

'What other matter is that, Mr Paterson?'

'The one which will have to be resolved after this is all over. I should like to hear from your own lips that Miss Rankeillor is in no danger.'

'She is in no danger from me, sir. I intend to take steps to ensure no danger threatens her from any other quarter. As far as that is within my power.'

'And her father?'

'As I have already assured Miss Rankeillor, I shall do what I can for him.'

'I have your word on both of these?'

'Aye, you have my word.'

Charles Paterson gave him a little nod of acknowledgement. 'May I suggest you do not don your uniform before you go to Eastfield? Likewise, whichever of your men you take with you. If you are going to take the law into your own hands, it might help that you do so when not dressed as an officer of that law.'

'Thank you, Mr Paterson. I had already made that decision.'

'Then good luck, sir.' He turned towards Christian, lifted her hand and bowed over it. 'Miss Kirsty. Please be aware I am at your service should you need my help in any way.'

❖

Christian returned from seeing Charles Paterson out, closed the library door, put her hands behind her and leaned back against them.

'I must go,' Robert Catto said. 'Before the day is very much older.'

'Not until you tell me what it is you and Mr Paterson fear may already have befallen Geordie. Why is time of the essence?'

He'd been pacing the library floor. Now he stopped, turning to look across the room at her. 'Don't you remember what Geordie said that day you came to the guard-house and I discovered he'd been hiding his sister there?' He grimaced. 'I can hear his voice in my head right now.'

'Remind me.'

'He said that of all things, he dreaded going back down the pit again.' He drew in a breath. 'That wasn't the worst of it. He said they would flog him before they condemned him to that fate. Which punishment the law allows.'

'Dear God,' Christian breathed. 'He did say that.' Pushing herself away from the door, she walked forward, pulled out a chair from the big table and sat down rather more quickly than she had intended. As she had done earlier with Alice Smart, Catto walked forward and crouched in front of her, reaching for her hands. 'But he's such a skinny wee thing,' she said in a cracked voice. 'Surely no one would flog a young boy like Geordie!'

'I shall not lie to you, Kirsty. We are talking here about Charlotte Liddell and her brother Cosmo and his friends. None of them are kind people.' He grimaced. 'Which is vastly to understate the case. I think perhaps they are the sort who take pleasure in the suffering of others.'

'Dear God,' she said again, placing the back of her hand against her mouth. Catto took it from there to his mouth, daring to press a gentle kiss upon it. 'Why would Charlotte even bother herself about Geordie, or know where he was to be found?'

'That's a mystery,' he said, releasing her hand. 'Perhaps something as random as spotting him in the street. It occurs to me that he might have passed the Liddell town house this morning coming back down here, depending on which way he went. Dammit!' He rose to his feet and took a step or two back. 'I should have warned him to avoid it long before now. He wouldn't necessarily have known where the house is.'

'You've been there this morning?'

He nodded. 'All locked and shuttered. I was to have escorted Charlotte Liddell to Leith today, to stay with Lady Bruce of Kinross for an indefinite period. I thought that might have kept the unpleasant Miss Liddell in check.'

Christian threw him up a speaking look. 'Poor Lady Magdalen. She doesn't deserve that. What do you intend to do now?'

'Head for Eastfield. Once you tell me how to get there. I know roughly where it is but not exactly.'

'I shall draw you a wee map of the final mile or so. Will that suffice?' When he nodded, she turned, drew paper and pencil towards her and started immediately on the task. He waited while she completed the sketch and handed it up to him. 'Is that all clear?'

He scanned the paper. 'Admirably so.'

'If Geordie is there, you will go against the law and forcibly remove him?'

'Aye,' he said, neatly folding the paper twice and tucking it into his pocket.

'But Mr Paterson is right, is he not? You are an officer of the law. It is highly likely you will bring enormous trouble upon yourself.'

'So be it,' he said grimly. 'I promised Geordie he would be flogged only over my dead body. If it has already happened, that promise has been broken. But they're not going to do it again and they're not going to send him back down the pit.' He muttered, as much to himself as her. 'I'll have to hide him somewhere. Though God knows where.'

Christian sat up straighter in the upright chair. 'He'll come here, of course. Apart from the necessity of keeping him concealed, if they have...' She faltered before she could say the word. 'If they have done this unspeakable thing to him, we can best look after him here.'

'Even though that might compound your – I should say *our* – current difficulties? Which are already complicated enough.'

'Och, Robert, need you even ask?'

'No,' he said, answering that wail of protest. 'It was indeed a foolish question on my part.'

'Which of your men will you take with you?'

'None of them.'

She gripped the back of the chair. 'You surely do not mean to go to Eastfield alone!'

'If I am unlucky, what I am about to do may raise a great noise. I will not have anyone else suffer the consequences of my actions.'

'Robert, please do not go alone! Archie Liddell would go with you, I am sure!'

'And subject himself to more insults and possibly damage to his future career and livelihood at the behest of his detestable cousins?' Robert Catto shook his head. 'No. My plan, however, is to do this covertly. Not through any fears of a warm reception but to keep Cosmo and Charlotte Liddell in the dark for as long as possible. They may very well have their suspicions once they discover Geordie is no longer at Eastfield but they will not have any proof of how he got away.'

'You are sure you will be able to find him and bring him back to Edinburgh?'

'I'm sure. I shall approach Eastfield only after darkness has fallen.

Which it more or less will have by the time I get there. I shall scout out the situation, find out where Geordie is, allow the night to wear on a little so that it's fully dark, and then bring him home.'

'Will that be so easy? To find out where he is, I mean?'

'I do not think it will be very difficult. They will not have thought they need to work too hard to conceal where he is. I shall not come back without him, I promise you that. You can tell Alice the same thing.'

She looked up at him. 'You're a good man, Robert Catto.'

He tilted his head a little to one side. 'Despite what you told me when I got here, does that mean I've earned myself a kiss for luck?'

She stood up immediately. Wrapping one arm about her waist, he pressed his lips against hers. Then he was gone.

'Livingstone. What the Devil do you think you're doing?'

Swinging up onto the horse standing next to Tam, Catto already mounted on the sturdy garron, the Sergeant's blue gaze was very direct. It always was. 'Coming with you, young Captain Catto.' Like Catto, he wore a short sword and had a brace of pistols at his belt.

'Oh no, you're not.'

'Oh aye he is,' came a female voice. The Sergeant's wife handed him up a small pewter flask. 'A nip of brandy,' Marjorie Livingstone said. 'The lad might need it.' Then, when Catto looked down at her: 'What do you think our bairns would say if they knew we hadna tried to help their friend? Good luck, Captain. You too, husband.'

45

He wanted his sister. He wanted the Captain. He wanted Christian Rankeillor. Miss Kirsty would know how to take away the pain raging in his back. She would bathe it in cool water to stem the fire, pat it dry with the softest of cloths, gently dab salve on his cuts and bruises. For a few moments he imagined her doing all of that, longing so much for her healing touch he thought he could almost feel it, until the pain in his ravaged back caught fire again.

Try as he might, he could not stop a sob from bursting out through his cracked lips. He had bitten down hard when the leather cords had hit his back. As they had been flogging him, he had damaged himself. Hadn't managed to stop himself from crying out. By the fifth crack of the whip he had been screaming. He was a daft gowk, a stupid wee fool. And now he was back where had started. Back in this place he hated so much. Back in this place he feared so much.

They'd untied him and thrown him face down onto the beaten earth floor of an old hut, a second bucket of cold water thrown over his bloody back, tossing him a ragged pair of breeches and a dirty old shirt before they closed the door on him. He thought of Sergeant Crichton yesterday, telling him he looked like a fine young gentleman in his smart clothes, and he let out a sob.

They'd told him he'd be going back down the pit tomorrow morning, doing his old job as a trapper. A boy's job, or a job for someone who was good for nothing else. Opening and closing a trap door, over and over again. That kept air circulating around the mine, sending it along the passages where the miners dug out the coal. It was lonely work. You could barely hear the men in the coal seam, see only the faintest glow of their lamps. He'd always been left without one.

'That'll keep you quiet, you wee shite,' said the overseer with a laugh. 'You'll be back down there in the dark wi' the rats.' He laughed again. 'And the ghosts.'

The low glow from along the coal seams served only to cast deeper shadows. It was months since he'd left the mine but in his head he could still hear the sound of the trap door opening and closing, shifting the air. It was like an unearthly sigh. On and on it went. Open the door. Close the door. Hear the sigh. People did say there were ghosts down below the earth. Once, many years ago, a passageway had caved in, burying three men. They'd never got their bodies out. Before Geordie's time, but he'd grown up hearing the story.

Footsteps. He was sure he could hear footsteps, moving stealthily towards him. Blind terror seized him.

The moon was riding high in the night sky now, which was both a blessing and a curse. They could see the road or the path in front of them but they could be seen too. To avoid houses and inns they'd taken a circuitous route at several points along the way, choosing to leave Edinburgh under the lee of Salisbury Crags and Arthur's Seat. They'd picked a path through whin bushes, skirted around mining villages. It all took more time than it might have.

Darkness had fallen shortly before four o'clock. They heard a distant church bell chiming the hour. Catto tried telling himself Geordie might yet be unharmed and that the end of daylight would stop any flogging from happening until the next day. Reaching the coast not too far west of Musselburgh, they stopped to let the horses take a drink from a burn which flowed down over a shingle beach. As Tam dipped his head, Catto clapped the horse's warm neck under his wiry mane and gazed out over the German Ocean. The moon lit up a silvery path through the dark waves. You could almost imagine you might be able to walk along it. Or dance.

'So much beauty in the world,' Livingstone said. 'If you look for it.'

Catto turned to him. 'Aye. But so much ugliness too. As we both know.'

'So you keep looking for the beauty,' Livingstone said. 'And the goodness.'

'As you did?'

'Aye. As I did. And found them in my wife and bairns. And a peaceful and convivial life as far away from the battlefield as I could get.'

'I do not think such a choice is open to me.'

'Perhaps you only have to be willing to make it, young Captain Catto. And find a woman who's willing to make it with you. One who's worth the effort.' Then, as Catto looked at his companion in the moonlight: 'I'm thinking you may already have met that person. Here in Edinburgh.'

'This is a very odd conversation for you and I to be having, Sergeant. Besides which, I thought you disapproved.'

Livingstone shook his powerful head. 'No. But I think you need to be cautious. Are the young lady's feelings as strong as your own?'

'Yesterday I thought they were. Today I am not so sure.'

'Are your intentions honourable?' The sternness with which the question was asked reminded Catto that Livingstone had not only two young sons but also a young daughter.

He turned his head to gaze out at the sea before swinging back round to the Sergeant. 'I wish to God my intentions could be honourable!'

'Genuinely?'

'Aye. Genuinely.'

'So it's more than desire. More than lust.'

'Much good may that do me. How can I hope for more when I have her under arrest and I'm about to arrest her father?' The despair he had felt after seeing Anna Gordon off at Leith came rushing back, the sense that he was an instrument in the destruction of other people's lives. He thought back to what Christian Rankeillor had said to him earlier in the day and knew she had spoken nothing but the truth. He repeated her words now to Livingstone. 'She and I are unsuited to each other in every possible way.'

'Except in the only way that really matters. Love.'

'Love does not last,' Catto said harshly. 'It dies. The people we love die. People betray each other.'

'Not everyone does,' the Sergeant said in his soft West Highland lilt, 'and the people we love do indeed die. But they live on in our hearts and minds. Do you think my Marjorie and I do not realize the chances are she'll spend years on her own once I'm gone?'

'But you're prepared to trade that for what you have now?'

'Aye. Because we both ken that true love never dies. It's the only thing that does last. Sometimes it has to be fought for, forbye. Not retreat when it finds boulders in its path. Find a way round those.'

'You and Mrs Livingstone had to fight to be together?'

'Aye. Her mother and father were not best pleased when she told them she wanted to marry a man so much older than her. I wasna so very sure either. Loved her to distraction but worried that such a pretty young lass would regret marrying me.' The Sergeant's smile flashed in the moonlight. 'She gave me a good talking-to. And has told me and shown me every day since how much she loves me.'

'And you her, Livingstone,' Catto responded, envying him.

The Sergeant gave a soft laugh. 'Aye. And me her. One thing I do know. If you find true love in this world, you hold on to it with both hands. Nor do you give it up without a fight.' He spoke quietly but with absolute conviction.

❖

Footsteps. Heading towards him. He was sure he could hear them. Geordie sat up, the abrupt movement sending shooting pains through his back. 'Who's there?'

There was no answer, and the footsteps had stopped too. His heart was thumping with fear. He peered into the gloom of the hut but could make nothing out. After a few moment's aching silence apart from his own panicked breathing, he felt the tension slowly leave his body. He had imagined the footsteps, thought the ghost of one of those buried miners was coming to get him, climbing up out of the pit during the night. What could a ghost do to him that hadn't already been done?

Another sob escaped him. His nose was running too. He lifted a shaky hand to wipe it and his mouth in one swipe. Not very gentlemanly. Then again, he was a long way from being a gentleman. Although he'd thought he'd looked like one yesterday, when he had got dressed up in his braw new clothes and he and the Captain had set off for Infirmary Street.

Only yesterday but a world away from where he was now. He'd never get back there to sit in that warm kitchen. Hoping Alice was going to mend, grateful beyond words that she had found refuge. His stomach full of goose and plum pudding and all manner of fine food. When he had sung *Balulalow* and the Captain had said *bravo* and everyone had clapped. It had been a grand day, the best of his young life.

He'd never get back there. Only a few miles away from here, yet he'd never get back there. He might as well give in and give up.

Only a few miles. The words echoed round his head. Over and over again. Then they were joined by other words.

Only a few miles. No distance at all. Not far to walk.

Geordie drew in a long breath. Only a few miles. He'd made it out of here once before. He could do it again.

❖

A few hundred yards away at the big house, Joshua was wracked with guilt. If he hadn't spotted Geordie and called out to him, the other boy wouldn't have crossed the causeway to investigate, wouldn't have been there at exactly the same moment as the footman opened the kitchen door, Charlotte Liddell at his heels. In the poky windowless cupboard which served as his bedchamber, Joshua couldn't stop thinking about Geordie. He'd overheard what had been said about sending the other boy back down the pit tomorrow, back into the darkness.

'Leave him where he is tonight,' Charlotte had ordered, her brother and his friend so guttered they could barely speak. She'd probably joined in with them by now. With no window onto the outside world, Joshua had no idea what time it was. It felt as though a few hours had passed, so it might be early evening. His stomach was growling with hunger. He hadn't eaten since breakfast the day before. He was cold too, although he'd pulled on his nightshirt and wrapped a blanket around himself as soon as they'd closed the door and left him alone here.

Geordie would have had his breakfast today but Joshua shivered at the thought of the other boy spending tonight as he had spent the previous one. It would be so much colder out there in that hut, and very dark. They would have left him on his own now too, part of his punishment for having dared to run away from Eastfield. Joshua wondered if the other boy was as scared of the dark as he was. He was more terrified than ever after last night in the coal hole.

The thought of Geordie out there in the cold and dark with an aching back and a long night ahead of him was unbearable. But there was nothing Joshua could do about it … was there? A plan leapt into his head, one so audacious he could hardly breathe at the thought of it. Yet he could see himself carrying it out, stealing down the stairs as quietly as a mouse, opening the front door – he'd have to do that very slowly and carefully, it could give a fearsome creak if you swung it open

– slipping out into the night and running through the darkness to the old hut where he'd seen them drag Geordie.

He could see himself doing it all, unfolding in his head like a series of pictures. The thought of actually carrying out his plan terrified him. He wasn't brave enough to do this. His fear of the dark was bad enough. His fear of getting caught leaving the house and going to the hut was even worse. How often had Charlotte Liddell told him she owned him, body and soul? How often had she told him she could do anything she liked to him? She often had, routinely slapping him, pinching his skin and pulling his hair. He'd endured more than one ferocious beating at her hands when she'd been really angry. She would half kill him if he did this.

If she can find me. He honestly didn't know if he had said those words out loud. Whether he had heard them inside or outside of his head they made him sit upright and straighten his shoulders. Why should she find him? He could hide for a while. Maybe yon nice Miss Rankeillor would help him. He'd seen her a few times when Charlotte had taken him to the apothecary's shop. She'd always given him a friendly smile.

Or maybe Geordie's Captain would help him. For a few moments Joshua lost himself in a wonderful dream. If he could somehow get away without Charlotte finding him he too could work for the Captain or Miss Rankeillor. He and Geordie would work hard but there would be time to have fun together too. There would be laughter, kindness, good food and good company. Nobody would get hit, ever.

It wasn't a physical force which struck him then but reality, as harsh as the cold water with which he'd been drenched earlier. His wonderful dream was an impossible one. His future was never going to be in his own hands. Nobody could make Charlotte give him his freedom. He had heard terrible stories of the awful ways in which some masters punished runaway slaves. She had told him, relishing every cruel, stomach-churning detail.

For a moment he sat immobile, despair flooding through him. It was all hopeless. He couldn't help Geordie and he couldn't help himself. He was useless. All he could see ahead of him was misery, years and years of it. No bend in the road, where his life might change for the better. Unless he made that bend himself. He could make the choice now to help Geordie and get himself away from Charlotte, even if only for a few days or a few weeks, even if she did beat him senseless when she caught up with him.

Joshua rose to his feet, gulped in a deep breath. Hands fumbling, he pulled his nightshirt over his head and started pulling on his clothes. Once he'd done that, he folded one of his blankets lengthwise and draped it over his shoulder. Geordie was bound to be cold, hungry too. Joshua swallowed hard. He should go to Eastfield's kitchens before he left the house, pick up some supplies. The thought terrified him, compounding as it did the possibility that he would be caught sneaking out of the house.

He had already opened the door of his room, only enough to allow him to look out at the upstairs landing. Now he stood with one hand gripping the solid wood, chewing his lip. None of the sconces on the landing were lit but there was a glow of light coming up from the ground floor of the house. So it wasn't so late that everyone had gone to bed. Besides which, he thought he could hear the sound of conversation, floating up to the landing.

He squeezed his eyes tightly shut, doing his utmost to summon up his courage. He couldn't do this. He really couldn't. The mere thought of going out into the darkness of the winter evening was enough to terrify him, let alone tiptoeing around the downstairs lobby and the kitchens. He could not do this. *He simply could not do this.*

❖

Footsteps. There they were again. Heading for the hut. Geordie managed to drag himself upright again. He'd tried several times to rise to his feet but each time he had been so shaky he'd had to abruptly sit down again, but whatever and whoever this was, he had to face them like a man. Like the Captain would. He felt around in the darkness, seeking a piece of wood or broken length of pit prop with which he might defend himself. There was nothing. He heard the door of the hut being opened. With the blood rushing through his ears, he spoke into the void. 'Who's there? If you're a ghost I'm no' scared o' you.'

'That's good,' said a voice he recognized. 'It's me. Joshua.'

'Joshua?' Geordie asked, hardly daring to believe his ears. 'What are you doing here?'

'Sssh. Dinna speak so loudly. We're no' wanting anyone to hear us. I'm come to take you away from Eastfield. What else?'

46

In Infirmary Street, Christian waited, keeping herself busy with every possible task involved in preparing to receive Geordie. She worked and spoke with Betty and the girls and comforted Alice. In body, she was fully there. Her mind was elsewhere, out in the cold and dark of the winter's night, willing Robert Catto and Geordie to return safely.

As the interminable evening crawled past, she imagined everything that might be going wrong. She worried about every possibility, constantly having to rein in her imagination. Most of all, she worried that Robert Catto would not be able to carry out his rescue mission covertly. What if he encountered violent resistance at Eastfield, whether inflicted by fists and feet or pistols and swords? She could see him at bay, prepared to fight all-comers, but up against impossible odds, surrounded by men set upon him by the Liddells and who had no choice but to obey them. Dear God, he and Geordie might not come back at all!

She was walking from the kitchen back through to the library to check for the umpteenth time that all was ready there when that thought struck. For a moment she froze, gripped by the most profound fear. Until she heard his voice in her head, responding to her impassioned question. *As to what we are going to do, we are going to put one foot in front of the other and keep going until we get through this.*

In that moment, her mind cleared. Her worrying herself sick was not going to help at all. She had to stay calm, she'd be of little use to either Geordie or Robert Catto otherwise. Decision made. Somewhere in the midst of all the worrying she realized she had made another decision too.

❖

'Ah canna go any further,' Geordie gasped. 'My back's too sore. And my feet. You go on while it's still dark, Joshua, you can easily make Edinburgh by the morning.'

'Dinna be daft,' the other boy said, lending Geordie an arm and lowering him down as gently as he could onto a sand dune. 'And dinna waste what breath you've got trying to persuade me. I'm not leaving you. We'll rest here for a wee while and then we'll press on.' He looked down at the other boy. The light of the moon allowed them to see each other clearly. 'Are you hungry, Geordie? I brought some food with me.'

Joshua pulled the soft cloth bag he wore bandolier-style across his chest over his head. He had been so nervous when he had crept into the kitchens before he had left Eastfield but he had known they wouldn't get far without some sustenance. 'Bannocks and a piece of boiling beef,' he said, bringing them out of his bag and digging in again to find the tin cup he had put there. 'We'll find a wee burn to get a drink of water. That'll keep us going.'

Nervous was by far too mild a word for how he had felt as he had walked cautiously into the kitchens. His heart had been beating so fast he had thought it might burst out of his chest. It was the same when he'd passed the dining room. The closer he'd got to it, the louder the voices within it had become. He could hear Charlotte and Cosmo and their friend. They all sounded drunk, talking raucously and giving out great hoots of laughter. After that he'd had to pass the servants' hall. By the sounds of it, they were all drunk too. The whole household had been too drunk to notice him.

He was in his cloak and he had draped the blanket around Geordie's shoulders to try to keep out the chill of the night. It kept slipping off,

Geordie having hardly the strength in his hands to hold it closed at the front. The other boy being barefoot was also a problem. Joshua couldn't offer him a loan of his own shoes either. His feet were smaller than Geordie's. They'd tried to keep to the dunes and the sandy beaches but they'd had to negotiate shingle too and the paths which snaked through the dunes and the winter-frosted grass were hard-packed, often with broken shells. The soles of Geordie's feet must have a fair few cuts and bruises by now. He saw his friend close his eyes and heard him give a little sigh.

'Have something to eat,' he said, handing Geordie a bannock and a torn-off piece of the boiling beef before sitting down, cross-legged, beside the other boy. For a moment the only sounds in his ears were of him munching his food and the wind stirring the grasses of the dunes. It was getting up a bit, which was worrying him. Geordie looked as though he was at the end of his tether, listlessly nibbling on the food Joshua had handed him. A cold wind blowing in from the sea wasn't going to help. But where could they go for shelter? And if they did, how could they be sure of staying concealed? Nor, to Joshua's mind, had they put nearly enough distance between themselves and Eastfield. When that household finally woke up tomorrow morning, the two of them had to be much farther away than here.

'Musselburgh,' he said, with sudden decision. 'We need to get over the river at Musselburgh. Once we're on the other side, we'll find a boathouse or a shed somewhere and rest there for a few hours, then set off again in the early morning before it gets light. That's what we'll do, Geordie.'

'Will we, Joshua?'

Joshua looked at him in alarm. That had sounded real faint, as though Geordie was drifting off somewhere in a haze of pain and exhaustion. He still hadn't taken more than a wee bite or two out of his bannock. Joshua gave his arm a little shake. 'You canna go to sleep now, Geordie. We need to keep our wits about us. Just until Musselburgh.

Then we can rest. We'll have to go up onto the road to cross the bridge over the river but that can't be helped. It's too wide to ford. Eat some more and then we'll move.'

By the time they reached the Esk, Joshua was pretty tired too. It was hard work helping Geordie with a supporting arm as well as encouraging him to keep going. His own twisted ankle was getting sorer too. 'Just a wee bittie farther and then we'll rest. I think I can make out the bridge now. Just a few more steps, Geordie. Then we can rest.'

The other boy mumbled something, an incoherent tumble of words from which Joshua could discern no meaning whatsoever. For a moment he thought he might succumb to despair, sit them both down on the grass and give up. Maybe they would die out here in this chilly wind and the dark of the night. Maybe someone would find them in the morning, huddled together trying to give each other their last bit of warmth. It would be a way out for both of them. It needn't hurt, either, might just be like falling asleep, nothing more. Only they would never wake up again. And a cruel and unkind world would have won.

Gathering the last remnants of his strength, Joshua half carried, half led Geordie up the brae that led to the stone bridge over the river. They had reached the middle of it, the wind whipping at them, when he heard the clip-clop of horses' hooves. Two horsemen, heading straight for them. This was it, then. Their escape attempt was over.

The clip-clop stopped. There were no lanterns on the bridge but one of the riders had risen in his saddle and was peering down at the boys in the gloom. 'Geordie?' the man asked. 'Is that you?'

47

'Where do you want him?' Robert Catto carried Geordie into the lobby, Joshua at his heels. Her eyes widened at the sight of him but she smiled a welcome. As did her housekeeper, standing behind her young mistress in the lobby. The boy looked so anxious, worn out too.

Keeping a secure hold on Geordie, Catto swung briefly around, nodding his head in acknowledgement of a wave of farewell from Livingstone. Having helped Joshua down from where he'd been sitting in front of him, the Sergeant got back up onto his mount, took the reins of both horses into his hands and led them away.

'In the library,' Christian Rankeillor said, answering Catto's question. Like the housekeeper, she was dressed for bed, in the frilled and flounced wrapper she'd been wearing the only other time Catto had seen her in her dishabilly. 'We've brought a mattress and sheets and blankets from upstairs and we've kept the fire in.' She smiled again at the black boy. 'Joshua, isn't it? Why don't you go through to the kitchen with Mrs Betty? The captain and I will look after Geordie.'

'I'm fair worried about him, miss.'

She laid a comforting hand on his shoulder. 'I know. But we'll get him settled and then you can come and say goodnight. You must be tired. We'll have to fix up a bed for you upstairs.'

'I'll see tae that,' Betty said. 'The lad can help me. After I've got him something to eat. Come on through wi' me noo, young man.'

'Where's Alice?' Catto asked.

'We managed to persuade her to go to bed.'

'Good. No need to disturb her.' Following Christian Rankeillor into the library, he saw the mattress and bed clothes laid close to the fire. 'I'm fair worried about him too,' he confided. 'Especially by how cold he is. I tried to keep this blasted blanket wrapped around him but it kept slipping off. I gave him some brandy, just a couple of sips. That was all he was fit to take, anyway.' He tossed the blanket over the back of one of the upright chairs set round the big table. 'He'll need to lie on his front, I think.'

Christian swallowed hard. 'They did flog him?'

'Aye,' Catto said grimly. 'Joshua says he counted twenty-five strokes.'

'Dear God.' She gave herself a little shake. 'Help me get his clothes off so we can assess the damage.'

He gently lowered Geordie down onto the mattress on top of the sheet already spread on it. The boy's eyes fluttered open. 'You'll have to sit up for a minute, lad. Just till we get you undressed.'

'Can't get undressed in front of Miss Kirsty,' Geordie mumbled. 'Wouldn't be right.'

'Havers,' she said and began pulling the tattered and dirty shirt off over his head. Geordie winced with every gentle tug of the cloth. 'Let's get you out of these breeches now and then you can lie down. On your front,' she added brightly. 'You should find it easier that way, Geordie. We'll soon have you more comfortable.'

'Miss Kirsty…' His protest was a whisper … and then his eyes rolled and his head fell back.

'Quick,' she said to Catto, 'let's get this done before he comes to again.'

Minutes later, they had Geordie lying naked on his front on the mattress, both of them momentarily transfixed by the angry welts crossing his back from the top of his buttocks to his narrow shoulders. The skin was broken in some places, blood drawn. It stood out now like rows of running stitches in red thread sewn through white linen. The bruised and swollen skin between the welts had turned an ugly shade of purple. His wrists were also badly bruised.

Robert Catto spoke in that low and dangerous voice. 'I want to kill whoever did this to him.' He looked across Geordie at her, saw she had raised a trembling hand to her mouth. 'Kirsty,' he said, his voice gentling.

'I'm all right,' she said, composing herself. 'Geordie needs me to be all right. Can you bring that basin and jug over for me?' She indicated both items, standing ready to the side of the fireplace. 'And the cloths and the pot of salve I've laid on the seat of that chair.'

He watched as she folded one of the cloths into a soft pad, soaked it in the water in the bowl, squeezed most of that out and began cleaning Geordie's back. 'Let me help,' he said.

'Take the other cloth, then. Dab. Don't rub.'

He gave her a speaking look. 'I do know what to do for someone who's been flogged.'

She looked up. 'Of course. I wasn't thinking. Has it ever happened to you?'

'No. But I've witnessed it too many times. Barbaric,' he added. 'As this is.' He tilted his head, watching the boy's face. 'I think he's regaining his senses.' He waited until the fluttering eyelids opened and stayed open. 'Geordie. Welcome back to the land of the living. How are you feeling, lad?'

'Happy,' the boy said. Christian Rankeillor and Catto exchanged confused looks.

'Happy?' she asked.

'Because I'm here,' Geordie said. 'And it's fine and warm. It was so cold oot there. So cold. I'm a wee bittie sore, mind.'

Catto laughed. 'A wee bittie sore?' Once again he looked across at Christian Rankeillor. Kneeling there on either side of Geordie, they grinned at each other in sheer relief.

'Aye. But that feels good. What the two o' you are doing to my back. And I'm happy because you came looking for me, Captain.' There was a tremble in the young voice. 'I thought I was never going to see you again!'

'Och, Geordie,' Catto said, hearing the emotion in his own voice and unashamed of it. 'I had to come looking for you. Can't do without my right-hand man, can I now?'

❖

Robert Catto sat opposite Christian in one of the armchairs in front of the fire. He had discarded his riding boots, loosened his neckcloth and stripped down to his breeches, waistcoat and shirt. Now, with a glass of claret in his hand and an empty plate on the table beside him —Betty had fed him as well as Joshua — he stretched out his long legs in their stocking soles to the fire. Geordie lay peacefully on the mattress in front of it, his head resting on his arms, his elbows crooked. The golden waves of his hair glinted in the firelight. Christian Rankeillor had applied salve to his wounds, on his back and round his wrists. Once that had dried, she had drawn the top sheet up over his back.

Joshua had been in to see him, Christian frowning as she saw how the other boy was limping. While he was saying goodnight to Geordie she had given him a small cup of ground willow bark and water for the pain in his ankle and prepared a cold compress to be laid over it. 'And I ken fine to put a pillow *under* his foot after he gets into bed,' Betty had told her. 'I've lived in this house long enough.' After they had left the library, Christian had helped Geordie drink a sleeping draught.

'That should see him through to the morning?' Robert Catto asked now.

'Well into tomorrow, I should think.' She raised her own glass and took a sip of wine.

'I should like to keep watching over him, all the same.'

335

'I'll watch with you.'

'I'd like that,' he said softly. 'But what will your housekeeper have to say about that? I don't think she'll approve. I'm surprised you got away with putting out the sconces. Or being in your dishabilly.' His eyes went to the cambric wrapper, adorned with frills and flounces and fastened up to the neck by ribbon ties. 'Not that it's the most revealing of garments. Unluckily for me.' He was testing the waters, tried to gauge the situation between her and him. When she made a face at him, his spirits rose.

'We did not know when you would return and I thought we had a better chance of persuading Alice to go to bed if we all got ready for the night in the usual way. As for the sconces, there's plenty of light from the fire.'

'Just enough,' he said, enjoying looking at her in the flickering firelight, wondering what she was thinking. 'We seem to be making a habit of this. Sitting in darkened rooms.'

'We seem to be making a habit of quite a few things.'

'Do you want us to do that? Make a habit of things?'

She looked at him, looked at the fire and then back at him. 'Yes. I want us to do that.'

His heart leapt. 'No longer confused?'

'I had time to think during the hours you were away. Are you tired?'

'Not yet. Right at this moment I feel wide awake.'

'Beginning to realize the consequences of what you've done tonight?'

'Those will soon have to be taken into account and planned for.'

'Although you already knew what they were before you did it. Including earlier on, when you showed your true colours to Mr Paterson.'

'Did I?'

'I'd say so. Against your own interests.' She nodded towards the sleeping boy. 'All for his sake.'

He shrugged. 'Maybe for my own, too. As atonement for what my duty obliges me to do here in Edinburgh.'

'I do not think redemption for yourself was your impetus. You thought only of rescuing Geordie. You're a good man, Robert Catto.'

'If you say so. Which observation you've made several times now. Please don't tell anyone else about my more noble impulses, will you? I have a reputation to maintain. Not going to stop growling at people any time soon.'

'You may have made life much more difficult for yourself. In the matter of doing your duty, I mean.'

'Perhaps. Probably. But I have a plan. Regarding your father. From what I know and what I have heard about him, Professor Rankeillor is a reasonable and rational man.'

'Yes. He is. What is your plan?'

'Firstly, I shall arrest him discreetly.'

'Oh, that will make all the difference, I'm sure.'

He threw her a long-suffering look. 'I shall ask for his parole of honour, so that I do not have to restrict his movements too much. Then the three of us, your father, you and me, will hold a council of war. In the course of which the professor and I shall contrive to knock some sense into that head of yours. Persuade you to say nothing about your involvement in any of the events of the past week or so.'

'Oh, you will, will you?'

'Aye. I'm guessing you'll listen to him if you won't listen to me.' He took another sip of wine. *Say it, Catto, say it now, you've got nothing to lose: and maybe everything to win.* 'Do you know that your chin goes up when you get angry? I find it quite enchanting. Makes your hair dance on your shoulders too.' His voice was very soft. 'I really like your hair.'

The aggressive posture relaxed but she wasn't ready for a climbdown yet. 'I thought it was my feet you liked.'

'Your head and your feet and everything in between. I believe you really like my hair too,' he added. Still not sure what she was thinking, he took refuge in teasing flippancy. 'My gleaming chestnut locks? Isn't that how you described them?'

'Stop trying to change the subject. You know as well as I do that we cannot keep the world at bay for very much longer. As well as being a rational man, my father is also a very observant one. As keen-eyed as Betty.'

'He will be coming home to a household which is rather different than the one he left,' Catto said. 'He will have a lot to observe. Do you want to keep the world at bay for a little longer?'

'What about what you want?'

'I think you know what that is. For the avoidance of doubt, I'll tell you anyway. Right now I'm where I want to be. With the people I want to be with.' He glanced down at the sleeping boy, then back up at her. 'I'm hoping you feel the same way. And that the people you want to be with include me. That despite all that divides the two of us, despite what we both feel we have to do and may have to do, that we can stop seeing each other as enemies.'

'Being honest about your feelings? How the mighty are fallen.'

It was the glint in her green eyes that did it. Thinking back to his conversation in the moonlight with Livingstone, he reminded himself that fortune favours the brave. 'Come over here and sit on my knee.'

He raised his eyebrows when she laid her glass down, rose from her chair, picked her way around Geordie and came to stand in front of him. Perhaps she was going to slap his face in revenge for that outrageous demand. He wouldn't blame her if she did. Instead, she pointed at his wine glass. 'Finish that off.' When he had done so, she took it out of his hands and set it down. Then she did as he had asked, settling herself onto his lap. His arms slid round her trim waist, finding the warm woman beneath the abundance of bows and flounces. 'How nice. No stays.'

'I don't normally wear stays to go to bed.' She slid one arm around his neck.

'No, I suppose not. You may need to fetch the smelling salts. I wasn't expecting such instant obedience. Are you feeling quite well, Miss Rankeillor?'

'Obedience has nothing to do with it. If you're expecting any kind of obedience from me you're going to be sorely disappointed.'

'I wouldn't have it any other way.'

'Really? You astonish me. But you don't need smelling salts. You need to be thanked for rescuing Geordie – and Joshua – and you need this.' Bending her head, she kissed him.

'I need the latter several times over,' he said a moment later. He was a little breathless. They both were. She touched her fingers to the bare skin of his throat beneath the loosened neckcloth. 'Mmm,' he said. 'That feels good.'

'Don't get too carried away.'

'I won't. Not with Geordie here beside us. Our sleeping chaperone.'

'As I recall, our sleeping chaperone didn't hold us back too much on Daft Friday in the guard-house.'

'No,' he agreed. 'Care to share your shameless thoughts with me? I'm all agog. Oh, you're blushing. How delightful.'

'I see you're not going to stop being sarcastic.'

'Unlikely. Although to see you blush really is delightful. Maybe we should leave the recounting of your shameless thoughts for another occasion. One during which we're less likely to be interrupted and have a decent amount of time for me to properly enjoy them.'

The mischievous glint was still there. 'I dinna think *decent* and *properly* are the right words somehow.'

'Is that so? I'm even more agog now.'

'When you smile at me like that...' she began.

He gave her a little squeeze. 'What happens when I smile at you like that?'

'It does strange things to me. In strange places.'

'Does it do nice things to your strange places?'

'Stop laughing at me.'

'I'm not. Well, maybe a wee bit. Nice things?' he asked again.

'Yes.' Her voice sank to a whisper and he saw that, for all her bravado, she was a little nervous. 'I do not know,' she said, apparently finding his loosened neckcloth quite fascinating, 'I do not know how to please you.'

If his heart skipped one more beat it was going to jump out of his chest. 'You please me simply by being you.'

'I mean,' she replied, her blush deepening as she returned her eyes to his face, 'that I do not know how to give you pleasure.'

'You give me pleasure simply by being you.'

She took hold of the neckcloth and gave it a tug. 'Och, Robert, you know what I mean!'

'Yes, I do. All that will come, I hope. But not yet awhile.'

'Not least because as soon as I hear Betty coming down the stairs I shall move like the wind. Fortunately there's a tread right in the middle of them which creaks like an oak tree in a storm.'

'I'll bear that in mind,' he murmured, his eyes dropping to her mouth.

'Oh, will you indeed? Are you not assuming rather a lot?'

'After this conversation? Kiss me again.' Funny how that was all he wanted at the moment. Here he was with her in his arms and he was feeling no urge to take matters any farther than kissing. Not tonight, at any rate. After a long and satisfying kiss they sat quietly for a while. 'Must be more than lust,' he said at last, hearing himself stumble over the words. 'What I feel for you, I mean.'

'I'm very glad to hear it.' Amusement bubbled through her voice. Affection too. 'You know, I don't think you're as wide awake as you think you are.'

He stifled a yawn. 'You might be right.'

'You don't always have to be the strong one, you know.'

'Don't I?'

'No. Even though you were tonight. I couldn't stop thinking about you and Geordie. All evening I was wondering where you were and imagining all the terrible things that might have happened to you, willing you both to come safely home.'

'Home,' he repeated. 'Is that where we are?' He went on, in an apparent non-sequitur. 'I think you might actually like me ... as well as my gleaming chestnut locks...'

'I do like you. Even though you are easily the most infuriating man I've ever met in my life. Haughty. Arrogant. Dictatorial. High-handed in the extreme.'

'Don't hold back...' he said, his voice drifting off.

'Close your eyes,' she suggested. He was aware of her slipping off his lap and putting a footstool in front of the chair. 'Lift your feet onto this.'

He obeyed her. Within minutes he was sound asleep.

48

'Robert,' she said softly. His eyes snapped open. Her hand was on his shoulder. She must have given him a little shake to rouse him from sleep.

'How nice to be woken by you.' He smiled up at her as she leaned over him. 'Good morning.'

'Good morning to you too. If you want to leave here and get back to the guard-house before it's gets light you'll have to go soon.'

'How long have I been asleep?' he asked, continuing to speak in the same quiet tones as she was. The fire was burning low and the sconces were still unlit but somewhere in the room a candle was burning.

'All that was left of the night. Several hours.'

He glanced down at Geordie, lying peacefully on his front on the mattress in front of the fire. Lucy the cat lay next to his legs. 'He's still fast asleep, I see.'

'All four of us were slumbering here through the night. Three people and one cat.'

'So you and I slept together?'

She narrowed her eyes at him. 'Very amusing.'

'I thought so,' he said smugly. 'I can't believe your housekeeper let us get away with it.'

'She's already warned me it won't happen again. Last night was a special case, she says. Never to be repeated. Never to be mentioned to anyone else.'

'That sounds like the wee witch. I had a very odd dream about her. She was spreading a blanket over me.' Sliding forward in the armchair where he'd dozed throughout the night, taking his stocking-soled feet off the low stool where they'd rested, he glanced down, puzzled. The blanket he'd struggled to keep wrapped around Geordie during the ride back from Musselburgh was puddled in his lap, falling down over his legs.

'That wasn't a dream. I was awake when she did it, dozing in the other chair. She brought another blanket down from upstairs and spread that over me.'

He looked up at her. 'Should I feel honoured?'

'Maybe you should feel accepted.'

'Really?' His eyebrows shot up in disbelief. 'I doubt that.'

'Well, she's put the porridge on early so you can have a bowl before you leave the house, so you must be more in favour than you were.'

'Wouldn't be difficult.'

'Will you come over to the table? I don't want to risk disturbing Geordie before he's had the full benefit of a good night's sleep. I'll take the blanket.'

He gave her a little smile. 'I have to do something first. Go somewhere.'

'Oh, yes, of course. I'll show you where.'

He came back into the library lightly brushing his newly-washed hands against each other. A single candlestick stood on the cleared corner of the untidy table, along with a wooden bowl, a ribbon of steam floating up from it, a jug of milk and a small dish of salt. He added some salt and milk to the porridge and picked up the horn spoon. 'I should really stand up to eat this.'

'In case your enemies are already riding towards your stronghold and you have to be ready to defend it to the death?'

He gave her a look from under his brows. 'Aye. And those within my stronghold. My fair lady and the orphans of the storm now under my protection. But it'll be a while before my enemies turn up, I reckon, so I'll stay sitting. You not having any?'

'I'll have some later. Your hair ribbon has slipped.'

'Slide it off for me?'

As she laid the black satin ribbon on the table, he shook his head, freeing his hair to spill over his shoulders.

'Aren't you going to tie it back again?'

'I'll leave it loose for the moment. Since that's apparently how you like it. Anything to please you, madam. If Geordie's going to stay in this room today, will you make sure the door through to the shop is never left open? The fewer people who know about last night's escapade, the better. Don't let Joshua go through there either.'

She nodded, stood up to lay the folded blanket over the back of a chair and sat down again at right angles to him. 'Mr Livingstone won't tell anyone?'

'Only his wife. And she won't tell anyone else.'

'I'm glad he insisted on going with you.'

'So am I. Although probably not for the same reason as you are.'

Puzzled though she looked by that response, she did not press him on it. 'We'll have to see how Geordie is once he wakes up. I'm guessing he'll be very stiff as well as very sore. We can maybe get him into one of the armchairs, with a soft pillow or two behind his back. But he might not be ready for that today.'

'As you think best. You will give him something for the pain?'

'Of course. Hopefully he will have an appetite too.'

'Hopefully. Then we'll know he's on the mend. Good porridge.' He addressed himself to it with some enthusiasm.

For a moment she sat and watched him eat, turning everything over in her mind. 'What are we going to do about Geordie and Joshua? Do you have a plan? I've learned that you usually do.'

'Several plans.'

'Care to share any of them with me?'

'Well, I'll come back down here in the late afternoon and bring *The Adventures of Robinson Crusoe* with me. Thought I might read some of it to Geordie until he's fit enough to sit up and read it for himself. After that, maybe you'll feed me.'

'In exchange for your kind thought? Joshua might like to hear about Robinson Crusoe too. And Alice and the girls. It's not what I meant, though. As you very well know.'

Finishing the porridge, Catto set the bowl and spoon aside and glanced across at Geordie and the small bundle of fluff curled up beside him. 'Trust a cat to find any new warm billet. Always looking for different places to sleep, aren't they?'

'We can talk about cats and their habits another time,' Christian said softly.

He looked at her. 'I'm not used to sharing my plans with anyone.'

'You could try. You did last night. About my father.'

'Because that directly affects you.'

'All of this directly affects me. If there's a storm heading towards us, much, much worse than the one we've just had, we're all going to be in its path. And it's going to make everything else so much more complicated. Is that not so?'

It took him a moment. 'Promises made and not kept are worse than promises never made at all.'

'Promises to do what?'

'Slaves and indentured servants can be freed.'

'Only if their masters agree to do so.'

'Pressure can be brought to bear. Bargains can be struck. Especially by powerful people like the Lord President.' He grimaced. 'Devil's bargains though they may be.'

'You really think it might be possible?'

'He's struck similar bargains before. Quite a number of them.'

'Including with you.'

'Yes. Including with me.'

'What is to be your reward for what you are doing for the Lord President here in Edinburgh?'

'A full captain's commission in my regiment.'

'Your real regiment, you mean. Not the Town Guard.'

'Yes. My real regiment. A captain's commission in Guise's.'

'Which is something you prize.'

'I thought I did. I thought many things. Principally, that after I had completed this assignment I would leave this benighted bloody country and never come back again. Scotland holds many sad memories for me.'

'And now?'

'Now there's you.' Once more he glanced over at Geordie. 'Him too. For some reason he seems to look up to me, even be fond of me. God knows why.' He looked back at her. 'I seem to be doing all the talking.'

'Finish what you were saying.'

'Very well. I've been thinking that it's possible for people to change, or at least to change direction. If they want to do it enough. If there's someone who makes the change worthwhile. Perhaps a soldier who's spent his life thus far racketing around Europe in the service of his king – or, as treasonous and disaffected Jacobite rebels like you refer to him – the Elector of Hanover – might decide he could settle down somewhere.'

She let out a little gasp but, leaning forward, placed her fingertips over his lips. 'Promises made and not kept are worse than promises not made at all.'

He lifted her fingers from his mouth, kissed her knuckles, laid her hand on the table and put his own over it. 'I'm not making any promises. Not yet. Especially not until I hear what conclusions you came to last night. What you were thinking while you were waiting for Geordie and me to return.'

Now it was Christian who hesitated, until it came out in a rush and tumble of words. 'I thought that if anything had happened to you last night, I would be distraught. As I would have been if the worst had happened to you on Daft Friday. I thought of how doing your duty means you so often put yourself in harm's way. Which you do willingly and fearlessly and are probably going to do for the rest of your life. I thought that if anything happened to you I would spend the rest of *my* life longing for the touch of your hand and the sound of your voice.' She took a deep breath. 'And I thought I should spend the rest of my life wishing we two had made love to each other!'

The hand resting on top of her hand flexed. She studied him in the light of the single candle, his hair loose about his face. Such a handsome face. Such a kind face. He had set the mask aside, his feelings for her clear to see.

He lifted her hand to his lips, locked eyes with her and kissed her palm. 'I'd make it so good for you. Do everything I can to give you pleasure.'

'I'd like to do the same for you,' she said shyly. 'If you'll show me how. Although I do not see how we can ever manage to be together in that way.'

'I'll show you how. And we'll find some way to be alone together and private, with no fear of interruption. So we can take our time about it. But not unless and until you're sure it's what you really want. We'll be careful, take it slowly.' He gave her that smile again, the one that sent tingles of desire coursing through her body. 'Although I could easily be tempted to advance to a position of reckless abandon.'

She took another deep breath. 'So could I. I want to lie with you, Robert. I want that so much.'

'Oh,' he said, briefly closing his eyes. 'Oh...' He opened his eyes again. 'To hear you say that... You have given me a gift, the best I could ever hope for. But there's something you have to know first. I'm not fearless, Kirsty.'

'I didn't think Captain Robert Catto was scared of anything.' When he didn't immediately reply she threaded her fingers through his. 'Dinna tell me Mr Sarcastic is lost for words. Tongue-tied?'

'Aye,' he said, 'I'm tongue-tied. Because I'm scared. Of lots of things.

I fear for you. I fear for your father and your friends. Dammit.' And then: 'And you scare me.'

'I scare you? How on Earth can someone like you be scared of someone like me?'

Now it was he who spoke in a tumble of words. 'Because you make me feel alive again. Make me think, make me feel. It hurts. Oh, how it hurts. But oh Kirsty, it's glorious too! I'm scared to have you and then to lose you. Because when I brought Geordie and Joshua here last night, it did feel like coming home. But this isn't my home and never can be. And if this all ends in tears, I'll be a husk of a man, even more empty than I was when we first met!'

'Aye,' she said slowly. 'It could all end in tears. We have probably both taken complete leave of our senses. What is you call it in the army when you mount a mission despite there being little or no chance of success?'

'The forlorn hope.' He swallowed hard. 'Is that what you think this is?'

She looked at him, saw the longing, saw the fear. 'I'm scared too,' she told him. 'But what if we gather our courage and choose to risk it? What if we can find the eye of the storm and ride it out together, you and me?'

'I'm ready to do that,' he said passionately. 'Oh, I am so ready! Are you?'

She nodded, momentarily unable to speak.

He lifted their joined hands. 'No more doubts. No more confusion. No turning back. Agreed?'

'Agreed,' she managed, finding her voice again.

'I love you,' he said. He unthreaded his fingers from hers. 'Give me your other hand. Cup them both. Like so.' He wrapped his own hands around hers. 'I place my heart here. For safe-keeping. This will be my home. In your hands.'

'I'll keep your heart safe,' she promised. 'If you'll do the same for me.' Then, after a quick little breath: 'And I love you too.'

'So it's decided, then?' he asked. 'We're going to do our damnedest to weather the storm together?'

'Aye,' she said, joy bubbling and fizzing through her. 'It's decided.'

As one, they rose to their feet and stepped into each other's arms.

…to be continued.

About the Author

A born storyteller, Maggie Craig is the acclaimed Scottish author of the ground-breaking *Damn' Rebel Bitches: The Women of the '45* and several page-turning historical novels set in Edinburgh and her native Glasgow. She comes from a family where writing is considered an entirely normal thing to do and numbers among her forebears Robert Tannahill, the weaver-poet of Paisley. She has two grown-up children and lives in the north of Scotland with her husband.

She has served two terms on the committee of the Society of Authors in Scotland and is a regular and popular speaker around Scotland's libraries and book festivals.

Visit her website at www.maggiecraig.co.uk or follow her on Goodreads or on Twitter @Craig Maggie.

All Books by Maggie Craig

Find these titles on Maggie's Amazon author pages and on her website:

Amazon UK
Amazon US
www.maggiecraig.co.uk

Non-fiction

Damn' Rebel Bitches: The Women of the '45
Bare-Arsed Banditti: The Men of the '45
Footsteps on the Stairs: Tales from Duff House
When the Clyde Ran Red
Henrietta Tayler: Scottish Historian and First World War Nurse
One Week in April: The Scottish Radical Rising of 1820

Historical Novels

One Sweet Moment
Gathering Storm (Storm over Scotland Book 1)
Dance to the Storm (Storm over Scotland Book 2)

Glasgow & Clydebank Novels

The River Flows On
When the Lights Come on Again
The Stationmaster's Daughter
The Bird Flies High
A Star to Steer By
The Dancing Days

Contributor to:

Twisted Sisters: Women, Crime and Deviance in Scotland 1400
&
The Biographical Dictionary of Scottish Women